PENGUIN BOOKS

362 Belisle St.

Susie Moloney was raised in Winnipeg, Canada, and still lives there with her husband and two sons. She is the author of *Bastion Falls*, *A Dry Spell* and *362 Belisle St.*

362 Belisle St.

SUSIE MOLONEY

PENGUIN BOOKS

PENGUIN BOOKS

Published by the Penguin Group
Penguin Books Ltd, 80 Strand, London WC2R 0RL, England
Penguin Putnam Inc., 375 Hudson Street, New York, New York 10014, USA
Penguin Books Australia Ltd, 250 Camberwell Road,
Camberwell, Victoria 3124, Australia
Penguin Books Canada Ltd, 10 Alcorn Avenue, Toronto, Ontario, Canada M4V 3B2
Penguin Books India (P) Ltd, 11 Community Centre,
Panchsheel Park, New Delhi – 110 017, India
Penguin Books (NZ) Ltd, Cnr Rosedale and Airborne Roads,
Albany, Auckland, New Zealand
Penguin Books (South Africa) (Pty) Ltd, 24 Sturdee Avenue,
Rosebank 2196, South Africa

Penguin Books Ltd, Registered Offices: 80 Strand, London WC2R 0RL, England

www.penguin.com

First published by Michael Joseph 2002
Published in Penguin Books 2003

1

Set in Monotype Dante
Printed in England by Clays Ltd, St Ives plc

Here's to the women in my life: Queen Victoria, Laurie, Jolanda, Helena, Mikell, Jane, Pamela, Sam, Brig, Noreen, Auntie Helen, Joannie, Linda, Janis Rosen. You made me go there and got me the hell out of there; for this, I shall be forever grateful.

Acknowledgements

The ever-resourceful Linda McAllister took me into the world of realty with enthusiasm and good sportsmanship; I took up far too much of your time for that measly 6 per cent. It was an adventure. Thank you, Linda, and the folks at Phoenix Realty, who patiently answered the silliest of questions. Many thanks to Louise Moore and Christie Hickman for their insight and tremendous skill with the knife. Thanks to Damon Rondeau for squeaking me through no fewer than four computer emergencies in the nick of time, and equal thanks to Laurie Marshall for food, drink, opinion and her heart-felt expression of terrors in the night because of something I wrote. Josh's comment to me in the early days of this manuscript about Mario Lemieux was the finest comment ever made to a woman terrified of time. Darling Michael kept me grounded. Mick read all the research material I didn't want to, and pointed out inconsistencies lovingly and sometimes carefully. The wonderful Riouxs – Gord, Earl and Noreen – got down in the dirt with me and pulled down my house, helping me to build it back up and, in the process, create a new beginning that led to this book; there are no words for the likes of you three. Thank you, Janis Rosen. All those house dreams had a purpose.

NEWLY RENOVATED, SINGLE FAMILY HOME. NEW HARDWOOD FLOORS THROUGHOUT, ALL APPLIANCES. BATHROOM, BEDROOMS, UNIQUE DÉCOR, MUST BE SEEN! WORKING FIREPLACE IN SPACIOUS LIVING ROOM, LARGE LANDSCAPED YARD WITH GARDEN. ATTIC READY FOR YOUR CONVERSION, NEW WINDOWS. A STEAL AT $95,900.

GLENN DARNLEY, SHELTER REALTY.

Glenn

I

There was a cairn at the front of 362 Belisle, glaring morbidly in the grey morning light. A grim shrine to something passed over, and Glenn hoped fervently that it wasn't opportunity. Number 362 was the only house on the street with a hedge *and* a cairn. The cairn was actually a four-foot concrete pillar with the name Waverley stamped up the side in block letters. The hedge, a caragana, would be pretty in bloom in a couple of months, but until then the pillar and the hedge together made the place look haunted.

Glenn tugged at the hair at the back of her neck, and absently brushed phantom wisps from the sides of her face out of habit. For fifty years, her hair had been kept long. Today, she'd had it cut. Short. It was driving her mad. Absently.

She leaned against her car, giving the house the once-over before going in. It was grey and cool out, the sort of spring day that isn't spring at all, but smells like winter and looks like threatening fall.

The hairdresser, a girl of about mid-twenties or so, had greeted her carefully. *Hello, Mrs Darnley, how nice to see you* – She'd stopped suddenly without finishing and blushed furiously. *Oh god, I'm sorry, are you still going by Darnley? I'm so* –

He died, dear. He didn't dump me, she said gamely, making the girl stutter and blush some more and ruining

3

the whole New Glenn experience for about ten minutes. How could a person be so stupid? Howard would have loved that story.

About two weeks after he'd died a woman from the church down the street – a church neither Glenn nor Howard had ever set foot in – had dropped by with some pamphlets and Glenn had been forced to give her a particularly ugly go-away stare. One of the pamphlets had been titled *Blooming after Widowhood*. She'd thrown them all into the fireplace and they'd gone up the next cold snap. But she wished she'd at least taken a look at that one. She bet it had a section called, 'Haircuts: Dos and Don'ts for the New Widow'. Glenn's hair, chic as it might be, felt hard and cold and indifferent to her, like a clerk in a jewellery store. It hadn't even known Howard, how dare it attempt to make her feel better?

How would have loved that one, too.

She swiped absently at a phantom wisp.

From the outside, there was little to recommend 362 Belisle. It was ordinary. There were two things that separated it from the neighbours that might help (excluding the vile memorial-cum-pillar-cum-grave-marker): there was the hedge, which *would* be pretty with yellow blooms soon, and the front door, which boasted stone stairs. The door was clearly new, and it brightened up the exterior, dragging the eye away from the common flat-front, which was a feature of literally hundreds of houses all over the city. It looked . . . different. It had been empty since the previous fall, and that was apparent. The yard had been neglected and it looked as though it could have used a paint job a couple of years earlier – also no different from a dozen other homes on the block.

It was not really a good day to look, if you were buying.

Early spring, before the snow was entirely gone, was the best time for a realtor to view a house. They were at their lowest ebb in the leafless, ashen surroundings, the litter and discard of winter clinging to their corners, unwanted, for sale, and for whatever reason, abandoned by the people who had once been a part of their walls and floors. There was a vulnerability about them then, caught naked in the daylight after god knows what infidelities. Houses in April were new divorcees with all the accompanying brittleness and desperation. The house on Belisle had all of those qualities. It looked as though it would fall and disappear out of courtesy, if you pushed it.

The letter from the insurance company said that numerous upgrades had been done inside and that would help in selling the place, but you had to actually get people to go inside, to call the number on the sign. Glenn was taking a look. She would probably take the listing. Her first in four months. Her last day of work, she'd had twelve.

Ah, How. See what ya done to me?

He would have refused to take the blame for his own death. He would have said it was the curry. Glenn smiled mildly and went inside, listening against her will to the sound of the cellphone in her purse not ringing.

If this was an ordinary morning How would have called her by now. Or she him. Retirement had made him easily lonely, a thing they were both aware of, and stepped around carefully. They met for lunch a lot. She might have called him from the front door and said, 'Okay, I'm going in.' And he would ask her what she saw. In her poshest voice – the voice that still held traces of an English accent, even when she wasn't being posh – she would rip the place to shreds, make it cry, and then, that done, would have begun to see its finer points.

Enormous hallway.

The fireplace works.

No wallpaper.

Miss Glenn, it sounds like a house among houses and you have been destined since birth to set it free amongst the people you are the messenger you are the –

The door opened easily with the key and swung wide smoothly without creaking or scratching on the floor. The floors had been redone, the smell of varnish still in the house, after having been shut up for so long. They were shiny and new. They looked stripped and done as opposed to replaced and that was good too, she would note it on her features sheet. Old floors have character and colour. The varnish smell would be good: it made the house smell new and clean. She hoped it would hold out. Nice large hall, the ceiling going to the top floor, culminating in a large, mostly unfinished, attic. Stairs ran up the left to the second floor.

Her heels clicked cheerfully and echoed back at her through the (*spacious!*) living room with working fireplace and into the dining room. It was chilly inside, and Glenn tugged her sweater closer and folded her arms under her bosom. The walls were freshly painted (*newly decorated!*).

She poked her head into the kitchen. Fridge, stove, dishwasher and waste-disposal unit. Four appliances. Too bad no microwave.

The floor was stone tile, also new. Would have cost a fortune if the kitchen had been any bigger. As it was there was only room for a small two-maybe-three-person table on the wall at the back of the house (*eat in the kitchen!*). In the corner was a wraparound that led back to the front hall and the stairs. The back door peeked between the wall and the corner. There was a small room built under the stairs, hardly large enough to be called a room.

She would see the backyard. It would be large. Nice thing about these houses.

She pulled open the heavy interior door. The outside door was new: a wood-look frame, sturdier for its plastic interior and wood-like veneer; the screen was black and the frame was somebody's idea of Old Atlanta Quaint. Not bad. The gingerbread frame had been painted a nice teal. *Frankly, my dear, I don't give a damn.*

There was a terribly tangled, but large, practically English garden along the back of the property. Even in the ugly spring light and the ugly pre-bloom stage of the season, she could see the garden would be lush. The property backed up into trees; she could see three varieties, all small, maybe young. In front of that was a tangle of last year's perennials. Like the front yard, it had obviously been neglected in the previous autumn, but that could be taken care of. The caragana hedge that had bordered the front yard wound its way around to the back on both sides. It needed to be trimmed, but the little yellow flowers would be pretty and add a touch of colour for continuity. On the west side of the yard was a row of three lilac trees that blocked out the neighbour's backyard on that side, effectively.

One very nice thing about these older houses was the lot size. Glenn sighed. An old English gardener herself, she and How had built their house on a little lot that cost what the house and lot here was asking. He had a small rose garden that he tended with more care than they might have given a child, and at least as much anxiety, and a utilitarian tomato and herb garden at the back of the house. There was room for a bench and an umbrella in her yard. The Belisle house had room for a gazebo. In fact the ground around the north-eastern corner had patches of black earth that showed in the shape of something large. Glenn bet the Previous Owners tore one down. And added a cairn to Industrialism in the front.

How about that, How?

Now, now. No accounting for taste, Miss Glenn, but room for us all.

She pressed her forehead against the cool glass for just a second and thought about the roses that would bloom in summer without him. When a breeze blew through the yard, it would fill her own kitchen with their scent. Summer seemed very far away, hard to imagine right then. It would be, really, her second season without How. Then it would be autumn and her third; then winter again. What would it be like to pass the seasons? How wouldn't even see his roses.

It was so grey out. She pulled away from the door before it left a mark on her forehead and closed the bigger inside door with professional snap. She locked it.

The house was now under Power of Sale. It had been a mortgage default, not that it mattered one whit, but the sort of people who got their second mortgage from

8

an insurance company and then made thousands of dollars' worth of investment in their property were very likely in marital default by now and Glenn had the feeling that the concrete moniker marker out front would not be listed in their assets. Although they were welcome to take it back. While it wasn't in the letter or the assessment sheet, there were rumours about a tragedy of some sort. Someone had either been badly injured or died during the renovation. They likely lost heart after that. Glenn wondered briefly where they were now. Did it split them up? Those things happened. About fifty per cent of the listings she used to get were out of divorce.

We never had that problem. I wish we had. I wish you were holed up in a mid-life crisis apartment dating a woman half your age. I wish I was crying over that.

The walls around the back porch, such as it was, were old plaster and lath, although freshly painted. The floor had been refinished down the hall right up to the back door and up to the narrow door of the room under the stairs, but as far as she could tell, the only adjustments to the house up to there were just that.

There was an old knob and cover with an old-fashioned lock on the door, a nice old, dark oak door. She turned the knob and pulled the heavy door open.

It was quite dark, having the disadvantage of the grey day, and no window to relieve it. And there was wood panelling, the bane of a realtor's existence. It made the room dark. She flicked at the switch and light popped into the room. The bulb hung low, with a green glass half-globe over it, obviously original or near. It was quaint; very thirties or forties or something. The shade did little to diffuse the light. It hung from a cord dangling from the ceiling and Glenn guessed that this was where the renovations had concluded.

The panelling was not as offensive as she first thought. It was wainscoted to just over half-way up the wall. The wall above it – original, it looked – was likely plaster and lath, confirming her opinion that they hadn't touched the back end of the house, save for the floor. They had painted, however, thank god they did, but had done it unfortunately in a paler than usual forest green, making the room darker. Under the paint, even though dark, you could see the ripples in the wall. On the exterior wall the wainscoting stopped partway before the door and ran suddenly up to the ceiling. On either side of the full-length panelling ran bars of some sort. It took a moment for Glenn to catch it.

Frowning she went inside and ran her hand along the wall. Up above, just above head level, was a small recess. She put her hand inside and gave it a gentle little tug.

A Murphy bed. She hadn't seen one in years.

She pulled it down, letting the legs fall naturally to their place from inside the recesses. They snugged to the floor. She leaned on the works. It seemed solid. There was no mattress, but that couldn't be hard to fix. The frame seemed intact, maybe replaced.

It was delightful, like a surprise. A grace note.

With the bed pulled down the room practically disappeared, but it looked very natural, like a tiny maid's room or visitor's quarters. The dark walls and panelling implied a man's room, and even fair paint of some sort wouldn't change the masculine view of it. But for some reason, Glenn felt a femininity in the space.

It was a good room for a sudden liaison. Instant bed. She blushed thinking about it.

Taken for a moment with the thought, she suddenly remembered the last time she and How had made love. The thinking made her lean with her buttocks pressed against the cold frame of the pull-down bed.

They had bought a trailer to pull and park some place close to the slip where they kept their boat. It had been a job-and-a-half, buying that trailer. There were – she was sure of it – more than a thousand trailer-sale outlets in the metropolitan area, and she and How had visited them all, peeking into tiny mobile homes that after the first twenty minutes all looked the same.

Sex had been something that had been put on a slow burn with the two of them. They flirted, they touched, they even exchanged innuendo throughout much of their time together, but the actual act became somewhat theoretical after Howard had retired. She suspected that he felt diminished in a way she understood, leaving his life's work. He puttered about the house in what he joked was a 'housewify' way, and hadn't quite found his retirement niche. They made love, but not with the frequency of even six months before he retired. Had he felt old?

You weren't, How. Not to me.

Point duly noted, Miss Glenn.

They had poked in and out of trailers for most of one day, getting punchy and silly by day's end. A salesman made the mistake of leaving them to it, after showing them nearly everything on the lot, from the obsequious to the cosy.

Glenn had spent her time poking in cupboard spaces

and finding dials and buttons. How had occupied himself with tanks and wheels and nuts and bolts and the like. They came together in the tiny little sitting space in one of the lighter cabins.

'Not much manoeuvring room,' How had said.

'And what would you manoeuvre to?' she said with futility. She was tired, by then, of the whole project.

'It's not so bad, everything right in reach,' he said, cheerfully. 'Lounging room,' he said, tapping the table. 'Kitchen.' He got up and slapped his hand on the three tiny elements of the equally tiny stove. 'Bath and respite,' he said, pointedly, opening the door chivalrously, like a game-show hostess. He took one step – all that was necessary – and dropped down on to the tiny bunk. Tagged a double, the bed hardly looked large enough for one. 'Bedroom.'

'There you go, all the comforts of home.'

He smiled deviously and patted the mattress beside him. 'Think there's room enough for two?'

'It's very little,' she said, giggling.

'We may have to double bunk.'

'One on top of another?'

'Come and see?' A dare. She did.

It had been jokey and silly and she climbed into the wall side of the bed, leaving little enough room for How. He crawled in beside her.

'I'll have to lose a few stone,' she said.

He rolled on to his side and put a hand on her substantial hip. 'It's pounds, dear, and not more than one.'

'How dare you, How?' They met eyes and were quiet a second longer than their normal quiet together. It was one of their signals. Perfectly naturally. Without speaking, How got up off the bed and went and locked the teeny-tiny door. And joined her again on the bunk.

'See if it works?' he said, in a whisper. She kissed him.

How naughty we were, How.

We were a couple to be reckoned with, Miss Glenn.

The room was chilly. The walls, so far back in the house, were likely uninsulated.

On the way out of the room, a terrible thought occurred to her.

She believed that might have been the last time she would ever make love. It surprised her at first, the thought coming like that. It sat in her mind. She didn't go past it. After a moment, she decided if that was it, that would be fine.

She slowly swung the bed up to its place in the wall. It disappeared easily, as though it had never been.

She shut off the light and closed the little door again.

The house was listed at $95,900. Not impossible. She gave the kitchen a once-more over and liked the stone floor even more. The dividing wall between the little (*cosy!*) kitchen had a lovely arch over the doorway that looked original. Those sorts of touches made a house.

On her way up the stairs she glanced out of the tall, narrow window between the new front door and the wall for the stairs. Two children, jackets undone, no hats or scarves, walked by the house with a glance. It would be noon, then, children on their way home from school for lunch. There was an elementary school (*close to school!*) about two blocks from the house.

They'd never had children. How hadn't wanted any

and Glenn hadn't had feelings one way or the other, although tipped in his favour was the fact that her family was in England. That would have made it more difficult, more awkward, growing up without a grandma. It had never made an issue of itself. Glenn had had her moments of regret, but nothing life-threatening, and they had passed through those years spending nappy money on a boat, went to dinner on birthday cash and drank margaritas in Mexico at Christmas after her mother had died. Tuition went to a cottage.

It was lately, in her fiftieth year, that she had had her regrets most seriously. And not because she longed for the pitter of grandbaby feet, but because she was alone in her grief. No one to mourn with her. There was no one to say, *Do you remember when Daddy* – no one who knew him the way she did. No one to rage at the gods with. No one who felt his absence with the same intimacy of his presence. She was alone in that.

The master bedroom was doubly blessed, with both a medieval arched doorway and matching, fitted door, and a large double window on the south side overlooking the street. The floors on the upper level had not been redone. They were in decent shape, however, with worn spots by the doors. There must have been a carpet runner in the hall, because no path had been beaten between bedrooms and bath. In places the varnish was nearly gone and the floor was lacklustre. There were no unforgiving gouges or broken boards or, worse, inept repairs. It was fine.

There were three-plus bedrooms (the room with the Murphy bed was the 'plus') and a bath. The master-bed door was directly at the top of the stairs, to the left, and got a south-facing window; the Murphy room was under the stairs to the peak of the wall, and beyond that the rest of the wall must have been dead space. She thought to inquire as to whether or not the Previous Owners had had it insulated. Such a large empty space could be a heating nightmare. She made a mental note. The rest of the rooms ran off the hall. A large house, but the rooms themselves were very small, excepting the master bedroom, which was comparable to most homes. The bathroom was equally small. Curious for the first time in the house, she popped in to see.

The tub had been bought at auction and hauled in through the bathroom window, enlarged for that purpose. It was the only item listed in the insurance letter and she felt it had been mentioned more for amusement's sake than anything else.

It was enormous, larger nearly by half than regular tubs. They'd used a hydraulic lift to bring it up to the second storey and she smiled imagining the show put on for the neighbours. It was quite a find. The feet alone likely justified the purchase.

They were beast's feet. Claws poked out from each rounded toe in sharp detail. The underside had been painted a soft colour, not pink exactly, more rosy than pink. A nice rose, not that eighties poofter pink that could still be found on walls in the city, if you weren't careful of the company you kept. The bathroom had been (at least) decorated with restraint. There was wallpaper, but nothing obvious, just a small white flower or something on a pink that matched the tub. The floor was tiled. It could not have been the original, of course, that would have been impossible, but still it was equally restrained and very old-fashioned-looking in the manner of the tub. It was very nice. Bathrooms and kitchens sold a house. Kitchens particularly, but a lady liked her bath.

The soft colouring of the underside of the tub seemed a direct attempt to set down the fierceness of the claws of the thing. If so, it had not succeeded. It looked like an animal. Of course, it was supposed to.

But still.

It looked like something that could eat you.

Across from the bathroom was a child's room. The walls had been painted a sky blue. It was a deep, rich blue, not robin's egg blue, which always seemed whiney to Glenn. You could almost imagine clouds and lying on your back finding trucks, elephants and an old man with a long beard.

The windows had been trimmed in recovered wood from some estate sale, or maybe a gem collected from somewhere special. The edges were crudely cut, and left roughly hewn, the wood stained dark, but not so dark that the character and age of the wood didn't show through. They had varnished it all to a gleam.

The baseboards and cupboard door, as well, were obviously scavenged wood from some lot or estate sale. The closet couldn't be rightly called that, the low door not quite reaching the sloped ceiling indicating a cubby-hole as opposed to something full-sized. The edges were not finished, but rough and uneven in places. It was very low. A child might like the size of it. The wood was scarred and aged, although the door had been freshly varnished and shone even in the limited light in the bedroom. She suspected there had been some sort of theme in mind that had not quite been fully realized, but Glenn got the general impression of something western or farm-ish: a barn or horse stall. It made sense with the sky-blue walls – the sky.

The little cubby door did not have a knob, but a latch, the sort you might find on a garden gate from a long time ago.

Glenn walked across the floor to the window, to see the view. It was of the front street. The southern exposure would give good light on a sunny day. It was very small. But there were three other bedrooms. This didn't have to be a child's room, it could be a home office, or a nice sewing-quilting room, that sort of thing. The dark trim seemed out of place, but it was interesting. A *feature*. She silently hoped the other rooms did not match. Her eyes were drawn to the little door, so small and yet so apparent, so dark against the blank, blue wall.

There was something inviting and whimsical about the latch that made you want to reach out and –

Put your clothes away, she thought, and smiled with it. Would a child like that? Would it promote good habits, putting your clothes away, toys in a row? There you go. Chores done. Good lad.

Come inside.

She lifted the latch and pulled the little door open. Darkness yawned back, terribly dark, without the sun shining in to light it. It seemed to go back very far. A child could get lost in there for days.

Cool, chilled air followed the opening of the door. A puddle of it seemed to settle at her feet. Glenn frowned, thinking of the space under the stairs not being insulated and how chilly it might be in the dead of winter in this little child's room when the sun was not shining. There was an earthy smell as well and she wondered if the space had been a cold shelf at one time. There was an unpleasant undertone to the smell, like something gone bad. Even in the cold. In the dark.

She swung the door shut and lifted the latch and closed it good. Properly. The latch was inviting. Something about the sound of it made you want to open it. And close it.

The other room was down the hall.

The door had been closed for a long time. Unlike anywhere else in the hall, there was dust, undisturbed in front of the door. She would just take a quick peek before leaving. She needed people. She would have liked to be back at the office, joking with Elsie about the pillar and Gavin Edwards' new toupée.

Instead, she opened the door to yellow walls and a smell that was both unpleasant and familiar. It was faint, leftover, like the varnish on the ground floor, but none the less present. It stung in her nostrils, dug into her memory –

– he's the same today no progress not expecting

Can we get you a cup of tea, Mrs Darnley –
the smell of swimming-pools and the custodial room off the parking lot at their building downtown. The smell of

Can we get you a cup of tea?
disinfectant.

She looked up at the white ceiling, the circular moulded pattern around the light fixture, like berries or grapes in relief. The walls were garish, the room bright and artificially cheerful, as though manufactured for a purpose. A sick room.

How's room at St Matthew's.

If she walked across the floor now, instead of the click of her heels over the wood planks echoing, she would hear the *squitch squitch* of rubber soles. She could almost hear the clanging of meal trays and whispers of guests. The hum and blip of machines.

Oh, How.

He'd been in the middle of a story, a not particularly funny story, but the only one he had from the day, about a lady trying to take back a skinny turkey at the butcher's. She claimed it was too skinny (he agreed), and that since it had been frozen and packaged when she bought it, it had been like buying 'a pig in a poke'. This was the part that How had found extremely funny.

Glenn had been tired that day, too, having unloaded (finally) a huge, expensive house that she'd had listed for nearly a year, to a couple that shouldn't have bought it. Ethically, she wasn't comfortable with it, but practically, she was glad to have it done. There had been a lot of paperwork that had sat untended while she walked the couple – nice older pair, the Reynolds – through the motions of buying what was going to be a large investment for two people who should have been past large investments and beginning short-term projects such as annual trips to Florida in some sort of large van. It was their third trip through the big old house.

They had signed, and while that had been lovely, it had taken up the rest of the afternoon with more paperwork and phone calls, and then she had had to stay later than usual to finish up some other paperwork that had waited long enough. By the time she got home How had supper ready and on the table and was bursting with energy and enthusiasm that Glenn had tried to catch, but couldn't. So she'd half listened to the story and let her mind wander in and out of the conversation, adding appropriate *hmmmms* in the right places.

He'd made a curry. Curry played havoc with her digestive system and even as she ate it, enjoying the flavour, she made a mental note to take an antacid later. How should, too, she remembered thinking. His digestive system was even older than hers and more susceptible to the cruelties of eastern food.

How coughed, suddenly, hard, deep in his chest. She frowned, something about the sound of it not right. She paused politely, smile moving back on to her face, about to ask him to excuse himself when he did it again.

One arm was raised in an arc, illustrating the posture of the old woman waving the skinny bird around, when his face went red and he coughed again.

'– S'cuse me,' he choked out. He forced another cough, his face red (always ruddy anyway, but the colour seemed to deepen with every cough), from low inside his throat as though trying to clear it.

'Are you choking –' Glenn started to say.

The arm that was held out swung into his chest and banged as though trying to dislodge something.

Glenn stood up then, fast, knocking her chair out from behind her. How still held his fork and it stuck out from his chest.

'*How!*' she called, not a scream, but close.

He shook his head, trying a smile. ''Sokay. Not choking. Pain here –' He shook his head again. 'Heartburn –' he choked out, just before his hand suddenly swung away from him again and the fork flew out, hitting the wall beside the table with a metallic clang. Glenn dashed around the table to his side, crouching down beside him.

How banged his chest again. He sucked in his breath, and made a low sound in his throat. All of these things happened in the space of time it took Glenn to complete her thought, if not her sentence, about how he – all of this happened in the time it took for her to get up from her crouch beside his chair and grab the phone. All of this happened in the second for her to know, *to know*, that her husband was having a heart-attack.

While she dialled the emergency number, never once taking her eyes off Howard, she remembered things like blanket, water, airways; portable phone in hand, she went to the bedroom, yanking the duvet off their bed and running back with it to the dining room shouting (for some reason she felt she needed to shout her address her name her problem or it would not be deemed an emergency); she was flinging the duvet over her husband, still in his chair, his face ashen and blank at the same time that she dropped the phone. She lifted him from his chair, words of comfort and nonsense coming out of her mouth, whispering, for some reason she felt she should whisper or the situation would be deemed grave, and helping him to lie on the floor. She undid the button on his trousers, and for lack of anything else, the buttons down the front of his shirt until the whole of his chest and stomach – his *beautiful broad chest just beginning to grey* – was exposed. His breathing was nothing more than gasps and the colour of his lips changed, or rather lost colour. When she hovered above him, the words coming strangely, 'Don't you worry a lot of times heartburn isn't something to worry – I'm going to get you water – you have a sip and that curry – no more curry, it's good for the Middle East not for us westerners –' she spewed and dashed into the kitchen grabbing not water from the fridge – it would be too cold, too jarring *maybe jarring would be good make his heart pump if he is having he is* not *having*, and took water from the tap where coming right out it would be lukewarm or room temperature and then she ran with it back to the dining room and looked into the face of her rapidly expiring husband.

His eyes were closed. His lips were grey, nearly the colour of the rug in the dining room that they both hated. His chest rose and fell with uneven rapidity and labour. She dropped to her knees beside him, hands shaking, spilling most of the water on the duvet and herself.

She held the water out from herself as though offering it up, but could not bring herself to move this man. Her man. It looked to her a danger even to make him open his eyes. Her body trembled and her own heart was racing, her breathing sharp and pained. She was afraid. So afraid. Afraid to speak to move him afraid to move herself, as though any ripple in the universe, in time, might tempt the gods to finish the nasty work they'd begun.

He breathed through his mouth. His body was held in such a way that she could feel its tension, its *labour*. He looked dreadfully alone.

She reached out and touched his cheek. With ferocity, How grabbed her wrist and gripped harder than she would have thought possible. It gave her some hope.

'Um 'kay,' he said, gasping out the words. He was as *not* okay as it was possible to be and Glenn couldn't help but let a small laugh escape and he smiled, slightly, just at the corner of his mouth, one corner, forced up. And, for some terrible, desperate reason, that too gave her hope. She expelled breath and believed entirely for one beautiful moment that it was going to be all right – *it will be hard he had some damage the way his mouth moves up on one side, he could be paralysed on that side that happens but we can work through* – and then the sirens outside and How opened his eyes and looked into hers a second before closing them again. He put the slightest pressure on her wrist and then loosened his grip, but kept his hand there.

'Cav'ry here –' he said. *Cavalry here.* She nodded and stroked his face, her mumblings and nonsense beginning again.

'All going to be all right, I hate that recipe and we're going to have a special burning in honour of its demise and, by the way, we are ripping out this carpet and when you feel better –' And then the cavalry was bursting through the front door dragging ruthless and monstrous equipment and she was shunted aside and she would not, *could* not cry in front of How. Not then.

He lingered three days in a room of indifferent colour, surrounded by whispers and the soft *squitch* of running shoes, fed through tubes – lips blue, face yellowed and slack, bits of gasped bravery and forced wit unheard or condescended. Then he died.

Glenn had stared at the wall throughout the remembering, one arm tucked under her breasts, the other hand touching the hair at the back of her neck. She had followed them to the hospital in her car. By the time she got there How was sequestered in a makeshift room, closed off from uncaring eyes by only curtains, with strangers shouting in abbreviations and they wouldn't let her in. Not even to touch him, comfort him by her presence. She had stood outside the curtains for as long as she was ignored, peeking through, terrified to watch, and absolutely certain that if she moved, if she wasn't there, then something would happen and he would need her. She was told to move twice and finally led away, when they were bringing a large machine in. For reasons unknown she thought of her compatriots over the water and their machine that went *beep*. She promised herself she would remember to tell How that one. He'd like that. That he had everything, she would say, even the machine that went *beep*.

She never told him. It was never funny again.

He'd been briefly awake (alive) the next afternoon. Glenn hadn't left the hospital. She hadn't slept. She had sat all night in the chair in the waiting room. When they put him in a ward with three other beds, she moved in there. There was a man in the bed next to How who looked much, much worse than he did and she comforted herself with that as though How would be graded on a curve. She never saw the third patient. His curtains had been drawn, maybe the whole time How was in the hospital.

He woke the once and smiled at her, fulfilling every dream and prayer she'd had in the last twelve hours.

He said, 'Big fuss, huh?'

She said, 'Nothing but the best for my How.' He'd

24

smiled at her and they held hands. He opened and closed his eyes and she whispered words of comfort and told him how much she loved him and how long did he think he was going to keep his sorry backside in that bed and would he *please* hurry up and get well because *Coronation Street* was on at three and she couldn't miss. He'd smiled once or twice more, when he opened his eyes, but he never said anything again.

Big fuss, huh was all she got.

She stopped tugging at the new hair and put cold hands on her cheeks. She had lost weight over the duration of her mourning and could feel it especially then, with her elbows loose at her sides, closer to the inside of her than they had been in ten years. She was regaining her girlish figure just as she was feeling twice as old as her fifty years.

It was the yellow walls, she decided. The room looked somehow garish, as though the Waverleys had gone one shade too bright near the end, perhaps in an effort to stave off the cheerlessness of their encroaching *situation*. A feeble attempt at cheer. Trying too hard. The *squitch squitch* of rubber soles echoed too plainly. A sick room.

'I'll have none of this,' she said to herself and to the room at large. The room listened politely, as though apologizing for its jarring colour by being extra nice and quiet.

On the way out she closed the door quietly, respectfully, maybe with a little too much relief.

At the end of the sidewalk she looked back at the house. The sun had not deigned to peek out from the endless clouds in the sky. The day was still grey. It would go on like this, she suspected, with few breaks, for a while yet. Like the home of her youth.

She felt very tired. It had been a big day. Her first house after four months. It was a good house, an *easy* house, and would be sold within a week to a nice young family. It was that sort of house, mid-priced, well renovated, good-looking, nice neighbourhood – not the best, but not dangerous, it was at least fifteen years from dangerous – and by then she would have another couple of listings and a few nice young families who hadn't acted fast enough to buy them and life would go on.

She didn't need a pamphlet to tell her what would happen. She would go first hours and then a whole day without thinking of How. Then a week would pass. Then she would box up his things and send them off somewhere. In a few months she would run across his slippers or a completed crossword puzzle and she would cry and cry and cry. And then she wouldn't think of him again for another week.

That was the way these things happened.

When she got into the car and started it, she wondered if she would miss the loneliness of these days. Regret losing the grieving, if only because it was now her closest connection to How.

2

The twentieth day of the Belisle house listing was the day that Glenn went hours without thinking about How. She had actually gone hours without thinking about him previously, but hadn't noticed in the active days. The house, of course, had dozens of calls, as she predicted.

No buyers.

It was practically a phenomenon around the office. They were beginning to refer to it as 'that house', without anyone needing an explanation as to which house exactly they meant. Since the ad had run, Glenn had shown the house at least once a day, but more often twice. On the weekends she showed three times sometimes, taking calls on her cell while she worked the cold, hard earth in the front of the yard, or sat in sweater and overalls on the little bench with a cup of tea. She went every time, and though she bitched along with the others at the office about weekend interruptions, she didn't mind at all, really. They took her away from her own empty house.

Out of showings, she had sold two other multi-listings and felt quite back in the saddle. (Oddly enough, one of the homes she sold could have been the long-lost twin sister to the Belisle house, same price range, same layout, fewer improvements; it went unmentioned, tempted as she was, to the buyers, but there really was no accounting for taste.)

Elsie said, on the twentieth day, 'What's on for that house today, Glenny?'

'Two showings, one's a repeat. Could be the end,' she quipped.

'So strange,' Elsie said. She said the same thing every time they spoke of the Belisle place. She had had a run-by a week before with the husband and wife of friends of hers. She had built it up in their eyes, in Glenn's opinion. The young couple had two school-aged children, and the wife worked at home in some sort of computer business. It was perfect for them. There'd been a lot of that.

They didn't buy it, didn't even offer on it, even though it was perfect, in their price range and had room for an office. The reason given, by the wife who had the computer business, was, 'It has the wrong vibe.'

'The wrong *what*?'

'That's what she said, "the wrong vibe".' Gavin Edwards and his toupée shook their heads, albeit at different speeds. 'You'll need a vibologist for that, I think, Glenny.' He laughed at the photocopier. 'You know, get a vibe expert in there, clean out the vibe and then offer it back to them, vibe free.' He laughed at his own joke.

Elsie said, 'Oh, no, they've bought on Lansdowne.'

'Elsie, your secret Santa is going to bring you a joke book.'

'Oh, oh, I see,' she said, and chuckled redly.

'Well, I'm showing again in an hour. Family. Just the wife and husband coming, I think. Yesterday I showed it to a woman and her mother. They seemed interested. The husband is out of town until the fifteenth. They said they wouldn't look at it again until he was back.'

'Oh, it'll be gone by then,' Gavin Edwards said, nodding, Fido bouncing in agreement.

'Oh, yes, absolutely,' Elsie agreed.

Glenn raised an eyebrow, but silently agreed. It was the buying season.

The Trents had brought along their teenaged daughter.

'This is Amber,' the mother said, after introductions had been made. Glenn smiled brightly at the girl, who half smiled back and then dipped her eyes to the floor, where they stayed, Glenn thought. She didn't know how the girl saw to walk.

They were motivated buyers. Mr Trent – *call me Don* – was about to leave town on business for an extended period of time and wanted the house question settled, and them settled in the house, before he left.

'We've got just over a month to find, buy, and move,' he said firmly. His wife smiled and nodded at everything he said. He worked in plastics for an international company and was away a lot. Mrs Trent stayed home, but inquired about business in the area.

'I'm going to need something to do,' she said to Glenn, as they walked through the house. 'Don is gone all the time and Amber has grown up. Don doesn't want me to work, but there is a limit to how dirty a house can get.' She laughed, but Glenn sensed a backbone somewhere in there about to be tested. Don squired his daughter about, his arm around her shoulders.

They were about to go out to the backyard and take a look at its size (Don would like a deck and a garage, one day). Amber asked if she could just look around on her own.

'Sure thing, little girl, you go right ahead,' Don said, and left the house to prowl the yard.

'Don't touch the walls, honey. They've been painted,' her mother said. The daughter rolled her eyes, something only Glenn caught, and then the two women went outside.

Don *liked* the yard. Don tended to say what he thought.

'That's a *nice* yard,' he said. 'You don't find a backyard that size any more.'

'It's a nice yard,' Mrs Trent echoed.

'Good size. Room for a deck. Can see a problem with a garage, though. All those trees back there.' The two women nodded. Glenn added that the trees were young and some could be moved.

'*Tough* job,' he said. '*Tough* job.'

The three of them went back into the house in time to hear the girl scream.

It was a terrible scream and paralysed them all for a split second, and then there was a crash of something heavy to the floor upstairs and Don was running for the stairs.

The women exchanged quick looks, and then the mother, with Glenn behind her, ran too.

They found Don with Amber, at the end of the hall, in front of the pull-down stairs that led to the attic. She was curled up in his arms, still screaming incoherently and sobbing.

'*There's a man! A man up there – he –*'

Don looked up at Glenn accusatorially, 'What the hell is going on?' he said.

All three of them looked up at the ceiling. The hatch

to the attic was wide open. A light shone, illuminating a plain, grey ceiling. It was all they could see.

'There couldn't be anyone up there,' Glenn said.

'*There was! There was! It was a man!*' Amber cried. She was genuinely upset. She dragged her hands down her face, rubbing her cheeks. Tears poured out of her eyes and she looked much younger than her fourteen years. Like a baby. '*He – he – he showed me his –*' and she began to sob harder still. Don's face went red with rage.

Mrs Trent went white. She dropped to the floor and began to croon, '*Oh my poor baby poor baby –*'

Glenn stood by helplessly, alternating between the open hatch and the trio on the floor. 'I don't know what to say, there's been no one –'

Don, red-faced and apoplectic with rage, called up the hatch, 'I'm coming up there, you bastard! Touch my little girl –' and he took the hatch ladder in two steps, disappearing into the attic.

Glenn urged the two on the floor to move away from the ladder. Mrs Trent helped her daughter up. The girl looked up towards the hatch and began her shrieking again.

'*He showed me his thing!*'

Mrs Trent covered the girl's head with her arms, forcing her almost to walk in a crouch. The three of them stood outside the blue room, looking up into the hole. The girl's sobs slowed and she sniffled. Glenn offered her tissues from her purse.

They listened to Don's footsteps, at first stomping, then not. Then just walking. They could follow him around the attic by the sound of his feet.

'Why did you go up there?' Glenn asked.

'It was open!' she said, defensively.

'It wasn't. I've never seen it open.'

The girl turned to her mother, her face indignant. 'It *was* open! It was, honest!'

Mrs Trent gave Glenn a look that could not be interpreted. But she suspected it was embarrassment. 'It's okay, honey. It's okay.'

Glenn went to the ladder. 'I'm going to go up,' she said. The girl was calming down. There was no one up there. She climbed the ladder carefully. It was steep. At the top she stuck her head through the hatch and saw a man. It was, of course, Mr Trent. He stood in the middle of the huge, empty room, clutching what at first looked like a spear. It was a hook for the ladder and hatch. There was not so much as a piece of drywall to hide behind. The attic was illuminated by a bare bulb that hung low from the dropped ceiling. It swayed. He must have banged it as he went past. It cast shadows.

'I think maybe the light played a trick,' Glenn said. She stood on the ladder, not going up. It was chilly up there. A window had been set in the vent. It would have cast very little light. As the bulb swung, it cast its own shadow. She pointed at the bulb.

Don looked at it absently. Slowly he nodded. He stuck his hands into his pockets. 'She got quite a scare. Someone could have run out between the time she screamed and we got upstairs,' he said feebly.

'We would have heard him, seen him. She would have said. I don't mean to question her, but I believe it was likely the light playing tricks.'

He nodded and dropped the pole. It clattered loud in the empty room, and Glenn jumped a little at the sound of it. He came to the hatch. Glenn backed down. Mrs Trent and Amber looked expectantly at the two of them as Mr Trent descended.

He shrugged. 'No one up there, honey,' he said kindly. 'I think you saw the lightbulb swinging –'

'I did NOT! There was a man, Daddy! Honest to god there was.' She looked at everyone in turn, wanting support. When she found only sympathetic glances, she buried her face in her mother's sweater and resumed her sobs.

'What the hell was that hatch doing open, anyway?' Don said, unwilling to leave his daughter undefended.

'I swear it was closed the last time I was here. I suppose another agent could have –' It was too late, of course, for the Trents. The four of them walked down the stairs. Don took over comforting Amber. At the door, Glenn apologized profusely and asked them if they would like to see something else.

Mrs Trent wrinkled her nose. 'I think, give us a couple of days before you call. I suppose Amber wouldn't let us buy this place over her dead body, now,' she said.

'I'm terribly, terribly sorry. Nothing like this has ever happened.'

'She's a little high-strung,' Mrs Trent said.

'I think they all are at that age, aren't they?' Glenn said, not really knowing one way or the other.

Father and daughter got into the back seat of the car together.

'I'm sorry, Mrs Darnley, thank you for your time,' the woman said. She took two steps down and said, oddly,

'She's Daddy's girl, you know,' as though by way of explanation.

Glenn repeated her own apologies and watched them drive away. Don looked back at the house through the back window. Glenn raised a hand; he didn't return the gesture.

After they'd left, Glenn went back up. The hatch had been closed, she was sure of it. She tried to think of the last time she had been upstairs, and it had been the evening before. She'd shown it to the Gillespies. If it had been open, she would have seen it.

She climbed the ladder and got up inside the attic to turn out the light.

The girl had been seeing things. The bulb was still now. To prove her point, she gave it a little push. Light flashed and blurred on the wood walls, throwing shadows around the room. Daylight tried to peer through the little window. A cold spot of air swirled around her. She shuddered.

She reached out to still the bulb, and to her right, something moved.

She swung around to where she'd seen the movement. 'Who's there?' she called. The room was bare. Empty.

'Who's there?' she said again, firmly.

She reached down, not looking, and picked up the pole. She realized she was shaking.

Glenn scrambled down the ladder, feeling foolish as she did it, and at the bottom pushed the ladder up and pulled the hatch closed with the hook on the end of the pole.

She'd left the light on.

She stared up at the hatch, listening. Imagining.

Mwa – ha ha ha . . .

Horror movie laughs from Hammer horror films of her youth.

Screw it. The light could stay on. She propped the pole in the corner of the hall.

There were two cards left by other multiple listing agents on the counter in the kitchen. She knew them both vaguely and that they had been there that morning. One of them would have left the attic hatch open, the light on.

She scooped the cards up and called them from the little kitchen on her cellphone.

Maggie Richards answered first ring. She'd shown the house around nine, to two people (they're not married, she almost whispered) before they went off to work. She had never been in the attic.

'Is it nice?' was what she said.

Mike Persher had dropped by with a woman that morning, just after ten.

'You left the attic light on, and the hatch open. I had an *incident* because of it,' she said sternly.

He was defensive immediately. 'I never went near the attic,' he said. He asked if it was worth showing.

Glenn heaved a sigh. He was lying. Had to be.

'Well, what happened?'

Glenn explained in brief, saying only that the girl had *thought* she'd seen a man up there. 'It was the light, I suspect. You'll have to be sure that you turn them out if you're going to show the property,' she said, poshly as possible.

'That's so weird,' he said.

'Well, her mother said she was high-strung.' Glenn heard his confused *hmmm* on the other end. It might have been amusement. She was losing patience.

He said, 'My client saw a woman.'

Glenn looked over her shoulder. She couldn't help it.

MOVE RIGHT IN! LOVELY TWO-STOREY HOME IN QUIET,
CONVENIENT RESIDENTIAL LOCATION. RENOVATIONS
THROUGHOUT MAKE THIS HOME MOVE-IN READY!
THREE+ BEDROOMS, UNIQUE BATH, HARDWOOD
FLOORS, WORKING FIREPLACE, UNIQUE ATTIC SPACE FOR
HOME OFFICE OR GAME ROOM! REDUCED, $92,500.

'Of course, he's lying,' Elsie said later. 'And he said the
thing about the woman to rock your boat. Don't you
remember the story about him and Patty Bunkle?' Glenn
did. Mike Persher had stolen a client right out from
under her *nose* and then sold it for more money than the
original asking. But they *were* talking about Patty Bunkle.

Glenn hadn't had time to dwell on either incident.
The constant showing and non-sale of the Belisle house
had brought her a number of listings as well as a number
of clients looking for 'the same but different'. It was a
buyer's market right now and she had two more couples
looking at houses almost across town from each other.
She didn't have time to do more than grab an apple from
the company fridge for lunch before heading out again.

'Your hair is so *modern*,' Elsie told her, and she couldn't
tell whether she meant that in the right way or not. She
tugged at it all the time. When she had switched from
glasses to contacts in her thirties, she had spent half her
time pushing glasses that weren't there higher up on her

nose; now she spent half her time brushing hair that wasn't there off her cheeks. Secretly, she was starting to like it. It was easy to keep and flattered her thinner face.

She was a half-inch from a sale with the second couple by five o'clock that evening. They were going to sleep on it.

It was after eight when she finally walked in through her own front door. Weighing most prominently on her mind at that point was her overburdened schedule for the next day. She had another Belisle showing (although she was near sick over that place and so familiar with the spiel that she could have cellphoned it in: *Look at the lovely high ceilings in this hall! The floors have been refinished throughout the main level and look! A working fireplace*) and she had a good strong feeling about the Vespers and the house on Laughlin.

A new woman, looking for a place for herself and her young daughter, was interested in a place on Sherber and there was the offer for the Durbin place in, they would hear about that tonight – *oh god not tonight I'm dead on my feet* – and she was showing an older couple a condo in Westwood Park. A gated place.

She put the kettle on to boil for tea and, while waiting for the water, she took cucumber and mayonnaise out of the refrigerator to make a little sandwich for her tea. She added some beansprouts that looked a day from going off.

A little Debussy went on the stereo and the day was just starting to slip off her. High heels were dropped beside the big chair in the sitting room and slippers went on. The kettle sang and she poured the water into the teapot, then carried a tray of goodies into the sitting room. She had her tea and a sandwich in the chair while making notes in her day book – when her pen ran out of ink and she had to go into the variety drawer in the kitchen to search out another. On top of all of the miscellaneous junk in the drawer, like a flag waving in the air, was an incomplete crossword puzzle in How's messy print.

Printed in block letters across the top was the answer to one across: *Bethune*.

Glenn pulled the folded-over newspaper out of the drawer and sat down at the little kitchen table with it. It was nearly filled in. Missing was thirty-six down: like pot-pourri. And forty-two down: *A-team* actor. And four-teen across: chip off Woody's block. She got up to find a pencil and sat back down.

Thirty-six down: *aromatic*.

Forty-two down: *Mr T*.

Fourteen across: *Arlo*.

She filled the little squares carefully, lovingly. She ran her fingers over the letters he'd printed and then moved her pencil, tracing them. Aromatic. She thought maybe he didn't know what pot-pourri was, although there was a little bowl of it gathering dust in the bathroom, a gift from one of his students when he retired from the high school. Glenn tried to remember the name of the girl and drifted off a moment.

I'm sorry, How. I lost track of you today.

Time marches on, Miss Glenn.

It was that stupid house and all the time it was taking up. It was being back with people that had done it. They talked to her about things that had nothing to do with

How or her life with him so she thought of those other things without combining them, the way she used to. Her conversations with people had always included him.

No one mentioned him now. Because he was gone? Or because they were being delicate? She felt a loss in there somewhere. That he was being forgotten by default, forgotten in favour of her.

Her tummy nudged her. There had been a little ache there all day, which she had attributed to having not eaten. She had assumed that the sandwich and tea would take care of it. It hadn't. In fact, she felt a little nauseous with it. It was a little burn that sat just under her diaphragm, not unlike heartburn, except that it hadn't really gone away. She rubbed it. There were Tums in the cupboard. She found them and chewed two, the cherry flavour over-sweet, making her cheeks pinch in.

If there was a way to honour How's memory, to make good for having forgotten him all day, she couldn't think what it might be. She wasn't very good at crosswords.

The music on the stereo penetrated for a moment. How had loved Debussy. The only classical composer he could stand, in fact. She hoped she'd put it on for that reason.

She stood up and swayed, slowly, imaginary arm around her waist, phantom hand in hers.

Sleep was long in coming.

The Belisle house added a mechanical problem to its list of irritations. Several weeks into the listing, the faucet of the tub – the tub itself had not been as big an attraction as Glenn had supposed it would be; in fact a number of people had commented on the feet of the thing as being 'a little scary' – began to drip. Being in and out of the house all the time, it seemed hard to notice. Glenn would only notice when they went into the bathroom, and on some occasions the shower curtain was drawn. Or not. It looked much better drawn, and whenever she showed the house, she made a point of drawing the plain white curtain around its maw (as it were).

The dripping tap left a little puddle in the bottom of the tub, around the drain, giving the appearance that the water did not properly drain. Which was true: it didn't. Although most houses have a lurch or two in their floors, this one had proven difficult enough to unload without the added issue of mechanical breakdown.

She spoke to Mr Cassevetes at the insurance company about having a couple of little things taken care of. There was an assortment of small items that needed attention that in the rush of the buyers' season, somehow, Glenn had simply not gotten around to asking for.

'In a week or so it may become necessary to discuss another reduction,' Glenn added, in the last seconds of the conversation.

'A reduction? What?' She had never met Mr Cassevetes, but he sounded the sort who always had something in his mouth, a cigar or a sandwich. She pictured him large.

'In the asking price, Mr Cassevetes. It doesn't seem to be moving. We've not had so much as an offer.'

He grunted and it sounded as though he might have swallowed. The pause on the other end became so long that Glenn was tempted to ask if he was still there. She waited patiently.

'I'll think about that. We're not in the charity business,

Mrs Darnley,' was his patient answer. He agreed to a workman for one day.

Glenn met the workman at the house in the morning, using a fellow she had used at her own home, Mr Gretner. She pointed out the pillar-cum-cairn at the foot of the path and asked that it be removed and the hole covered as best possible. She explained about the tap in the upper bath and added that she believed a washer was all it would need. She asked him to measure the Murphy bed frame in the small room off the kitchen downstairs.

'I'd like to be able to tell people what they need,' she explained. 'I'm not going to buy a mattress.' There was the problem of the back screen door opening and swinging in the wind. 'I can imagine the damage to the spring,' she said, by way of explanation. She also asked that he install a lock and latch on the attic hatch, lock it and give her the key.

'How long do you suppose, Mr Gretner?'

Tom Gretner walked around the pillar in the front and Glenn followed him around to the back of the house where he took a look at the screen door, well latched and firmly closed at the moment. He glanced at her questioningly. 'Well, it's latched now, but it seems to be at its own whim. I arrived here yesterday and found it banging against the side of the house.'

Tom opened and closed it cleanly a couple of times, peered meaningfully into its workings and closed it again. 'Can't see what the problem would be,' he said.

Glenn popped two Tums into her mouth from her pocket. 'Look over there, Mr Gretner,' she said, pointing to the wall on the outside of the house where the screen door had already left a mark. 'It's banging against the paint,' she said, defensively. 'Just tighten something on it. The wind may be catching it.' Tom opened and closed the door again, and the two of them ran their eyes around the edges of the door. It fitted smoothly, no place for wind to catch.

'Okay, Mrs Darnley, will do,' he said.

'And you suppose it will take how long?'

'Lock and that's going to take an hour – I'll have to run to the hardware for that. Pick up a washer while I'm there . . . wouldn't mind a look at the tap before I go. Washer won't take long if that's the need of it, and then the pillar out front –' He licked his lips, staring off into space. He checked his watch. It was after nine.

'Could be packed up and out of here by two–three. Does that suit you?'

Glenn smiled. 'That will be lovely,' she said. And left him to it.

After leaving the Belisle Headache, as she had come to think of it, Glenn showed a little two-bedroom on a pricy street to a young nurse straight up from the country. The nurse loved it and put in a respectable offer on the $75,000 place right away.

Now why couldn't that happen with the Belisle place?

Around one thirty Glenn dropped by the Belisle house. Mr Gretner's patchwork truck was still parked outside. The pillar was gone. She walked up the stone path, hardly glancing to see the earth filled in, and went inside. She could hear the terrible whine of a power tool. She waited for it to stop or subside. When it did she called up. 'Mr Gretner! How goes the lonely battle?'

Tom came to the top of the stairs and down two or three steps to look down at her. He looked odd without his cap. He was quite bald-headed and looked chubby and baby-like with the sun streaming down on the top of his pink skull from the window on the stairwell. 'Just putting your lock on for you, now,' he said. 'That post outside took a little longer than I thought it would. She was dug in deep. I put it out back in the yard by the trees till someone comes to claim her. Put a new washer in the bath tap. Should be all right for you now,' he said. 'Be another half-hour or so. Two's what I said, right?'

'Oh, yes. Don't mind me. I was in the area, is all. I'll leave you to it. I'd like to show it today at three if I can. I have a couple interested,' she said, casually. Mr Gretner would have no idea (or interest) in the epic Selling of the Belisle House.

She turned to go and he called back to her: 'I – um – tightened your screen door for you,' he said.

She could hear the smile on his face without turning around to see it. 'I'm very pleased,' she said, hoping he could hear hers.

The Armstrongs met Glenn outside a truckless 362 Belisle at three on the nose. She had hoped they would be late so that she could just walk through the house and see that everything was tidy after Mr Gretner had been there.

They pulled up in a green, late-model Volvo station-wagon, thankfully without their apparent children. The Armstrongs were Cal and Effie, a dentist and his hygienist wife. Effie explained right away that they had to practically 'run through' the house, as they had to pick up the children in a half-hour.

'Traffic will be terrible,' she said, tilting her head and looking over the place. They waited for Glenn's lead.

'Shall we, then?' And she led them up the walk, with Cal bringing up the rear.

'What happened here?' was the first thing Cal said. Glenn and Effie stopped and looked back at him. He was toeing the ground at the end of the path, where the pillar had stood. The ground was turned up, but not filled in. The earth was black and rich-looking. Not at all frozen.

'Oh, I'm sorry. That was something we had taken care of today.' She explained about the pillar, saying only that it was monogrammed and that the Previous Owners had wanted it back, not bothering to add that the thing looked like a headstone for a very narrow memory.

'That will be filled in tomorrow,' she said. 'The hedge goes all the way around the house. Caragana, you know. It will bloom, come summer.' She led them inside.

They did, indeed, run through the house. They did the upstairs first. 'We're practically there anyway!' Effie said. The tap was not dripping in the bathroom and there was no tell-tale puddle at the drainway.

They liked the little blue bedroom. They had two children, Effie said. 'Earl's nine and Katie's thirteen. She wouldn't mind the yellow room. You're sure that smell will come out?'

Glenn assured them that it was just a matter of airing the place. She said it had been shut up a long time. They nodded agreeably to everything Glenn told them.

The back door stayed shut. The three of them piled out of it, and Glenn shut it herself to be sure. It latched securely and snugly. He had tightened *something*.

'It looks a little like a graveyard.' Cal snickered. Glenn turned with a smile, about to explain the style of the English garden, when she saw what they were referring to.

Perched against the back fence, almost but not quite buried behind the trees and tangles, was the pillar, boldly white against the black and grey of the hibernating perennials. Spectral.

'So that's where they're buried?' Cal laughed. 'Waverley, is it?' he read, tilting his head sideways. Glenn glanced over at Effie, who had a hand to her throat and was grimacing.

'It looks awful there,' she said.

'The owners are picking it up tonight. Those are all perennials planted there. And the trees are young, but very healthy, wouldn't you say?'

A breeze came up and blew dead, year-old leaves around the yard.

'They're picking it up tonight,' she said.

The Armstrongs admitted they hadn't given the time necessary to really look at the house. They admitted it was most of the things they were looking for. They asked Glenn if she would mind if they slept on it and gave her call in a couple of days. That was most often the code for 'no, thank you'.

Glenn thanked them and gave them another issue of her card and told them that there were a number of houses on the market in their price range. 'None are as lovely as this,' she added.

'Not as convenient either,' Cal said. 'This one'll take you from cradle to grave.' He laughed and winked at

Glenn. She smiled gamely and let him have a little chuckle, but the joke was wearing thin.

They didn't make an offer.

After they drove away, she walked through the house, checking to see if all was at rights. She thought briefly of propping the window in the sick room open again, she couldn't help but think of it as that, and decided it was a bad idea. She also didn't want to go in there. She left the door open. The attic hatch was locked. The keys were on the counter in the kitchen, along with the carefully printed measurements for the Murphy bed frame. She found herself walking slowly and thoughtfully through the rooms once more, the light starting to fade outside, the house looking sleepier in the dull light.

She went down the stairs in the same way, eyes roaming up and down walls, as though trying to discern something that she couldn't openly see.

Her footsteps spoke on the bare wood floors through the living room and dining room. She checked the back screen door. It was latched and behaving like a child warned enough times.

On the way back through she stopped in the living room. She stared into the clean, untried fireplace. Up the walls. Through the window.

Eyes upward.

'You're going to have to do better than this,' she told the house. 'I'm going to wash my hands of you. I mean it.' She stuck her hands into the pockets of her raincoat and flapped it open and shut a few times as though in supplication.

She looked sternly around the room once more. She locked up before leaving.

She did so tenderly, as though to make up.

The house sold the following Monday.

The couple, Dan and Rebecca Mason, were in their mid-thirties, childless, but wanting a larger home. They were a very attractive couple, although he was on the softer side of masculine and that wasn't necessarily Glenn's type, but she could see how very lovely his face and form were. She was tall and slender and dark and very self-assured. They both were. Glenn actually found them rather bold at first, when they separated from her (and from each other) and wandered around the house unaided. She respected confidence, of course.

For once, the whole house behaved. The back door had decided to stay put since Mr Gretner had fastened or tightened or bewitched it, the tap did not leak and, as predicted, the earth in the hole where the pillar had been had blown over, or whatever it had done, and looked less craven and conspicuous. The Waverley cairn had been picked up. By whom she did not know. She had simply put in a call to the insurers and they had had it removed.

She decided she liked them when she heard Mr Mason scream from the room with the Murphy bed, 'I *love* it! Becca, come and see!' The two women joined him in there and couldn't help but catch his enthusiasm. The Murphy bed was pulled down and took up much of the doorway space.

'It's so funky,' he said. Becca touched it delicately with a long, manicured finger. She was a director of some sort at a medical administrative place or something downtown. She did not say it so much as elocuted it, and Glenn wondered if it was a new promotion. Something about a health professional with long nails bothered Glenn, but she, of course, kept her poker face. Dan was a graphic artist at Clayton and Marks. The agency had used them once, Glenn had mentioned. She believed they did the Shelter logo.

'It's my studio! Totally!' Becca looked dubious as far as Glenn could see, but she could, for the first time, smell something good in the house.

'I knew I would find someone who would appreciate that particular little gem if I waited,' Glenn said, smiling. 'I have the dimensions for the mattress, if you're interested.'

'It's beautiful,' Becca said. The couple met eyes.

And Glenn took her cue. 'If you don't mind, I'll leave you two for a moment. Please enjoy the house, I've got a call to make. Do you mind?' She was bluffing, giving them a chance to get on to the same page.

She disappeared on to the front step. She called the office and chatted briefly with Elsie. She wanted to say she had a nibble, but would not for the world charm it. She would give them ten minutes. She called her drycleaner. Her skirts were ready. They had not been able to get a spot out of her jacket. She chewed a couple of Tums.

After ten minutes had passed, she went back inside, glad of it, the spring air crisp that morning, although the sun was warm and would be warmer. Already summer seemed a possibility. 'Well, I'm done with my calls,' she said casually. 'What can I show you?'

49

'How about the deeds?' Mr Mason said, grinning broadly, his arm wrapped around his wife's waist. She smiled at her husband and laughed, a tinkly laugh.

And that was that. How would have been pleased.

Company You Keep

I

Rebecca Mason dipped the shammy in the bucket and rinsed it in the warm water. Carefully she squeezed out the excess, and as she did, the scent of pine filled her nose. It was a good smell. Clean. She liked things to smell clean. She folded the cloth in half, and then in half again, forming a neat, hand-sized square. Then she ran the damp cloth over the baseboard from the corner, an arm's length from her, to the end of her other shoulder, precisely; in this way she kept track of where she had washed, and what was yet to be done. She repeated this when she moved the bucket an equal distance each time, so that it stayed just four inches to her left. Her eyes followed the motion of the cloth, and she moved gracefully, but her thoughts were not in the yellow room at the end of the upstairs hall at all.

In her head, a cocktail party was in full swing.

Ice tinkled gently in glasses. Laughter was discreet and elegant. Conversations were quiet, and thoughtful, murmurs really, in a large, high-ceilinged room, with a ceiling moulded with ivy leaves intricately woven and forming an enormous circle around a giant chandelier. Hundreds of crystals hung suspended in light, casting stars on the four walls surrounding it. Sometimes, instead of a chandelier, the room was lit with hundreds of tiny white lights strung on cord so fine it was invisible. Becca spent a lot of time constructing that room.

It was an old fantasy.

How do you do? I'm Rebecca Mason. She wore, usually, black Armani, cocktail-length, of course, and carried a small, discreet Prada bag. Her hair differed each time, according to the time of day. If it was an early-evening affair, she wore her hair loose. If it was later, her hair was pulled back and held fast with a clip covered in black velvet; only rarely was it up. Her jewellery was minimal and well chosen. It also varied, tastefully.

What do you do?

If there was music, it was strictly in the background. The music in Becca's fantasy cocktail parties was the low rumble of important voices, from the mouths of important people. Who they were in reality was less important to her than who she was in their midst. At the cocktail parties in her mind, Becca was an equal among giants. She was a success.

How do you do? I'm Rebecca Mason. I'm the Director of Patient Services at the Centre for Improved Health. We were featured in the Atlantic *last year.*

The cloth swept efficiently across the south wall, and Becca turned herself around in a swivel on her bottom and repeated the process with barely a missed motion. She was nearly done. The floor had been washed, rinsed, and rinsed a second time already, early that morning. The walls had been washed the night before. They were clean, bright and without streaks. It was mid-afternoon, and they had been in the house a week. The previous weekend had been entirely taken up with the steady and constant movement of boxes, endless boxes, more boxes than she was sure she had packed, and she had mentioned to her husband that she believed they were breeding. It had been a joke, of course, but a joke was rare enough from her that he had looked twice at her before laughing.

Under his breath, not more than a beat later, she had been sure she'd heard him say, *I'm glad someone's getting it around here*, but when she asked him to repeat what he'd said, he said, 'Nothing.'

You're very young to be a director.

Yes.

The room smelled heavily, and pleasantly, of pine forests as replicated by Johnson and Johnson. Under the pine scent was the fainter scent of oil soap; she'd used the oil soap on the floor, but had decided the baseboards required something stronger. She thought of bare feet rubbing up against them for years and years, the flesh leaving its traces, never washed off, just sitting and breeding its germs and filth; no one ever thought to wash a baseboard.

She could feel the water cooling through the thickness of her rubber gloves. Her hands were sweating under them, and would likely be puckered, but they would not be dry and flaky and itchy at work on Monday. It was important to keep up appearances. Under the gloves each fingernail had been carefully wrapped in cotton batting and taped with surgical tape to protect it. She'd had a manicure on Wednesday, and although she was trying very hard not to think in *those* terms, she could not afford another this month.

Intermittently, she could hear the whir of Dan's drill from the room under the stairs, the one with the bed that folded out of the wall. The Murphy bedroom, the realtor had called it. Dan called it no such thing: he called it *the studio*, as though it were some loft in New York, instead of a room hardly bigger than a closet, hidden under the stairwell.

The drill sounded for a couple of seconds and then stopped. Becca worked her way across the last baseboard, on the east wall.

Sun poured in from the west window, making a shadow on the wall. Out of the corner of her eye, she saw her own head bob and rise with each swipe of the shammy. It was probably after four already. She looked up from her work, and arched her back, stretching out from her diaphragm. She rolled her head on her neck.

They were having friends of Dan's for coffee.

You're very young to be a director. You must be very good at what you do.

Ice tinkled in glasses. Conversations around her were of portfolios and state dinners, private schools and senate races.

Yes. Her dress was custom fit. In it, her breasts were high and discreetly perfect. Her stockings blended subtly from her discreet black pumps to her modest hemline, just two inches above her knee, knees smooth.

Downstairs the drill sounded again, twice in rapid succession, as though the first attempt hadn't quite been right and he was forcing the issue. Which was probably true. Dan wasn't handy. The drill was his only real tool, although they had a motley collection of screwdrivers and hammers. The rest of the items in their 'toolbox' were odd things that were rarely used for their purpose: a large heavy file that had pried open a little crate of Christmas oranges sent to them by her mother from Florida one year; an awl that had been used to punch air-holes in a jar when Dan's nephew caught a butterfly at their old house a year earlier. Nothing matched. Nothing was particularly useful. They kept it all. Just in case.

And what does your husband do?

Sometimes in her fantasy (and more lately) she danced. Her partner would be older and urbane rather than handsome, with a moustache and a smile that seemed to know more than he gave away. She would relax in his arms, neither leaning nor leading, and yet he would almost carry her with every stride. There was an assumption of what he did for a living; it was never entirely defined in her fantasy, drifting over a multitude of occupations that were titular rather than hands-on: publisher, CEO, president, director, politico.

What does your husband do?

Becca reached the corner where she had started and gave it a last wipe with the cloth. The water was murky, but not dirty. Dust floated serenely on top in little patterns. She sighed and stood up slowly so as not to bump the bucket, which was resting on a square of newspaper. She gave the room a once-over. It was remarkably yellow. The sun brightened it considerably, and there was a moment of adjustment for your eyes when the sun was at its fullest in the room. There were two windows, a south-facing window that overlooked the street, and a west window, which mostly overlooked the windowless side of the neighbour's house and the hedge that wrapped around their place. Their new house. The house that they might not be able to pay for in a couple of months, unless she made director.

She would make director.

Her heart pounded when she thought about money.

To make it stop she leaned over and picked up the bucket with her rubber-gloved hands. Her fingers felt moist under the cotton batting and she would be happy to get it off. She made herself think only of these things. Becca was a very focused person. When she had a will, she could do anything.

From downstairs, Dan hollered, 'Becca! Come hold the shelf!' At the sound of his voice, Becca closed her eyes. It was just for a moment, but in that moment she could feel her body turning inward on itself, away from the voice downstairs.

Becca was going to talk Dan into ordering Chinese. To do that, she was going to have to be sweet and accommodating. *Please, not too accommodating.* Max and Kate were coming for coffee after supper. Friends of Dan's. Max was Dan's new partner. Which sounded much better than the truth.

And what does your husband do?

He has a partner.

That sounds impressive.

Yes.

What do they do, these partners?

They're making a comic book. It's about a superhero.

Becca carried the bucket out of the yellow room at the end of the upstairs hall and into the bathroom. Inside her head, the atmosphere of the cocktail party changed dramatically. Gales of laughter overtook genteel conversation and elegant chuckles. She dumped the bucket in the tub and watched as the greyish liquid rolled slowly down the drain and then rinsed the tub efficiently before pulling off her rubber gloves. Without the gloves her fingers looked like oversized Q-tips. She smiled at that.

She peeled the tape off and was pleased when no glue was left behind.

He used to be in advertising.

He won an award.

'Becca!' Dan called up again.

'I'm coming!' she called down, and took her time, unwrapping each finger slowly, lovingly, and wondering if she should have sex with him before Max and Kate came and that way get it over with for the night, or if putting it off for the evening until she had at least had a glass of wine would make it easier.

The studio, as he was calling it, and had been enthusiastically calling it since the moment he and Becca had put in the first offer on the house, was filling up fast. There was a serious lack of room, but as the boxes emptied and were put out in the hallway, it was beginning to take on a cosy feeling, as opposed to the crowded feeling he had briefly been afraid of at the beginning of the week. There was not much left to go inside. Once the books were unpacked and on the shelves, it would free up the rest of the floor space and he could unpack the rest of his stuff, put up the drafting table, his floor lamp (the overhead was just a bulb, and cast a horrible glare over everything, it would be a disaster at night, when he was tired), and his supplies table. Then he was set. There would be just room for the bed to come down and room for a bedside table if he so chose – although he didn't anticipate using the bed too often – and that would be it. Cosy.

Next year he would put in a window on the outside wall. It would be useless for light for most of the day, being an east window, but it would be very nice in the morning. He did his best work at night anyway.

That was habit. He had always worked at night because he'd had a day job, or he'd been in classes during the day. He could work any time he wanted now, and that was both a total bummer and excellent.

For the first time in his twenty-eight years, Dan Mason was gainfully unemployed. Unless you counted college. Even then, he'd worked part-time, framing prints for people whose conception of art rarely went further than making sure it matched their sofa.

He realized too late that instead of putting the upper shelves on first he had anchored the frame to the wall and attached the lower two shelves to the frame, using his eye as a level (he had a great eye). The bottom three shelves were in place, and only the top one remained. But he couldn't quite get under it. He would need Becca to hold it while he stood on a chair with the drill.

Dan shrugged and took a break, slipping out of the house into the backyard for a smoke. Becca didn't like smoking in the house. During the day he often broke that rule, taking a smoke break in his studio as he pondered or unpacked, and so far she hadn't said much. He kept it contained in the small space and usually stopped doing it long before she got home from work, so there was time to air the place out. When he put his window in, he was going to smoke all he wanted in there. *Second-hand smoke kills, Dan.*

Not reliably. He smiled, thinking of the line from the movie. He'd used it on her a few times, but she never got the reference. She never remembered things like movie lines, or bits of poetry or famous quotes. If you told her the reference (which spoiled using it at all), she would smile falsely and sometimes laugh, if they were in a group, but it wouldn't reach her eyes and he would know that she didn't get it. It was, in a way, part of her charm. At least, he used to think so.

The backyard was a tangle of untended garden. He was still mildly high from a joint smoked early in the afternoon and so, looking at the garden, he imagined himself getting in there and untangling it and replanting, propagating and creating something of unearthly beauty, a little Garden of Eden. He had time, after all. One afternoon when he wasn't working, he would get out there and dig around in the dirt. It would be great. Dirt smelled great. Earthy and green. It was creation. He felt a surge of creativity that made him flick his lit cigarette to the side and wander over to the garden. He bent over, hands on knees, and stared into the tangle trying to recognize something in there. He thought he saw some columbine, some *impatiens*. He was no plant expert, but they were plants his mom had grown.

He stretched into the sun, squinting against it, and looked at the back of the new house. Big place. Nice big yard. Nice place. Lots of atmosphere. A good place to be creative. He wished for a cigarette and patted the pocket of his denim shirt for the pack, but he'd left it on the table by the back door. He liked a smoke while he thought.

Place could use a coat of paint; roof might need work; some gingerbread to match the back screen door would be cute as hell at the peak of the roof. Wouldn't take anything at all to do and Bec wouldn't scream about the money if he did it himself. In his mildly stoned state he felt both capable of anything (creative) and sort of tired, like he needed a shower. It was mid-afternoon. Max and Kate would be there in a few hours. In a perfect world, he would have liked to have the studio all finished for when Max showed up.

And it was a perfect world. Dan was finally doing what he had been made to do. He was doing his art. At home. No more bullshit job; no more nine-to-five kissing ass.

Perfect world.

He went inside and called for Becca to come and help with the last shelf.

Becca fixed her hair before going downstairs. She would have a shower before their guests, Dan's guests, came, but for now she pulled out the elastic gently and brushed the tangles from her long hair. All gently. She took very good care of her hair, and in return it was thick and glossy, poker straight. With her fair complexion it gave her an exotic look, she liked to think. Her features were thin and even, broken only by a high, round forehead. Her shirt – actually an old shirt of Dan's that she used to clean in – was dusty at the front and she brushed at it carefully with the palms of her hands, holding her fingertips outward so as not to catch a nail on a button or pocket. That was how accidents happened. If you were aware and alert, accidents were avoided and so was the disappointment. It was focus. She was a very focused person.

'I'm coming!' she yelled. She would have sex with him now, and get it done with, then she could shower and be clean for the rest of the night. It wasn't good for the skin to shower too often, and she felt dirty and dusty, as though a film was encasing her.

The cup in the bathroom had a white-grey film in a circle on the bottom from toothpaste. She took it with her.

She walked erectly down the stairs. Chinese would be a forty-dollar order, but she was in the mood for it and then wouldn't have to cook or clean up before Max and Kate arrived. It was logical.

And (for god's sakes) it was her money, wasn't it?

The front door was closed against the sun, making the hallway dark after the brightness of the upstairs and Becca paused, slowing down on the stairs, blinking to let her eyes adjust to the light. Through the wide doorway into the living room, she could see that light flooded the room. The front window spanned almost the whole wall, and was at least six feet tall; she'd added a rider to their house insurance to cover it against breakage. That had been another twenty-five dollars. Of course, Dan had still had his job then.

She took the cup into the kitchen to put it into the sink, only half registering the open door to Dan's studio. As she passed it she called back, 'Will I need gloves for this?' noting that the leather gloves were in the toolbox, which she could see open on the kitchen floor.

Dan answered something back, but Becca hadn't heard him. Deciding she did (wood splinters, hard edges), she picked up the pair of heavy leather work gloves and walked back through the kitchen, to the studio. She could see Dan, bent over in front of the shelves with the tape measure.

She heard the snake of the tape running back into the metal casing (a sound like nails on a blackboard) as she approached the small door to the studio. It was wide open, pressed against the west wall.

Just in front, a cold breeze hit her from the front, swirling around her, cooling the sweat on her back and freezing her. Gooseflesh broke out on her arms. She crossed her arms over her breasts, feeling her nipples harden. She opened her mouth – *it's so cold in* – taking a single step in the room.

BANG! The door slammed shut just as her foot crossed the threshold, smashing hard on her big toe.

'*Oh!*' She took a reactive jump backwards, staggering, cursing inwardly. She bent over and grabbed her foot, rubbing her toe. (*Shit.*)

Dan said something on the other side, alarmed, but it was too muffled to make out.

'The goddamn *door* slammed in my face!' she called out angrily, at least as much at the door as to Dan inside.

Becca straightened up, face screwed up in a pout – *felt like the nail cracked that's going to hurt in heels on Monday* – and grabbed the knob, turning it and pushing, stumbling again when her weight did not open the door. She turned and pushed again.

It did not open. She rattled it gently, coaxing, turned it and pushed again, but it was stuck. 'Dan,' she called, leaning over to feel around her toe again, checking for the cracked nail, 'let me in. The door's stuck.'

From inside he called, 'What?' She pictured him looking up, not even having noticed or heard the slamming door, *he can just ignore everything completely oblivious to the world must be nice*, colour rose in her cheeks, annoyance making her voice rise shrilly, hating the sound of it when it came out of her mouth. She hated yelling. Dan yelled from wherever he was, regularly. Like a fishwife. It was unattractive.

'The door is stuck! Let me *in*.' She said the last part through gritted teeth and then banged hard on the wood twice, not knocking, but *smacking* it, angry; she tried turning it again, but it gave no quarter.

Then it swung open easily, the knob tugged gently out of her hand. Dan stood behind it. 'You have to be gentle with it, Bec. It's an old knob,' he said, pushing it open, all the way to the wall.

'It was *stuck*.'

'You have to go easy,' he said, firmly.

'Well, it wouldn't open. You should change the knobs.'

'I don't want to. They're funky. They're *cool*.' The knobs were white porcelain and they were attractive; it was a look, as they say, that matched the interior of the room. It was a part of the house untouched by time or renovators. For whatever reason.

'It's probably not safe,' she said, not willing to let it go, feeling the tension rise in her, the wanting to pick a fight, that she had been feeling lately whenever they were in close quarters. Picking a fight seemed better than the alternative. It just seemed like he was always crawling on her. Always wanting to.

It will pass. This is a phase. That was what Donna at work said. *We went through it; now we're fine again. Moving's hell.* She hadn't told Donna, of course, that they weren't having sex. Not much anyway. Not like they used to. She hadn't mentioned to Donna and she wouldn't, god knows she wouldn't. Especially not the part about how she just didn't want to any more, about how the sight of his hands, his too-long fingers and wrists sticking out of the ends of his sleeves like pale, sickly little tree branches, made her shudder. She and Dan didn't even talk about it. Not directly. Just the odd shot. *Nice to know someone's getting it around here.*

'Maybe the stairs have shifted or something,' she added. He didn't answer her (didn't take the bait), the routine well established by then, and his way of dealing with it – *like everything it's how he handles everything* – was to avoid it.

'I need you to hold up this shelf,' he said, briskly. She gave the room a good look, her arms crossed over her chest again. He watched her. 'Pretty good, huh?'

She shrugged, 'It'll look better when you get the books unpacked.'

'Then hold this while I fix it to the wall,' he said, pointing at the board leaning against the rest of the shelving. She slipped the gloves, large, over her slender hands. She felt her nails push against the ends of the fingers. It felt confining.

He marked a spot on the wall that she could barely see and had her hold the board from the centre over the line. It was awkward. She was at an odd angle, her arms up over her head, her buttocks sticking out, her body bent in a V from the middle, her weight on the board to hold it steady.

From behind her, Dan said, 'Keep it steady.' She heard the click of a bit into the drill, but nothing else happened.

'Mmmm,' he said. 'Nice view from here.' In her mind's

eye she could see the leer spreading across his soft, almost girlishly pretty features. She closed her eyes. Waited. As if on cue, she felt his hand, hot, small, on her thigh. It rose and curved smoothly over her buttocks.

'Nice,' he repeated. She did nothing, least of all react. In a moment she heard him sigh. Then it passed. He got up under her and anchored the board to the wall and to the frame, she kept her eyes shut against the flying sawdust. The little space between them smelled of Dan's sweat and burning wood. It took only a few seconds and the unit was complete.

She let go and the two of them stood back to look.

'Pretty good. That wood goes very well in here. I wasn't sure it was going to,' he said, almost formally to his wife, the mood shift firmly in place.

'Mmm-hmm,' she said agreeably. *I want to be agreeable, I really do. This will pass.*

'I was thinking we should order Chinese,' she added once he ducked to unplug the drill and started wrapping the cord around the base of it.

'Sure,' he said guardedly.

'Okay. Is there anything you want?' *With my money?*

'I'm open.' *It's your money.*

She nodded and took a big breath and let it go, in some sort of gesture of finality. The two of them turned at the same time, and found themselves face to face, his face only inches from hers. They locked eyes. For a moment it was natural, familiar. Then Becca felt a too-familiar tightening inside herself, bracing herself for what might (would) come next. His mouth was very close to hers. He had a broad mouth, the sort with an easy smile. His teeth were even and white. Even though he smoked, he didn't have the same trouble keeping his teeth white as Becca, who had never smoked.

His eyes seemed to bore into her, not pleading like sometimes but worse, somehow, as though he were trying to see inside her, to know what she was thinking. His lips were parted. She looked at his mouth. She could see two flat slivers of white, and beyond that, a black maw. His lips were red. He had a woman's mouth. She was momentarily mesmerized by it. His lips would be warm; they were always warm. There was, in spite of everything, something appealing about his mouth.

Cold air seemed to puddle around her feet and it broke the mood. She shivered, and pulled back slightly, enough to break whatever had held them there.

'It's so cold in here. Why is that?' she said. Her voice sounded loud after the silence.

He reached out and put his hand on her arm. It was warm on her bare flesh, hot, really, in the cold air of the room.

For a long time, too long, he didn't say anything and she felt trapped by him. She looked at his arm on hers. It was bare. In a T-shirt the alarming length of his arms was unnoticeable. His fingers were long; his hands were smooth. An artist's hands. The fingers tapered at the ends. His nails were always clear, they never got white spots or cracks. They were dirty, though. Always. She knew intellectually that it wasn't dirt; it was ink. The tool of his trade. She wanted to snort at that. *Trade. You married a tradesman.* But it was.

(In college she had liked the idea, *welcomed* the idea, of his dirty hands trailing over her clean white flesh as though the ink on his fingers would stay on her skin and make her in that way a piece of what he made with his hands – lovemaking as art.)

'*Bec* –' he said. She looked back up at him. His eyes were soft; sad. Like a dog's. The air, cold, swirled around her. *Let's get this together. Fix it.*

She turned her head away from him. 'Cold,' she said mock shivering again. 'What time are they coming?' and the moment broke, as loudly as if it had been glass.

His hand dropped from her arm and he turned away. 'Seven,' he said, flatly.

'Okay, then,' she said, and left the room. In a minute, he heard her on the phone, ordering Chinese, reading off the order with clipped efficiency, enunciating each word carefully, so she did not have to repeat herself.

They gave Max and Kate the grand tour, of course. Dan changed the moment they arrived, his whole *posture* changed: his mouth became a perpetual smiling organ, he laughed easily and was more physical, even, hugging Kate and slapping Max on the back a few times, as though he hadn't seen them in years, instead of since just before they moved. He even seemed taller, walking straight down the hall when they knocked at the door, galloping the last couple of steps like a randy horse. Becca was hurt by it. He was so changed by the appearance of his friends that she couldn't help but compare it to their (mostly) silent afternoon.

Becca didn't like Max and Kate. (*You don't know them*, was Dan's answer to that when she had brought it up once.) It was too difficult for her to articulate to Dan, but it was almost an impersonal dislike, the way you don't like someone because of their politics, although it wasn't their politics that she didn't like. It was the way that Max seduced Dan out of the very natural funk he was in after Clayton and Marks had let him go, into the current foolish, practically maniacal enthusiasm for their project, the comic book. They were calling it a series of *illustrated novels*. But it was, as far as Becca could tell, a comic book. To call it anything else was what her mother would call (and had, when she told her) gilding the mule. Kate, she disliked by association.

Under other circumstances, such as circumstances previous to Dan's losing his job, Becca might have enjoyed having them around. They were interesting people, people of the sort that Dan had always had in his closet of strange friends. She had met them once or twice before the project, usually in passing at someone's Bohemian house party, the kind of party where the food was exotic and laid out on a long table, buffet-style, and you ate sitting cross-legged on the floor, and took your drinks standing up. Fridges full of beer. Half-empty bottles of wine – some of it very good – strewn about on tabletops, manteltops, coffee tables. The music too loud, the conversations peppered with talk of grants, funding, projects, theatre, and art. Max and Kate were alternative. And Kate had recently had a showing at a large gallery downtown that had been well reviewed.

('It smells so clean up here,' Kate remarked, when they looked in the yellow room.

'Yes,' Becca said.)

The four of them went down the stairs, crowding into the little room under the stairs, with their bottles of beer.

'My room,' Dan said.

He'd pulled it all together for the evening. The shelves were up and the books were on them; he'd set up his drawing-board, a large, tall, slanted surface with a glass plate in the centre that lit up when you turned on a switch. His tall stool was in front of it neatly, and beside the stool he'd laid out his art table, and his inks, pens, pencils and brushes. A closed sketchbook rested on the drafting table.

'That for me?' Max asked, grinning.

'Later, buddy,' Dan said. He opened his arms in a magnanimous gesture. 'This is the inner sanctum. Head-quarters of *The Headhunter*.'

'Good thing I'm doing the writing,' Max said, joking.

'You should spread out a bit in here, Danny,' Kate said. 'Use the room.'

'Aaah,' he said, waving his finger at her. 'There's more to this room than meets the eye,' he said mysteriously. He ran his hand along the wall, tapping it lightly. As he got to the space where the bed was tucked away, the taps were hollow. Kate and Max followed him with their eyes, half smiling.

'What's that? What's that?' and he stuck his hand in the recess near the ceiling and pulled what looked to be the whole wall down. It came down with a cranky groan of metal on metal and hit the floor a little hard.

Kate laughed and clapped her hands. 'That is so *cool*,' she said.

'I had one of those in a college apartment. They're not bad. You kick him outa your room, Becca?' Max joked. Becca laughed. Dan met her eyes, smiling. She smiled back.

'Yup, this room speaks to me,' Dan said. He leaned

up against the mattressless bed. Kate peered through the metal frame to the wood underneath.

'It looks like a coffin with a bed on top,' she said.

Dan patted it affectionately and nodded. 'Could come in handy that way,' he said, joking. 'I ordered the mattress for it,' he added casually. Becca looked up, surprised. He hadn't mentioned it. *What had it cost?* She tried to catch his eye, but he avoided hers. 'It should be here by Tuesday.'

'Then you'll have a place to sleep,' Becca said sweetly. Max and Kate laughed, and so did Becca, pleased to have made a joke. Dan met her eyes briefly, sheepishly. She shook her head dismissively. It didn't matter.

She was going to be a director soon.

The three of them, Dan, Max and Kate, went out back to smoke a joint. Becca passed. When they were pleasingly altered, Dan and Max went into the inner sanctum to look at what Dan had for sketches.

Kate was left with Becca in the living room. 'Great house. You enjoying it?' she asked her.

'Yes. Thank you. I heard your show went well at the gallery.'

'Yeah, it was great. Did you see it?'

'No,' Becca said.

'So, how's the job. You're still at the . . .'

'Centre for Improved Health. It's good. Thank you.' She nodded. They both took a sip from their beer.

'Are you planning another show?'

'I'm just starting a new series,' Kate said. Becca nodded. Kate smiled. So did Becca.

And on like that.

*

They said goodbye to them just after midnight. Becca and Kate had managed to make conversation for more than an hour while the men were holed up in Dan's studio, talking about the *illustrated novel*, which they were calling alternately *the pages* or *the book*. When they came out, finally, the four of them sat around in the living room and made stilted, general conversation, but it wasn't long before they got back into *The Headhunter*, the name of both the book and the title character. Kate got into it with them.

They talked mostly about the Reporter, still nameless and still faceless.

'She's got to be serenely beautiful, like a beautiful *nun* or something,' Max said.

'The face of an angel,' Kate said, distantly. Her pupils were very small. Her eyes glassy.

'Yes! Exactly!' Max nodded thoughtfully. They would retreat into periods of thoughtful silence. Thoughtfully stoned silence. Then they would all talk at once.

'The kind of chick you would call a "beautiful crea-ture", you know?'

'Chick? *Chick*?' Kate punched Max lightly on the arm, her face amused and frowning. 'What're you, a sixties throw-back?'

'You're such a chick,' he said, with mock derisiveness.

Dan seemed not to be listening. He would periodically lean back on the sofa and hold his hand near his face, his eyes automatically squinting against phantom smoke. It was his smoking posture, Becca recognized it. When he was working at the old place, he would get that look, that posture, when he was thinking about some project or other. They had agreed that he wasn't going to smoke in the new house. Seeing him like that, she felt almost guilty, the two seemed to go together so completely. She supposed she should give him credit for not smoking.

'I sort of see her as strong, but vulnerable. That nun analogy is good,' he said, looking off into space, nodding. 'Short hair, I think. Something framing her face. You got a name for her yet?' Max shook his head.

'The Reporter,' he said.

'She could be nameless; it could give her a mysterious quality,' Kate said. The three of them nodded. Stoned thoughtfulness.

They smoked more dope, outside. Kate and Dan went out into the yard a few times to smoke regular cigarettes and more beer was drunk.

Becca had a beer and two glasses of wine, and by the time the evening was wrapping up, she felt light and relaxed. The two of them stood out on the front stoop to say goodbye. It was dark out, and warm, a lovely beginning to summer. Soon it would be barbecues and lawn chairs and Saturdays spent tanning with the radio. The thought filled Becca with hope and anticipation. Summer was nice.

They closed the door when the car pulled way and Dan draped a happy, loose arm around Becca's shoulders and she didn't shake him off or wiggle away. She felt good inside. Warm, from the wine and the sweet, outside air.

He flicked off the hall light and in the same motion – his arm still around her – turned on the porch light outside. The hall got dark at the same time the porch light shone in through the small, narrow window at the bottom of the stairs. Then he turned and kissed her.

It caught her by surprise and she kissed him back. They stood a moment in the dark hall, their mouths moving familiarly through the steps of their kissing, moving this way, then that way, warm, soft, then pressing, releasing. Dan ran his tongue over her lips and through the wine, it was good. He tasted of beer and cigarettes. Like always.

'Let's go to bed,' he whispered wetly in her ear. It was nice, his breath in her ear. She wanted him to breathe into it, it tickled sweetly, warmed her neck, made the flesh rise. She wished wistfully that that was what sex was, just warm breath. She nodded slowly.

The lights were on in the kitchen and the living room. Beer bottles and glasses and bowls of chips, the jar of salsa, were all still out. She pulled softly away, wanting to be agreeable, knowing that it was time, and that it would be all right.

'Lemme just put a couple of things away, and I'll be right up,' she whispered back. His mouth was still at her ear. He was leaning on her, not moving much. He was a little drunk. So was she. That made her giggle. He laughed in her ear, from his throat. She felt it on her shoulder, a rumble.

'Want me to help?' he said. Breath in her ear. They spoke with long pauses between words. She because of the breath in her ear; he because he was a little more drunk than she was.

'No. I'll do it.'

'Don't be too long,' he said, singsongy, promising. He

swayed away from her as much as turned and thumped heavily up the stairs.

Becca grabbed beer bottles and put them on the counter in the kitchen. She went back for glasses and just dumped them into the bowl of chips. She giggled, shutting off the lights in the living room, flooding the downstairs with darkness.

In the hall she noticed light coming out from under the door of Dan's studio. She debated only briefly, thinking of the electricity bill and the fact that they already left the stove light on in the kitchen at night, and lights at both the front and back doors.

Her footsteps echoed in the dark hall. Upstairs she heard footsteps from their room to the bathroom and the clunk of the toilet seat being lifted up. She smiled into the dark. Paused to hear the splash of his stream. Thought of his penis. Realized it really *would* be okay. Maybe she even wanted to, a little.

Maybe it was *a phase*. She didn't let herself think any further than that.

She grabbed the doorknob of his studio and turned and pushed. The door didn't open. She sighed, disgusted. Tried without effort once more. Gave the door an unenthusiastic little shake. It stayed closed. She looked down at the floor, at the light spreading over the toes of her shoes.

Fuck it.

It was almost funny, or should have been. Like a sitcom moment. Lucy trying to open the door that Desi opens without effort time and time again, a vaudevillian act played out in silence with large-eyed, pursed-lipped mugging for the camera and *'Luuuucee –'*

It should have been funny. But it wasn't. It was annoying.

Before going upstairs to make (dutiful) love to her husband, she gave the door a little surreptitious kick. Not hard. But her foot bounced back from the door. She moved back in surprise.

The door had resisted. It had felt, distinctly, like it had kicked back.

Eyeing the full length of it, she stepped sideways away from it and into the hall. With one last backward look over her shoulder, she mounted the stairs.

Becca was taking her husband into her mouth, to his great delight, when downstairs the light sneaking out from under the door to the little room under the stairs spilled out into the hall.

The knob turned (easily) and the door slid open wide, coming to rest against the wall. It stopped just before hitting the plaster and stayed put.

Dan woke up briefly at nearly four in the morning, still half drunk, but awake enough to feel the pounding starting in his temples. The room was dark, the only light coming through the window from the street-lamp outside. The window was as yet uncurtained. He shut his eyes against it and thought about getting up and taking a couple of aspirins.

The thought passed, *I'll still have the headache in the morning*, and he settled his naked body against the warm, naked body of his wife, the smell and memory of their sex still lingering enough to make him smile as he put his head on the pillow and began to fade.

Just drifting off, he thought he heard a car pull up

outside. Footsteps. Somewhere distantly, a door closed. She tugged at him.

Downstairs?

Then music, tinny and low, something jazzy, from another time. He moved his body, eyes lightly shut. His face buried into Becca's hair. He smelled her. Soap and skin.

After you've gone and left me crying . . .

An old recording. A record player, or the sound of one.

Sounds like someone's having a party, he thought, and fell into the dark fog of sleep.

Victoria Warwick had woken up on Friday morning with a hankering for potato latkes. But there was no sour cream in the house. The only thing to do was to pack her old bones into a sweater and running shoes and walk herself down to the grocery, only five blocks from her home. She was eighty-eight years old and sure to remind anyone who crossed her path of the fact. 'I'm eighty-eight years old. I still do my own cooking and, goddamn it –' she would at that point wave her cane high enough in the air, so that whomever she was speaking to was, literally, taken aback '– I'm still doing my own walking!' Often as not, she had with her a yellow mesh bag, a gift from a planet-minded granddaughter, for carrying the few groceries she could manage. Her son Donald did the major shopping every Tuesday afternoon. Recently, Donald and Victoria had stopped talking; it wouldn't last long, it rarely did, but came about regular as clockwork every few weeks when Donald tried to get Grandma, as she was known, to live with him.

'I'm eighty-eight years old, and I'm still able to do my own cooking!' was her invariable reply, thick with indignant anger. The fact was, and even Donald, in the extremities of his own anger, was reluctant to state, she wasn't cooking quite as well lately. Fire had become a major source of concern. Linda, Victoria's middle daughter, had taken to calling every night around eight, to remind Mom to turn off the elements on the stove. A small incident the previous November had given every-one (Victoria included) a heads-up. Victoria, for her own safety – and so those goddamn kids couldn't accuse her of being senile – went meekly about the house, checking elements, toasters, kettles and heating pads.

She had lived on Belisle Street since her marriage, in 1935, to John Warwick, ten years her senior and, by the time she married him, well on his way to the ulcers that would take his life just neatly after Victoria had given birth to the last of their seven children, Graham. John, however, had been a prodigious saver and a thrifty man, not to mention a man with a deep and abiding faith in insurance. His death had paid off their house and left them comfortable for long enough to get all seven chil-dren started on the path to goodness and success. Gra-ham, the baby, was already ten before his mother had to begin to take in boarders in the large three-storey house at the east end of Belisle.

The last boarder had departed nearly fifteen years ago. The top two floors of the house were closed off, to all intents and purposes (she had no idea that for three years her young grandson Lawson had been growing pot, quite successfully, in a boarded-off room in the attic), the two floors a favourite storage place for her many children, grandchildren, and suddenly, over the last few years, great-grandchildren. The milestones of a changing nation, technologically and ethically, could be found up there, and Victoria depended upon her sons and grandchildren to keep it maintained and critter-free (for three years, a job taken over enthusiastically by Lawson, a most attentive and regular mouse hunter, 'Hi, Grandma! Gotta check the traps!').

Victoria sighed with remembering, lumbering her way slowly up Carson and not waiting to cross the street to Belisle, but just stepping out on to the busy road, waving her cane in front of her. Her bag, small as it was, was getting heavy. In it was a pint of sour cream, and while at the store she'd seen some fresh strawberries and found she had a sudden hankering for those, too. So she'd bought a small container and a tub of that ready-made whipping cream (she berated herself for this all the way up the street). There were also two purple onions, and a bar of pretty lavender soap that she had picked up in the sale bin at the druggist's.

It was Friday afternoon already and she had to haul herself home, because Donald would be coming in the afternoon to pick up her list for next week's shopping. Like clockwork, he picked up her list on Sunday afternoon and spent an uncomfortable hour sitting with her (*Ma! Don't make me nothing to eat! I just ate!*) and then left on his way back to his own family, duty again fulfilled. It would be an interesting and quiet visit this week, because they weren't speaking. But she just bet that wouldn't keep him from staying the hour and making strained conversation. She would pout at him the whole time. Drove him batty.

She had to make her list for him, and it was a chore she dreaded. He was a precise (somewhat prissy, in fact) little man, who got too excited over things like a poorly written list, and she herself was used to shopping by whim and sight. Instead she had to think ahead and decide on Tuesday afternoon what she wanted to eat the rest of the week. Damn shame. She shook her head.

She was nearly half-way up the street, and could see the tall oak tree in her own front yard. So, because she was nearly there, she looked to her side, pausing to get her bearings, because she could never quite remember which house it was any more. Though she thought of it often and sometimes smiled while she did.

Half-way somewhere, up Belisle, she could sometimes hear a bit of the old music coming from the house.

Lovely stuff, songs of her youth.

Marion Harris, Paul Whiteman and his orchestra, Ruth Etting. All the old songs. They were played quiet, and you had to stop and listen and hope the wind was blowing the right way.

She saw the hedge up ahead and stopped a moment to see if she could hear. All she could hear was the traffic, a block distant yet, and further still, a lawn-mower running. There was nothing wrong with her ears.

They reminded her of the days with her best friend Joannie, dancing at the Baltic Ballroom, or Sunday after-noons in Joannie's bedroom listening to the phonograph when they were supposed to be looking at the Bible. Joannie was an only child, and was permitted the most liberal of privileges.

Victoria plodded the rest of the distance, one foot about as sore as could be, the other tingling like it had gone to sleep a mile back and was loath to wake itself up just for the walk home.

At the edge of the yard, identified by the hedge – still untrimmed, she noted with an internal *tsk tsk* – she stopped and listened. *Maybe they wouldn't be playing it today. Sometimes you couldn't hear a thing.*

Victoria had no idea who lived in the house, or where they'd come from, but they had lovely taste in music.

The sound of something strained to be heard from the house. The wind was a little off, but Victoria pricked up her ears and kept walking, closer to the sidewalk. Only a foot away, she heard not music but growling.

A little dog stuck his head out through the hedge and growled at her. Instinctively, Victoria put out her cane, waving it in front of her legs. She was not afraid of dogs, but that little one had caught her by surprise, and his growl was vicious. Sometimes the little ones nipped. He bared his tiny teeth at her, snarling so hard, his lips curled up over his teeth, she could see the brown spots on his gums.

'There, there, dog,' she said firmly, 'that's enough of that! G'wan!' She waved her cane at him. The dog didn't move but continued to growl menacingly, and Victoria felt the first pangs of fear. There would be little she could do if he decided to come after her. She could hit him with her cane, was all; swinging her bag at him would only throw her off balance.

'Git! *Git!*' she shouted at him. He had not yet come on to the sidewalk from the hedge, but he was between her and her house. She looked around up and down the street for someone to call to, but the streets were deserted, everyone off to work.

Afraid for real now, her voice lost some of its strength. Her arm did not, was in fact made stronger with the threat in front of her. She slammed the end of her cane down on the sidewalk; the noise was nominal, but the aggression apparent.

'You *GIT!*' she hollered loudly, giving another glance around – quickly, not wanting to take her eyes off the dog for even a minute – for someone, anyone, a postman on rounds, a little kid slipping out of school. The streets were still bare.

The dog hung its head low and its growl disappeared into its throat – a sure sign of something worse being contemplated. Victoria swung her cane at him, swiftly, sparing nothing, her face twisted into its own fierce snarl –

by god two wars the depression a hundred funerals raising seven children on my own a goddamn little dog is not going to scare –

The cane swept right through the dog.

Victoria's mouth dropped open and her arm stopped in its return arc, while the two met eyes for just a split second before the dog's little head tucked into the hedge and left her sight. A small, fierce bark was offered and then nothing. She looked over the hedge to see where it went, but it was gone, completely.

You are seeing things, Victoria.

On weak legs, she stumbled past the rest of the house, her heart doing its level best to pound, her mouth gone dry, because she had seen what she had seen and she must be going senile.

Those eyes. She could have sworn she had looked into eyes as dead and flat as the eyes of a shark she had seen on the Discovery channel not two nights earlier. Flat, black, dead; she'd had her share of dogs through the years, with seven children there was no avoiding a dog or two (and no avoiding the scraping of them off the road when it was over), and never before had she seen such eyes.

They'd had a dog with some sort of brain defect one time, Oscar it was called, and it was clearly a shuffle short of a decent hand. He had never looked like that, and he was dumb as they come.

Becca had spent a couple of minutes watching through the large front window as the old woman hacked away at their hedge with her cane. She shouted something that Becca couldn't hear, and seemed to be talking to whatever she was hacking at. Maybe even the hedge itself. The woman was very elderly. Frequently, in the early years at the Centre, Becca would make trips to the various 'retirement' homes they represented, and considered herself to be compassionate in the face of the eccentricities of people on their last legs. However, attacking a person's hedge at a private residence was not acceptable. Sometimes you just had to deal with things firmly to set the tone.

Dan was working in his studio, sneaking cigarettes that he obviously thought she couldn't smell, but she was reluctant to spoil the nice mood that had been established overnight, and so far hadn't said anything. She wasn't going to bother him with this, either. She would just poke her head out the door and see what was going on. The woman might be confused or lost. Maybe she'd dropped something in the bush and couldn't find it.

She pushed open the front door to find the woman

staring blankly up the path, (slinking away, it looked to Becca), a look on her face that was like confused terror, but it was hard to tell expression in the road map of lines that was her face.

'Excuse me,' Becca said firmly, the frown on her pretty face determined and authoritative. You had to deal with people in a certain way.

The old lady looked up at her, and continued to stare blankly. Becca took a step down the front porch steps towards her, but did not go down as far as the path.

'Huh?' the old woman managed. Her eyes, which looked intelligent and not the least bit deranged, did a quick trip around the yard.

'Can I help you?' Rebecca said.

The old woman raised her cane off the ground, but not so much in a threatening way, as an added means of emphasis. 'Your little dog tried to bite me,' she said, loudly, angrily.

'I don't have a dog, ma'am,' Becca answered patiently. She looked around the yard quickly to see if someone's animal had snuck in, but there was no sign of a dog, big or little. 'You must be mistaken.'

'Your dog tried to bite me! I live on this street, I have lived on this street for sixty years! I'll not be bitten by some little animal that needs to be put on a leash!'

'You are mistaken,' Becca repeated, angry now. 'And I don't appreciate having you *hack* away at my hedge, ma'am.' The two of them stood there, each confused in their own way: Becca, unsure as to how to finish the conversation, the old woman now just confused.

'Maybe a stray,' the woman mumbled. *Victoria, you are seeing things*.

Becca softened. 'You may be right. I'll keep an eye out, thank you,' she said, but by then the woman had begun back on her way, a large, full bag of groceries hung from a gnarled, almost claw-like hand, and Becca felt suddenly sorry for her earlier tone. She debated offering the woman a ride, but did not. She watched until the old woman had made it past the middle of the other side of the hedge and then went inside.

Mistaken. I was mistaken. While she had not appreciated that young woman's tone – *not at all, not at all snippy young thing we would never have spoken to our elders that way* – she understood how it must have looked to her.

Victoria's head swung on her neck, looking back at the house and yard with each step, looking front only to check her own progress. The dog did not come back out. But just as she passed the end of the hedge and started walking past the next house, she heard the sweet, low strains of 'Lonesome Hours'.

Past the yard she was sure she heard Paul Whiteman start up again behind her, but she was glad when she couldn't hear it any more.

2

Monday morning, Becca dressed carefully. She'd risen early, earlier than she usually did. She showered quietly while Dan slept on, towel-dried her hair to barely damp and then blew it dry, curling it under slightly with a round brush. It wouldn't last, but it might last long enough. She was going to speak to Gordon Huff after the morning meeting. Her hair had only to last until ten. Then it could do what it wanted. By the time she got out of the bathroom, Dan was out of bed and somewhere in the house. The sheets were bunched up at the end of the bed. Looking at them, she blushed, thinking of the other night, after Max and Kate had left. Had she really done those things?

And liked them. It gave her a small feeling of power.

She stood in front of her closet, a frown marring her high forehead. She was wearing matching dark lilac lace bra and panties from Divawear, a set she had paid $250 for just after they'd signed for the house. She had felt on a roll. The colour perfectly set off her dark hair and fair skin.

Four of her suits had come from the cleaner's the week before and she concentrated on those. Pastels were best for her skin tone and colouring, and her wardrobe reflected that. Under plastic was her pale yellow suit (too understated), a pink suit with delicate white trim around the pockets (too springy), her lilac suit and a personal favourite, her mint suit – which always made her look like she had a tan.

She fretted between the lilac and the green.

Above her head there was a loud *thud!*, as though something heavy had fallen over. She looked up. *What the hell was he doing up there?* Footsteps shuffled across the ceiling in the opposite direction of whatever had fallen, but by then she'd chosen the lilac suit and didn't care about distractions.

She would match all over, and only she would know it. Power lingerie.

It might not hurt to lean forward once during the interview. The lilac suit jacket had a slight gap at the neckline. Things had been said about Gordon Huff. And Becca listened to office gossip. She had seen *Working Girl*.

Footsteps paced across the length of the ceiling while she dressed. She tried to dress quickly when they sounded as though they were approaching the hatch in the hallway. If Dan came down and saw her in her underwear it would be a wrestling match to get dressed, and she wasn't in the mood. She had to stay focused.

She zipped up the skirt and gave the jacket a sniff before putting it on, checking for the smell of dry-cleaning fluid. It just smelled clean. She looked herself over in the full-length mirror. Dan called her suits TV-lawyer suits, because the skirts were short and the jackets fitted. She didn't care what he called them: she had a body made for those suits. She was tall enough to pull off the short skirt with ease. A perfect size six, but tall. She was five nine in sock feet. She tried to remember if Gordon Huff was tall or short; it wouldn't do to tower over him. Or would it? This created a debate over shoes.

She had two pairs that matched the suit, a low-heeled pair, and a damn-you-to-hell pair that put her to six feet.

Upstairs Dan dragged something slowly across the floor.

What's he moving, sacks of grain? She thought that was pretty good. She nodded to herself authoritatively in the mirror.

Cocktails tinkled in glasses in her head.

How do you do? I'm Rebecca Mason, Director of Patient Services at the Centre for Improved Health.

Oh, how nice.

We were featured in the Atlantic *last year.*

She said it into the mirror. 'I am Director of Patient Services at the Centre for Improved Health. I'm Rebecca Mason,' she said. She added, as an afterthought, 'How do you do?'

Then she went downstairs. A little positive visualization never hurt.

'Good morning, *Gorgeous!*' Dan called from the kitchen as Becca approached through the dining room. He low-whistled.

She stopped dead half-way through the dining room and stared wide-eyed at him.

'Whassamatter?' he said, pouring her a cup of coffee and holding it out to her. She glanced up at the ceiling. '*What?*' he repeated, wandering into the dining room and looking up at the ceiling.

'I heard you upstairs,' she said.

'Heard me what?'

He handed her the cup of coffee and she took it automatically. 'In the attic.'

'I wasn't in the attic. What did you hear?' He slurped his coffee, unconcerned, going back into the kitchen. She heard the toaster pop. Dan muttered an *ouch!* and the toast hit the counter. Nothing wrong with her hearing.

'Heard me what?' he said, again.

She shook her head. 'Never mind,' she said slowly. 'We have mice. Or something. I heard something up there. Moving around. Better check.'

'Ditto on the mouse check. All ready to be a big-shot director?' He poked his head around into the dining room and gave her a wink. It was lost on her. Becca stood in the dining room and stared up at the attic, head tilted, listening.

The minute Becca was out the door, Dan stuck Sheryl Crow on the stereo and cranked it. He danced his way into his studio – *my studio!* – and flipped open his sketch-book to the first page. He turned the pages slowly, checking out the characters in various poses, one leg bopping up and down to the music, his hands in a different time zone, moving with patient slowness through the pencil and charcoal sketches from the weeks before.

The Headhunter. Great fucken idea. He and Max had come up with it one night over beers in the bar near their old place. Sitting around shooting the shit, Max had mentioned he wanted to write a quick book. What he actually said was that he wanted to write *an illustrated adventure story for adult males.*

'A comic book?' Dan had offered, bemused.

'An *illustrated novel*,' Max said, firmly.

Dan had laughed. 'Pardon me.'

Max was undeterred, though. 'Something meaningful. A superhero for our times.'

'A fighter for truth, justice and the American way?' Dan laughed again.

'Sort of. But more *now*. No bullshit. No punches pulled. I wanna take shots at the establishment.'

Dan groaned. 'This is too much. Like shots at *Da Man*?'

Max nodded, and Dan realized he wasn't kidding.

'I'm open,' he said. 'Not much else going on.'

Max tossed around ideas. After his initial amusement, Dan got into it. It was something different. And comics were hot. The beer flowed. Somewhere between the Green Machine, a pollution fighter, and a group of four superhero terrorists called Dark Hour, they came up with the Headhunter. They broke loose then. After sneaking out back for a toke, they went back to their table and Headhunter came alive on a series of bar napkins.

Dan had the first impression sketch of the Headhunter on the napkin (in tiny black script across the bottom was Rye Wit, the name of the bar), taped on the edge of his drawing-board. It showed a tall, skinny guy, hair blowing around, thin face filled out only by a square jaw. The defining factor was a long coat – originally a trench coat, but now it was an oilskin like the Australian cowboys wore – billowing around his legs. If things got tough in the future – after *The Headhunter* hit, and it would – he would sell the sketch on e-bay.

The Headhunter masqueraded as a corporate raider, slowly making his way through a list of companies with the worst records in environmental and social malfeasance.

Born and raised in Love Canal, he grew up with unexplainable super powers that were a bane to his personal life. Unable to get an erection, he has channelled his sexual frustration into combating corporate evil once and for all. He scours company lists for top heads. When he finds them, he offers them spectacular work at a developing company – an offer they cannot refuse. Trailing right behind him are two bounty hunters, Hanus and Malicia, each with their own super powers, hired covertly by the World Trade Organization to destroy him at all costs. Headhunter has the amazing ability to hear only the truth, his brain translates corp-speak into real truth, which enables him to seek out and destroy the real masters of deception. When he puts on a suit, he is able to blend in and assume the bland, bloated features of the corporate demons who feast at the trough of mankind. Only slightly tongue-in-cheek.

They surprised even themselves with the ideas. It was funny, ironic, and real.

Within a week, Max had given him an outline for the first issue. More or less. They'd been arguing about layout, some story details, bullshit stuff. It would all be worked out.

It beat the *hell* out of advertising.

Around the time *The Headhunter* was born, he and Becca went looking for a house. They had looked at about six when they found the one on Belisle. They fell in love with it. They put in their offer. They bought it. He had been talking non-stop to Becca about *Headhunter*; she had been talking non-stop about the upcoming director's job. Somewhere in there, they weren't listening to each other. There had been an atmosphere around the house then, the sort of feeling like they were arriving at some kind of threshold. They were moving forward.

Dan's day job started to go bad a few days after the purchase of the house went through.

There were murmurs around Clayton and Marks about cutbacks. Downsizing. Two weeks later, Dan was let go. And the endless round of the same conversation began.

What the hell does that mean?

It means I've been laid off.

For how long?

I don't know. Maybe for ever.

Unsaid, but said just the same in a million other conversations and a tone of voice that was at first afraid, then shamed, then contemptuous, was the Rebecca Mason version of How My Husband Fucked Up.

What did you do?

Why were you fired?

How could you do this to me?

Where Becca had seen disaster and chaos, Dan saw the light. Since his first job after college, he had wanted to leave the corporate world and work on his own. Creating. Making art. He and Becca had talked of little else in the narrow single bed in his rented room off-campus the last year of college. She was going to be a CEO before she was forty. He was going to make truth and beauty with ink and paper.

I love you. She would say it fiercely, when he talked about what he wanted to *make*. I love you. She would arch her body against his. He would draw on her, in secret places that no one would ever see, angels, winged creatures, castles, colouring her flesh with pastel crayon paints. He would wash her slowly in the shower down the hall, taking his time. The other guys in the apartment would bang on the bathroom door and they would ignore it. They had fucked like weasels then. Rabbits. Guppies.

Now she wanted a portfolio and retirement savings.

Dan opened the sketchbook to the pages he'd roughed out the week before they moved. They were for the first scene in which Headhunter (going by one of his many corporate names, Ted Michaels) dons a suit to infiltrate a pharmaceutical R&D company that is promoting a diet drug taken from the bark of a tree on the endangered list. They received clearance with a fake report that they had synthesized the material, when they had not even begun attempting it.

He tilted his head and backed up some, taking in the work. He grabbed the second sketchbook from the table and began looking through it. In it were his initial sketches for the characters.

Headhunter was a skinny guy. An anti-hero. He had a head topped with too much black hair, he was tall and skinny, and had a slightly prominent nose, with heavy-prescription glasses he could discard only when wearing his corporate suit. Chicks, of course, weren't really an issue, although he planned the on-going, unconsummated relationship with the Reporter. She was a youngish girl, the bloom of youth just off her cheeks, secretly working in an underground press. Headhunter would dazzle her with Chomsky and Zim quotes and then disappear into the night, leaving her panting and wanting. It would all be very (hysterically) sad, given his condition. Unrequited love in the extreme.

He had good, solid sketches of Hanus, Malicia, the Headhunter *nemesi*, and of the Headhunter (plus various minor characters who would appear and disappear, a couple of moles, and the WTO leader, who looked like a weasel from exposure to a so-far-unnamed chemical that made his family rich). Malicia had cold, patrician good looks, the over-groomed dark beauty of someone who has never had a day of indecision. Her hair was long and dark, her skin fair. The sort of woman who is over-groomed but looks entirely natural. Hanus was a compact, silver-haired machine with the ingratiating smile-while-garrotting-you look and speech of a major domo. They were perfect or near so. Max was pleased.

The Reporter escaped him. Still nameless and faceless – although he would give her a killer body under her Guatemalan sweater and no-logo hemp pants. He stared into the wall in front of him. His mind wandered to the window he would put there.

He decided a toke would free the muse. He dipped into the kitchen and took a quick hit from his pipe, drawing deeply and holding the smoke reflectively. He exhaled.

Face of an angel. A sexy nun. He nodded. Ready to work. He left the pipe on the kitchen table and went back into the studio, pleasantly buzzed and pumped.

He closed the two sketchbooks. He needed a bit more room to free form. He grabbed his portfolio case, tucked neatly between the table and the shelves and zippered it open. Inside was an oversized sketchbook, still clean and empty.

He propped it up on his drawing table and opened the flap cover to the first page. He pulled his stool up close and with his pencil, began drawing voluptuous, soft circles that were forming flesh in his mind. The comic-book (*illustrated novel*) women of his youth flashed through his mind as he worked – Vampirella, Red Sonja, the girls of Conan, what they had in common: for quality, look to the classics.

He was a man. He started by drawing her breasts.

Dan worked silently without stopping for an hour. The music from the stereo ran out without him noticing. His cup of coffee sat cold and half full on the table beside him.

She was beautiful. Ethereal. All six versions of her.

The first sketch was too comically disproportionate. Enormous breasts stretched the woollen Guatemalan sweater he'd put her in. Just looking at that sweater made him feel itchy. He would dump it. Under the sweater was a pair of tight black pants. The woman had impossibly long legs. Long, tangled black hair flew out from her face as though caught in a wind tunnel, untamed. She was hot, but hardly political. Only the eyes were somehow right, or close. They were wide-spaced and large. Too large in that version, but there began the element he wanted. A sort of innocence, but not with those breasts. Not those legs. Wrong hair.

The next two were toned-down versions of the first one. The pants flared out in the second. The breasts were remarkably reduced, the work of a skilled (if somewhat disappointed) surgeon. After some of that had worked its way out of his system, and he began thinking *nun-like* she began to take on a sort of personality.

He cut off her hair, curled it around her face. Kept it

dark, as a foil of sorts for Malicia – whose hair was dark and long and straight. He made the Reporter's hair short and curled, soft-looking. He made the eyes smaller, but kept them spaced: it gave her a young-old look, like knowledge unwanted. Dark eyes. He rounded her face, made it heart-shaped.

Somewhere between sketches four and six, he gave her a skirt and a little sweater. Nothing débutante, but short, to show off a high waist. The skirt was fitted through the hips and then flared out, to her ankles.

She looked old-fashioned, maybe a touch too feminine. A politically correct Betty Boop, with her curly hair and the figure not quite hidden under her clothes. He frowned at the last sketch, unsure of what to change to sharpen the character, remove some of that overt femininity. He started a seventh sketch after deciding he didn't need a cigarette just then. One more and he'd take a break. Maybe a couple more. The house was quiet around him. A stillness that felt like breath held, but it might have been his own breath, held and let out in gasps, little moans sometimes, noises that went unnoticed by him.

Unaware, he hummed as he drew. A tune that seemed to fit his mood, the sketches. Something old and dreamy. Something he'd heard, but didn't know. Jazzy. Once, far away, he heard something in the attic, which he ignored or simply didn't acknowledge. Once, he thought he heard water running in the tub, but it was discreet and quiet, muffled as though through a closed door, and it went away before he'd really even thought it through.

Around him, the house went about its business.

In front of him, the Reporter came to life, taking on

form and feature, growing in detail, both visually and in character. She was quiet, but every emotion showed on her face; she liked jazz and dark rooms; she had a weakness for the wrong men; she was in love with the Headhunter. She was not as innocent as she looked. She looked very innocent. The last sketch betrayed that best. Her mouth was twisted up at the corner, in a smile that *knew*. At some point, he had a name.

Maggie.

Something moved in the attic, a shuffle across the floor. A door slid open in one of the bedrooms. Water in the tub drained. A whiff of fresh hay. Dan hummed, hearing nothing but (his own) breathing.

After you've gone . . .

Becca's hands were shaking as she stood in front of Gordon Huff's solid oak door. His name was stamped into a brass plate just above eye level. She checked her watch. It was one minute before ten. She rapped twice on the door, willing herself to relax.

'Come in, Rebecca,' he called, from behind the door. It was muffled. But she'd heard him say her name. That heartened her. She pushed the door open, her face a fiercely willed mask of efficiency and determination.

'Mr Huff,' she said, firmly, nodding once. No wasted motions. In her mind she repeated, *Director of Patient Services, Director of Patient Services.*

'Sit down, Rebecca,' he said, waving towards a large chair angled to his desk. He leaned forward as she sat (and *she* leaned forward as she sat, willing her face not to blush, not to heat, not to redden even as she did, shamelessly). 'What can I do for you?' He looked her straight in the eye. He was not an unkind man, this she already knew. He was not unattractive, either. He was about fifty or so, and had not run to fat as some executives did. He was married, of course. Becca knew nothing of his family. Theirs was not a company of family picnics, Christmas parties or retreats. For that she was truly grateful.

'Thank you for seeing me,' she began, steadily. 'I understand the director's position in Patient Services is opening up. I'd like to put myself forward.' She was firm, but not aggressive. She smiled to soften the words, but not servilely. Her heart pounded so hard in her chest, she was sure he could see it; or at least hear it.

He nodded thoughtfully. 'How long have you been with the Centre, Rebecca?'

'I started in Nutrition right out of college, Mr Huff. I've been here six years. I was committee head two years after I started with the company, and I now hold – as you know –' her hands continued to shake, and she held them tightly in her lap where he couldn't see them '– an executive assistant position in Patient Services.' It came out in one fast breath. She hoped he hadn't noticed. She smiled, warmly, she hoped. 'I'm just one step below the director's position now.' It was true. Everything she had said was true and it gave her a sudden burst of confidence. She continued, 'The only logical next step is the director's position. I've worked closely with Mr Anderson. I have experience.'

Gordon Huff raised an eyebrow and allowed her a small smile that faded quickly. There was a pause during which Becca's heart resumed its serious thudding. She swallowed. Her mouth was filling up with saliva.

'I have an updated résumé in my desk. I can put it in your mailbox, if necessary,' she said.

Mr Huff nodded. 'You understand that there are six other exec assistants, equally qualified, also applying for the position.'

Was he testing her? 'They are all from other departments.'

'Tom Higgins is from your department, Rebecca, and he's also expressed an interest. I'm not saying anything at this point. Decisions won't be made until the end of the month, as you know. And it isn't entirely up to me. There's a committee that will choose amongst the qualified candidates. All of your qualifications will be taken into account.'

'I'd like a recommendation from you, Mr Huff,' she said quickly, firmly, before he had a chance to dismiss her. They met eyes. His flickered quickly to the V of her jacket and back again. So quickly it was hardly noticeable. *I saw that.*

Her mind flashed possibilities as quickly as her heart skipped in her chest. Director of Patient Services was a good gig. A *very* good gig. The sort of position from which there was no (or little) looking back. From the Centre she could move into an executive position. It was also an extra twenty thousand dollars a year.

With slow, uncertain deliberation, she said, 'I would like to take you to lunch, Mr Huff, in an effort to better familiarize you with my experience and qualifications for the position.' She dared not look at his face. She swallowed. 'Would tomorrow be a good time?'

It wasn't a terrible idea, and it wasn't anything below board. Huff had had lunch last week with Lynn Sanderson from Accounting. No one had said boo. Craig Pollack had lunch with *everyone* and he was Huff's boss.

She dragged her eyes up to meet his. They were a clear, wet blue. They bored into her. Finally he said, 'I'll have Mary check my schedule and get back to you later today. What would you say, one?'

She nodded briskly, just once, lowering her chin and bringing it back up. She stood on weak knees, squeezing her hands together to force them to stop trembling. 'That sounds exactly right. Thank you, Mr Huff.' She extended her hand over the desk. He rose and tugged his jacket down as he did, over a slight paunch. So he wasn't without vanity. His hand was warm and steady in hers. They shook and she excused herself.

When she was half-way to the door, he said, 'Slip your résumé into my mailbox this afternoon, will you, Miss Mason?'

She started at the name, paused just a beat before turning. 'I'll do that,' she said and left his office, without correcting him.

3

Dan took a break around one and found himself eating his sandwich in the studio. He was terribly pleased, in an offhand sort of way, with his diligence. He was rarely so motivated when a whole day like this one – which would soon be a whole raft of days, months – stretched out in front of him, and he took advantage. Who knew how he would feel in a week.

He decided to try some group sketches for the afternoon. See how the characters looked together. The first storyline, introducing all the characters, ended with the Headhunter meeting the Reporter – Maggie (he supposed he would have to discuss her name with Max, but already it had wormed its way into his head and it was not just her name, but *her* by then) – on the roof of an abandoned building in the heart of the city. It offered beautiful, poignant possibilities. He itched to start it.

There was also Hanus and Malicia in their office, dull but necessary, phones, computers, all edges and angles. He hated drawing furniture. A lot of furniture in that one.

There was Headhunter in his disguise, the Supersuit, mixed in at a corporate meeting or, better still, wandering in a subway crowd, Hanus and Malicia somewhere distantly in the background of the crowd, searching him out – good possibilities for drama in that one; and *de rigueur*, the Hideaway. He planned a nerdy, adolescent boy's dream cave, deep in the catacombs of the city. He smiled. That would be *cool*.

On the walls all around his drawing-board, he taped up individual sketches of the characters. Then he opened his sketchbook to a fresh page, and began the rooftop scene, the first meeting, between the Headhunter and the Reporter for the underground newspaper.

He fell immediately, deeply, into the page. It was not just a sketch, but became, slowly, as he worked, a scene. He put the pencil aside after a while and worked with the charcoal. Darkest night with light pouring from a full moon; the Reporter, books primly covering her bosom, as seen over the shoulder of the tall, thin Headhunter. Fear on her face, as she looks up at him, sensuous lips parted.

He hardly noticed his erection, or the fact that the door had swung closed slowly during the course of the sketch, the sound of his breathing, small gasps and murmurs, occasional grunts, as he moved pencil, charcoal, fingers around the page, executing life from dust. Under his breathing, his sounds, made when he worked since childhood, the auditory equivalent of the tongue in the corner of a mouth, were strains of music too low to really hear, something that moved in and out at such a low decibel that it might have been the hum of the fridge, a car driving by outside, the buzz of electrical wires in a distant power plant.

Sometimes he spoke, real words: 'Rounder, yeah, like that . . . good. Arched . . . angled light . . . good. *Good*. Right.'

No one answered back.

Not really.

*

It was after six when Becca pulled in front of the house, parked her late-model Volvo behind Dan's ancient Mustang. In the terrible days just after he'd lost his job they had discussed, briefly, getting rid of one of the cars to save on insurance and the like. She had been horrified when he suggested her car. He said maybe they should trade it in on something smaller and cheaper. 'Like a Taurus,' he'd said.

She nearly died. She wouldn't be caught dead in even a Ford Handivan if both her legs fell off, was her answer to that. He hadn't brought it up again.

His car was parked in the exact same place it had been when she'd left that morning, which meant he hadn't left the house all day – unless he'd *walked* to the grocery store, and there wasn't much chance of that. She was late because she'd stopped at the store on the way home. She was going to make veal Parmesan. Dan's favourite. They hadn't had it in months and soon it would be too warm to cook anything fancy.

Just before leaving work at five, Becca had slipped her updated résumé into Gordon Huff's mailbox. He'd emailed her at four and said that Tuesday at one for lunch was a go. That's what the email had said: *Lunch is a go for one tomorrow.*

All systems go. *And how far, exactly, will I be going?*

Veal Parmesan.

She juggled two bags of groceries on to the front stoop and twisted the knob, but the door was locked. She knocked a couple of times, but while she waited she rested one of the bags on the stone step and fumbled with her keys. She unlocked the door and, holding it open with her elbow, grabbed the other bag and went inside. She pulled out her keys and pushed the door shut with one heeled foot.

'Hello!' she called. The hall was dark. The sky was cloudy and very little sun managed its way into the house. Most of the sun was blocked during the day from the hall at least by the neighbour's huge tree. It would help keep it cool in summer.

There was no immediate answer to her call. She wondered if he was napping, the thought instantly pissing her off, but she cut it. She was going to be *nice*. In the back of her mind was the reason why, but she cut that off, too.

Instead, she slipped off her heels with a delighted sigh and picked up the bags of groceries again to take them into the kitchen. Stepping once off the mat, she was greeted by the distinct growl of an animal.

She stopped dead, listened, feeling ridiculous. *We don't have a dog.* She didn't like dogs as a rule: they shed hair, and needed too much attention. They drooled. What she had heard was likely air forced up from the furnace, or the pipes or something. Really, in an old house, it could be anything. It was part of the charm and character of an older home. That and the lower taxes.

She took two brisk steps down the hall and heard it again, the growl of a dog, clearly, distinctly, and it sounded right in front of her.

Low. Menacing.

Her head swung round, she looked quickly into the living room and by her feet, blocked by the bags. There was, of course, nothing there. Radio? Nothing else could be heard in the house.

'Hello?' she called out, weakly. There was no answer. Then she moved.

The dog barked, loud, once. Becca dropped the bags of groceries hearing something break (that would be the salad dressing, goddamn it) and, unable to stop herself, she let out a small scream, in reaction. Her hand flew to her mouth.

The door to the studio flew open. Dan appeared in the hall, hair dishevelled, in the same T-shirt he'd had on when she'd left; the same T-shirt he'd slept in.

'What the hell happened?' Anger twisted his feminine features.

'I heard a dog bark. Did you buy a dog, now?' she said, angrily back.

'*What*?'

Becca leaned down and poked through the bag. The dressing bottle was intact. 'I heard a dog growl! And bark! And why are you yelling at *me*?'

He stared unbelievingly at her a moment. Then shook his head, anger dissolving, but slowly. 'Sorry,' he said crisply, 'but *obviously* there's no dog in here. I didn't hear you come in.' He ran his hands through his hair and for a moment looked disorientated, like he'd just woken up, or didn't quite know where he was. He looked around and low-whistled. 'I was working. What time is it?'

'There was a dog in the yard the other day. It could have gotten in,' she said, not letting go.

Becca stood up, awkwardly with the two bags, her purse still over her shoulder. Reacting, finally, he rushed forward and took the bags from her. She muttered a sulky *thank you*. 'What's all this?' He peeked into the bags as he walked them into the kitchen.

Becca looked around the empty hall suspiciously. There was nowhere for anything to hide (unless it was in Dan's studio). She shook her head. 'This house has the strangest noises,' she said. 'It's after six and all that's veal Parmesan. I thought I'd cook tonight,' she said, dropping her purse on the dining-room table and going into the kitchen.

'Oh, wow. Are we celebrating? Are you *Rebecca Mason, Girl Director*?' He did not begin unpacking the groceries. His face still had the faraway look of earlier.

'Not yet,' she said evasively. He didn't notice. He didn't ask about work. She didn't ask him, either.

Over dinner, two hours later, she mentioned that she was having lunch with Gordon Huff the next day. She kept her eyes on her plate and hoped he didn't see the blush rise on her cheeks.

'Oh, yeah?' he said, disinterestedly. He sipped wine, preoccupied.

'It must be going well,' she said, just a trace of sarcasm escaping.

He nodded, and looked at her, sheepish. 'I think I'm going to get back at it after supper. You mind?'

She shook her head. 'I'm going to move some things into *my* office, I think,' she said. Transforming a bedroom into an office. There was just something about that room that seemed to mark it as an obvious bedroom and nothing else. She wondered if she should try the other room. Even with a desk in it, she had a feeling the yellow room was always going to look like a bedroom.

With the image of a bed in her mind, Becca imagined lying across one in a hotel room, listening to Gordon

Huff brush his teeth in the bathroom. Waiting. She wondered if he visited a tanning bed after his workout, or if his skin would be pale from too much time spent indoors.

'Great.' And as an afterthought, he said, 'Think you'll be needing it soon?'

'What's that supposed to mean?' she said sharply.

He raised an eyebrow. 'An office. You're having lunch with the guy. I just thought – *Christ*. Never mind.'

She recovered quickly. 'It's just lunch,' she said, to him, and to herself.

It's just *lunch*.

Becca noticed the mark on the wall when she was moving around the little antique desk her mother had given them for Christmas one year, trying to find just the right place for it.

It was a long mark on the interior wall of the room. She thought at first that it was a shadow, but there was nothing in the room that would cast such a shadow. It was too long, and too large. All that was in the room were a couple of boxes and the desk and the matching chair. The desk was too small to do any real work on. Even her laptop would take up most of the surface, but that was something to worry about later. It couldn't be a shadow, anyway, because she could see her own shadow move over it, and there was nothing behind her.

She bent low for a closer look. The overhead light was dim, only a sixty-watt bulb under the frosted glass – which, although cleaned on Saturday, still did not let as much light through as she would have liked. She would have to get a desk lamp, if she expected to work in here.

She was going to put the overstuffed chair from the bedroom in the corner, and move one of the small occasional tables from the living room to go beside it, and get a floor lamp, for reading. That would leave a huge, empty space in the over-large bedroom, but when she was director, she would buy something elegant for it, and bigger, like a *chaise-longue* or a small love-seat.

The mark ran from about six inches from the wall that faced the hall to about six inches from the opposite wall, the one with the south window. It was oblong, and solid, with a lip at both ends, the lip taller at the end by the window. She frowned and ran her fingers along it. She had washed the walls herself and hadn't noticed anything. She hoped it wasn't something under the paint. Wall stains were notoriously difficult to get out if they had bled through paint.

She stood and stepped back for a larger perspective, still frowning. Her own shadow cut the mark in half, and the two were indistinguishable, making her think again that it was a shadow of something. Behind her were two brown cartons (books and papers, knick-knacks and desk things) about a foot apart. They were barely tall enough to reach her knee. The mark on the wall was higher than that. Past her knee, up to her thigh.

Getting closer again, her shadow walked through the mark. She bent low to it, eye level. Her shadow-head stuck up in the middle of it, and no edge that separated the mark on the wall from her shadow could be seen. She licked her finger and rubbed. Nothing changed on the wall. Her finger was clean.

She stood up and backed away, surveying the whole thing again. It was coming through the wall. It was a mark under the yellow paint, and it had bled through. She would have to have the whole thing painted. Glancing up and around at the room, the decision to paint lifted her spirits. It was not undue hardship. She hated the yellow. Rose. She would paint it a nice rose.

The long, dark mark stood out against the yellow paint more obviously now that she'd decided it was bleeding through. It reminded her of something, but she couldn't think what. After a minute, she let it go, and decided to put the desk almost at the corner between the two windows. She would deal with the wall later.

They lay in bed that night, not touching. Becca had fallen into sleep only with difficulty, her mind raging over the next day. Her clothes (the mint green suit, to be worn with her white DKNY matching undies, no pantyhose) were hanging off the door of their armoire. White heels. Mr Huff was at least two inches taller than her; she was safe in her higher heels.

She fell asleep to her cocktail party. She had on her pink suit. Everyone else was in dark colours, subdued tones. She was explaining to someone about *it's only lunch* and realized her dress was actually red. She wasn't wearing the pink suit at all. Ice tinkled in glasses. Gordon Huff approached her and cupped her breast. *I enjoyed our lunch*, he said.

Dan did not have trouble falling asleep the first time. By the time he gave up for the night and crawled into bed, it was after one and Becca was lightly snoring, the sheet tangled around her body as though she was having a restless night. He untangled her with the greatest care, so as not to wake her. Then he fell into a deep, dreamless sleep.

When he woke, stumbling out of sleep much the way people fall into it, it was after three. Dan opened his eyes and propped himself up on one elbow. Saw the lighted numbers on the clock, moved to the table on Becca's side of the bed. His brain registered it, distantly: *after three*. He groaned and flopped back down on to the pillow and closed his eyes. A second later they popped back open. He flexed the fingers of his right hand. They were stiff. He hadn't done so much work in a day for years. It was a good feeling. He felt productive, alive, thick with possibilities and meaning; he smiled into the dark, *truth, justice and the* Mason *way*.

Outside the house, on the street, a car pulled up and stopped. The door opened and slammed shut, echoing off the pavement, making it sound very close. Dan stiffened.

Déjà vu.

He listened, slowing his breathing down, making it shallow. The front door opened.

Someone's in the house! He did not panic. The door closed quietly, but not silently, the way a burglar would try to close a door. Just normal. He sat up in bed, carefully. The sheet tugged where it was tucked under Becca and he eased it out from under her, careful not to wake her.

Sound is funny on concrete, street is lined with trees, sound bounces. It was warm out, maybe the first really warm night after spring, people had their windows open, this occurred to him in a surface sort of way, the lines preaching to him in his head, while he listened intently to the sounds downstairs, under the pumping of his heart. *Some drunk. Mistaken house. Could be anything.*

Heels clicked briefly down the hall, not mincing, TV-tiptoe burglar steps, but just steps. He listened, fascinated, as they went from the door to the end of the hall. *Tick tick tick tick.*

Sound carries. Dan felt every nerve-ending light up, go on alert.

The door to the studio opened and closed. He heard the small *snick* of the tongue into the latch. A rational part of him screamed after that, *Someone is in the house!* His mouth felt dry. He couldn't move. His heart went *boom boom* in his chest. He could smell himself, his underarms. Fear sweat. *Sound carries this time of year. Some drunk mistook the house. Kids, fooling around.*

Muffled, tinny, low, up the stairs drifted the sound of music. A woman's voice thinned through ancient recording, sad and simple at the same time, filtered up through floor, walls. He didn't know the song, didn't think he'd ever heard it in his lifetime. But the words came to him.

> *You'll feel blue, you'll feel bad*
> *You've lost the sweetest thing you ever haaaad –*

The music faded out. He listened, intently. The silence of the house fell down around him, seductively. A minute passed. Then several. In listening, his mind wandered: the possibilities of *someone downstairs!* became the possibilities of the utter hush – a palatable thing, a thing that surrounded him like a blanket. The sounds came from outside then, the burr of distant traffic, the bark of a dog far up the street, the electrical hum, always present. Ten minutes passed. His eyes glanced over at the clock. It was nearly three thirty by then.

Nothing from downstairs. The press of silence was all he could hear.

Sleep came back, his muscles lost their tension, as though he was unable to fend off what he couldn't coax over before. Now, sleep wanted him.

Dream. It was a dream. He'd been dreaming (*sitting up?*). His conscious mind told him it was a dream. He hadn't really been awake at all. There were lots of names for it. Sleep paralysis. Sleep psychosis. Day-dream.

Just falling down the rabbit hole, his first real dream of the night was about to take place on the roof of an abandoned building in the heart of the city and when it started, he thought he knew *oh yes absolutely* that if he went down the stairs the light in his studio would be on. The door would not be closed, but open a crack, just enough to invite you to push it open (*come in*).

The door would open with a yawn.

Come in.

Sleep took him.

4

Whatever fascination had kept Dan in his studio for all hours of the day and night, he managed to avoid it for most of the next morning.

Becca left early for the office, not having said much at all. She told him that she'd called the painters and they would be in on Friday.

'What painters?' he said.

'For the bed– my office upstairs. I told you last night.' Had she? She didn't meet his glance, but it seemed only that she was lost in thought rather than avoiding him. The rest of breakfast – just coffee for both of them – was quiet: they seemed to have other things on their minds. Becca had said she might be late coming home, not to wait on her for dinner. He said okay. She kissed him lightly on the cheek without making eye contact and he smiled a goodbye. It had the formal feel of mornings after a fight. Except, as far as he remembered, there had been no fight.

There had just been doors opening and closing and footsteps and things that go *hum* in the night. (Not hum, exactly. But something about *leaving* or *going away* or *leaving me lonely*.)

Dream.

He drank a cup of coffee in the living room and called Max on the portable phone. Max wasn't in, and he left a message. He called his mother in California and told her about the new house; he gave her the new address. He thought about calling the employment agency that Becca had mentioned, but didn't. She hadn't brought it up; he wouldn't either.

Around ten he wanted a toke. His pipe was in the studio. He went upstairs and had a shower.

Under the pelting water, he found himself listening for something.

In the bedroom, standing in clean boxers and nothing else, towelling his hair (and listening, *listening*, feeling foolish), the doorbell rang, and Dan nearly jumped through the roof. He stopped completely for a second or two, brain dead, unable to place the sound in the lexicon that had developed over the last couple of days (overnight, really). When it rang a second time, he dropped the towel.

'Shit!' He fumbled around the room for pants, grabbing the pair he'd discarded yesterday. They were dirty, but he didn't care. He called down, 'I'm coming!' fully aware that it was unlikely that anyone would hear him. He ran down the stairs shirtless, water still running casually down the centre of his back.

He jumped down the last two steps and flung open the door, panting. Standing there were two blue-shirted men awkwardly propping a mattress. Dan stared. 'Oh! *Shit*,' he said, laughing. 'The mattress. Right. Come on in.' He pulled the door wide and held it with his foot. 'I just got out of the shower.'

The large man, very large, in front ignored him. The heat from the day came in through the door. Summer was coming, sending its calling card early. Another couple of weeks and it would be shorts and shirtless. The big guy's face was reddened and already wet with perspiration. *The body Doritos built.*

'This going upstairs?' he breathed.

'No, down here.' Dan thumbed down the hall.

'Where?' said the other one, letting out a breath as though it were a piano and not the narrow, super-single-sized mattress that it was.

Dan pointed more directly. 'It's a room under the stairs,' he said. 'Lemme get the door,' and jogged in front of them.

He pushed past the large man and his end of the mattress, which looked abnormally large in the cramped hall. 'In here,' he said, almost so that they didn't get away. The door was closed. His eyes dropped to the floor quickly, but he knew the light wasn't on – *it was a dream*: no light shone out from under the small crack.

He turned the knob (had he felt something? Heat? *Absolutely not*) and the door opened easily. With a little shove, it opened all the way. He flicked the light switch, turning his head slightly and backing up unconsciously. The light popped on, he heard the tungsten snap to life.

The room was empty. (*Of course it was.*) Everything was as he had left it. There were no party hats, no discarded shoes or clothing (*what am I thinking?*); no crank gramophone in the middle of the room stacked with records '*my lonely heart,*' '*don't leave me,*' '*dancing alone*'. He looked for a moment, eyes scanning the room boldly. With an internal nod, he said to the men, 'In here. Just a sec.' By then they were waiting at the door.

Dan reached up and pulled on the bed frame. It held

for a second and then came down. Legs appeared under it as if by magic.

The men paused at the door and let the mattress fall to the floor with a soft, solid *thud*. They checked out the room, sizing up the situation with gape-jawed astuteness.

'Hey, that's one of those beds that come out of the wall, right?'

'Yup,' Dan said, holding his laughter. 'You think you can just toss it up here?' The bed was higher than most, almost three feet off the floor when down.

The big boy changed places with the smaller guy, giving the bed frame a little push down as he passed. 'That's pretty sweet,' he said, smiling.

The two of them shifted the mattress on to the frame and wiggled and pushed it with a professional sort of speed and finesse that didn't seem possible. Once it was settled into place, they pressed down on it with their hands, as though testing it.

'These things really work?' the littler one wanted to know.

Dan shrugged. 'I don't know. I've never had one.'

The fat guy's eyes twinkled, like a child's. 'Let's close it.'

Dan opened his arms generously. He grabbed the underside of the bed and tentatively raised it. It didn't give much.

'You have to be careful, but firm,' Dan said, and the man moved over. The two of them put their hands under the bed and raised it a few inches, and it closed easily, sliding up on a spring. It closed with a solid, woody *thunk*.

The three of them stood, staring at the wall for a moment, where the bed had disappeared. It fitted snugly, as it had before the mattress had been added. The room was thick with inspired awe.

Then the fat guy turned his head slightly, as though listening, hearing something. He got closer to the wall, a serious expression on his face.

'*Gee-zus!*' he said, alarmed. 'Did you hear that?'

'What?' Dan said, eyes widening.

The big guy raised a hand for quiet and pressed his ear to the false wall. Dan and the other fellow leaned in towards it, listening also. Then the big guy dragged his hands down the wall. 'Help me! Help me!' he said, his voice raised in falsetto. Then he turned to them and said, with exaggerated concern, 'Somebody wants out.'

Very funny.

They laughed, none harder than the big guy, who insisted on pulling the bed out again, and then sending it back up, as though it were a toy.

Max called at one, excited. He wanted to know how far Dan had got on the first scene. 'Are you sitting down, buddy?'

Dan had grabbed his pipe off the table in the studio and was sitting on the back step, having a toke. He told Max he *was* sitting and then drew deeply on the pipe.

'I got a meeting with *Apex* on Friday. Fuck! Friday afternoon. You too, right? They'll want to see characters and at least a scene of story with an outline and a bible. This could be it –'

'Who's Apex?' Dan said, exhaling at the same time.

'Who's Apex! They're a publisher, boyo! A small one,' he conceded. 'They publish *Brat Boy* and *Tunnel of Time*. Not a bad company.' He waited for Dan to comment.

'How small?' Dan asked. 'They got any money?'

'Fuck off, dickbrain! You're sucking the life outa this. *They are a publisher* who wants to see our book. So shut the fuck up, draw some pretty pictures and phone me when you're done. Like tonight.'

'*Tonight*! Fuck you,' he said, alarmed.

'I'm a married man,' Max said, with mock primness. 'I'm banging ya. But Friday bring something. It doesn't have to be anything more than the story pages roughed for the first scene. Atmospheric, original and . . . I dunno, haunting or some kind of shit. Meeting's at three at Jester's on Oak. I can't believe it! Apex! I am so *pumped*! Phone me –' His voice rose and fell with a few more *Apex, shit!* and then he hung up.

Dan clicked the phone off with his thumb and took another hit off the pipe. He sat a moment more, taking in the sun shining on the tangled back garden, which looked less appealing, somehow, than it had.

Then the idea of a publisher and something to offer Becca (*gee, a couple of months out of work and I'm a working artist and how was* your *day, you director yet?*) and he smiled, not without a little cruelty, and then felt bad enough and pumped enough to pull his ass off the back stoop and put himself into the studio to work. Stoned, he hardly paused at the door. But he thought, however briefly, *Bring it on, if you're gonna* –

All was quiet (empty) in there. But, just to be sure, Dan put Aerosmith on the stereo, and cranked it. Loud.

Becca was back at her desk by three. It had been a long lunch.

She tried to get back to work but the two glasses of wine, combined with her nervousness, had made her quite light-headed. She had no idea if it had gone well or not.

He had read her résumé, he'd said. It was complete, he'd said. He'd asked her some questions about her department and the work that she was currently doing. She had answered everything with dignity and confidence – a confidence that went up and down as the lunch progressed, veering wildly in both directions.

While she had no reason to be thinking about beds and hotel rooms, the conversation did get personal. Mr Huff had Scotch straight up, and it had seemed to Becca terribly CEO-ish of him, and she wondered if he was doing it to impress her (it had). He had downed the first one quite quickly and she wondered if that meant he was nervous. But even then the talk had been entirely shop and she had been starting to relax. Her career was not, in general, a source of anxiety for her. While they stayed in the realm of the current, she was fine. When they moved into the director's position (a position she could practically taste, almost reach out and touch) the nervousness returned. Ambition made her tremble with anticipation and fear.

The conversation did get personal. He asked her almost nothing about herself.

'Do you have children, Rebecca?' he asked her. When she said no, she braced herself (*why?*) for the married question, but it didn't come. Instead he told her he had two children, both in university. They talked of schools for a while. She used the opportunity to mention her education and a course currently offered by the local university, and *What do you think? Is it worth looking into?* By-the-book flattery; men rarely noticed.

And so it went.

Becca looked at her watch several times – each time discreetly – but he did notice that. She wondered unkindly (and a little gleefully) if that was because her arm was attached to her chest, and whenever she looked away, his eyes wandered back there.

'You're very conscious of the time, Miss Mason,' he said, and she wondered about his vacillating use of her name, Miss Mason one minute and Rebecca the next. She frowned inside, thinking it meant something and she would have to figure out what: was he moving randomly between intimacy and distance, or was it a power thing; Miss Mason when she was being a bad girl, and Rebecca when he was condescending (*good girl*) to her? She tried to pay closer attention. She enjoyed such challenges: they were easier, in a way, than sitting back and hoping for the best; it was like working a room or being a wallflower. Math as opposed to guesswork. Active versus passive.

'Do you have a meeting?' he asked.

'No, but I have some things I would like to get off my desk today,' she said, importantly. In fact, she was checking out how long they had been at lunch. How long she had been listening to stories of his university days and the time he caddied for Jimmy Carter.

'When you're a director –' (*he said when!*) '– lunches will take up your afternoon. It's part of the job. A director has to spend a certain amount of his – or her – time *making nice*. Do you know what I mean?'

It was then that she became most confused. Making nice. Her mouth went dry and she casually took a sip of her wine. 'I think so,' she said. 'I think there's a certain amount of time that most of us spend advancing the Centre. On or off the job.' She tilted her head to the side, exposing her neck. She looked at the table. Remnants of lunch. Her salad had gone mostly uneaten. Her head was light.

There was a momentary pause in the conversation that seemed important. Her head was buzzing. She was having trouble focusing. She would have liked another glass of wine, something to take the spin out of her head and make it stay put in an easy place. *Do you like to dance?* she would have liked to ask him. *Do you think Prada will come out with a new line for fall or do you think this heavy-heeled, masculine thing is going to go on for ever? I'm thinking of painting my office pink. What do you think of pink as a working environment? Do you like my shoes? They were three hundred dollars.* Easy things. Things with answers. She put her glass down and reminded herself not to touch it again.

If he had said at that moment that a room was waiting for them at the Houston, she would not have refused. She would have gone meekly, just to lie down. Just so the unanswerable portion of this thing would be over. *I will sleep with you for the job. There it is.* If only she could say what she thought he might be thinking. It was all very exhausting. Innuendo was hard for her.

She would rather he just gave it to her because her work was good, of course. It just didn't feel likely. His eyes on her body made it feel less likely. Her work flashed occasionally before her eyes. She had no idea if she was the right person for the job. She couldn't have said at that moment that the current holder of the job, Mr Caldwell Anderson, was the right person for the job.

They all felt the same to her. She was the *logical* choice for the job; of that she had no doubt.

I am the logical choice for the job, for Chrissakes. Don't make me have sex with you.

She looked him in the eye. 'I'm the right person for this job, Mr Huff,' she said, anyway. She didn't say the rest. *I will do anything to have it. To be it.*

He might or might not have known that. He reached over and put his large hand over hers. She looked down at their hands. His was covered in hair. It was white. It would be demanding. She could tell.

He rested it there a moment and then shook it a little. 'I'll see what happens,' he said. 'In the meantime, this has been a very pleasant lunch. We'll have to do it again some time.'

And the lunch was over.

Ambiguity. A job description for women.

Just before leaving work, packing up her desk, memos, notes, phone messages that had gone unreturned through the course of the afternoon fog, and with the beginnings of a headache probing her temples, she decided that if he wanted her to sleep with him for the job, she would just do it. It wouldn't be cheating. It would be business. It wasn't as though she'd like it.

It was just the way things were. Probably (maybe not) everyone did it.

She loved her husband. This was just business. In a perfect world, he would understand.

Dan's afternoon had not been particularly productive, although he had started out with good intentions.

The jumpiness of the morning had simply had to give way to work. He started with his pivotal frame, the Reporter and the Headhunter locked in an emotional and politically savvy embrace on the rooftop of the abandoned building. It was good, great even. And he worked backwards.

He ran quickly through preliminary sketches of Hanus and Malicia in the office headquarters. He had a nice early sketch, an overhead view of Hanus on the phone, Malicia pacing patricianly. That was the first frame. They wanted the Headhunter.

He roughed out five frames with those two, then backtracked for another with the Headhunter, the first study of him. He's in his bat cave, head and shoulders illuminated by his computer screen, face pensive, reading headlines out of indymedia.org. He had to come up with an expression other than pensive for the Headhunter, so far he had only pensive and longing. Weren't they very nearly the same muscles?

Dan worked through the afternoon without pause. Repeatedly, he slipped outside for another toke. He smoked cigarettes (four) in the studio. Becca would probably freak, right up until she heard the good news. Then she would back off.

What's Apex?

A publisher.

I've never heard of them.

They're small. They do illustrated novels.

(Snort).

She would be happy, once she figured it out. She loved that he was an artist. Or used to. He had had a show in college that made her cream, made her his virtual slave for weeks. When he and his partner won the award at Starmon, she'd cooked every night for a month. And he'd never had to ask for it. *It would be fine.*

He worked frames until he got as far as the moment when the Headhunter, in his Supersuit, is in the crowd at the subway station. It's rush-hour, early morning. A New Yorky scene. The crowd is surging forward on to the subway. The Headhunter hears something. It is Hanus and Malicia (whom he's never seen) not far away. They are sketched into the crowd, full-frontal. The reader sees them. The Headhunter only senses danger.

In profile, he looks for them; looks for what he knows is there, but cannot see.

Dan glanced up at the wall in front of him for the profile sketch of the Headhunter. And it was gone. The wall was different and he registered it. He ran his eyes along the wall.

Marching along the wall were only sketches of the Reporter.

Maggie.

Huh?

She stared back at him, innocent, knowing, smirking, breasts pressing out against her little sweater, nipples (when had he drawn those? Had he given her *nipples*?) pushed out against the coarse fabric of her top. Eyes longing, wide-spaced.

All the other sketches were gone.

He looked on the floor, leaning up over his drawing-board. Nothing was there. He looked up again. She stared back.

Dan backed away from the drawing-board, backing into the table where he kept his pens and ink, his pencils and small smudgers, the pastels, the nibs for pens, his straight edge, compass set that his dad had given him. He spun around, as though he'd tripped over (a body) something.

In a tidy pile on the table were the other sketches. On top was the Headhunter, the full-frontal sketch, coat blowing in a dark night wind, like wings, around his body.

I took them down.

He stared at them from his ungainly position, half leaning into the table, his buttocks pressing against it.

I took them down. Of course I did I was obsessed with getting her right yesterday I took the others down to focus.

Self-consciously, he turned slowly and pawed through them, leaving the pile as untidy as it had been tidy, digging out the profile sketch that he needed. He did not tape it to the wall with the others, but propped it on the lip of the drawing-board and went back to work.

The breathing that he heard was his own. Consciously, he put a new CD on the stereo when the other ran out. Loud. He played it loud and jumped, sometimes at shadows.

5

In the night, there were sounds.

Dan woke up at three o'clock. He did not, at first, search out the clock. Instead he raised his head and looked around the room. Everything was as it should have been: the room was lit with the streetlight that shone just outside the window. *I have to ask her where the curtains are this room needs a set of curtains.* Regular breathing came from Becca's side of the bed. He realized he was naked, except for shorts. He looked down at his wife. The sheet was tangled around her again. *She's getting to be a real cover-thief,* he thought, anything to drown out the sound that was coming next, and he knew what it would be. He dropped his head and pulled the pillow over it, pushing it close to his head on either side.

Outside, a car pulled to a stop. *I don't hear this.* The door opened and closed.

Footsteps up the concrete path. *I don't I don't hear this.* The front door opened, boldly. And was shut.

I don't do not *hear this.*

Tiny heeled steps down the hall. A door opens and closes.

Before the music started, Dan was out of bed and at the top of the stairs. *This is a dream.*

Come in.

★

He crept down in utter silence, his feet nothing more than fleshy pads on bare wood. The stairs did not creak. Upstairs he thought he heard movement and paused briefly. It was not coming from the bedroom (Becca), but from somewhere else. The attic. Mice.

Dan stepped down off the last stair. All had been quiet until he reached the floor. Then, as though whoever (what) knew he was coming, the first strains of music began.

Lilting, hesitant, jazzy; tinny like from a record player that wasn't very good.

After you've gone, and left me crying

He heard it clearly. He must have heard it many times before that night, because he knew the next verse and could have sung along with it, but did not.

After you've gone, there's no denying
You'll feel blue, you'll feel bad –

Dan inched his way down the hall, strangely calm, the only giveaway his dry mouth. He moved carefully, so as not to bang anything, not to step on a creaky board, the one by the phone – he passed the phone easily, not reaching to pick it up.

He simply did not think about what he would find.

The door was open a crack. Light spilled out into the dark hall in an arc, as he knew it would.

He stood in front of it and reached out with his whole hand. He pressed his fingers against the cool wood of the door and pushed. It protested a moment, a slight *squeak* on old, unoiled hinges; he pushed it all the way open. As it swung forward, the smell of flowers – maybe lilac – filled his nose, a sweet, pungent scent that lasted only a moment, the sort of smell, not entirely pleasant, that you got off the sweaters of old ladies at funerals. Too sweet, like something gone over that hasn't been found. The door caught, not caught, but paused like a breath, and Dan saw that the bed was down. The door snicked past. The light in the room was from candles. Shadows danced with the opening of the door, flickering everything in shadow.

In the middle of the room, as though waiting, was a woman.

Come in. She smiled, lips parted. Tiny white teeth showed through, like pearls.

Come in. She was naked. Beautiful. Her smile, her mouth was of pleasures, secret things he would like to know. Candlelight flickered off the glow of her skin, smooth, supple, inviting. Blood pounded in his ears. The music played, in the back of something. He could no more have moved than not. A standstill. Stalemate. His erection – there, always – kindled, pulsed. The woman's eyes glanced casually down at it; her smile deepened, a red smile (*was it really red?*), something knowing.

Come in.

He must. He did.

Time went somewhere, but he did not follow it.

Dan lay on his back on the Murphy bed. In his hands were the first curve of buttocks, the buttocks of a woman, round and soft and full. Dan was buried deep inside her heat. She threw her head back in pleasure and tightened muscles that he knew the name of, but at the moment couldn't name; he could not think, but only respond. He responded by pulling his body up, tightening his own muscles, the ones in his abdomen, and a groan escaped his lips. He felt her move under his hands, and he gripped her, pressing his fingers into the soft flesh there as presented. His leg was caught under the sheet at the bottom of the bed, confining him, restricting him. It added, in some way, to the pleasure. He tried to move a foot, and gave up. He was caught.

Briefly then, *This is real I can feel it I am caught.*

When he opened his eyes, her breasts, perfect and high, bounced delicately in front of him with each upward motion. His hands reached out to grasp *round beautiful firm soft* her breasts and she leaned forward to accommodate him. He cupped her breasts as best he could as she rode him, powerful thighs tensing and releasing in turn against his own tensed thighs, her breasts bouncing appealingly in his hands. He wanted to swing her off, drop on top of her, pound himself inside her, but he was beyond such physical control by then.

'Ah ah ah ah ah,' he said, gasps barely coming out of him. Just air. He squeezed her breasts, under his palms he felt her nipples, hot, hard little lumps of separated flesh, standing out in lurid detail; he thought if he looked he would see the pink-brown flesh puckered around them. They would taste of soap and rouge. He worked one thumb over to a sweet hard bud to *play* –

Just as it brushed the pad of his thumb, just as he was thinking about how it would *taste feel* in his mouth he went over the edge into sweet, black darkness, pressed his eyes shut tightly and –

Red, everywhere. Then nothing.

6

Dan woke to Becca talking on the phone.

He sat up suddenly on the Murphy bed. He'd been sleeping, splayed across the bare mattress, legs akimbo, arms up over his head. He felt vulnerable, waking up. He covered himself, oddly, with his arms a moment. The door was wide open. Light in the hall. Morning.

She was mumbling (whispering?) something into the phone. He heard it click on to the cradle. The sound of disconnection. All around.

Quickly, very quickly, he sat up. He heard her move into the kitchen. Water ran. The clink of glass on the counter. He heard the fridge open. Heels clicked on the tile floor as she moved around. She was dressed for work. The fridge door *whooshed* shut, nearly silent. He heard it.

Memory flooded. He swung his head round. The room was in shadow, but silent. Empty.

Dan jumped, literally, out of the bed. The bed bounced on the floor.

'Becca?' he called. There was no answer. He stepped (very fast) out of the studio, glancing just once over his shoulder at the bed, laid out, sheetless. Blameless. The black, empty space behind it, where it went folded (when not in use), yawned lazily at him.

'*Bec* –' he said. He rounded the corner into the kitchen to his wife.

'Why did you sleep down here?' she said, not concerned, but mildly annoyed, like being left out of the joke.

He blanked. Blinked. 'You were restless,' he said.
'Kicking up the sheets.' She was. He remembered the
tangled sheet. Or was that something else?

'Coffee's on,' she said. That was enough of an
explanation.

He stared, still blank. Still wandering. 'You look nice,'
he said.

She looked up quickly, blushing, guilty? Thinking,
searching his face, for something missed. 'Thank you,'
she said, finally. 'Did you sleep well?' she asked. The
coffee chugged. She sipped from a glass of orange juice.

He sat down on the stool by the counter. 'I don't
know,' he said. She wasn't listening. She watched the
coffee pour into the pot with the distant look, the Sunday-
morning stare. The room smelled like coffee.

'I guess I'm getting in the shower,' he said, tried to
make it cheery, discountable, when in fact he felt filthy,
sweat-stained. Then she looked at him. Looked him over.

'You should. Doesn't look like you had a restful night,
either,' she said. She indicated his head, sticking out her
chin in his direction. 'Bed head.'

And he smelled. A sweet smell, like perfume, gone over.

Gordon Huff had called. Asked for a meeting. Ten
thirty. No, she didn't have to check her book, she was
free. His voice had been light, different. An equality?
He'd called her Rebecca. Was she a good girl?

In the shower, under the stream, his head hung low,
water pouring over his neck and shoulders, he realized
he had to go in there at least once more. He would get

his shit out of there and work in the dining room. The light was better in there anyway. In and out. And when he was finished with the stuff for Friday, he would set up in the attic, or the little room upstairs that Becca wasn't using. And then whatever went on in that room *just bad dreams* could go on without him.

And today, he'd skip the pot.

He put off going in for as long as possible, doing the supper dishes and sweeping the kitchen floor with extra caution, the way Becca did before she washed it. He carted some empty boxes out of the bedroom and stuck them by the back door. He opened them up and laid them flat. He gathered some laundry and then thought better of throwing it into the washer: the machine was in the cloakroom, just a few paces from the studio. He wasn't ready to go in there yet.

Max called. He wanted to know how it was going and could he drop round after work and see anything? Dan gave him a brief on the work he'd done the day before (giddily thinking about saying *and then* but ultimately not saying a thing, not betraying himself by word or tone, and as for thinking the penultimate *who who* he did not even go there). It had been good work. The conversation turned long. Some of Dan's anxiety started to drop away as they talked about the work. The prospects.

When they hung up, he geared up. But even as he approached, sweat dotted his upper lip and around his hairline. Close to the door, he could smell her. His erection rose, a mind of its own.

Becca watched the clock nervously, in a way she hadn't watched the clock since her college-years job at

Starbucks. Little work was accomplished, mostly papers were shuffled from one side of her desk to another. Her computer glared at her, figures without meaning.

When she knocked on Gordon Huff's door at ten thirty her hands were not shaking nearly as badly as they had been that first time. She took it as a sign.

She knocked and went in, poking her head with false concern around its corner before pushing it all the way open, 'Mr Huff?' she said, wishing she had called him Gordon. 'It's ten thirty.'

He waved her in; he was on the phone. His face was a frown when he nodded a greeting to her and motioned to a chair. He put his hand over the receiver companionably and, like a conspirator, mouthed the words, *This won't take a minute*. She nodded her acquiescence, fitting her hands into her lap and crossing her legs at the ankle. She breathed deeply and hoped he didn't notice. He finished his call and hung up, pulling his chair closer to his edge of the desk and flopping his arms across it with that same companionability.

'You wanted to see me,' she said, a statement, not a question.

He sighed and looked off into space a moment, as though gathering thoughts. 'Well, Rebecca, I thought I would let you know that Don Geisbrecht has expressed some interest.' For a moment she didn't understand. Expressed interest in what? In *her*? In the hiring process?

'In the position,' Huff added, noting her confusion.

'But he's from outside,' she said.

Huff nodded. 'He's a good candidate.' A scowl she couldn't control marred her features. Her stomach twisted and she wished she'd had breakfast. She thought it might rumble. She opened her mouth to speak, but wasn't sure what to say.

Mr Huff said, 'I'm not sure how the board is going to look at this – he hasn't applied, of course. But I understand he's been talking to Ben King.' She nodded with growing understanding and a small sinking feeling. There was a long pause between the two of them.

Finally she said, firmly, although her voice wanted to shake, 'I think I am a good candidate for the job. I've worked in this department for six years. With this company. I hope that you will recommend me to the board. I appreciate the information, Mr Huff. Thank you.' She rose to leave, her mind going in a million directions at once. He had wanted to see her to prepare her. It was as good as saying she didn't have the job. She was angry, and embarrassed.

'Rebecca,' he said, from behind her. She turned half-way round. 'I enjoyed our lunch yesterday very much,' he said, watching her face. She met his eyes. In the pause, she turned and faced him fully.

So here it is. This is the part where he tells me what he wants.

'I was hoping we could have dinner some time,' he said. The words were spoken carefully. He leaned back in his chair. *Bastard prick bastard.* Even as she thought it, she knew what she would say.

She blinked twice. Thinking and not. Sleepily, she said, 'That would be nice.'

He nodded, half smiling. 'Monday evening?'

'All right,' she said. She slid to the door and turned the knob, her heart thudding so hard that it was hurting her ears, or maybe it was another headache. She did not turn and look back at him, and did not say goodbye. It seemed unnecessary; *uncompanionable*. And, anyway, she would see him later.

In her head, the cocktail party sprang to life. *I'm Director of Patient Services at the Centre for Improved Health*, she said.

Oh, my. And how did you get that?

I earned it. Diamonds twinkled discreetly on her ears. She wore Armani. Her shoes were Prada. Somewhere, distantly in the background, Gordon Huff stood with his wife.

The door was open, the light off. The bed was down. *I slept in it that's why it's down.* A small patch of light from the hall filtered in, no further than the end of the bed. Through the shadows he could just make out the chrome legs of the drawing-board, the stool.

He leaned in through the doorway and flicked on the light.

Hello, big boy.

The words weren't said, not out loud, but he heard them, as though they were coming from inside his own head. *Hello, big boy.* Said with a twinkle; a grin. There was no direction in which to look, but he spun his head round – nowhere to hide. The room was empty. He walked in, the room scented with lilac and sweat, warm. His breathing became shallow and he went to his drawing-board without conviction.

Movement behind him. He turned.

She was on the bed. She lay on her side, the curve of her hip inviting, the smile on her face promising, her skin white and smooth, breasts, hips, thighs, curves that undulated like a mountain road. The door swung shut lazily, closed. He jumped in a slow, delayed reaction.

'I have to work,' he said weakly. She wiggled her hips playfully.

His penis tented the front of his jeans, pressing painfully against the seam there. It throbbed like it hadn't since high school.

I have to work. Even as he walked to the bed. Even touching her, inside he recoiled, something curling up as though burned. Even as he slid his pants down over his hips, even as she leaned forward, her red, painted mouth opening, light glancing off little teeth like pearls, even as he slid into the dark maw of her throat, even as he closed his eyes and let her swallow him, he retreated inside, breathing through his mouth so he didn't have to smell what persisted under the sweetness of something rotten.

Intermittently, he opened his eyes from one world into the next. He would be standing, naked, at the drawing-board, charcoal or pencil in hand, fingers poised as though to swoop. The overhead light would sometimes be flickering like candlelight, but filling the room and he would blink against it, as though the light shed itself on things he'd just as soon not see. At those times, the room would be still and silent, like a room should be. Unable to help himself, his eyes would sneak around it, lighting on items and ticking them off mentally in their normality. Drawing-board, table, books, wall. His hair would be corkscrewed around his head, his eyes heavily lidded as though he had just woken (or been crying). His penis would lie limply, in retreat, against his leg, hardly rising to bob with the movements of his body.

Pencil to paper, he worked. On the wall in front of him, his pictures of the Reporter stared back. Subtly, they looked different, as though someone had come inside in the night and altered them. The heart-shaped face was rounder; the hair a little longer, less coiffed. Some of the intelligence had been replaced in her eyes with a *come hither* stare. He took note of all of these things.

But he worked.

He drew quickly, and well. He fell deeply into the paper, so deeply, the flesh over his top lip grew moist, as did the band of skin around his hairline, sweating with the force of his concentration. He did not notice when cool air climbed his back, stroking up from the small hollow there, as high as the place where he broadened across the shoulders, and rested there for a moment.

He did not notice, but he welcomed it.

Time slipped around itself like a snake swallowing its tail. He thought that, when he realized that he wasn't separating the day very well. He was here again, spread open on his back and she rode him. The light was off sometimes and candles burned. Sometimes the light was on. When the candles burned, unfamiliar shapes appeared just beyond his sight, in the flickering darkness that yielded randomly, like a woman.

A phonograph in the corner. A tall lamp. An over-stuffed chair piled high with silks or scarves or the sort of filmy night things that women wore. A hat hung on a hook. All of these things were just beyond his sight and they appeared and disappeared with disarming frequency: the hat became books stacked in rows; chair became table; lamp became stool. He preferred, after a while, not to look.

He grabbed her hips and pulled her down on himself hard, felt bone through flesh and that was both better and worse. He squeezed and pinched, felt her wriggle and tremble on him, felt her heat, the sweat that trickled down her back and that was both better and worse –

Because sometimes he held only air.

His cock pointing up to a white corked ceiling, hands above him, muscles tightening against nothing. His head became light and he would close his eyes and, slowly, pleasure would take him past thought, and if then he opened his eyes again he would have forgotten the moment before when he held nothing, and the room smelled stale, like yeast and old fruit.

Becca took off early, claiming a headache, and headed for the mall on the outskirts of the city. She rarely ventured to that particular mall. It was very, very expensive. She visited only once a year – the last time was to buy the pair of shoes that she had worn yesterday to her lunch with Mr Huff. They had cost three hundred dollars, and were not the most expensive pair that she had tried on; in fact, they had been a compromise. Three hundred dollars for a soft little pair of pumps. There was about two thousand dollars in her checking account. She had both her Visa and the Amex with her. If all went well, in a couple of months' time, she would have a little gold company card and this day would be a memory.

Becca drove slowly past Beemers, Jags, softly tinted subdued little Mercedes, and lots of other Volvos. Her older, but well-cared for Volvo was still okay among the cars in the lot. Volvo owners, she had found, tended to be a loyal group and often drove a favoured Volvo to the point of exhaustion. It was an appropriate eccentricity. (Especially now that Suvies outnumbered Volvos by twice.) She looped up another row and searched the lot keenly.

She found a parking space near the entrance. She decided that it was a sign. Divine approval for the line of attack, while shopping for body armour.

At very least, she would have to have a new outfit for dinner. And shoes. Probably underwear. It was unseemly to expect her to appear at dinner as the fatted calf in underwear the previous farmer had already pulled off her body, wasn't it? And the outfit had to be spectacular, something that spoke of her lofty grounds for execution. Something spectacular, in fabric so expensive and fine that it would raise her up by its very perfection above the dirty little engagement that instigated its purchase. And shoes to match.

Women strolled elegantly through the mall in clutches of twos. From jewelled, dainty fingers dripped richly coloured shopping bags, with matching tissues stuffing out the tops of some as though they were barely able to contain the secrets inside. Others gaped openly, their contents peeking out above the straps of the handles. On the sides of the bags the names of shops were discreetly pressed in black. Martel's, Ambrosia, West, Lamprey, Anne Klein, Versace. Becca breathed deeply, her body relaxing familiarly into the rhythm and pace of the aisles.

She went first into Martel's. It was very likely the same place where Mrs Huff shopped.

★

When Becca pushed open the front door, both hands were fully occupied with shopping bags. There were two from Martel's, and an Ambrosia bag, tiny and sexy with its rose-petal montage and scented paper, containing undergarments so light and engineered with such perfection that the bag hardly seemed necessary – the items seemed almost capable of walking home on their own. There was a Veda bag, with a new pair of slingback pumps – jumping the gun slightly on summer, but by then she'd thought what the hell? and a pair of more sensible shoes for the moment (*the* moment you could say), which matched perfectly the suit in the large suit bag slung over her shoulder.

The trick would be getting it all upstairs before Dan noticed. *This old thing? I've had it for months. I hardly ever wear it because it's not flattering.* The bags crinkled excitedly, cheerfully, discreetly expensive, and she realized the *real* trick was going to be keeping her own excitement down and resisting the desire to try everything on once she got the bags upstairs. Her stomach was tight with exhilaration and utter terror. She had put everything on her charge cards (distributing it relatively evenly between the two). In all she had spent just over a thousand dollars.

A thousand dollars. The figure left her out of breath. It was half of what was left in their checking account.

None of it was out of line, really. The suit – white, how fitting: she'd thought at the time, but only fleetingly, that she would wear white like a bride or a virginal (hardly) sacrifice – had cost just over six hundred dollars, not outrageous. The shoes had been an absolute *bargain* at two hundred dollars. The dainties were also two hundred and fifty, but she had paid that before. Stockings had put her over at fifty dollars, but they were the sort that clipped on to the delicate and delightful, practically *invisible* pair of garters that the salesgirl assured her would not show under the slightest of fabrics. The garters had been a hundred and fifty dollars. That was the fly in the ointment, and the one serious regret (and the most stimulating impulse purchase). She would likely only ever wear them once. It was almost a done deal now: she would have to do what she was ready to do, or she would have shopped in vain.

A thousand dollars. Thirteen hundred dollars, give or take. She preferred her rounded-off figure.

She stepped quickly and quietly into the deserted hall. There were no lights on in the kitchen and she assumed Dan was still in the studio working on his book. *Let him. Soon we'll be able to afford that little indulgence. And mine.*

The bags, in spite of her holding everything carefully away from her body, made their happy crinkling sound, which seemed loud in the empty hall, but wasn't the sort of sound that carried at all. Just as she was about to mount the steps, she heard the studio door open and the scrambling sound of someone rushing out. She was caught. She thought of dashing up the stairs quickly – *Hi I'm home I'll be right down* – but then he would come up, and what would she do? Shove the bags in the armoire before he got up to the bedroom, like a common thief?

She backed down the step and stood, brazenly with her bags, in front of the door.

Dan was not in the hall. Instead, she heard him fumbling just out of sight, and then the familiar sound of a zipper hastily raised.

'Hello?' she said, curious.

He came around the corner then, hair dishevelled, shirtless, looking like he'd just crawled out of a dumpster. Or a bed. Had he been napping?

'What's going on?' she asked. He ran a hand through his hair, succeeding only in making it worse. It stuck up at the back, stiffly, as though he had lain on his back for a long time.

'Nothing,' he said quickly, and she recognized a flash of guilt on his face, even in the dim light of the hall. She leaned sideways, peering behind him, almost, but not quite, expecting to see someone (a prostitute, a tramp, a fellow *artiste*) standing behind him. Dan followed her gaze, cheeks pink, and reached beside him and closed the studio door. It clicked shut boldly.

'Is there someone in there?' she said, her voice rising. 'You have someone in there?'

He snorted indignantly. 'For Chrissakes, Bec!' he said. 'What the hell are you talking about?' His cheeks blazed then, and it might have been from indignation or anger.

'Why aren't you dressed? What's the matter with your hair?' she demanded, her bags and their contents forgotten.

He looked sheepish then. 'I had a nap,' he said, apologetically. 'I guess you woke me up. Sorry.'

They stared at each other. Of course. She sighed and nodded. *A nap. Must be nice.* She was just about to say as much when anger crossed his face. He looked down at her packages. 'And where the hell were you?' he said, turning it all around. She was trapped, caught (a thousand dollars! Half the account!).

'I was shopping,' she answered, daring him to say something about it. Defiant.

'I can see that. Looks like a pretty successful trip.' She nodded, the same nod she'd given Gordon Huff, that first day: a duck of the chin and not much more.

'I thought we were going to discuss spending more than a hundred bucks at time. Wasn't that your idea?'

'Who says this is more than a hundred dollars?'

He laughed. Shook his head. 'Anyway, *hello dear. How was your day?*' he said, sarcastically. Then he brushed past her in the hall and started up the stairs. 'I'm getting in the shower. Then let's go out to eat –' he paused on the stairs, and turned to her '– unless, of course, we're all out of money now. And in that case, I'll have a pair of Prabas. Maybe a left one. Fricasseed. What do you think?'

'Prada,' she corrected, automatically.

'Right. *Prada*. Nice soft leather, easy to chew. I'll be but a moment, darling.' He ran up the stairs, taking them two at a time, leaving Becca to stand in the hall, her egregious tokens dangling elegantly from her fingers. Gilding the mule, as her mother would say.

Dan bent over the toilet, sure he was going to throw up. His body felt like it had been battered. His stomach was horribly empty, the only thing that kept him from vomiting was that there was nothing to throw up; he hadn't eaten all day. Toast in the morning. He hadn't left the studio.

He'd heard her come in. His body had shuddered and stiffened as though a piece of piano wire had been strung from his head to his groin. In an instant, the room was brightly lit again, electric light beaming into his eyes from the ceiling bulb. He was alone, strung out on the sheetless bed, naked, sweat filming his torso, his breath still coming in gasps. He heard the crinkle of bags and thought she was home with groceries. The fact that he hadn't been shopping in a week – one of his new duties as home-all-day guy – flooded over him just as the world flooded back over him. Max, drawing, groceries, eating, Becca's drycleaning – *mice in the attic* – and he had jumped, literally, off the bed and grabbed for his pants, pulling them over his legs, jumping comically about, like some rake caught by his lover's husband. He tumbled, nearly into the door, and flung it open, pausing only long enough to zip up his pants. He almost caught himself in his fly. Then he stepped out into the hall.

There she stood, staring at him with (what seemed to him) utter knowledge. *Honey it's not what you think . . .*

Then he saw the guilty look on her face, saw the bags, the packages and his sheer, perfect world, utter luck.

Tears sprang to his eyes as he leaned over the toilet and a wave of self-pity and loathing struck him hard enough to make him shudder. *What's happening to me?* He cried a minute, standing over the toilet, utterly wretched and afraid.

What the fuck is happening to me?

'I'm done with it,' he said. The sound echoed up at him. 'I'm done with it.'

By silent agreement, they went to Vesuvio's, an old hangout from the early days of their marriage. Dinner was friendly. After his shower Dan had asked her for a truce. She had been on all fours in front of the armoire in the bedroom, stuffing her shoes with tissue. New ones, he guessed, and they certainly looked expensive, but he didn't say anything.

'Truce,' she said, standing up. She was two inches shorter than he was in bare feet and looked terribly sad when she looked up at him. He'd held his arms out to her and she walked into them, not a word about the fact that he was still wet. No grumble, no admonition to watch her hair, nothing.

'I don't know what's happening to us, Bec,' he said into her hair, which smelled clean and fresh. 'But let's stop it, okay? Start fresh, be nice, all that?' She nodded, her chin bobbing on his shoulder. They stood like that, swaying together, her body moulding lightly into his, a posture he knew was, if not an invitation, at least a yielding to sex. To lovemaking. He pressed his eyes shut together and tried to will his body into it, but it did not happen. When he broke their embrace, he couldn't tell if it was relief or disappointment on her face. But the moment passed.

At the bottom of the stairs, ready to go, Dan stopped a second.

'What's wrong?' she asked.

He held up a finger. 'One sec, would you just come here for one sec? I have to do something,' and he went down the short hall to the door of the studio. She followed him. He looked at her, wide-eyed, for a moment and then turned the knob and pushed open the door. The room was pitch black without the light. He flicked it on.

He stared into the room a moment. 'I just have to get something. Just stay here,' he said, planting her in front of the open door. Inside, he grabbed two sketchbooks off his drawing-board and then held them flat like a tray beside his supplies table. He brushed everything on the surface of the table, pencils, pastels, charcoal, smudgers, erasers on to the flat top. A piece of charcoal rolled off and broke into two on the floor. He looked down at it, alarmed, hands full.

'I'll get it,' Becca said.

'No!' he said. 'Just leave it there. I have lots.' He carried the books flat, the edge pressing against his stomach (and his clean shirt, she did not point out) and all the supplies shifted to that end, in danger of falling over.

'Okay,' he said, cheerfully. 'Shut out the light, baby.' She flicked the switch and closed the door behind them. As Becca walked towards the front door, Dan stared up the full length of the door, and tugged once more on the knob, making sure the door was firmly, resolutely closed.

He took everything upstairs and came back down again, in good spirits.

'Let's go and get some grub!' he said, and smacked her affectionately on her bum. She squealed, as much from surprise as delight, and they locked up and drove off in the Volvo, Dan at the wheel.

Over plates heaped with spaghetti (by silent agreement once more, both of them had ordered spaghetti, a favourite during those same early years), Dan told Becca about Apex and the meeting. He explained who they were, and when she was unimpressed by their pedigree as publishers of *Brat Boy* and *Tunnel of Time*, he told her they were a small publisher of illustrated novels, adding 'comic books' at the end of that by way of explanation, who were well thought-of in the world where such things are thought of at all. He tried to make light of the opportunity, but she could hear the pride in his voice.

'So this might be a thing, huh?' she said. She twirled spaghetti on her fork and nibbled at the result daintily. She looked a little like a bird when she ate that way.

He shrugged. 'I don't want to get all excited about a meeting,' he said modestly, but he was grinning. 'But, yeah, I guess I'm pretty happy about it.' He wanted to tease her. 'Not bad for a guy out of work a few weeks, huh? Published.' She made an agreeable murmuring sound, but didn't say much. She looked pale.

'You'll be a director soon, I'll be a famous illustrator. You'll be rich and I'll be famous. What a team. Just like we said in college, huh? Brains and talent. Huh? Admit it, it's all happening now and you're secretly thrilled.' He laughed, and she didn't join him.

'What?'

She shook her head and said, without enthusiasm, 'I'm very happy for you.'

He let it go. 'Tomorrow after we meet with the Apex guy, we're going to go out and celebrate – hopefully, keep those gorgeous painted fingers crossed – me, Max, and Kate. I'll call you at the office and you can meet us, but we'll probably get started at Jester's. What with all the available beer and all –'

She nodded. 'Okay.'

Becca stared down at her spaghetti. She felt like there was a moment being offered up to her here, like a lifebelt thrown to the guy caught in the swirls of the sea. She could pass on dinner on Monday. Dan was going to bring in some money. They would get by. She could wait and see what the board decided on its own. She could throw herself to the mercy of legitimacy.

Certainly, she could; but even if she was thinking about legitimacy and talent, even if on the surface of her mind she was thinking about doing the right thing, it stopped there. She simply didn't want to go that route. She simply wanted the job. The means of getting it were no longer in dispute. She'd made her decision, and she was going with it.

'The painters are coming tomorrow,' she said, brightly. 'In the morning. I'm sure it will be all right if you just leave them there when you go to your meeting. Just ask them to lock up. I'll stop in there and change before I meet you and make sure everything is cleaned up,' she finished. She took a big bite of the spaghetti off her fork and through it, in unBecca-like fashion, she said, 'Tell me all about the first issue of *The Headhunter*. I'm dying to hear the story.'

It was just a tiny dishonesty, and just business. A wall, thin but there, dropped between them and she felt a little as if the hand that had been pressing on her chest all week had let up the pressure just a bit.

'Okay: the scene opens in the Headhunter's "cave" – it's not really a cave, I'm just calling it that until Max gives me a name for it. Ah, man, fuck! Max thinks of stuff at the last second and then calls me with changes, unbelievable. I *love* working with the guy, Becca. So Headhunter's in his cave, sitting at the computer. The screen is illuminating his face . . .'

Dan told the story of Headhunter to Becca, in detail. Somewhere in the course of the evening she dropped in the information that she had a supper meeting on Monday. Somewhere in the course of the night he mentioned he was going to be working in the other bedroom upstairs for the duration. Neither of them asked for further explanation. Dinner was lively and full of the unsaid.

The door to the Murphy bedroom did not stay closed long. Some time after Dan Mason pulled the front door to the house on Belisle shut and locked the deadbolt with his key, the pretty porcelain knob on the door to the little room under the stairs turned and freed itself from the restraint of the latch. The door was pulled open by invisible hands. From inside came the regular *skritch* of a needle on vinyl, the echoing, tinny sound of music recorded long ago.

Elsewhere also, the house awoke.

In the attic, an old resident of the house paced uneasily, sometimes dragging a heavy bundle from one end of the room to the other. In the bathroom, water ran into the tub, over the despondent form of a Mr Hendricks who appeared and disappeared, and even when apparent, seemed not to be whole, and the swirling eddies of the water as it filled the tub could be seen through him.

Behind the small door in the blue room came the distinct and pleasant scent of sweet grass and hay, just cut.

The yellow room was cold. The shadow on the wall, a permanent part of the décor, could not be seen in the dark.

The music faded in and out of one dimension to another from the room with the quaint, old-fashioned

Murphy bed. Re-enacted again and again, over and under the voice of a generation, was someone's lonely and horrible end.

The room veritably spun with heated anger.

Under the stairs, the high, sweet voice of the Sweetheart of Columbia Records, *circa* 1929, Ruth Etting sang her plaintive song.

Jazz feeds the soul.

7

Dan helped Becca move the few pieces of furniture in the yellow room to the blue room. He set up the desk midway, in line with the window. When she asked him why he was giving up the studio, he mumbled something about needing the light. It was accepted without question. He put his sketchbooks and supplies on the little desk. It was too small, but it would do. He felt a tremendous relief at not having to be back in that room again. Whatever had happened to him in there, he was willing to let it go in exchange for it not happening again.

While his wife ran water in the tub for a soak before bed, Dan opened his sketchbook to the last sketch he'd done in the afternoon. Headhunter scanned the crowd at the subway station for Hanus and Malicia, without success. They could be seen just in the background, through the crowd of mid-town commuters. They could not find Headhunter, either. He was in his Supersuit. The scene was full of movement and drama. It was pretty good. Considering.

He'd read a book once by a therapeutic hypnotist who practised in a city large enough to provide him with plenty of clients. Over the years, he began to notice a group of people suffering for the most part from post-traumatic stress syndrome. Other than the obvious symptoms, there seemed no other connection between them. They were from wildly varying walks of life, differing age groups, socio-eco status, and mixed fairly evenly between the sexes. They matched society on sexual orientation, as well, about ten per cent.

The patients themselves offered no real clues to the sources of their anxiety, only that it was real and not contrived. Their phobias were similar: about half of them had night fears, and the remaining half experienced a variety of situational fears, but the majority of them were basically afraid of being left alone.

During a session of relaxation with a woman in the group, the hypnotherapist stumbled upon the source of the phobia quite by accident. He was regressing her to a time when she did not have her night fears, taking her backwards along a time line, and paused her (apparently) too soon along the route. The woman went into a full-blown episode of terror. The hypnotherapist was unable successfully to draw her out of the scene to save her much anguish, but in the course of the attempt, she described what was happening to her.

She was being abducted by an alien from outer space.

Night fears, afraid to be alone, strange feelings of being watched and followed, memory loss, so-called 'missing time', all fell into place in the session. Once discovered, the woman began to recall her terrifying experiences at the hands of aliens and was able, eventually, to recall her stories without the aid of hypnosis.

Heartened by his success with the woman – but by no means convinced of the experience, and in fact believing it to be covering something less fanciful and more unfortunately mundane, such as childhood sexual abuse – the hypnotherapist began regressing his other, equally vaguely diagnosed patients. He found nearly all of them had claimed to have had an experience with aliens, and most, with abduction by the aliens.

Situations were all nearly identical. They followed the same types of patterns, even though the details might vary, they were all essentially the same circumstances and outcomes.

So he studied them. He invited in a small group of researchers and shared his information with them. The study itself was a landmark. The conclusion was scientific and final, in the eyes of the researcher.

What the people who had come to the hypnotherapist for – treatment of symptoms of post-traumatic stress syndrome – had experienced was a memory cover-up. Their traumatic experiences, while not detailed in that particular study, were covered up with a less-than-plausible tale that was more palatable to their human minds than the reality of whatever had really happened to them. As a result, in order to make true what their mind was attempting as a cover-up story, they found themselves experiencing a combination of sleep paralysis and deep meditative dreaming.

They imagined their abductions by alien beings – the human-like qualities of which proved to researchers that the traumatic sources were indeed very human – and their subconscious mind planted the stories so firmly that they were able to express the symptoms of their stress without danger of their real trauma being discovered, for whatever reason.

Clearly, that was what had happened to him. A bizarre and more twisted version of the same story. Stress, the eternal catch-all.

Somehow between moving, losing his job, embarking

on a new avenue in his career, the insecurity of revisiting a world that he hadn't even hoped to be able to rejoin with *The Headhunter*, the tension between him and Becca, her disappointment in him and withdrawal, all of it had combined somehow and, without his knowing it, had tossed him on his ass.

Post-traumatic stress syndrome. That was all it had been. Hallucinations and day-dreams, sleep paralysis inventing a wild but more acceptable story than the truth for him to deal with in order to express his feelings. *Which were what?* Unimportant.

Why not?

Dan pulled a chair under the small desk in the blue room and flicked on the light. He flipped through the sketches in the book and played around with ideas lazily in his head, without coming to any conclusions, without defining any sort of plan. He and Max would meet with the Apex guy the next day and then he would go from there.

And since he had to relax, since it was now discovered to be very important for him to relax, big-time, he went downstairs and out on to the back stoop and had a toke. He stayed out long after the pleasant effects had smoothed the edges of the day and smoked a regular cigarette, watching as the smoke curled up into the air slowly above him, the night darkening on all sides, the air still, the street noises undemanding and easily recognized.

Post-traumatic stress syndrome. Absolutely. *Why not?* Could happen to anyone. They wrote a whole bloody book about it; it had to be true.

Just the same, when he went back inside the house

about an hour later, he bypassed the room under the stairs, and cut through the dining room and the living room to go upstairs instead.

It was too dark in the back-door cloakroom to take note of the door to the room with the Murphy bed. Dan averted his eyes, in any case. The door stood wide open, propped uneasily against the wall, a dark, yawning maw, like the mouth of a cave.

Becca soaked, lying in unrest against the sloping back of the oversized tub. She was indulging herself in examination with the fascination of someone who has found an unknown rival in her midst. She heard Dan go downstairs, and the back screen door squeaking open. *Having a cigarette*, she thought absently.

Steam rose lazily above her to the ceiling of the bathroom. The mirror had fogged over and the whole room, in fact, was overcome with the mists of her bath. She kept her eyes closed. Her face was in repose, betraying her lack of inner turmoil.

I don't have to. She repeated it after and throughout certain thoughts, not in hope of assuaging any upset but more as a litmus test for her true feelings. Nearly on the heels of every such thought were practical and dogmatic womanly thoughts, such as the fact that if she abandoned her course of action now, it might well be premature: Dan had nothing so concrete as a contract or even a verbal agreement; what Dan had was only a meeting. Not unlike her meeting of that week, her lunch meeting. From her point of view, the meeting was only a starting point and, in fact, was still of no more consequence than her handing Mr Huff her résumé. Just a small step towards a larger goal. He had a meeting. Big deal. That meant nothing in the scheme of things.

They still, all in all, as the way things were (*in this day, in this moment, as of this second*) needed a second – or at least *larger*, much larger – income. As of that moment, in spite of what might happen at Dan's little (she couldn't help but lower it in her expectations, condescend to it somewhat by adding *little*) meeting, they were exactly at the point they were at the moment Dan lost his job at Clayton and Marks. Nothing had changed.

I don't have to sleep with Gordon Huff: I can take the chance. I can wait and see. At very least I can put off the . . . dinner meeting, until I know what is going on with the comic book. Illustrated novel. The one with the evil villainess who looks just like me.

I don't have to rush forward.

And she would. It was confusion to her. She understood, vaguely, that she didn't have to do what had been almost proposed at all, that she was, in fact, the *logical* choice for the director's job; her résumé was in perfect order and she had the unsettling feeling that Mr Huff had mentioned Don Geisbrecht only to frighten her into something rash. He still hadn't even said that Don Geisbrecht had applied for the position – only that he'd expressed 'interest'. Such an obvious ploy. *Yet I missed it.*

Or ignored it.

She swished her legs around in the warm water and slid further down the back slope of the tub, ducking her shoulders under the water and exposing her knees. The water in the tub was cooling. She opened one eye and, with her toe, nudged on the hot tap. Water rushed out, and to move it around to raise the temperature evenly, she waved her hands under the surface wanly. Steam rose anew and she watched it. The room was quite clouded. She felt cocooned. When the tub had filled to the point of water running out of the overflow drain, she shut the tap off with her toe and noticed with disgust that the flesh under her natural pedicure was discoloured from the week before, when the door to Dan's studio had slammed shut on her foot. She closed her eyes again. Relishing the heat of the room. Summer was coming and this would soon be an undesirable luxury, like a sauna. She disliked sweating.

It certainly wasn't the prospect of sex with Gordon Huff that was keeping her from breaking off their dinner meeting. She found she didn't really like sex. *It's not that exactly: I'm bored with it. It is the same act repeated over and over, it would hardly be any better with someone else. If I don't enjoy it with my husband, who at least has an interest in keeping me satisfied, how could I like it with a stranger? An old, paunchy stranger.*

She dangled her arms at her sides and let the water hold them up. She relaxed her body as much as she could and tried to doze. She tried to imagine sex with Mr Huff. Unable to prevent it, she felt herself distracted by the décor of the hotel room, hanging curtains, changing fabrics, choosing bedding. Well-appointed furnishings, of course. There would be a full bar instead of the more likely mini-bar. Not content with just that, she made Gordon Huff a CEO of a large corporation, and much, much more handsome. He gave her a long velvet box. Changed it to a pendant. Then it was a watch. Then it was the bracelet.

They had a drink. Dark amber with ice. Ice tinkled. *Miss Mason, is it true you are a director of your company?*

We were featured in the Atlantic *last year.*

She dozed on this for a while.

Her arms dangled at her sides. Through her reverie, she became aware of a tingling, like a foot asleep, in her hands. They were cold, suddenly, although the water was warm around her. She moved her hands about.

They hurt. She flexed her fingers and found it caused pain and she opened her eyes.

The water was red with blood. She stared gape-mouthed for just a moment and then sat up, fast, her head lightening with it. She stared at the water, swished her hands through it; it was blood. Confusion would have lasted longer – *my period?* – if not for the sudden sharp pain in both wrists that hit her suddenly, like knowledge. She pulled her hands out of the water and blood rushed down her arms, painting her red from her hands to her elbows.

She screamed. The blood flowed freely and with alarming speed down her arms, flowing as though from the tap, her hands freezing now, not just cold but dead cold, and from there she saw her wrists were great gaping wounds that coursed blood. The water was red with it, not even pink but *red*, and she stood up, holding her arms in front of her, fingers curled into weakening fists, and screamed and screamed and screamed, finally stumbling out of the tub, grabbing for the towel that was just out of reach on the rack beside the toilet.

She screamed for Dan, calling his name. She turned, naked, to the door, wrapping her hands in the towel, fumbling with the knob, wiggling out the fingers only of her right hand in order to open the door. She pulled it open, crying then, tears running down her cheeks, flushed from the heat, her hair clinging to her neck and back, and over her face, damp from the steam and sweat.

She screamed through the open door.

'Dan Dan Dan Dan Dan!' pausing between fits of his name, to gasp, to sob and scream again. She spun around back into the bathroom to find bandages, tape, something to staunch the flow – *bleed to death* – and in confusion and horror she tried to imagine what had happened and could think of nothing. Her eyes, frantic around the bathroom, glanced into the tub to see – *glass? a piece of metal sharp tape?* – the water in the tub was clear.

The scream that had been on her lips stayed there.

The water was pure and clean. The bottom of the tub winked passively through the surface of the water, sparkling with the overhead light.

The towel wrapped around her hands almost to the elbow was a white one. All of their towels were white. Becca took care to keep them utterly, purely white, adding a half-cup of bleach to every load, washing only white towels with white towels. The end result was snowy – if destructive to the fibres, they went through a lot of towels – and this one still was.

She unwrapped the towel with trepidation, still hiccuping in fear and sobs.

Under the towel were her arms. Intact. Her flesh was pink and flushed from the warmth of the bath. Becca collapsed on to the closed seat of the toilet. She buried her face in the soft, damp towel and breathed in its fabric-softener scent.

Spring Morning, she believed it was called.

*

Dan had turned off the light in the hallway, and locked the back door when he heard what he thought was Becca, upstairs. It sounded almost like a groan, or a sob, maybe. Frowning he called up. 'Bec?' There was no answer. He flicked off the lamp in the living room and closed the front curtains. It was dark; the light from the street flooded weakly into the front room, blocked by any number of obstacles, the hedge and the neighbour's tree among them. The street was deserted, in spite of the fact that it was not very late, only after eleven. *Work tomorrow, for everyone.*

Him too. The meeting was at three. He would put together a portfolio to show the Apex guy, but there was not much else to do. Probably Max would want to meet earlier, before –

'*Dan?*' Becca called from upstairs, her voice soft and strained, as though she was crying.

'I'm coming,' he said. At the foot of the stairs he stepped in something warm.

He paused just long enough to look down before going up. His sock was soaked. A small puddle of water sat at the foot of the stairs. On each stair, all the way up, was an identical puddle.

Becca had come down from her bath, looking for him. He must have been outside.

It took some time to calm his wife down. She had a fright, she'd said, but hardly elaborated more.

'You haven't been sleeping well,' he said. 'Maybe you dozed off?' She shook her head, but with less conviction than before. She kept looking at her hands. The fingers were pruny from the bath. He rubbed her shoulders through her robe and held her. She had been crying, he had seen that her eyes were swollen and her nose was red at the tip. She blew her nose once or twice and recovered. She accepted his offer of a drink and he went back downstairs to pour her a shot of something – they had some Scotch left over from an ancient party, and there might be a glass of wine in the fridge. He decided on the wine: it was white and he thought maybe that would be more appealing to her than Scotch without – as far he knew – any rocks. He stepped around the little puddles of water, bubbled up against the heavy layers of varnish on the wood floor, and thought only fleetingly that he should wipe them up before they left a mark.

Concerned as he was with getting Becca a drink, he went directly down the front hall, passing the room under the stairs without thinking. He flipped on the kitchen light, found a wine glass and poured her a full glass from the bottle in the fridge – emptying it – and grabbed a tea-towel from the door of the stove to wipe up the footsteps from the wood floor.

The recycling bin was beside the washing-machine in the foyer and he flicked on the light in there to toss the empty wine bottle into it.

I closed that.

The door to the studio was wide open. He shrugged, but without conviction. The skin at the back of his neck tightened and he felt his balls actually retreat into his body. He backed his way into the kitchen and shut the foyer light off from there. He went the long way, through the dining and living rooms, wine glass in one hand, tea-towel, momentarily forgotten, in the other.

At the bottom of the stairs, he stepped into the same

puddle and bent over and mopped it up. He mopped up the spot on the first stair. He looked around for another.

The puddles retreated down the dark hall.

He stared. *Becca came to get me. I was outside.* He turned on the hall light.

The trail of puddles stopped short of the back door. They stopped at the corner to the little room. He knew without looking that if he walked down there – and he would not – the puddles would go right inside that room.

I was outside. Becca was looking for me. She looked in the studio. I wasn't there. She was upset. Too upset to think that I might be outside having a smoke.

That was it. Of course.

Becca called him from upstairs and he went.

Becca began to snore softly beside him and he tried to read. He picked up a novel for distraction, but couldn't concentrate. Didn't really care. He ran over the sketches in his head, wishing he had done more work on the set pieces, and did not dare to think about why he hadn't. He wanted a drink himself. He settled, instead, for a toke, and went into the blue bedroom, where they had moved Becca's things in anticipation of the painters the next day, and breathed out the smoke through the little window that overlooked the street. It was just after midnight. He hoped the toke would help him sleep. Or at least take him away somewhere. His sketchbooks were stacked on Becca's small desk, the tools of his work lined up beside them, tidied. Ready for the next day. The whole thing had the look of makeshift; of fast retreat. Of exile.

We have to get out of this house.

He went no further with that thought, but it was a firm thought. A come-hell-or-high-water thought, a conviction.

We have to get out.

When he went to bed, he closed the door to the bedroom, like a child.

The music, not withheld by barriers, filtered up into the bedroom. Dan moaned against it, covering his head with his pillow; he held it tight against his ears with both hands, until his breath was hot in his own face. His body tensed as though against certain attack and his heart started its familiar pounding. His flesh recoiled, tightened into goose bumps, and he listened for what would come next, not wanting to hear it, but listening intensely for it. Wrapped only with a light sheet, and that only to his waist, he was covered in a thin film of sweat and cool air breezed above him and he was chilled.

After you've gone . . . and left me crying. It was far away and low, almost a murmur.

'*No*,' he muttered through the safety of his pillow. Beside him, Becca shifted in her sleep. He held his body stiff, so as not to wake her. She moved over on to her side beside him and was still.

He waited it out. Waited for the inevitable opening and closing of doors, the footsteps, the car. None of it came. The music, low to begin with, was fading out completely. Dan loosened his grip on the edges of the pillow. Cool air hit his face. He waited. A minute passed. The muscles of his back and arms lost some of their tension. He breathed into the pillow.

Hello, Daddy.

Dan jumped in his skin. He pulled the pillow off his head and turned his head to the door. It stood open. He rolled on to his back, eyes frantically searching the room, corners, shadows; his head swivelled as though on a pole.

Hello, big boy.

Beside him, Becca lay on her side, facing him. Her eyes were closed, her mouth still. The sheet that had covered them had been tugged off her. She lay naked. One breast rested on the bed, the other dangled, jauntily. One slender arm was perched on the rise of her hip. She did not move.

Her lips parted. *How's my big six?*

The arm on her hip moved, rose towards him, hand hanging limply as though operated by an unseen lever. Her body shifted weightily with the change and the arm jerked its way inanimately to his shoulder. Dan opened his mouth and screamed.

And sat up in bed with a jerk. The room came quickly into focus.

'Dan?' Becca said sleepily beside him. When she touched him, he jumped, and another, smaller scream escaped.

'Oh, shit!' he said. '*Christ.*' It came out with a breath.

Becca sat up and blinked, rubbing her eyes. She put a hand, cool, on his back. 'What is it? Are you all right?'

He nodded. She rubbed his back slowly, automatically. He turned to her. Looked closely. Her hair had flattened to her head from sleeping on it wet. She was she.

'Just a dream, honey,' she said. He reached over and pulled her to him.

'You're just covered in sweat, Dan,' she said, but enveloped him in her arms, anyway.

He rested his chin on her shoulder and felt her lean against him, sleepy. He felt her breath, warm in his hair. He started to relax. *Bad dream.*

'I'm okay,' he said quietly. She rubbed his back ineffectually a few more strokes and then leaned away from him.

'Yeah?' she said. He nodded.

'Let's go to sleep.' She said okay and stretched a little before yawning and collapsing on to the bed on her side, reaching down and pulling the covers up over her. She tucked her fist under her chin. Dan sighed deeply and it turned into a yawn.

'Catchy –' he started, but the words stopped. The door to the bedroom was open. Just a little, as though someone had meant to close it, but hadn't.

He lay in bed until he heard Becca's deep, regular breathing, which meant she was asleep, then got up and closed the door. He lay on his back, watching it as long as he could. Until sleep came, and took him.

The painters arrived at seven thirty in the morning, when Dan was just groaning awake. Becca had risen and showered (a moment of trepidation overtook her when she entered the bathroom but passed rapidly) and let Dan sleep through all of it.

She came into the bedroom and closed the door behind her, shaking him gently awake. He resisted for a moment and then his eyes flew open. Becca leaned above him.

'I let you sleep in,' she said magnanimously, 'but the painters are here.' There was a commotion outside the door, the clank and thud of large apparatus and the heavy footsteps of large men. Something slammed against a wall and there was a grunt and a low, rumbled *sorry*.

'Why the hell are they here so early?' Dan groaned. The night before began to come back to him. His terrible dream.

'I wanted them to get here before I went to work. With any luck they'll have the first coat done by tonight. It's a very pretty colour – do you want to see a colour sample?' Her voice was cheerful and busy-sounding. She seemed rested. She got up off the bed and went to the armoire, doing something out of Dan's line of vision. She stood up again and, gracefully, balanced herself on first one leg and then the other. Putting her shoes on, he realized. 'Anyway, they're on their own, they know what to do and you can just pretend that they're not here. All taken care of.' She picked up a small square of paper from the dresser and handed it to him. He took it automatically, hardly glancing down at it.

'The door – was it open or shut this morning?' he asked suddenly.

'Huh?' She half turned to him, but turned away again, picking up her watch and adjusting it on her wrist.

'The bedroom door, was it open or closed when you got up?'

'I don't know. I never noticed. Pretty, isn't it?' she said, gesturing at the colour sample in his hand. He nodded vaguely. 'What time is your meeting?' she said, walking to the big mirrored dresser in the corner, where the chair used to be. With the overstuffed chair in the blue room, the bedroom looked terribly under-furnished. The blue room, on the other hand, looked like a storage room – everything crammed into too small a space.

'Three,' he said. He sat up in bed. The squeal of a ladder opening was heard through the door and the low murmur of voices bled through the wall. It reminded him unpleasantly of low, distant sounds.

(*come in*)

'Becca –' Dan started. She brushed her hair and adjusted her fringe. She leaned in close to the mirror for an inspection. She dabbed at her lips. She caught Dan's eye in the mirror.

'What?' she said.

'We have to get out of here.' She blinked and tore her gaze away. She found earrings in the small jewellery box on the dresser top and fixed them to her ears.

'Get out of where?' She checked her watch. Dan glanced at the reflection of the clock in the mirror. She would be leaving soon.

'Get out of this house. Right away.' He got up out of bed and pulled on the jeans that were tossed across the only chair in the room. He pulled them over his hips and zipped them up. They were dirty. He could see a smear of charcoal on the right leg – sometimes he cleaned his hand by rubbing it across his thigh. It drove Becca crazy. She refused to wash his pants with anything else. When had he done that? When was the last time he worked? It seemed a long time ago.

'Well,' Becca said, watching him, 'we're going to go out tonight and celebrate. I'm meeting you later –'

'No!' he said, loudly. 'No. I mean we have to *leave* the house. Move out. Get out.'

'What the hell are you talking about?' Her eyes widened in surprise and her forehead wrinkled in confusion. 'Move out? Move out of the house?'

He opened his hands in a gesture of understanding. 'I don't want to be here even through the weekend. Tell me what you can't live without and I'll pack it today, before I go. We won't come back tonight. We'll go to a hotel. Just tell me what you need.' He started looking around the bedroom, as though for what to pack.

Becca grabbed him by the shoulder and made him look at her. 'I can tell you what *you* need, Dan,' she said sarcastically. 'What the hell is this all about?' She looked at her watch. It was nearly eight. 'I have to go.'

'Becca – there's something wrong with this house –'

'There's nothing wrong with this house,' she said, moving towards the door. She pulled it open just a crack, but the sounds of the painters in the room at the end of the hall became loud. They would be able to hear them. She lowered her voice. 'I have a dinner meeting Monday. I'm having a room painted. We have barely unpacked. Tell me what this is about because I'm going to work now.' One hand was on the doorknob and she planted the other on her hip, making Dan think of the night before.

It probably wasn't a dream.

'I think the house is haunted,' he said weakly, knowing how it sounded. He looked away from her. For her part, she stared at him, through him, eyebrows raised. Her lip curled up at the corner, unattractively.

She shook her head. Snorted. Laughed. She started to speak and stopped. 'I have nothing to say. If you want to talk about this tonight, fine. I'm going to work. I'll see you later.' And she went out of the door, pulling it shut behind her. He heard her on the stairs. Hesitating only a moment, he ran to the door and pulled it open, dashing down the stairs after her.

'Becca! Wait –'

She stopped at the door and put her purse over her shoulder. She looked very fresh and clean. And good. 'What?' she snapped.

'Promise me you'll come to Jester's right from work. Don't come back here, okay?' His eyes were narrowed, serious.

She sighed heavily and rolled hers. '*Dan* – I'm not going into some dirty, smoky bar in this suit. I'm coming home to change and then I'll meet you guys –'

'I'll bring you something. I'll drop it off at the office on my way to meet Max. Okay? If it's a big deal, you can phone me and tell me what to bring. I can throw something into the wash, even. Okay? Promise.'

She looked heavenward. And she shook her finger at him. 'You're smoking too much pot,' she said, and left, yanking the door open and pulling it hard shut, slamming it. He stood on the stairs, deep breathing. One of the painters upstairs dropped something and Dan jumped.

I don't have time for this, Becca thought in the car. *I have other things I have to deal with. He had a bad dream and he's turning it into – ha ha – a nightmare for me.*

Traffic, heavy anyway in the morning, seemed to single her car out for delays. She missed a turn signal and a guy in a big sports utility vehicle behind honked angrily. She honked back and checked for his reaction in the rear-view mirror. He flipped her off.

Fuck you too. Ass.

Traffic seemed unduly heavy. In fact, the lane that she would be turning into was backed up into the inter-section. She peered down the road as far as she could to see what was going on. Bright orange signs indicated road construction. Two lanes were being funnelled into one. *Great.* The light turned green, and Becca pulled out as far as she dared. The lane was still backed up, starting to move only very slowly.

The SUV honked again. She honked back, angrily, slamming her fist unnecessarily hard on the horn, and glanced narrow-eyed in the rear-view.

Instead of the SUV behind her, Becca's rear-view mirror reflected the back seat of her own car. And the upper body of a dark-haired woman. Sitting in the back of her car.

She grinned at Becca, red lips exposing small white teeth.

With a start, Becca spun her head round. The back seat was empty.

Honk! She jumped. Glanced in the mirror again. The back seat passenger was gone. The mirror flashed the angry face of the SUV driver. He pointed, agitated, ahead of them. The lane in front of her was clear. She pulled her car forward to a series of other honks and found herself sticking out into the intersection, behind a car trapped in traffic in front of her. Everything was at a standstill.

She checked her mirror again. Behind her, the SUV driver gave her the finger. For good measure, he honked again. Becca did not react.

Max called, his voice high and excited, talking too fast.

'The Apex guy checked in. Everything is a go for launch! You got your shit together, buddy?' The smell of paint was everywhere in the house. Dan was getting a small headache from it.

'Yeah, I think so.' He realized that his portfolio and his character sketches of the minor players and of Hanus and Malicia were still in the studio. He took the phone into the living room and sat down on the couch. He would have to go in there and get them.

'You at work?'

'Yeah, where the hell else would I be? How far did you get on the storyboards? You got any more?' Dan ignored the question. He was just making conversation anyway.

'What time are you taking off?'

'Probably at two. I'll go from here to Jester's. Kate's not coming to meet the Apex guy. She's got some grant thing at three thirty. You might as well show up around two, two thirty, hey? We should go over our shit – our *presentation*. I gotta stop using "shit" as a noun, man. I gotta go. I'll call you later,' he said, and hung up.

Dan had to drop Becca's clothes off at her office before he met Max. He looked at the clock on the mantel. It was ten thirty. Becca's office was across town – of course – from Jester's. He would need a half-hour, minimum, for that. Fifteen minutes in the office, yadda-ya, twenty minutes from there to Jester's. Meeting Max at two thirty. He would have to leave the house by quarter past one, just to be safe. Eat, shower, pack. Get the portfolio, the sketches.

He dialled Becca's office.

Becca answered on the first ring. 'Rebecca Mason, Patient Services,' she said, authoritatively into the phone.

'It's me,' he said.

Her voice changed immediately. 'You gotta stop this,

Daniel Mason! You are freaking me out. I just had the worst experience in traffic –'

'What happened?'

She signed into the phone angrily. 'Never mind. Nothing. But you're creeping me out. So stop it.'

'All right. Tell me later. I don't have time now, anyway. What should I bring you to change into?'

'I'm just going to go home and change.'

'Becca, come on. You promised.'

'I didn't promise anything. *You* promised. I have to check the work the painters did. I have to make sure the door is locked. I don't want to jump in the car and drive to some bar. I need a buffer.'

He made a face into the phone, pressed his lips together hard. 'Fine. I'm packing something for you and I will drop it off at your office. I'm also packing stuff for the weekend. We'll go to a hotel –'

'We can't *afford* a hotel!'

'Then we'll crash at Max and Kate's. We can talk about it when I get there.'

'*Do not come to my office!*' She almost yelled it into the phone. He imagined her face, red, angry. He held the phone away slightly from his ear. 'This is out of control,' she said. 'I'm hanging up now. I will see you later at Jester's. Good luck with your meeting. Goodbye.' She hung up.

What exactly was he supposed to tell her by way of explanation? *Honey, sometimes I hear music coming from the room under the stairs. Oh, and also – there's a woman in there and she makes me –*

There was no way to explain it. He would pack a bag for himself, nothing too dramatic. It wasn't like he was going to start throwing everything back into boxes. Just a fresh T-shirt, clean jeans, socks, underwear. He'd get his toiletries after his shower. Enough for the weekend. Maybe after the weekend they could get someone in and –

What? Exorcize the place?

Maybe Becca was right. It was nuts. The living room had the unlived-in look of a place that had yet to hang pictures or toss magazines around. There hadn't been time to live in it yet. The TV aerial was down. The VCR wasn't even hooked up. Pieces of art he'd been collecting since college leaned up against each other, and the walls, unhung. The rug bore traces of popcorn Styrofoam from packing boxes.

The bedroom window – all the windows except the living room – was uncurtained.

Post-traumatic stress syndrome. Sleep paralysis. *And nothing actually happened last night, except for a bad dream. It was just a bad dream.*

What about the door? The bedroom door was open last night. He closed it.

The house shifts. It's old. The doors in old houses – especially on the first floor – must be hard pressed just to stay hung. The latch could be loose; the tongue-in-groove thing could be off. It could be anything.

(hello, sailor)

He could be losing his mind.

But Becca had said something happened in the bathroom. And the footprints, water. She hadn't said she'd come down. What about that?

He stared at the phone in his hand, tempted to call her back, demand she tell him what had happened in the

174

bathroom. What had frightened her? His thumb played across the on/off button, but he didn't press it.

Earl Connelly rubbed the grizzle on his chin. He hadn't had a chance to shave that morning. He and his partner, Cal, had been finishing another job until after eleven. Earl had pretty much fallen asleep eating the reheated roast beef his wife had nuked for him. She'd made him get right to bed. The alarm had rung at six forty-five. There hadn't been time.

'I think it's a shadow,' Earl said to Cal.

Cal tilted his head first one way then another. He shrugged. 'I dunno. She says it's a stain.' The two of them looked behind them. The room was conspicuously empty. There was nothing, literally, to cast a shadow and, in fact, the way the light in the room was the two of them did not cast a shadow.

'It's something,' Earl said, dismissively, and went back to covering it with a heavy, stain-special primer. The customer is always right.

'The customer's right,' Cal said, grinning. 'Fifty-two bucks an hour, I'm not arguing.'

Earl nodded thoughtfully. 'As long as she doesn't come back to us in a week and tell us we didn't do it right.'

'Should we get the husband up here, take a look? Back us up?'

Earl thought about it. Husbands were unreliable, as far as decorating work went. They could get him up there and point to the wall until they were blue. A lot of times they still didn't see what they were talking about. You get a woman in a room and she could find a wrinkle in wallpaper from a hundred yards away. He shrugged helplessly.

'Looks like a bed,' Cal commented.

Earl nodded. 'Yeah, sort of.'

'Should we get the husband up here?'

'Nah. Let's just get it done. I'll leave her a note, like a disclaimer. We can stick it with the can of primer. We covered it. That's all we can do.' They nodded, glad to have decided.

The two men worked mostly in silence. In their overalls, with the constant labour, neither of them remarked on how cold the room was.

In spite of what Becca had suggested, Dan figured he needed a toke if he was going to go into that room. And he had to go into the room. He needed a bunch of stuff. Especially the portfolio. It wouldn't do to arrive at the meeting with a bunch of crumpled pages torn out of a sketchbook. Even if it was a comic book.

Illustrated novel, he corrected himself. With a guilty glance over his shoulder, he slipped outside to the backyard – the nicest place in the whole house, as far as he was concerned.

He did everything else, first. He packed a small overnight bag, and after a serious amount of deliberation, he packed one for Becca too. He was alarmed at the variety of clothes that faced him in her side of the cupboard and her drawers. The underwear alone was daunting.

He picked out a set of casual clothes (did women change their underwear when they changed their outfits? He decided to be safe and packed a fresh brassière and panties, and a package of pantyhose – adding a pair of socks at the last minute). He laid out a pale blue T-shirt, one that he liked on her, and a pair of jeans that he hadn't seen her wear in a while.

For the weekend – and he did not think of anything beyond that – he packed her a nightgown, more socks, underwear and two more brassières; he packed a blouse and another pair of jeans, and another package of pantyhose. Unopened.

That had seemed easy compared to what faced him on top of her dresser. There was makeup in a little case – he figured he would just take the whole thing. There were hair brushes, three of them. He packed the one he'd seen her use that morning. Sometimes she wore her hair in a ponytail. He didn't know if it was for practical reasons, or for utilitarian reasons, but he packed one of her cloth-covered elastics in case it was important. She had creams and lotions and *equipment*, and he had no idea as to what the essentials were. He had seen her use all of it at one time or another, but what was it she used every day? She was terribly fastidious. He debated just throwing all of it into a bag.

It was overwhelming. Finally, he went mentally through her routine, the parts of the routine he saw, and packed what was familiar. He wondered suddenly about tampons and pads and all that. As far as he knew, she didn't have her period. Even if it seemed like it.

Satisfied, he separated it all into two piles, sending her makeup and a brush along with her change of clothes, pleased that he'd thought of it all.

Then all there was left to do was to get his stuff. *What can happen with the painters here?*

He started in the little blue room.

*

Gordon Huff stopped by after lunch. He perched himself casually on the side of her desk, pushing aside some papers to do it. She was in the middle of a statement for the accountants on the Nutrition budget. Seeing him pleased her.

'How goes the afternoon for Rebecca?' he asked, familiarly.

'Well, I think I just saved the Centre about seven thousand dollars annually, on the Retirement Homes budget,' she said, terribly pleased.

He raised his eyebrows. 'Oh? And how did you do that?'

'I have included a codicil here for the individual homes to choose a picnic ham, instead of . . . the other kind,' she finished delicately. It wouldn't do to say 'real' ham. There wasn't quite another word for it, though.

'Well, well. Impressive. Have you saved any other fortunes today?'

She chuckled. He seemed very cheerful, almost as though he had a secret or something. 'You're in a good mood, sir.'

'Sir?' He leaned in discreetly towards her. 'I thought we were friends. Call me Huff. I'm looking forward to dinner on Monday.' In spite of herself, Becca blushed, her cheeks heating up. She didn't dare glance up at him, in case he took it for something that it wasn't.

'Have you got plans for the weekend?' he asked. It sounded like pleasantries to her, rather than any sort of real question. *My husband may have sold his comic book. We're going out to celebrate at a dirty, smoky bar where the only kind of cocktail you can get is a shandy. And you?*

'Nothing special,' she said. 'What about your plans?' *And your wife? Will she be joining us for dinner?*

He shook his head, dismissively. 'Golfing with Paul Nusome tomorrow. Feeling pretty rusty, it's a new season. Do you golf, Miss Mason?' She cringed at the error and did not correct it. She felt suddenly tired. Paul Nusome was head of their pharmaceutical division – everyone's pharmaceutical division. Impressive.

She shook her head. 'No. I haven't had the opportunity, I suppose. I'm not very athletic.' She was sorry she had said it as soon as the words were out of her mouth, because they gave him an excuse to drag his eyes over her sitting form. Sitting duck.

'Well, we'll have to get you out this season.' *The royal we? You and the missus? Does your wife golf?* She smiled sweetly.

'That would be a pleasure,' she said. She met his eyes. 'Have you heard any more about Don Geisbrecht?' She tried to gauge his expression, but it was inscrutable.

'He's still interested,' he said. His voice was controlled, his eyes steady on hers. She felt suddenly that it was true, that the great Geisbrecht was indeed going to apply. If that was true then, under ordinary circumstances, he would get the position. He was part of the Group. The Old Boys. He was a man. He was forty to her twenty-four. He was old blood, and while in the real world new blood might have made a genuine difference in operations and in the future, in the world she moved in old blood ruled. Old *male* blood was at the top.

I am the logical person for the job.

That was of no consequence. She widened her eyes slightly in an age-old (old blood) way and smiled. 'Will anyone else be joining us for dinner?' she said, sweetly.

He let a grin spread slowly over his face. Not an unhandsome face. She glanced away demurely. Her eyes landed on his hands. They were large. Thick-fingered. Soft. His nails were clean. Hands of cellphones and palm pilots; hands of checks and credit cards. He drove a Jag. Not a new one, but a Jag. Thick-fingered hands on the leather-covered steering-wheel. Briefly, without any control over it, she thought about them on her. For just a second, maybe less, she felt small, and submissive (powerless) and, maybe, just a little curious.

Maybe even aroused.

'No,' he said simply. 'I was thinking Donovan's. Have you ever been?' he asked.

I'm married. It was on the tip of her tongue. Did he know? Surely he would have access to personnel files. Surely, if he was interested, he would have looked. A woman would have. *I would know his sign*, she thought giddily. She snuck a look back up at him. *And where afterwards? Hôtel de Chandai?* The Jag was a convertible. He drove it even in the winter. Dan behind the wheel of his old Mustang flew through her mind. Guilt coloured her cheeks. *He'll think it's him.* Donovan's was very expensive. She hoped he knew he was buying. At least.

'No, I haven't,' she said. The fact that he might know and just not care was frightening and intoxicating. *I am here because I want to be. This is what I want.* The thought occurred to her all at once, and it was a relief.

She understood. Dan faded into the background. It was one fifteen.

The house reeked of paint. After his shower, Dan had stopped in and said hello, again. He asked them if they wanted some coffee or something. They were eating their lunch, each of them sitting on the floor on a dust-sheet, old-fashioned lunchboxes opened beside them. Thermos caps filled with creamy liquid. Coffee and milk, packed by their wives.

'We're good,' said the older fellow.

'You know, your wife said there was a stain on the wall,' said the other one. The older man looked plaintively at him when he said it, but said nothing. Dan checked out the walls. The west wall had a coat of pinkish paint. The rest of the room was more or less white. Faintly under the white, Dan thought he could still see yellow. It had been a rude sort of yellow.

'Yes?' Dan said, politely.

'Well, I'm just saying – we painted over it with primer. I dunno. It looks a little like –' He didn't finish. Dan peeked around the corner where the man was looking. He didn't see anything.

'I really don't know anything about it,' Dan said. 'This is going to be my wife's office,' he said apologetically.

'Yeah, I know. Just letting you know. We primered and we'll paint over it. In other words, I guess we've kind of done all we can. If there's something in the drywall, there's not much we can do about it.'

Distracted, Dan just nodded. 'I'm getting some stuff together and then I'm taking off. Did my wife tell you about locking the door?'

The older guy nodded in agreement, 'Yup. We're aware,' he said. He took a bite of what looked like a big, thick roast-beef sandwich. Dan was suddenly hungry. There wasn't time. He'd grab something at Jester's.

'Great,' he said, and nodded his goodbye. He would just get his stuff and go.

*

He loaded the car. He put the bags in the trunk and Becca's change of clothes on the passenger side of his car. He would stick his portfolio in the back, propping it in the back footwell. It was stand-up. It was hard-sided. Nothing would get bent.

He just had to get the portfolio and his sketches. Then he could leave.

On the front street, everything was quiet. People at work. It was a beautiful sunny near-summer day. *Nothing bad could happen on such a day*, he thought. And then he wished he hadn't. It sounded to him too much like a threat. The last words uttered by a prom queen in a slasher movie. Strictly B grade. Like good porno, the plot is predictable, but satisfying.

He had a smoke on the back step. He had considered taking his smoke in the living room, rationalizing that the smell of paint would cover everything for the next few days – *not to mention I'm not coming back here* – but decided to take up his peaceful, pleasing perch in the back.

When his smoke was finished, he tossed the butt into the yard. So far he had been snuffing them out on the concrete step and putting them carefully into a pile for later disposal, much the way he had done at their other place. Beside the step was a tidy little stack of butts, faded and damp. He flicked it away, but felt bad after. The yard was okay.

There was, of course, a plan of attack as he opened the screen door and let it swing shut unaided behind him. When it clicked into place, he shut the inside back door and locked it.

The door to the studio was open, and had been all day. (*come in*)

At the door, he flicked on the light. A quick look. Business. His portfolio was propped against the west wall. The sketches were in a pile on the table. He would grab just one of the Reporter off the wall. He had decided on the wide-eyed, innocent one, the one where she was unsmiling and pensive. It was, at that moment, the sketch that was least offensive to him. He wiped his forehead with the back of his hand, but his skin was dry. Like his mouth. His throat. He tried to take a deep breath, but couldn't.

He went in through the door without incident. He looked only straight ahead, feeling foolish and stupid but – *at least I don't have a* – very focused. Becca might have been proud, if she had known. He went directly to the portfolio. It was zippered shut and he opened it. This was all done in a smooth, unfettered motion, and went well. He propped the portfolio on the little table, now devoid of his paints and inks and pencils.

He stuffed the stack of sketches straight into one of the pockets. He would make it nice and pretty once he got to Jester's.

Just get out of here. That was all. Job one. Job infinity. *Get out of here.*

Just as he was thinking that, the door to the studio swung closed. Dan turned, heart nearly stopped in his chest, body on alert – *alert! alert!* – and stared at the door, breathing shallow, not daring to move.

'I'm not staying,' he said, his voice loud in the room. Firm. His eyes swung around, lighting on every little thing. The overhead bulb shone indifferently into every corner. The room was empty. Something tickled in his abdomen, like fingers. He shut it out. He turned slowly back to his portfolio. He grabbed the sketch off the wall, pulling it so that the tape tore. He checked the edge with deliberation and tucked it into another pocket. His hands shook. He closed the portfolio and zippered it shut.

He walked to the door. Behind him, a cool breeze whispered. He heard the remaining pictures on the wall shudder. Temptation aside, he did not look back.

(*hello, big boy*)

The door opened for him. A tug. He shut off the light and closed the door behind him. As he walked down the hall to the front door, the sound of the men moving around upstairs, the smell of paint heavy in the air, he became aware of his hard-on, almost like an afterthought. His nipples, sensitive always, pressed against his shirt. There was a familiar langour in his belly that threatened to climb. His mind was tight. Afraid.

I'm not coming back, he said, a whisper, to himself.

Becca wasn't at her desk when Dan arrived (flushed and pleased, and finally anticipating the meeting with the kind of focus that he needed) at her office with her change of clothes. He walked past Reception – a new girl – and into the inner offices, not much more than cubicles, doorless rooms with standard equipment. He stuck his head into hers and she was not there. Her purse was not in evidence either.

'Can I help you?' asked the young girl he had passed at Reception.

'I'm looking for my wife,' he said. 'Becca Mason. Do you know where she is?'

The girl peeked over Dan's shoulder into her office. 'She's not at her desk,' she said pointlessly. She looked quite young, probably fresh out of secretarial college with all the infirmities and authority conferred there.

He smiled indulgently, hurriedly. 'I'm just going to leave her some things. I'll write her a note. When she comes back you can tell her I was here, all right?' The girl looked at him dubiously, at his denim shirt and jeans with the permanent black slash across the right thigh. He could hear her think it: *Rebecca* Mason's *husband*? She took in the small black duffel bag that hung from his hand. Her eyes narrowed.

He lifted it. 'It's a change of clothes. The Uzi's in my *other* bag.'

'*What?*' she asked, alarmed.

'Joke. *Joke*,' he said. The clock on the wall behind her gave him fifteen minutes to get across town. 'I'll leave this by her desk. And a note. Just tell her I was here,' he said, and brushed past her into the office, dashed a quick note to Becca and dropped the bag beside her desk. He was back in traffic in five minutes.

Rebecca was coming down the hall from the coffee room when she saw Dan pass the reception desk. She ducked into a bathroom and waited. She peeked out only once, and saw him talking to Heather at the door to her office. She waited another ten minutes in the bathroom, then felt it was safe to leave, her cheeks red with the anticipation of running into him.

It just wouldn't be right. Not with Huff's office at the end of the hall. She had no idea if it would have any effect on their arrangement – if it was an arrangement at all (although she was sure now that it was) – but she did not want to (*Miss Mason*) take the chance.

When she returned to her desk Heather buzzed her and told her that her husband had been in and had left a note and a bag. She thanked her.

'So that was your husband, huh?' Heather said with interest.

'Yes, thank you, Heather,' she said, and hung up before the girl asked the obvious *what does he do?* question. She could just imagine: *He's an artist. Oh, yeah? Like what kind? He draws comic books. Oh, yeah? I read them.* Her lip curled into a sneer.

The note said, 'Hey baby, guess I missed you. Here's the change of clothes. Meet us at Jester's right after work. We'll wait for you. *Do Not Go Home.*' 'Do Not Go Home' was underlined, twice, in heavy strokes. The note would read through on the next page, and maybe the page after that.

She opened the black bag at her feet. Inside was a pair of jeans she hadn't worn in months and a blue T-shirt she thought was a little too tight. There was also a full change of underwear And pantyhose. What exactly did he think she did at work? She rummaged through the bag. There were no shoes. She went quickly through the bag again, looking even into the pockets on the sides. No shoes. On her feet at that moment was a pair of pink pumps. She had a change of shoes in the car, but they were the mint green shoes that she had worn at the beginning of the week. There was a black mark on one of the toes and she thought it might be tar. They were resurfacing the road behind the building. She had decided to take them to the shoemaker's and see if he could clean them. She had a cute pair of tan shortie boots that she wore with casual pants. She would just have to go home and get them. And shower, and change.

Max was waiting for him at Jester's. He jumped up when Dan walked into the place – noticing first the low, dim lighting and thinking, *Not exactly a place to show sketches* – and stuck out his hand, grabbing Dan's and pumping it wildly. His other arm came around and slapped him on the back. His face was split in two with his grin. Dan had the idea, horribly, that at any minute he was going to start jumping up and down like a little girl. But he didn't. Instead he pulled out a chair for Dan and had him push another table over to make enough room for them, the Apex guy and the portfolio on the table.

'This is fucking amazing!' he said. His excitement was catching and Dan signalled the waitress for a beer. They checked their watches in unison then laughed about it.

'Ten minutes!' Max said. The two of them tried to relax, tried to drink their beers, but their heads swivelled to the door every time it opened. Dan flipped through a copy of the proposal and read the synopsis of the first book. Max had done a synop for ten other storylines.

'This is totally impressive,' Dan said.

'You think so?'

Dan nodded reverently. 'Oh, yeah.'

The Apex guy's name was Gib Sanchez and he was fifteen minutes late. He had a Van Dyck and a nose piercing in the soft nib of flesh between his nostrils. He wore a T-shirt with Brat Boy emblazoned on the front.

Max exclaimed over it. 'Man! I love Brat Boy!'

'Oh, yeah? I'll get you a T-shirt,' Gib said, magnanimously.

Gib explained how it worked. He wanted to see what they had for pictures, and hear the storyline, plus a few from the series, and a projection on the length of the series. Max gave him a copy of the storyline's synopsis. At the back of the booklet were character descriptions and relationships.

The Apex guy took his time reading the synopsis and then, without commenting on it, wanted to see the pictures. He kept calling them the pictures, and Dan caught on right away and referred to them ever after as 'pictures'. He thought it might be an industry thing.

He brought out the character sketches first, one by one, in order of importance, starting with the Head-hunter. The Headhunter full-length sketch went over very well, getting a grunt and a nod.

'He's a good-looking frame,' Gib said, mysteriously. Dan and Max exchanged confused looks, and grins.

He liked Malicia a lot and speculated as to a need for Hanus. 'I love the name, man. *Love* it. But a chick bad guy is super sweet right now.' He ducked the picture of Hanus under the table on to a chair seat and added, 'I don't know about the chick–prick team-up, it's sort of Rocky Bull-winkle, you know? Like with Boris and Natasha. Chicks don't need an evil partner any more. We should talk about that later. Love the name, man, Hanus. Malicia's good too, but Hanus.' He laughed. 'Chick is great. She is so sweet. Chick bad guys are great. Could do a bit more with her body, though,' he said, gesturing at chest level with his hand. Dan nodded, unconvinced.

He went through the sketches one by one, asking

188

about this one and that, remarking only that the weasel-faced WTO guy would make a great recurring character. 'He's a bad guy, right?' Both Dan and Max nodded.

He looked over everything again, reading parts of the synopsis.

'This is great. *Love* the concept, it's completely under-looked. Totally original. Nice deal. Nice. *Love* the concept,' he said, nodding. 'I'm taking this back with me. I'm in love with it. Totally in *love* with it. I will show it to the boys and I'll be calling you in a week, maybe less. Tad's on vake, but he's back Tuesday. We'll probably meet on the whole thing on Wednesday. I can try and call you Thursday. No promises but, you guys, it's totally original and love the sketches. They'll want to meet with you too, probably – no, for sure – and then we'll talk some more. Cool? Anything you need to know?' He stood up and tucked sketches and synopsis into his own portfolio and Dan had a moment of panic.

'Um, could I have a card?' he said. Max nodded.

Gib dug around in his back pocket and pulled a grimy card out of his wallet, handing it to Dan. Almost with hesitation, he pulled out another one and gave it to Max. 'That's my last one,' he said. The card said, *Apex Point Publishers, Gib Sanchez Associate Publisher*; there was a phone number and address, and under that in smaller, groovy script was *illustrated works of fiction and comic books in Spanish and English*. Dan felt Max sigh beside him. They stood up with Gib and shook hands, thanking him for looking at their work.

'You guys are going to be great,' he said, and smiled. His teeth were very white and gave him somewhat of a smarmy look.

The whole meeting took less than twenty minutes. Gib hadn't even had a beer.

They waited until they saw him pass by the length of the window, then jumped up in the air, high-fived and screamed, like little girls. Little girls after the big game.

'Fuck!' Max kept saying it. 'This is it, man! Man, oh, man, *oh man!*'

'What's a vake?' Max shook his head. 'Vacation, maybe? For sure.' He nodded crazily. It didn't matter. As Gib would say, it *totally* didn't matter.

Kate came around four and the three of them ordered another round. The mood was high. The waitress asked what they were celebrating. Max told her they had probably sold their comic book to a publisher.

'Like *Superman?*' she said.

'*The Headhunter,*' Max said, dramatically. 'Remember that. *The Headhunter.* Big.'

They drank. They snuck outside at the back and had a toke behind the garbage bins. They ordered another round. Six o'clock came and went. At around six thirty they were talking about going somewhere to eat and Kate said, 'I thought Becca was coming.'

Dan looked at his watch. 'She was off an hour and a half ago. *Damn!*' He hit the table. 'I told her to come here right after work. I told her not to go home.'

Kate raised her eyebrows in surprise. 'You *told* her?' she said, incredulous.

'You *smack* that bitch down!' Max said with mock severity, and hit the table.

Dan got up and grabbed his portfolio. 'I'm gonna go pick her up,' he said, and headed for the door. They yelled at him as he left to meet them at Shirt and Thai. He spun round and waved and was out the door.

The house smelled sharply of fresh paint. Becca dropped her purse by the door and kicked off her heels. The floor was cool and hard under her stockinged feet, which were hot and sweaty. It was the best she'd felt all day.

No, the best I felt all day was when Huff took a peek down my jacket when he thought I wasn't looking. Down the new director's jacket. She'd stayed late enough that the place was empty when she left. She chanced a peek in Anderson's mailbox on her way out. Two résumés were in there. Hers was on top (a position that did not escape her). The other one was *not* Don Geisbrecht's and that was all that mattered. As far as she knew, the decision was being made at the end of next week. They were meeting Tuesday at Mario's about something – she'd seen it on the schedule. It had to be about the director's position. Which certainly explained Monday night's *dinner* meeting.

This time next week I'll be decorating my new office. Becca walked slowly up the stairs, humming a tuneless song without lyrics.

She slipped into the bedroom and went to the armoire to pick out something to wear. She thought about calling Jester's and telling them she was on her way, but it was a passing thought. She had other things to think about.

He'd told her to call him Huff. *Huff, for Chrissakes.* She giggled at the thought. It was the sort of thing that kids called their soccer coach. He reminded her a little of her dad. Of course, he was younger than her dad, but not by much.

Call me Huff. She thought it was very funny. She had a feeling that everything was going to be funny, all night. And she was in the mood for it. She chose a pair of low-riding black pants from the clip hanger at the back of the armoire. They sat just below her navel. She had a pretty navel. An innie. From the dresser she picked a little sleeveless white T. Not sleeveless exactly, but with delicate little cap sleeves. Very flattering for the shoulders, and no worries about a bra strap showing.

And, as a matter of course, she picked new underwear. She decided to have a shower. She grabbed her robe.

The paint smell was heavier upstairs. She couldn't wait to see how the room looked. Light filled the hall from the south side of the house, but she flicked on the hall light anyway. It wasn't dark out – in fact the days were long, it didn't get dark until eight or nine now. But for some reason, the house was always a little darker. The neighbour's tree blocked out –

Ice tinkled in her head, distracting her.

How do you do? I'm Rebecca Mason. I am the Director of Patient Services at the Centre for Improved Health.

Oh, my.

Yes, I know.

She tried, but could not stop grinning; it was all she could do to keep from squealing with delight. Becca took her robe and hung it on the back of the door in the bathroom. She would just have a peek and then have a quick shower and meet those guys. If things had gone well (and she sincerely hoped they had, she felt generous and beneficent right then and wanted everyone to have their wish – she really, *really* hoped they were going to have their little comic book published. It would be *so nice* for Dan) then they would be drinking and celebrating. If things had not gone well they would be drowning their sorrows. Probably they wouldn't even miss her.

She pushed the bathroom door back against the wall.

'Becca?' She started. She had thought she was alone. Becca grabbed her throat a minute and tried to place the voice. It had come from the bedroom. The end of the hall. A woman.

'Hello?' she called back.

'Becca?' the voice called again. Small-sounding; feeble, shaking. Confused, she stepped out into the hall, and leading with her head, she wandered down, cautiously. One of the workers? She had assumed they would be men –

'Hello – ?'

A bed was pushed against the wall in the room. Becca's mouth opened, but nothing came out. It was a metal bed, of the sort you saw only in hospitals.

'What is going on – ?' She stepped into the room, which was not pink at all but an alarmingly bright shade of yellow. An undertaker's impression of cheerful. Under the window on the south side was a small table. It was littered with bottles.

Sitting in the middle of the bed was a very old woman. She reached out with a skinny, clawed hand to Becca. 'Am I cold?' she asked.

The woman's eyes were a watery blue. Flesh seemed to just cling to her skull. She could see the edges of the woman's eye sockets. The skin around her eyes puckered and hung. 'Who are you?' Becca said, her hand going to her mouth. The room no longer smelled like paint, but had an equally distinct and pungent smell. The smell of disinfectant. Strong. Under that was the sour smell of age and illness. She yelled, '*Who are you?*'

Downstairs she heard the front door open and close. Footsteps down the hall. *Dan.*

The woman on the bed rose, and a rasping sound followed. Becca looked down. Her feet were shod in paper slippers. They scraped across the floor. Her brown gnarled legs were covered in sores.

'Am I cold?' She reached out to Becca, her arm long, the flesh paper-dry to touch. Becca's mouth hung open. 'Don't touch me!' she cried. The woman stopped dead in the middle of the room.

'*They've found each other, you know,*' she said firmly. Becca backed out of the door. The woman called her back, but feebly, as though she wasn't entirely sure.

'Dan!' Becca screamed. Downstairs the door to the studio opened and closed. Becca ran for the stairs. *He's right there's something wrong with this house something in it* – Her foot in her pantyhose slipped on the first stair, sending her head first into the wall. She let out another scream, a littler one then, of surprise, and whipped her head sideways to look down the hall before running down the rest of the stairs, sliding and nearly falling down, twice.

From the studio came the sound of music. Upstairs she heard the attic hatch open and the ladder drop down.

Music played in the studio, muffled by the closed door. He hadn't heard her over it. She ran down the hall watching over her shoulder.

Dan parked behind Becca's car and got out. He jogged to the house. The front door was closed. Everything looked all right. He would just pick her up and go. He wished he'd said something to Max and Kate about bunking at their place. It seemed a shitty thing to spring on them in the middle of the night. On the other hand, everyone was in good spirits. It wouldn't be a problem.

The door was unlocked. Becca's purse was hung on the banister. Her shoes were kicked off and in an untidy pile in the middle of the floor. He nudged them aside with his foot so that he didn't step on them.

'Becca?' he called up the stairs. 'Big news, babe! Big news! Your man, *he da man!*' he called up, and his voice echoed back to him, then eerie silence.

His stomach tightened. 'Becca?' he called, louder. And listened.

Quietly, weakly, came the reply. '*Dan?*' she said. It sounded like she was crying. 'I'm in here.' Where? The sound came from everywhere.

Oh, fuck. He leaned back against the door. *Fuck. Fuck.* He stuck the heels of his hands into his eyes and pressed. His body shuddered. Sweat began to trickle under his arms, the hairs on the back of his neck shot up, tightening the skin there, his scalp seemed to shrink.

'Becca?' he tried again. 'Where are you?'

In answer, music blasted out at him, so loud he cringed against it. She was in the studio. Of course.

'Becca!' he called, trying to sound strong. 'I'm coming!'

His knees shook. He clenched his hands into fists. *How bad could it be? Maybe the door was just stuck. She went in there, maybe, to take a look at his stuff or something, and she couldn't get the door open. It had happened before. She got stuck in there, maybe for an hour, maybe since after work. She knew he was out. She was frightened. Thought she would be stuck in there all night. That was probably what it was. Door was stuck.*

He didn't know who that was in the room. But he didn't think it could hurt her. He walked the hall. The music drowned out most of his thoughts.

The door was closed. He turned the knob. The moment he touched the door, the music cut out suddenly, in the middle of a word as though the singer had been gagged.

– the slickest friend you ev–

What replaced it was much worse. A voice, a whisper, breathy and girlish, came not from the room, but from everywhere, as though the walls were breathing it into his ear.

Stay with me. Stay with me. Stay with me. From the hall, and upstairs, and the stairwell. The kitchen. Outside.

He shook the door and it trembled. 'Becca!' he yelled, pressing his mouth and ear close to the door. He could hear fumblings inside. A groan.

'BECCA!' he screamed. He backed up and threw his body against the door. It shook but did not open. He rattled the knob again, frantically, all the while calling his wife's name. He was coming. He was going to break the door. He was coming.

He shook it, twisted it. Kicked. Backed up and kicked. 'Let me in!' he shouted. And the door swung open.

Stay with me. Stay with me. Stay with me.

Becca stood in the furthest corner of the room, her face twisted in a sob, cheeks smeared with tears and makeup. Her jacket was unbuttoned and he could see her bra. She was shoeless. She stumbled towards him, reaching out.

He went to her. 'Oh, baby – it's okay. I'm here . . .' he mumbled. She fell into his arms, a groan of relief came out of her mouth. He rubbed her back, tangled his fingers into her hair. She sobbed against him.

''Sokay. 'Sokay. I'm here.'

'Stay with me,' she said.

He started, grabbed her shoulders to pull her away from him, see her face. Her fingers curled into claws and dug into the flesh of his neck. He howled in pain and pulled her roughly away from him, reaching under her, between them, and pushing, the issue of his wife and what might not be his wife fighting his pressure. He didn't want to hurt her.

He forced her from him and her face twisted again into tears. 'Dan!' she cried. He let go, uncertain. Becca fell to the floor. Beside him, there was movement.

He turned his head. The bed was down. Had it been down? Becca stumbled to her feet in front of him. She grabbed at him. 'Dan!' she cried again.

'Hello, big fella,' came the voice, coquettish from behind his wife.

The woman stood against the back wall. She wore a dress. The front of it was rent with jagged rips, as though torn off and put back on. Through the holes he could see her flesh. Becca pulled herself to her feet.

'Get me out of here!' she screamed, and pushed past him. He grabbed at her and the two of them staggered out into the hall. Becca was screaming and crying alternately, hysterical. They lurched their way to the door, hanging on to each other. Heels clicked on the floor behind them, above them, in front of them.

Becca sobbed. 'Let's get out of here,' Dan said.

Stay with me, the voice came distinctly from behind him and Dan turned his head to look. Maggie stood behind him, her arms outstretched. Her face was wrenched into the saddest expression of longing. Her arms reached for him. Like a waif. Please.

Stay with me. He paused. Becca yanked on him.

'Let's get out of here!' she cried. He couldn't move. She pulled on his arm. 'Dan!' she screamed. She called from a distance, as though her voice were at the other end of a tunnel. Dan tried to pull his eyes away from her.

Please.

'Please,' he repeated, dully.

The front door flew open. Sunlight poured in, splashing on the floor of the hall. Becca shrieked and stumbled towards it, letting go of Dan. At the threshold she turned and screamed at him to come. She tumbled out, bending at the waist, she screamed, no words, just a long shriek.

The door slammed shut.

Maggie smiled, softly, her bottom lip trembling appealingly. Dan's body turned full towards her. He was unable to stop it. She was so beautiful. Under the terrible rents of her dress, her breasts quivered prettily, with fear or promise. A strip of fabric, hardly held to the rest of the dress, clung to the soft curve of her hip. Her throat was long. Her head tilted back. Her skin was white and smooth.

Sweat gathered on his upper lip. His eyes closed for just a moment. Heat swelled in his belly. From far, far away, he heard the sounds of the house. Someone lay on a mattress that squeaked. The attic hatch closed.

From outside, his wife called his name. All very far away.

Maggie lowered her arms. She backed away. Dan followed – the lure of her already ruling his body. He followed her into the little room under the stairs. Enticed. Beguiled. Bewitched.

The door swung closed behind them.

Stay with me.

On the bed then. He pressed himself to her. Pressed his penis, hard with wanting, against her soft belly. She opened her mouth to receive his kiss. Her tongue found his. His arms wrapped themselves around her back, he felt the knobs of her spine through the thin, torn fabric of her dress. It was wet. He buried his head in her neck. Tasted her. Tasted copper.

He pulled away from her.

Everywhere, she was torn and rent. Her throat was a gaping wound. He was soaked through with her blood. He pulled his hands away from her body, his mouth still hanging open, wider now, from her kiss. He looked down. He was covered in her.

When his eyes reached up to hers, she enveloped him. His throat gagged with the taste of her until he couldn't breathe. His heart fumbled for purchase on a beat. He did not breathe. It thudded mercilessly for a while, then became erratic. She was in him. She was of him.

Stay with me.

Becca stood on the steps for a long time. She leaned against the front door, which would not open. Her screams had brought neighbours. Someone said the police were coming. She heard these things outside herself. Her ear was pressed to the door.

Inside, the same song played over and over. Something old. Jazzy.

> *After you've gone, and left me crying*
> *After you've gone, there's no denying*
> *You'll feel blue, you'll feel baaaad*
> *You've lost the slickest friend you ever haaad.*
> *After you've gone.*
> *After you've gone awaaay.*

Glenn

I

A roll of laughter overtook conversation for a moment as Gavin held up a full-sized garden spade on which someone had painted the words 'Better Get Started!' Under that was 'Happy Retirement!'

Elsie leaned in to Glenn and said, 'Is that supposed to be for gardening, or digging his own grave?'

'Oh, I think Helen started digging his grave the minute she heard he was retiring.' Glenn smiled.

'Or her own.' The two of them laughed. Glenn had a bit of cake left on her plate and decided against eating any more of it. It wasn't sitting well. She tucked the plate and the napkin in her hand behind a photo of Gavin and his dog, Trigger. She smiled wryly at the photo. Trigger wasn't going to know what hit him.

Gavin Edwards was retiring at sixty (the office joke was that his toupée was also retiring – some time next year, *ba boom*). He was hanging up his pager, as he put it, to spend a few years enjoying his garden, dog and wife (in that order, he said, *ba boom*) before he forgot what to call them. There had been a mumbling of reassurance when he said that, but he raised his hand for quiet. 'I've put in a lot of years, a lot of miles, and it's time to spend some time in my *own* house.'

She tried to listen to the speeches. Boss Paul was making some crack about how 50 per cent of all listings came from divorces, and the leading cause of divorce after fifty was retirement.

'I guess I just want to say that, as an old friend, I hope Helen will list the house with Shelter Realty,' he finished sombrely, to great amusement.

Elsie leaned in to Glenn and clucked. 'Not very funny, if you think of the truth of it,' she whispered. Glenn nodded in acknowledgement, if not agreement. Elsie was the very voice of the disapproving (and shrinking) middle class. Who was Glenn to disagree?

There were more speeches, few as amusing, and then the last act of a realtor, the distribution of Gavin's current listings. It was turned into a game. Gavin gave each listing a sales pitch and then a realtor's name was drawn from a hat. There were fourteen agents and only six listings.

'A beautiful bungalow on lovely picturesque Waymar Avenue in the faltering but-never-giving-up west end. Only six miles from the river! Four bedrooms! Close to bus, school and train yard. A self-seller! Stand around and watch her go! And the listing goes to –' John Peterson did an impromptu drum roll on the desk and everyone laughed.

Merle got the listing on the draw. 'How long have you had this?' she asked with a frown.

Gavin shrugged. 'Long enough to know the lonely divorcee vendor will not be pleased with her new girl realtor. Good luck, darling!' More laughter.

Carl Wall got the next listing. A two-bedroom condo that really would sell itself. Merle groaned and offered to trade.

'Now as you know,' Gavin moved on, 'I shouldn't

have been on the rotation this week, but our next rotation, Benji, has broken his leg and is using that as an excuse to get in a little more golfing this week.' Everyone laughed. 'Mark my words, he'll be back in here next week, tanned and looking fit and relaxed with a plastic cast on his foot, with "Made in China" stamped on the bottom.' He raised his hand against more laughter and wondered what people were going to do for laughs once he was gone.

Tom called out. 'I'm next on the rotation for "class clown",' he said.

'Enough, you people. As I was saying. I decided to take the rotation that came in this morning – should have been Benji's, too bad for him, and raffle it off in this afternoon's festivities. So here it is: an old, familiar favourite.' Everyone groaned. 'A peach of a house, a plum of a listing, a piece of cake – I'm getting hungry – a three-bedroom plus, two-storey, landscaped, hardwood throughout, many unique features, on – don't take it too hard, Glenn darling – Belisle, in the near heart of the city, and the listing goes to –'

Glenn frowned at him, drawing a blank for just a moment and then (*Belisle*) smiling at the reference. Gavin pulled a little piece of paper out of the hat and grinned when he read the name. 'Well, what a surprise. Ms Glenn Darnley!' He laughed and held out the stats sheet for her. She held her frown as she came forward to get it.

'You remember how to get there, dear?' he said.

She smiled sportingly and glanced quickly down at the address: 362 Belisle. 'You're kidding,' she said. 'It's the same house.'

Gavin nodded. He leaned in and gave her a wink. 'I'll tell you all about it when I'm done here.'

Glenn walked back to lean against Gavin's desk. She quickly looked over the details on the sheet, thinking it had to be a mistake. *I just sold it. When was that?* She couldn't seem to pull it out of memory exactly. Not long. Late spring.

I just sold it.

A notation at the bottom, photocopied but legible, said, 'Selling due to death in the family.'

Oh, my.

It went on like that, the listings getting better and more exciting, saving the best for last. Glenn was anxious for it all to be over.

Then it *was* over and Gavin was shaking hands and someone was passing out champagne to toast him. Glenn took a glass and a polite, single sip, no more than required for form's sake. She didn't think her head could handle the sweet, thick, cheap champagne.

When people started making their way into little groups and chatting, Glenn walked over to Gavin to congratulate him. He shook her hand, his grin nearly bursting.

'Can't wait to get the hell out of here,' he said. 'I got a golf date tomorrow morning at eight. With any kind of luck I can squeeze in a nap before dinner. Hey, Helen's got a little "do" planned for the twenty-second. Can you make it?'

Glenn smiled warmly. 'I'd love to. Shall I bring something?'

'You shall bring yourself,' he said, affectionately. 'And your *bathing costume* of course.'

Glenn snorted. 'You won't get me in a bathing costume, or *suit*, either, but I'll bring a lovely bunch of roses
for the table.' The roses weren't doing so well in the
garden. She would have to pick some up and lie.

'I'm awfully curious, Gavin,' she said. 'What's going
on with the house on Belisle?'

Gavin's eyes widened. 'The fellow. The husband.
Mason? He died.' Glenn shook her head.

'Just dreadful,' she said. 'I can't believe it. They're so
young.' Gavin seemed near bursting with some kind of
news, but Glenn didn't notice. 'Was it a heart-attack?'
she asked suddenly, thinking of Howard.

'Uh-uh,' he said cryptically.

'What, then?' Car wreck. Cancer. There were so many
terrible ways to die young.

Gavin leaned in and whispered with careful enunci-
ation, as though he didn't want to get it wrong, '*Auto-
erotic-asphyxiation.*'

'*What*?'

'No kidding,' he said. 'The guy choked to death while
– how do you say? *Pleasuring* himself? Is that the love
that dare not speak its name? Or is that something else?'
he asked, frowning.

'That's something else. And we don't call it that any
more.' She gazed past him.

'Uh, yeah. That's right. Anyway, auto-erotic-asphyxiation
is when you choke to death doing that. Self-damage, as
my dear mother used to say. Not to my face, of course.'

'I know *what* it is,' she said. 'I'm just . . . shocked, I
suppose. My goodness.' She grimaced. The image of
such things rose and was quickly quelled in her head.
'Terrible thing for his wife.'

Gavin said, 'Oh, yeah. She found him. In that little room under the stairs.' He shook his head in disapproval. 'Why couldn't he just take it to the bathroom like the rest of us.'

'Gavin!'

He patted her arm. 'Don't forget about the twenty-second,' he said, and wandered off towards Merle and Paul.

Glenn found the package in her briefcase, under a heavy stack of current and pending listings. How could she have forgotten? A large brown manila envelope. It was addressed by hand, the address, *362 Belisle*, written smaller and in a different ink than the larger, *Dan and Rebecca Mason*. Their names (*that poor woman*) had been centred across the middle of the envelope, throwing off the balance of the rest of the address. Inside, as she recalled, was the various paperwork that had come with the house, forgotten in the process of the transaction. Receipts from the renovation, the letter from the bank, descriptions of the work done on the house and the names of various contractors, etc.

Originally, she had intended to drop it by and hadn't. The details were vague but, for whatever reason, she hadn't delivered the letter. She did remember coming across the envelope in her briefcase later and addressing it. The postage was already on the package. She'd never mailed it.

It was strange of her to be so forgetful. She was usually so efficient. And now this. The package felt electrically charged and cumbersome in her hand, as though there were an electrically charged and cumbersome connection to it all, a series of ripples in the universe. Absurd, but there, lurking; small.

Terrible to think of it, but the whole thing had likely just slipped her mind because, at the time, the house was sold, it was a completed deal by *months*, and in all truth, it simply wasn't her house any longer.

It isn't mine now. She opened her bottom drawer and stuck the envelope into an empty slot in the hanging files for the new (next) owner.

The car turned quite naturally down Gibbons and Lane Drive. She stopped at the stop sign on Gibbons and smiled at a little girl riding her tricycle on the sidewalk. The little girl's eyes followed the car unsmilingly as it went through the intersection. *Probably thinks I'm a stranger.* She pulled on to Belisle and slowed the car, leaning forward so that her head was nearly touching the steering-wheel, taking her eyes off the road at intervals finding the house.

She checked numbers, although it was unnecessary: 372, 370, 368.

Scaffolding veiled a house of similar construction on the south side. It was being painted; the upper half was complete, the white so clean and bright she could smell the paint through the closed windows, by suggestion only. They'd trimmed it in a deep, rich green. Very nice. Big windows. Excellent kerb appeal. People didn't realize what a difference the little things made.

Through the large tree in the neighbour's yard, she caught a glimpse of 362.

Peek-a-boo.

The street was full of parked cars, on both sides.

Everyone home from work by then. She took note of the SUVs, Volvos and Japanese cars, most of them clean and shiny as though they, too, had been recently painted. There were few signs of children in the yards. It was a starter neighbourhood. The people behind the Suvies and foreign cars would climb their ladders and in two or three years buy a place with a severely groomed landscaped yard, backing on to a golf course or the river with a house with no asbestos or history, on McGillvray or Somerset or something in the east end of the city, tripling their taxes, and then their yards would bloom with play equipment of the sort that blended in with nature.

She slowed the car to a crawl.

I won't go in. There really wasn't time. Not really.

Then, there it was. She tilted her head slightly to the left to get a better view from under the windshield. The windows were curtained and shut, giving the impression that it couldn't see her. She considered it.

It looked the same.

She rubbernecked all the way past and then picked up speed.

Not the same, exactly. In her brief, concentrated glance, it had looked cleaner, taller, brighter, and she wondered if someone had washed the front of the house in anticipation of its listing. That seemed too much to hope for. She glanced up at the last moment before she was in front of the neighbour's house and caught a glimpse of the upstairs window. *The little blue room. The children's room. Pretty.*

Pretty stone walk. Lovely back garden. (*English-style garden! Three bedrooms+! Close to school! Newly renovated!*)

She wondered hopefully if the Masons had at least tended to the garden before he died, and then promptly chastised herself for it.

At the stop she checked her watch and her beeper went off. Juggling traffic, she checked the beeper number. At the next red light she called, on her cell, a realtor she had been trying to reach all afternoon about a showing of their listing. They made a tentative arrangement for between eight that evening and not after ten the next morning. After that she would have to rebook.

'I'm showing a bungalow in fifteen minutes,' Glenn said precisely, into the tiny phone. 'I will attempt to reach my client at the next stop. Shall I call you back to confirm?' The light changed and Glenn expertly swung the car into a left turn. The realtor said it wasn't necessary and gave her the location of the lock box at the house. She hung up politely and curtly and dialled a client's number by heart, with her thumb, driving the car carefully with her left hand, watching the road and mentally organizing her time.

Twelve and a half minutes later, she was parked outside the bungalow waiting for a Mr and Mrs Winkler – driving a blue-green Honda Civic – to appear; she had booked her other client into a nine thirty showing, which would give her (depending upon the promptness of the Winklers) half an hour to grab something to eat. It would be fine.

The Winklers were two minutes past their appointment time. In the waiting period, Glenn had updated her book, made her list for morning, adding to the already lengthy list a note to write the pitch for Belisle and to have the sign placed out front, and a reminder to send a condolence card (*so young*) to Rebecca Mason. Discreetly, of course, signing just her name, not mentioning who she was. With any luck it would be received in the spirit intended.

The Honda Civic pulled up behind her and Glenn shut her briefcase and was out of the car door. She pasted a smile on her face and stuck out her hand in greeting.

'Hello, thank you for arriving on time. The house is lovely. I've just been in it. Shall we take a look?' she said, and before the Winklers had an opportunity to do much more than nod their greetings, Glenn was manoeuvring Mrs Winkler by the elbow in the direction of the house, with the same deft touch she used in the car.

'You were looking for a place with appliances, isn't that right? I think you'll find this home ready to enter! There's brand new wall-to-wall carpeting throughout, just imagine the expense!' and the three of them went up the walk, Glenn by then in the lead.

By nine they were still in the house. Glenn checked her watch covertly once or twice, but didn't concern herself. The next showing was not more than five minutes from the bungalow. And she smelled a sale. While the two of them spoke in low whispers in the kitchen, Glenn busied herself in the living room.

At nine ten they wanted to think about it. Mr Winkler asked about any others who might have looked.

'It's the busy season,' Glenn said. 'A seller's market, this year, I'm afraid. There haven't been any offers thus far, but it's a newer listing. Why don't you sleep on it and we can talk about it tomorrow?'

On the sidewalk Mr Winkler said, 'If someone was

going to make an offer on this house, say, what would be a good one?' In the seconds it took to size them up, their glassy-eyed, half-terrified look, and the dubious nature of the next showing (third showing for that couple, didn't need something until October), Glenn decided. She explained that she had another showing in twenty minutes, but if they were serious about discussing it, she could meet them (and there she looked interestedly at her watch) at ten fifteen at the coffee shop half-way between this house and next.

'Okay,' he said, looking nervously and happily at his wife. For the first time, Glenn noted that she was pregnant. How had she missed such a thing?

'Won't that be too late for you?' Mrs Winkler asked.

Glenn flashed her brightest, most motherly smile at them. 'Oh, no, not this time of year. I'll see you then.'

In the car before the corner she checked her watch again. Nine eighteen. There wasn't time to stop for a bite, not even at a drive-through. Her stomach rumbled. Eating was sometimes (lately) difficult for her, and there was no need to stuff something dreadful down at this hour. They had a saying at Shelter. *Eat in January*. It was the busy season. She could eat any time.

Glenn crawled into bed at twelve thirty after a half-dozen crackers and a glass of water. She certainly wasn't gaining back any of the weight she'd lost after –

After Howard died. She said the phrase in her mind with trepidation, the way she still did, as though testing herself. It settled there, inside her, and she waited just a moment or two before the next thought, to take stock.

She had showed the second house and sold the first.

Tomorrow she had three showings only, a sure sign that things were slowing down. In June, just three weeks ago, she'd shown on average five houses a day, with seven being her record. (*My husband is dead. How died. He's never coming back. Never.*) In another two weeks, she would be trickling down to two–three a day and hold steady there, probably until a couple of weeks after school started. In January she would eat. And she would eat out. A lot.

Lists rambled over and under the other random thoughts. The bungalow on Washington should be reduced. It wasn't moving. Neighbourhood was just not in that range any more. She would talk to the wife. The Dalls would probably make an offer tomorrow on the condo in Billingsford Estates. The Winklers' offer had to be dropped off in the morning. First thing. First. Then the Garfield house showing.

Dunston. Crane Street. Ledbetter Road. Columbus. Belisle.

Belisle. Glenn opened her eyes a moment into her dark bedroom. Moonlight filtered in through pretty lacy curtains, dappling the silver light across her duvet and the two small mounds that were her feet underneath. The Belisle house had been her first listing; the first listing when she went back to work after –

How died. She tested herself. Felt her resignation, the dull pain sitting there, the disappointment under that, the sadness, an ache, and somewhere in the midst of it, a familiarity with the pain that wasn't as unpleasant as it had been, but which was not yet strength. It seemed both a long time ago and almost something that hadn't even really happened, but something that was going to happen, an event of some anticipation. Each day, waking up, remembering that there was something new and different in her life, and the heavy remembrance that while there was indeed something new and different, it was not something good. That day she'd gone back into the world, *cutting off her hair!*, she had been so shaky and unsure, almost sick with the newness and differentness of a world without him. Standing in front of the house on Belisle. That had been very nearly as terrible as the first few weeks after he went. Had she really wept? She remembered how raw she had felt in the beginning as though her very flesh had been scraped from her bones, every motion cost something dear; it seemed a long time ago. If nothing else, it was easier to move around.

I'm getting used to it.

She tested herself and thought thoughts loudly in her mind, her exhausted body fighting back by drifting off and jerking awake, the intervals between longer and longer until finally she was no longer in control of the thoughts at all. It was the way she'd come to fall asleep in the last few months. It was better than lying there and listening while the silence of the empty house bore down around her without How in it.

Her last thought before succumbing was of the Belisle house. The smell of varnish almost tingled in her nostrils with it and then –

Sleep.

2

Two days had passed and Glenn hadn't done a thing about the Belisle property, except drive past it twice on her way to other properties. Her book was full. By Thursday, with the weekend approaching, she had a decent nibble on the Ledbetter Road place, a nice couple from Ohio who were looking for something small to start. One of them had family in the area and they were relocating. That usually meant one of them (Him? Her? It was hard to tell these days) had lost a job and they'd run out of money and were relocating to save a little. Thursday morning she had gone directly from her little house to the Ledbetter place to meet them and was at her desk by eleven, ready to do some paperwork. Not much.

One bit of paperwork was the ad for the Belisle house, which really should have gone in directly on Tuesday. First thing upon sitting, she quickly jotted something down, a standard first-run ad. Appliances were a big coup, especially for first-time home buyers.

TWO-STOREY HOME IN QUIET NEIGHBOURHOOD, UP-DATES THROUGHOUT, REFINISHED HARDWOOD FLOORS, NEWLY DECORATED, ALL APPLIANCES. $96,500. SHELTER REALTY.

(She couldn't believe Mrs Mason was asking $96,500. The Masons had bought it on their first offer, a low-ball

at $89,000. Even Glenn had been surprised at the accept-
ance. Now the widow was wanting to make a profit.
It was somehow unseemly. And entirely none of her
business.)

Glenn read it over. It didn't say much. She frowned
and fiddled with her glasses. Took them off her nose
and polished them with a tissue. Bad form. Howard
always claimed that tissues would scratch glass. Seemed
impossible. She put them back on her face. Read the ad
once more.

It was a nicer house than could be read in the ad.

LOVELY THREE BED+, NEWLY REFINISHED HARDWOOD
FLOORS ON LOWER LEVEL. QUAINT CHARACTER
THROUGHOUT, ARCHED DOORWAY TO MASTER BED,
ANTIQUE TUB IN UPPER BATH, LARGE, OPEN, INSULATED
ATTIC SPACE FOR YOUR HOME OFFICE, COSY ROOM UNDER
STAIRS, WORKING FIREPLACE! THREE APPLIANCES –

That was just too long. She tapped a fingernail on her
desk and stared blankly at the computer. Appliances and
working fireplace – those were the big sellers.

APPLIANCES INCLUDED IN LOVELY 3-BED WITH WORKING
FIREPLACE. CLOSE TO SCHOOL, SHOPPING IN QUIET
NEIGHBOURHOOD.

She decided simply to re-run the original ad. Glenn
opened her file drawer and while thumbing through in
search of her *Sold* folder she ran across the still unopened
package addressed belatedly to the Masons. It was fat
and inviting. She pulled it out.

With her letter opener she scored through the gummed flap, frowning over the wasted postage – out of pocket – and emptied the contents out on her desk, beside the computer. Tiny bits of paper scattered out along with letters and forms, the accoutrement of a house's paper trail.

In barely legible handwriting, on what looked like the corner torn from a child's school tablet, was the receipt for one grille sold as is, twenty-five dollars; a name was scribbled underneath that might have been Roy Leg or Ray Ley, but no buyer was listed. Another receipt was for PVC tubing from a large hardware chain. Receipts, for the most part computer- or cash-register generated, were for everything from screws to tins of varnish for the floor. Stain, paint, brushes, clothes, dust-sheets, all came from the same local paint and wallpaper wholesale company. There was a large, detailed receipt from Stanley Mann Wood Finishers – another local company. In the bottom corner, before the sub-total of an outrageous amount, was the notion 'Expenses', with the bracketed reminder, 'receipts attached'. It appeared that the Previous Owners paid a great deal of money to refinish the floors on the lower level. Glenn nearly blanched at the figure, even though they had been perfectly refinished. There were many little handwritten receipts, including one for the tub in the bath. She smiled, reading, 'One tub. As is Scratched and Chipped. Antique. $1,000'. It was signed, but again there was no mention of who did the buying. She pawed through the papers, suddenly very curious about the installation of the beast, but couldn't find a receipt amongst the little receipts for the crane that brought the tub to the second floor. *Maybe they just wanted to forget about that particular day*, she thought wryly. *I would have.*

There were more receipts for the little things, screws and nails and sealants and wire and pipes. Taps, the sink. The floor tiles in the kitchen had come from Fleur de Lisle Flooring, a very high-end manufacturer, with no store mentioned, so Glenn wondered if they had had Stanley Mann or someone get it for them on a regular trip.

On lined paper, folded in the midst of the larger documents, was a letter that Glenn didn't think she'd seen before. She unfolded it. It was a few pages thick, and written prose style. Unlike the little note that had accompanied the letter from the insurance company, which listed the renovation in point form, this appeared to be a detailed description of the renovation itself, from bow to stern. She unfolded it.

Simply, at the top of the legal-sized white, blue-lined paper, it said, '362 Belisle'. It was handwritten in what was probably a woman's handwriting. She flipped through it quickly. It was unsigned.

Obviously, it was written by the elusive Previous Owner.

She began to read. It started as though in the middle of an as-yet uncompleted thought, but there were no other sheets, and the address at the top appeared to be the title of the piece.

We renovated most of the house. The rooms more or less left were the master bedroom upstairs, the bedroom at the end of the hall, both were painted, though, and the small room under the stairs. I understood that at one point in the house's background the owner

*had rented the rooms out to boarders. The room under the stairs
was exactly as it had been then – it was originally a servant's
quarters, and was also used as a guest room – so we just left it. It
was fine the way it was.*

*The plumbing in the bathroom was entirely replaced – a process
that consumed the upper floor and the east and north walls for more
than three weeks. The toilet went in next and then the sink. The tub
was a different story.*

*The claw-footed tub, more than a hundred years old, was part of
an estate sale, purchased from Jack Reimer at auction, for $1000.
The house that it had been in (his brother's) was razed after his
death and the pieces sold bit by bit. The tub, due to its size and
weight, had proven difficult for Mr Reimer to unload (in retrospect
I wonder if he 'saw me coming'). A beautiful piece of work even in
its neglected state, it was refinished by Lorimar's before it was
installed. This proved to be somewhat of a nightmare. The window
in the bathroom was not large enough to accommodate the width of
the tub. It was taken out, the hole enlarged. Scaffolding was built
along the side of the house and the tub brought in by a rented crane.
The whole proposition took weeks of planning and booking and then
had to be co-ordinated to be done in a half-day in order to save the
money on the crane. It took the whole day. The rough opening for
the new window was damaged by the tub on its way through and
the wall had to be redrywalled before the new window could go in.*

*In spite of new plumbing, there have been problems off and on
with the tap.*

Glenn scanned ahead in the letter, but nowhere was
there a mention of how much the whole process cost. It
must have been horribly, prohibitively expensive. She
shook her head.

'The kitchen was tiled in stone –' The letter detailed

the kitchen floor, the process of the wiring, insulation throughout, the cupboard on the west wall in the kitchen gutted and the built-in dishwasher installed, the gingerbread screen door added to the back of the house. The banister and stairs were refinished by another company – which explained why they seemed to have less lustre; Glenn suspected that Stanley Mann Wood Finishers proved to be a little too expensive, either that or they had got in too deep financially by then and were cutting corners. There was no date at the top of the letter and no indication of year or real time frame of the renovation. The descriptions seemed to jump around as though the author had sat down and just written what she remembered.

The barn board in the baby's room [Glenn assumed she meant the little blue room at the top of the stairs, across from the bathroom] *was also bought in the country. Driving by one day, we happened to see a crowd of people, trucks and cars parked up and down both sides of the highway, watching a barn being pulled down. We watched too, and I asked the fellow what he would like for some of the wood. I told him about the house and how I would like to do the baby's room like a farmyard – with the clouds and sky and a little fence rail around the room, with hooks and such to hang things from. He said I could take what I could haul. Got the whole barn door intact. I asked him how old the barn was and he said he wasn't sure, but that it had been there since he was a little kid and the place had been abandoned for years. It was the county, he said, that was pulling down the barn because it was a hazard. We got a truck and piled enough wood on it to do the whole room. While I was there I grabbed some big rocks for the corner, thinking maybe I could do some kind of diorama or something. That renovation is* incomplete. *The fence posts never made it up. And I didn't get the clouds painted. By the time I would have done that, this had mostly all started happening.*

The foreclosure? Their marriage breaking up? For surely that must have happened, with this loose wire running all over the state shopping with impunity, only to have to pay later when they were insolvent. She wondered where the rest of the barn board was, but she supposed it was sitting in someone's backyard, still. And the baby?

The attic is also an incomplete renovation. It has been fully insulated and vented, sealed and the drywall installed. It has been completely taped, but the plastering is only at the first coat. We are leaving the three decorative beams (bought at Carlisle's Restored Hardware) along the wall in the attic, for future renovation, since they have been cut to order. The beams are solid maple and apparently cut from trees on a fellow's land just outside of Brockville. That's what the Restored Hardware people said. My plan had been to install the beams abutting the east and west walls and then to centre the last beam and hang 'pool hall' type lights along its length, because of the original plan of having a family room up there, and with the low ceiling, it seemed like a nice plan. The renovation in the attic is incomplete.

The whole house was painted. The paint numbers are as follows: living room, dining room, lower front hall and foyer: sun sand #38 Houston Cover –

Paints and numbers for every room were listed neatly, with names and finishes. All were placeable in her head, except for what was called 'the back bedroom', which could only be the godawful yellow room at the end of hall, but the paint name was 'lilac dust', which (although you never really knew with paint, you sometimes began thinking, reading the colours on the samples, that they were named by deranged teenage girls with an inappropriate interest in Victorian romance novels) could have been anything, she supposed, but seemed to her that it would at least have some kind of 'lilac' hue to it. As far as she remembered it was the yellowest room in all the world.

'*Roof was reshingled on the west and south sides –*'

The letter went on and on. It was apparent, from its tone, that the renovation was entirely about the *renovation* rather than any sort of resale value being added to the property. It had to have been, given the number of foolish, expensive choices they had made. The time, expense (and likely, contention) that had gone into that house, and the Masons had got it for $89,000. It was a travesty, more so now, she thought, because they (*she*) were attempting to make a profit. How difficult it must have been for the owner to give it up.

'Get rid of that albatross, yet?' Glenn started a little at Paul, behind her.

She sat back and pulled her glasses off, rubbing her eyes. In the meantime, she raised an eyebrow at him over her shoulder. 'I've only just got the listing. Am I that good a salesgirl?' she said.

'The Columbus place?'

'Oh,' she said, and sniffed. 'I thought you'd meant – never mind. *That* listing is strictly charity. I shall carry it to my deathbed, I think,' she said, the deathbed sticking in her mouth, unseemly given her train of thought and the house she was writing up. The Columbus property was being sold by an older couple who wished to move to Florida. They had bought the house some time in the forties, likely for not much more than a small car, maybe less. A small *used* car. Through the years they updated carefully while the neighbourhood collapsed indifferently around them. It was now not much better than a war zone.

'They're asking sixty,' she said ruefully. 'That's nearly twice as much as the assessment. I've had one call, an out-of-town couple, and they wanted an evening viewing. Against my better judgement, I actually drove them into the neighbourhood at night, terrified I would have to park my car on the street. It appears my terror was unfounded. There was a gang of teenagers in full, dangerous bloom on the corner and they started asking questions –'

'The questions will get you every time,' Elsie said, seriously.

Glenn chuckled. 'Anyway, they were very suddenly "uninterested".'

'How old are the couple?'

Glenn shrugged. 'I would say in the middle sixties.'

'Appeal to their children. Tell them to talk to their children about the asking price, if you've had no luck. You've had no luck, right?'

'Well, I haven't gotten difficult with them.'

'Tell them to talk to the kids,' he said. 'What're you writing up?' The Belisle ad glowed on the computer screen. The letter was open beside the computer and, for some reason, Glenn casually leaned her arm over it, hiding it from his view.

'Belisle,' she said.

Paul rolled his eyes. 'Well,' he said cheerfully, 'keep a good thought.' He wandered off in the direction of coffee.

Elsie leaned in conspiratorially, screwing up her face sympathetically. 'What're they asking?'

'$96,500.'

She sighed meaningfully and shook her head slowly.

Glenn faced her. 'It's a lovely house. Good neighbourhood. *It's in the range.*'

'I guess,' she said. 'But *still*. Such a terrible thing right in the house.'

'People *do die*. They *do die* in houses. I'm not putting it in the ad.' Her face reddened and she couldn't quite put her finger on why. Maybe *protective*. She turned back to her computer screen and away from Elsie. She'd have it sold in two weeks. At $96,500, it was robbery. (The grieving widow could make a profit like blood money, oh, god, she thought unkindly.) It was a lovely steal of a house.

She looked at the ad on the computer screen.

APPLIANCES INCLUDED IN LOVELY 3-BED WITH WORKING FIREPLACE. CLOSE TO SCHOOL, SHOPPING IN QUIET NEIGHBOURHOOD.

Then she carefully picked up every little piece of the house's most recent history and put it back into the envelope. She would just drive over there, and get a new feel for the place. Then she'd write something up. Something worthwhile.

The hedge had grown over terribly since the last time she'd visited the house and it was most apparent from inside the yard. The sides had grown in, casting shade over a good half of the lawn – no big deal itself, overgrown and crabby – but it gave the front of the house a cosy feel, like a pair of protective arms. She supposed it could also feel claustrophobic, if you were so inclined.

Everything was so grown over in the front. She suspected the back would be as bad or worse. The house could use some paint. The outside of the windows was grimy with the dust and exhaust of the summer. The patch of flower garden under the large front window and the smaller flower garden on the other side were devoid of flowers. In their place were a lot of weeds, some foxtails and the sad remains of dandelions. She looked upwards, bending back to see the roof, and gave the whole house a once-over. She half expected some sort of *déjà vu*, but none came.

Flitting through her mind, but not settling (probably some sort of self-defence mechanism), was the fact that the last time she was selling this house, standing in front of it with an eye to going in and taking a look around, was her first day back after Howard died. She had missed him that day as she had in the month previous to that. At home she'd gotten used to him being gone; once she was back at work, it was all new again, and she'd had to get used to him not being at the other end of any phone.

But no *déjà vu*. She was thinking in terms of real estate. In reality, there had been likely a hundred walks up other paths to other houses since that afternoon when she'd first looked at the Belisle house.

The door opened smoothly with her key and slid wide as if to welcome her in. *Hello there, Glenn. Welcome back. Long time no see.* Instead of hot, dry air, the air that filtered out of the door at her was cool, if a little stale from having been closed up for so long.

The smell of varnish had disappeared from the front hall and she noted that with disappointment. A layer of dust across the floor hadn't helped and the house had a slight, indefinable odour from being shut up tight in the summer. In spite of the curtains being off the windows and the large front window allowing sun into the front part of the house for most of the day, it was surprisingly cool. She went first into the living room and took a quick look around.

The floor was dusty. It might not be a bad idea to give the Grieving Widow (*I've got to stop calling her that or it's going to pop out once when I don't want it to*) a call and see about bringing in a spruce-up crew. Maybe for a day – take care of the yard, get rid of the dust, that smell, whatever it was (a horrible option occurred to her and she shook it off) and get it all bright and clean and . . . smart. The way it deserved. Oddly, other than a quick brush-up, it was as if time had stood still for both of them. Absently, she tugged at the short hair at the back of her neck.

That first day back, she'd talked to him in her head. That had been both awful and comforting. The memory made her smile. He always said the same things.

Glenn stood too long in the sun patch of the front window and stared into space above the fireplace, tugging at her hair and trying to hear the sound of his voice. It didn't quite come.

Eventually, she wandered through the living room and the dining room, noting a place on the wall where the vague outline of a hanging picture could be seen.

There was the faintest smell of cigarette smoke lingering here and there. Someone had smoked in the house and she wondered which of them it was. It was likely her. Those skinny ones always smoked to keep their weight down. It needed a good airing. She would make a note of it for the cleaners.

The refrigerator door had been propped open and she peeked inside. It had been cleaned. She supposed a mother or friend had helped Mrs Mason (*that poor woman, must have been horrible to pack after unpacking and because of –*) get packed and cleaned out. The stove was also clean.

After peeking into a cupboard or two she stood in the centre of the little kitchen and looked back through the door at the length of house between her and the front window. The space was deceptive. It was really much larger than it looked from the outside.

'You're a rather *large* house,' she said poshly, and a touch too loudly, mocking her own accent. The voice echoed back at her, a vibration of sound only, no words, like a responding *hmmm*.

Hmmm. Quite right.

Who are you talking to?

She was very curious about the garden. While neither of them had looked much like gardening sorts (not to be offensive, of course, since she herself was more of an aficionado as opposed to a maestro), she wondered if they might at least have begun to clean things up out there. It had been terribly disordered. Terribly perennial (terribly *English*, really). The inside back door stuck slightly, probably due to the humidity. The screen door held fast, and opened only after a deliberate push. So it was staying shut then, after Mr Gretner's patient ministrations. Good for it.

The door opened into shade from the house, cool and hidden. The rest of the yard was bright with sunshine, the sort that hurt your eyes upon first glance.

It was a very nice day, with a clear sky and a slight warm breeze, the sort of August day that would turn quickly into September. Glenn longed for fall and cooler days, although this was the first time she felt that she had truly noticed the weather. Most of her summer had been spent in transit, moving from one house to the next, home to sleep, the office. In and out of climate-controlled buildings and the air-conditioning in her car. She hadn't been down to the beach even once. It was no wonder How's roses were doing so poorly. Such delicate plants needed a little ministration of their own. She'd hardly chosen to be home, flittering about like a bee. In fact, Saturday's party at Gavin and Helen's, with their pool, would be the closest she came to having a day at the shore.

Water. Now there's a thought. Have I watered them?

Her heart sank. The backyard was, indeed, an indecipherable tangle. She stepped out into the cool shade of the overhang and let the gingerbread green-painted cheap outside screen door snap shut behind her. The springs creaked appropriately, sounding exactly like childhood and summer and Popsicles.

All screen doors sound like summer. Funny.

She took a walk slowly through the yard, flying insects lazily stirring with each step. The sun was right overhead, reflecting off the green of the grass. Glenn had to squint even to look down.

The worn patch on the lawn, where she had formerly suspected a torn-down gazebo, had grown over green and thick and was no longer noticeable. It was all open space now, a large backyard with ample room should someone desire a patio or a jungle of children's play equipment and toys. Bicycles, swing sets, maybe a little blow-up pool, squeals and splashing. Lots of room.

The silence of the yard and the neighbourhood bore down against the thought and it occurred to her how heavy the silence was on a summer afternoon in a neighbourhood like this. The sound of naps, the slow, deep breathing of sleep.

That might be just what the place needs. Children. Something to wake it up.

She wandered along the edge of the neglected garden. Some perennials had gone completely wild along the back row, a path of irises had nearly taken over the east side, their flowers long gone; only their green knife-like leaves and hard, brittle stems were left, the leaves slowly browning, in need of water. It had been a dry summer.

There were peonies, their blooms drooping in the heat, but their leaves fat and waxy and bright. They looked healthy enough and brightened up the middle of the long garden. Tall along the back end were stalks of something quite dead that she thought, with a crestfallen heart, might have been hollyhocks in life. One of her favourites. Their stalks were nearly yellow, small dried buds of indeterminable colour dotted their way up, while dry yellowed heart-shaped leaves hung limply off the stems.

Thick stalks of witchgrass had all but taken over from whatever ground cover had been planted in its halcyon days; bits of it still poked dry heads up under the grass, tiny round leaves in bunches like grapes. Here and there the last remnants of the early summer's dandelions stood folded up, waiting for fall. Midway through the garden the plethora of plants thinned out and the weeds were smaller and fewer. It looked as though someone might have been digging; had they given up upon realizing the enormity of the task?

It was a shame there was no one to care for it.

Glenn checked her watch and was horrified to see that she had been at the house for nearly forty minutes. In another half-hour she had an appointment. The back door snapped shut behind her and she pushed closed the inside door with difficulty. The heat. The humidity. What was it How used to say? It wasn't the heat, it was the humiliation. She smiled. She knew exactly what he would say about *that* little production.

She went inside for a quick look around.

Directly in front of her, down the short hall from the mudroom, was the little room with the Murphy bed. Where the man, Mr Mason, had died. It was a unique feature, the Murphy bed, a grace note, for a house of this sort. The room, as she remembered, was almost untouched in the original renovation, and had a distinctly antique look to it. A selling point. It had been a cute, if cramped, little room. A good temporary guest room. He had used it for something specific. An office, probably. She couldn't recall, but it had been his room.

The door was shut.

(*Now it's his room for ever. Whooooo . . .*)

It was silly, of course, but she felt reluctant to go inside. (She wondered suddenly if he had done *it* on the Murphy bed and realized immediately that of course that was it, and was instantly horrified. Such a lovely feature. And then *that*.)

Glenn strode purposefully forward, thinking that this was the part of the film when the spooky music would rise up, just as the heroine reached out and touched the knob, opening the door to whatever horrors –

The room was pitch black until Glenn ran her hand up the side of the wall for the switch and turned it on. Light bounced into the room from the bulb overhead, revealing an empty, darkish-but-charming, tiny, tiny room. It had that very strong, closed-up smell inside, due to the fact that it was windowless and, with the door shut, airless. The bed was closed up in the wall.

It was . . . small, not up to the task of its new reputation. There was hardly room enough for any sort of living creature at all to do anything except stack a box or two. There was a feeling of mild disappointment; it had been larger in her memory (and in its current reputation). There was room enough for the bed to come down, and not much more. Maybe room for a lamp and an overstuffed chair, maybe a phonograph and a small dresser.

She tapped on the wall where the outline of the bed frame could be seen. The sound that echoed back was hollow. But of course it would be.

It was . . . *fun*. And small.

She flicked off the light and the room went dark, except for a small patch of light that made its way down the hall, stopping nearly at the little door. She hoped some air would get inside. She left the door open, pressed as far against the wall as it would go, and headed upstairs.

*

She was again startled by the size of the master bedroom, so deceiving from the hall or the outside. It wrapped around the corner of the house, giving it an odd L-shape, unusual for a bedroom. The doorway was arched, the door cut to fit. Very nice. She noted that the Masons hadn't done anything tragic to it, like wallpaper or carpet.

The bathroom and the enormous, wild-looking tub had remained the same too. The clawed feet of the creature were still disturbing, beast's feet. But it was clean and shining, its new porcelain finish holding up. Very nice.

She looked into the other two rooms, whose qualities were unfortunately buried in the glamour of the other rooms. Whatever painting Mrs Mason had planned to do had obviously not been done. The little child's room was still a pretty sky-blue and the other room was the garish yellow that she remembered all too well. She did not linger in the end room. Its colour and odd scent or atmosphere – she could not put her finger on which – reminded her of unpleasant moments. Hospital rooms. Breathing apparatus. The soft *squitch* of rubber-soled feet. If she lingered she would be able to hear that *squitch squitch would you like some tea, dear? He looks much better today* – and hear the regular hiss of the machines.

I'm better now.

They hadn't done anything new, and they hadn't seriously damaged anything. Very nice. Very good.

As she walked away she could have sworn she heard, behind her, the soft step of a nurse and the whispering hiss of oxygen through tubes, *Would you like some tea, dear?* It passed quickly.

*

233

She checked her watch again and did a quick calculation. There was plenty of time to get to her next appointment. She would run past the office after that. (The next 'people' was a woman doing a prelim search without her husband, she was looking at everything and would then choose a few for the two of them to look at; it was a poor arrangement and one with which Glenn was very familiar. The husband never liked anything the wife chose and, as often as not, they went through the whole list again. 'I'm sorry, do you mind showing us the one I looked at Tuesday? Jim says he *likes* the idea of living on the highway.')

Her feet on the stairs muffled the sound of the door to the Murphy bedroom slowly sliding shut. She didn't hear it over the sound of her steps, or under the thought in her head: that it was really quite a nice house. If she didn't sell it by the first of the fall, she would eat her hat.

Upstairs, something in the attic shifted, as though having held still a very long time. By the time Glenn was locking the deadbolt on the front door, there was a soft sound, like a breath or a giggle that no one acknowledged from somewhere in the walls. The tap in the tub dripped into unseen water. Glenn stood beside the car a moment, very aware of the house in sunlight, so bright and empty. *Within the month*, she thought. *Even at this point in the season.*

Lazily, sleepily, the house stretched in the August heat.

3

On the Saturday of the Edwardses' party, Glenn showed the Belisle house to a couple who praised it effusively, but did not stay long. While in the kitchen, showing off the appliances, Glenn noted a tidy little pile of cards in the corner of the counter. The house had already been shown three times, all by other agents. She knew it, of course, but busy as she had been hadn't given the fact much thought. The sight of the cards on the counter bothered her some. The couple gave the house only a cursory walk-through (*It's beautiful! Do you have something smaller and on one level?*), and left after just twenty minutes or so.

There had been lots of time to go home and change before showing up at the Edwardses'.

Glenn believed she was looking forward to the party. The roses she had hoped the garden would produce in time for the occasion did not appear so she bought a dozen short-stemmed roses (briefly considering passing them off as hers) and a large watermelon, which was the most summery thing she could come up with that didn't involve cooking. Helen met her at the gate with a great deal of enthusiasm, some of which Glenn suspected had come from the glass in her hand.

'Glenn!' she squealed, and opened both arms for a hug. 'I'm *sooo* glad you came! Come on in! Did you bring your suit? I hope you brought your suit! Everyone is in the pool.' When Helen let go, she looped her free arm through Glenn's rather trapped arm and all but dragged her into the fray.

Once she had discarded her watermelon ('*Ohmigawd! It's enormous!*'), and the flowers ('*They're just the prettiest things I ever saw!*') disappeared into the house with one of three hired helpers – one of whom was Helen and Gavin's granddaughter Eliza, so Glenn assumed the other two were chums – she was given a Manhattan and left to her own devices.

The party was very large, something she had not given much thought to. She supposed she had thought it was going to be just 'us', us being the folks from the office, and maybe Helen's constant companion Reba and husband Mark, who they frequently got together with on 'occasions'. But many of the faces at the party were unfamiliar – meaning for Glenn, at least, not 'us', not of the small world of real estate, although real estate appeared to be just as well represented, not just Shelter realtors, either, but other agencies appeared to be out in force. The Edwardses threw a well-documented good time. She was introduced to several people by Helen as she glided by on her way to or from someone or something, and every other person seemed to be someone from 'the club'. She realized that would be Gavin's golf club; they appeared to be a very social bunch.

It was just a moment or two before Gavin spotted her. He was in the pool and swam up to the edge in one smooth motion, that would have been quite impressive if it had not been for what looked to be a small soggy mink on his head. 'Glenny!' he called.

She covered her mouth to hide a small, inevitable

smile. He was really so earnest about himself, it wouldn't do to laugh. 'Shore to water: hello, Gavin,' she said, allowing the smile then.

He waved, disappearing under the water for a moment, then bobbing back up to the surface.

He pointed disapprovingly at her. 'Get your suit on, Miz Darnley, or else!' to which Glenn laughed coyly.

Helen had been right, it seemed everyone *was* in the pool. She waved to Cindy Graham and Elsie (*Elsie in a bathing suit!*), where they clung to the side and talked soberly amidst the chaos and noise behind them, oblivious. They each waved back; Elsie offered a broad and cheerful smile. The men were tossing an enormous sponge ball of some sort around in the pool and periodically it landed somewhere, shoreside, sending water splashing two feet in circumference, causing squeals of surprised delight. A long table had been overlaid with food (among it all, her mutant watermelon) and set up against the fence. The food was covered with Cellophane and wax paper, and from somewhere in the distance came the tantalizing smell of barbecue.

'Glenn!' called a familiar voice, and Glenn spun around until she noticed Miriam West of Shannon Realty, whom she had worked with briefly a few years back, waving her over from the other side of the pool.

She worked her way through the utterly and oddly mixed crowd of well-dressed, over-groomed realtors and the bathing-suited, wet (or at least damp) members of Gavin's club.

'Miriam,' Glenn said, warmly. 'How are you?' The two women shook hands and Miriam said that she had shown one of Glenn's listings just the other day. It was a standard realtor greeting, much like *and what do you do* was in the real world. If Miriam had last shown one of Glenn's listings four years earlier, she would have opened with *that*.

'Oh?' said Glenn. 'And which one was it?'

Miriam winked at her. 'Braggart. I know you're having a good year. It was the two-storey on Belisle Street.'

Glenn smiled, broadly. 'Oh, yes. That's a lovely house. How did it go?' So Miriam's would have been one of the cards on the counter. Her smile began to feel pasted and stiff.

Miriam shrugged and then guffawed loudly. Glenn had forgotten how loud she could be. 'Well, I got me a Miriam story to have lunch on next week!' she said, with a loud, mildly offensive, Deep South accent. People turned and looked. Once they saw who was talking, they smiled in recognition and went back to their own conversations. Everything was a Miriam story.

'What happened?' Glenn asked, with just a touch of curiosity, thinking that it must have been something with the newly varnished floors, a Miriam-landing-on-her-ass in front of (what would be by next week) clients who were, respectively, a priest, a rabbi and a nun.

'We lost a whole goddamn kid in that place!' she hollered.

Glenn cringed, but kept smiling, raising her eyebrows in an almost defensive motion. The smile was real, however. Miriam was one of those people, in spite of herself. 'Oh? A whole child. Not a large one, I hope,' Glenn said, getting into the spirit of the thing.

Miriam laughed. 'That's funny, girl! Not a big one, no. It was a little one,' she said, inflecting every few words. 'We were upstairs, looking in the master bedroom, talking about that layout – very unusual, the L-shape – and the little kid is squirming in Mommy's arms. She's about three, I guess. Squirming, bored, you know. Mommy puts her down, I was telling them a story about another house I had listed, and it couldn't have been more than – and I'm not kidding for once – maybe five minutes. *Bang!* Kid's gone.'

Glenn clutched her throat primly. 'Oh, my,' she said. 'That doesn't sound very funny. What happened to her?'

Miriam gestured, largely, spilling some of her drink and not noticing. 'We couldn't find her. We called and looked. We checked the cupboards and the yard, the bathtub – that's quite a creature in there – the little room under the stairs, the fireplace, for Chrissakes –' She screamed with laughter then, drawing sets of eyes from the crowd again.

'We looked every damn place in the house. The mother was in tears. We searched the place, calling her, *shouting*, for god's sake, "Cindy! Cinnndeeee!" Nowhere. The father by then has started going up and down the street, the parents are absolutely frantic –'

'I should say,' Glenn said.

'I've got my cellphone out and we're going to call the police, the father comes into the house, saying the same damn thing, "Call the police", and just as I'm starting to dial – and I gotta tell you that is one helluva situation to be in, I was just shaking crazy. I've got kids of my own. You know what it's like –' Glenn, of course, didn't, but she did not correct her. Somewhere the story had lost its loud, guffawing Miriam-story edge and had become a touch more serious. Instead of gesturing wildly, Miriam had begun leaning into Glenn and her voice had – for Miriam – dropped considerably.

'Just as I'm dialling, the kid shows up at the top of the stairs!' Now Miriam clutched her throat. 'She says, "Hi, Mommy." Just like that. Like a ghost, she's standing at the top of the stairs. We all just about die. Her mother tears up the stairs to her. Grabs her and between hugging her to death, screams at her about where she was.' She shook her head, remembering.

'Where was she?'

Miriam shrugged effusively. 'She said she was in the closet. Upstairs. She says, "It's nice in there."'

Glenn frowned. 'The closet in the blue room?'

Miriam nodded. 'Except we looked in there. We looked everywhere. She just says, "It's nice in there."' Miriam leaned in a little closer to Glenn and said, conspiratorially, 'No offence, but it's not "nice in there". It's *pitch black*. She wasn't in there. We looked in there. It was empty. At least, as far as you could see,' she said. Then, as though recovering, or remembering that it was a Miriam story, she ended with a huge guffaw. 'Needless to say, they're not buying it!'

Glenn smiled politely. Miriam took a deep drink out of her glass, nearly draining it.

As if to make up for what hadn't been a particularly funny story, Miriam launched into another, this one about the rather tiny man who got his foot caught in the mail slot at another house she was showing. It was funny. Glenn laughed out loud at the part about the fire department arriving and the man yelling at his wife for panicking and calling them.

Barbecue was steak (to order) and chicken, burnt and dry. Glenn had the steak, her first in months (probably since How died, but she didn't think about it). There were three kinds of potato salad, many green salads, fresh fruit, cheeses, dips, pies, *watermelon*, sherbet, cheesecake, and Glenn ate to busting.

'Helen, this is all just too much,' Glenn said, when Helen passed by with a tray of canapés during the meal. Glenn helped herself to two. 'I'm going to be as fat as a peahen next week.'

Helen nodded her approval. 'You could use a little,' she said. Glenn hadn't gained back much of the weight that she'd lost in the last eight months, it was true. In fact, sometimes in her bathroom when she caught a glimpse of herself getting into the shower, she wondered if she hadn't lost just a little more. She'd certainly had what Howard used to call 'wiggle room'. Wiggle room was losing just a couple of pounds more than you intended, and then allowing yourself a whole chocolate cake on a Sunday night.

The two Manhattans Glenn had consumed before dinner were sitting nicely between her and stark reality in spite of the huge meal, and she said to Helen, 'It's my *wiggle* room,' and then chuckled to herself.

Helen patted her on the head and told her to have another drink. 'It's nice to see you loosening up, Glenn. We've been thinking about you,' she said, solemnly.

Glenn stared. Helen's face was so serious. She sighed, internally. *Oh, my.*

'I think I might just go for a little walk around your yard. I've yet to see your garden,' she said, and stood, heavily, the meal she'd eaten pressing hard against her diaphragm. 'A walk is definitely in order,' she said.

*

The Edwardses' house was on an acre and a half of fully landscaped yard. Gavin had done very well, all his career, and Helen had been a nurse before retiring last year. She did most of the gardening herself, with Gavin's help when he could in the summer – always real estate's busy time – but she could see that they had really put the effort in this year. Likely, golf and gardening were what Gavin did now.

Helen had a passion for peonies and the entire west side garden was dedicated only to them. The scent carried far up the yard on the light breeze and filled Glenn's nose long before she got close enough for a good look. They were of all colours, the deep rich mauves, the pale pinks, a profusion of colour, their bulky round heads drooping only a little, their wire casings well hidden in the foliage. They smelled heavenly (they would also die soon and leave only their leaves and repulsive, rotten-looking heads – they were not a Darnley favourite). The back garden was devoted entirely to annuals, those fickle consistents that bloomed well into fall, but never came back again.

Large trees covered most of the half-acre at the back of the yard and, with the sun dappling through them, it looked like an ethereal forest, something that the fairies might be photographed in.

It was all very soothing.

The light had slanted to that angle that warmed even the darkest earth and shadow to a state of gold. It was prettier (and happened earlier) in the fall when even the grass looked like waves of gold, but it was very pretty then. The air was slightly moist, and if you breathed in the right direction, you couldn't smell the chlorine from the pool. That made Glenn smile.

Behind her, the party began to get noisy again, as people finished up their food and filled their glasses. She turned her back on the garden and looked over at the party. The people from the club seemed a jolly bunch, laughing loudly at every remark or retort, in a way that made a casual listener feel very much like an outsider. The two groups hadn't mixed entirely well, but that would come later, maybe. The party itself seemed to Glenn, suddenly, rife with twos. Elsie stood – bathing suit now discreetly hidden under a brown and black animal-print muu-muu – with her husband, his arm draped casually around her waist. A younger couple, for this crowd, stood in deep conversation at the end of the pool. Miriam and Mark Bingham sat next to each other on chairs by the food table – Miriam was eating and, for once, listening to a story. Gavin and Helen stood close together with another couple and Gavin was telling an amusing story, judging from the look on Helen's face.

Retirement seemed to have suited them. Gavin hardly stepped away two feet from Helen without giving her a squeeze round the waist or a peck on the cheek. It was quite natural. She supposed they had rediscovered each other or some such Oprah thing. The heavy bags from under his eyes had disappeared so dramatically that Elsie had speculated to Glenn that he must have had some 'work' done. She had said nothing, but believed it was just a combination of everything coming together. When How retired from teaching he had lost ten pounds, but it hadn't suited him, ultimately. He had found retirement difficult. Perhaps if, like Gavin and Helen, they had retired together, things might have been different.

She'd never know, now. *No, that's not true. I do know. It would have been glorious.*

The moment of peace in the garden had been used up. She wandered resolutely along the rest of the path, however, pretending that it hadn't.

Gavin caught sight of her, just as she was turning back to the party. He waved and walked towards her, leaning just a little to his left. A little in his cups. The sight of Gavin, friend that he was, rarely failed to make her smile and she did then. The mink on his head had been tamed over the last couple of hours (likely at Helen's insistence) and he looked more or less his usual self. As he got closer she could see two bright spots on his cheeks: he looked flushed and happy.

'Gavin,' she said, with real warmth. He surprised her then by scooping her into a warm, friendly hug that he held a touch too long for her British sensibilities.

'Why, Gavin,' she said jokingly. 'I'm overwhelmed.' She leaned uncomfortably back from him. He seemed unwilling to let go.

'Glenny, hon, you are one of my favourite people in the world,' he said, with mock gravity. 'I want you to live a little.'

'Gavin, now I'm utterly moved.'

He turned serious. 'I mean it, Miss Glenn,' he said, and she cringed a little with the use of How's name for her. She supposed he must have heard it a time or two and was trying to be cute. It stung a little, after the garden. 'You seem like you're . . .' he continued, searching for the right word or phrase, his arms still pressed around her waist. His breath was warm and ginny. 'Like you're fading,' he said, finally.

She raised her eyebrows. 'Fading?' she said, offended.

He nodded broadly, drunkenly. 'Working, working, working. You know, this is the first time you've been out with us since –' and they both realized it at the same time and the sentence hung there, unfinished. She attempted to wiggle discreetly from his embrace. Before she could get an explanation from him, Helen came upon them.

'My god!' she yelled. 'Not retired a full month and already bored enough to cheat! And with our good friend Glenn, too!' People looked over at them and Glenn blanched. 'Gavin, how could you?' She smiled at Glenn.

'Who better than the lovely, the talented Glenn Darnley? I ask you that, woman,' and with that he let go of Glenn completely and made a grab for his wife. She shrieked and darted away. He swiped at her bottom and hit it. She squealed, delighted, and Glenn finally laughed.

When she did, she caught Gavin's attention again. He stuck a defiant finger in her face and shook it. 'There's someone I'd like you to meet,' he said, and Glenn noticed that the sun, finally, had started to sink and the sky behind his head was a brilliant pink that faded into orange at the horizon.

Fade. Fading. Faded.

'All right,' she said, and they wandered companionably back towards the thick of the party.

Glenn was introduced to a man from Gavin's club.

'This is Calvin Doon,' Gavin said. She looked questioningly at him, waiting for the rest of the introduction, *this is my cousin from France, this is the man who built our house, this is Helen's childhood sweetheart/dentist/podiatrist.* None came. Instead she caught the two of them, Helen and Gavin, exchanging glances, and something like recognition began as a cold ball in her stomach.

'Cal, this is the lovely, the talented, the *hysterically* funny Glenn Darnley,' Gavin finished effusing.

Glenn blushed, 'My goodness, Gavin, you are smashed. I assure you I am no more than clever at the best of times,' she said. 'How do you do?' She put out her hand and the two of them shook lightly. His was warm and soft.

'Nice to meet you, Glenn.' She thought she noticed a slight flush across Mr Doon's face as well, not so much from drink as from embarrassment. 'Gavin and I play golf at the same club,' he said, realizing perhaps that Glenn was searching for a connection.

'Oh,' she said, nodding.

Gavin watched the two of them like a father. 'Calvin teaches high-school history,' he said, bursting with it. Glenn nodded politely, horrified.

As if noticing, Calvin Doon added quickly, 'Gavin mentioned you were British. You have just a trace of an accent. How long have you been here?'

'Most of my life, it seems. Actually thirty years,' she managed.

'Surely the first thirty,' he flattered.

Stop calling me Shirley, she thought hysterically. Gavin would have loved that. Hysterical, indeed.

'I just came back from there. I try to go as often as possible. I'm an Anglophile, I guess they're called. I spent a month in London. Where are you from, originally?'

She fought an urge to snort and stomp away with a disgusted *oh, please*. She could imagine Gavin's glee.

High-school history, the British connection and the fact that he was single (*was he also a widower? Would that be too much?*). It must have sent poor Gavin into gales of hysterical serendipity. Fading! She imagined him rushing home, perhaps forgetting even to remove his singular golfing glove, and anxiously explaining Mr Doon to Helen, who was bursting to have him to the barbecue. Couples abhor the vacuum presented by the empty right side of a single.

Mr Doon talked and Glenn pretended to listen. She was surprised that she wasn't utterly furious. But she wasn't. In fact, it had only made her feel tired. Elsie brought her another Manhattan and joined the conversation briefly before moving on to someone else. Calvin Doon spoke of London and she added the odd bit here and there, but wasn't really listening.

Instead, with surprise, she looked at the big picture. *This is it, Glenn. This is what it comes down to.*

(Oh, Gavin, how could you?)

Mr Doon was around his mid-fifties, with a roundish face and not-unpleasant features, but bland. His hairline had likely receded back as far as it was going to, and there was still hair on the top of his head, which had turned grey and which he kept short. His skin had a pink tone that didn't belong to summer, the sort that would burn. He was thick through the middle without being fat and, all in all, there was nothing remarkable about him. He seemed to have a passion for London, and all things British, but it seemed a dull sort of passion, the kind that people who collect documents of the Civil War and stamp collectors have.

The empty right side of her, that had so offended the

Edwardses that they sought to fill it only eight months after her husband's passing, began to feel wholly empty to her at the moment as well. More than just simply empty: a yawning, cavernous hole so vast it spoke, loud howls into space that couldn't be heard.

'Excuse me, Mr Doon,' she said, interrupting his story as delicately as possible, 'I really must go.'

The streets were dark and quiet when Glenn drove away from Gavin and Helen's and into the urban sprawl that they would face in the next few years. Front porch lights gleamed in the dark, but the front streets were devoid of life. No dogs roamed, no walkers walked; in the backyards there would be clusters of people, laughter would tinkle and barbecues would give off waves of heat. Fairy-lights were strung on some trees visible from the street, cut off at the trunk by high, solid fences of cedar and pine.

She wound the car over on to Alexander Avenue, once a gravel road serving as a connector between the city and the country, but now a conduit from which people drove in and out of their suburban homes. It was paved and duly signed, with tall, brightly lit signage indicating exits and highway numbers and directions for the neophyte upwardly mobile. Glenn exited on to Washington for no deliberate reason, but just because she wasn't quite ready to go home.

The feeling that had chased her away from the party dulled and became something heavy inside her, neither sadness nor anger, neither fish nor fowl. She felt heavy and cold, as though her skin had been exposed too long and the air had cooled so slowly it was only just noticeable. Like the frog in slowly boiling water. Raw and heavy, aware.

Downtown was better. The lights were bright and garish, pulsating, some of them, like breathing. People walked from place to place in twos or threes, or groups, indistinguishable in the glare of false light, silhouetted against broad store fronts, their lights on, open for business, or lit anxiously against the temptations of others.

From Washington she drove to Pillar, a roundabout route. More apartment blocks appeared, lighted windows dotting the sides. She passed an elderly lady sitting sentinel outside one in a lawn chair, hands clasped in her lap, under the lighted awning of the block, staring out into the street, waiting. Pillar fed on to Belisle. At the stop sign she paused. There were no cars behind her, no others at the four-way stop. The sound and colour of downtown had faded, although traffic could still be heard distantly through the open windows of the car. Street-lamps were all that were on the street then.

She parked without thinking about it and got out of the car in front of 362. She could hear muffled laughter from another barbecue party, and from somewhere further away, music played softly. Something old and torchy, a contrast to the heavy-handed noise at the Edwardses'.

Light from the street-lamp reflected off the large front window, giving it an expressionless look, something that could be either acquiescing or watchful, but guarded. No light shone from any of the windows, of course. Not even a front porch light burned and yet, somehow, it seemed living.

The air was very warm, and yet something about walking up the path to the pretty red front door reminded Glenn peacefully of autumn. *You'll be sold by then. Someone will own you.* Cool evening walks, fragrant and crisp, everywhere the smell of apples and the pungent scent of fruit going over, the hunkering-down look of the light by five o'clock, the house protectively wrapping itself around you, closing you in, closing you off, in anticipation of the hostility of winter.

You'll be sold.

With her key, she went inside. Light from the street flooded in behind her, the orange halogen light of the city, like the poor-quality sepia of an old photo. Glenn quickly flipped on the light for the hall.

She walked gently (reverently) through the house and flipped on all the lights.

Upstairs she stood in the bathroom, her parade complete.

She looked down into the glossy, light-reflected face of the tub for a long time. She ran her finger along the soft, smooth, cool surface on the edge. It was perfect, unblemished and gleaming white. The overhead light shone subdued in the bathroom, soft, artlessly. It was so cool upstairs, she realized, in spite of the heat outside. The house would be well insulated, or perfectly placed to catch the air.

Glenn left the bathroom somewhat reluctantly, glancing down at the feet of the tub with amusement. At the door, she looked down the length of the hall, taking in each sconce, each imperfection in the wall, each soft corner. She wandered down and looked into the yellow room, which didn't seem quite so glaring in the night, and then into the joyfully decorated blue room, so eager-looking, so eager for a child's things.

It needs a growing family. Small children, the noise and glee of toys. The right people simply hadn't been found for it yet; the Masons hadn't been right. She was sure of it suddenly, feeling in tune with the market value of the place. It needed a family.

Light was flooding into the master bedroom from the hall. The arched doorway and the bright light gave it a look of a small cottage she remembered from home. All it needed was a four-poster bed and some filmy curtains and it could be a place transported. The hardwood floor upstairs was not as smooth or shining as the one downstairs, but endless feet had given it a character that could only come from being part of a home. The Previous Owner had likely noted that; the little wears and scratches on the floor in the bedrooms and in the hall gave the upper floor an intimacy. What more could you ask for than intimacy while you slept? The Previous Owner had seen that and decided against refinishing upstairs. It hadn't been about money at all.

She took the stairs slowly, her hand lightly on the banister, feeling its smoothness, wrapping her fingers around the delicate curve, very aware of how it warmed under the heat her hand left, and how that warmth trailed behind.

Either the moon or the streetlight left a patch on the floor in the living room, as if to show off its lustre. It would be cool there. At the bottom of the stairs she slipped off her shoes and stood flat-footed on the moonlit patch, the colour of the light so vague, pouring over her bare feet and on to the floor. It was so smooth and cool, a tonic for the soles of her feet, trapped in high heels for most of the evening. She wiggled them around until they had absorbed all the coolness from the floor and it was hard to tell where they ended and the floor began. She walked through the house once more barefoot.

The door to the Murphy bedroom was open. She left it open. As though inviting it back to join the rest of the house, in spite of, or in forgiveness for, its recent, most tragic event. A sad little room for a while, but that would fade. And no one would have to know what went on in there.

It is my secret.

The living room had a moulded ceiling. Not the original tin, but it looked just like the old pressed-tin ceilings from the era. It was painted to match the walls in a slightly lighter colour, which gave height and dignity to the room.

It was a most beautiful house. It deserved to be lived in.

A thought very nearly occurred to her: *Do I want to buy it?*

She walked slowly through the moon-flushed living room, her bare feet soundless in the empty room. She slipped her shoes back on. She stood in the middle of the great hall and breathed in the blameless silence, more of a waiting silence, and some of the heaviness of the past hour drained out.

Most of the houses on the street shone their own light from front rooms and porches on to the darkened street outside. Through some windows she could see the bluish glow of television sets. The Belisle house looked darker (waiting) by contrast. The windows were so dark they looked black now, even in the reflected light, as though the contrast of having been inside and coming out, taking her beating heart out through the door, had taken something out of the house. There was not even a porch light to give it a semblance of life.

All sorts of things ran through her mind. Vandals, squatters, break-ins. She decided she would speak to (the grieving widow) someone about having the porch lights put on a timer. People driving by at night could see the house and the Shelter Realty sign in front. Something else tugged, almost guiltily, at her as she got into her car and drove off. She glanced at the place once more in the rear-view mirror as she pulled away and saw it again. A quick impression.

In the dark summer night it looked haunted. And that would never do.

4

Whatever had happened the night of the Edwardses' party persisted for weeks. She was blue without being depressed, feeling a general sort of malaise that took her no lower than a few nights blind-eyed in front of the television, entertained enough by the flickering of the pictures to hold her there until the early hours of the morning. Days moved by with both surprising speed, in retrospect, and with snail-like sloth. If she didn't feel exactly bad, then she felt as Gavin had described, as though she were fading. Maybe just a little. At night she performed her ritual of testing, *How is dead. He is dead and he is not coming back*, feeling around inside herself for metaphorical broken bones, and found only bruises. They, however, felt fairly permanent.

She sold the house on Dunston. Calls were fewer suddenly, as though business had gone from boom to bust in a matter of days. Glenn spent more time at home than she had all summer.

Her across-the-way neighbours went away during August and asked Glenn to take in their mail and to water their profusion of plants, and she said she would. The week limped quietly into the long weekend and it was on that Saturday that Glenn realized her pager hadn't gone off for several days. Her phone hadn't rung, and the road was sleepy and void, as though dozing in the heat. She busied herself in the garden, did a crossword puzzle and kept the radio on for company. The silence got to her, too: she tried to coax herself into dinner at a restaurant on Saturday, but couldn't summon the energy to clean herself up enough to go. Around four o'clock that afternoon she opened a bottle of red wine that had sat unopened in the cupboard since June, and had a glass on her deck before strolling across the road, the preternaturally muted road, to water the plants.

Two houses could hardly have been more different than Glenn's house and her neighbours'. She and How had loved the convenience and country feeling of their one-level ranch style, but the neighbours had an enormous bi-level, split into two sections, each section with its own, oddly placed, sunken-something. In the front of the house, the family room was three steps down from the dining room. In the back of the house, there was a den from which ran their three bedrooms, and all of this was the same three steps down from the kitchen. It was an odd place, where it seemed as though the kitchen was elevated to some kind of throne-room status. Yet instead of a large, eat-in kitchen, there was a fairly small cooking area and a too-wide island in the centre, around which had been placed six chairs. It was a strange layout and, all in all, an attractive house. Even denied its people, it somehow managed to feel full. The neighbours had three children, only two of whom were still at home, and those two were teenagers, about to launch out on their own. She wondered (routinely) while she carefully watered their profusion of African violets on the west side of the house, if they were planning to sell.

Signs of life were everywhere: magazines and clothes were strewn about in a tidy, yet haphazard way, as though they were about to be picked up at any moment. Pots hung from a ceiling grid. Plants grew wildly in windows and from hanging baskets. Books were overturned, their spines bent out, as though the reader had just gone off to answer the phone, or let the dog in or stir a pot. The phone rang twice while Glenn was there the first time, and the answering-machine picked it up. The youngest daughter's voice told the caller that no one could come to the phone because 'We're all outside playing football in the backyard, like the Kennedys,' and this was followed by a giggle, as though she were doing something naughty. Each time the caller left a message for one of the children.

In the middle of tipping the bright yellow watering can over a healthy, green and white spider plant, she had the strangest feeling that she wasn't there. It was not a feeling entirely unknown to her.

There were times that summer when Glenn would find herself entirely lost. She would suddenly pause in whatever she was doing, oblivious to the moment before or the moment that would come next. She would be walking along a street somewhere and find that she didn't have a clue where she was or how long she had been in arriving there. This happened once or twice while she was driving. She would find herself stopped at a red light as though wakening from a dream and she would not know where she was. The streets of her city were as familiar as the halls of her own home, and yet she wouldn't be able to place them. Then her foot would press on the accelerator at the end of the light, or she would come to a full and complete stop at the stop sign and everything would be clear. *I am on Oak Park. I am on*

Washington, I am on Larabee Avenue. I am on Belisle. And everything would be fine again.

But it terrified her. She thought she was losing touch.

She locked the door to the neighbours' house and walked back across the lonely lane without bothering to look for cars.

Glenn slipped her shoes off outside the large patio doors off the deck and pulled the door open.

'Hello,' she said into the empty house, a statement. It was not answered, because no one was there. She poured herself a glass of wine.

Crawling into bed that night, wanting to read, she turned off the light instead and lay in the half-dark of her room – no longer sleeping on her side of the bed exclusively but settling usually, naturally, in the deep of the night to somewhere closer to the middle – staring at the doorway to the hall.

You aren't even a ghost. Why hadn't he at least come to her as a ghost?

She lay there like that for the longest time, willing him to come back as a ghost and wondered if he couldn't because he simply wasn't there, wasn't in their house. Maybe he was on a boat somewhere in the Caribbean; in Greece at the market that he loved; in Mexico, waiting outside the bus station in the heat.

Glenn was glad to see the neighbours pull into their driveway the next day, the back of the station-wagon full to the window with various and sundry items. She was glad to see them pile out and fill their house up with their things. She was glad to not go back there. There was something about being in that house, so full of absent noise, that made her silent house much, much more silent. She watched from her front window and waved when they looked over. They did not wave back, couldn't see her through the flat reflective surface of the glass.

Later, the neighbour lady brought her a tin of banana muffins for her trouble. Glenn walked out into the yard to meet her and they spoke lightly of her trip and Glenn's week. The woman looked tired and it filled Glenn with a sort of pleasure that someone else was made tired by the efforts of living – even though her efforts were likely more exhausting than Glenn's. Glenn thanked her kindly for the muffins and took them into the kitchen. She ate two of them without tasting and then, with the deliberation and precision of someone with only one task, wrapped the rest up and put them in the freezer for some time in the future.

The house surrounded her. She thought she might go into town and rent a movie, something funny with lots of characters. Something like *Around the World in Eighty Days*. Something populated.

The muffins did not sit well.

Her stomach churned them over, turning them hard inside her. Her need for antacids had diminished since spring but the imagined ulcer that inspired them seemed to be back. She put up with it just a moment and went into the bathroom.

It was terribly tidy and starting to look fussy, down to the too-carefully managed towel rack where a large, fluffy towel was artfully covered with another in a contrasting colour. Her bathroom suite was beige, something they'd always talked about changing, but never had. She could do it now. Anything she wanted. Purple. Orange. A garish yellow.

She pulled open the mirrored medicine chest and found a bottle of Tums. Without closing the door, she popped open the lid and shook out two tablets. She stuck them into her mouth and chewed, wincing at the sweet, chalky taste. She replaced the lid on the bottle and put them back on the shelf where she'd found them. She swallowed the bits and pieces, waiting patiently for the moment when the hot, bitter feeling in her stomach would pass. She swung the mirrored door shut.

The image in the mirror behind her was not the beige tub, but a familiar, brilliant white tub of enormous proportions and just before she dismissed it, *trick of the light*, she caught sight through the bottom of the mirror of two large, clawed feet. Light winked off the gleaming white enamel.

Wink.

She spun round.

Her own neglectful taste stared back, uninterested, square and muted. Glenn leaned back on the sink. Her heart pounded, for she *had* seen something else. She turned her head and looked back into the mirror. Her face, pale, stared back, framed chaotically by the dull beige tub and tiles of her own bathroom.

Just to be sure, she turned and looked once more, almost wishing she would see it again.

Fall and winter passed.

She sold two houses before spring, something she had never managed before. She was hard pressed to find a time in the past when she'd sold a house in February at all, and within a month (she did not hesitate to point out to Elsie several times that February was the *shortest* month of the year) she'd sold two.

Both sales renewed her interest in her work, just in time for spring. Interest in realty at all had been waning and she had begun thinking it was time to find something else to do. There was, of course, nothing else and her renewed interest came like a breath held too long, a gulp of air followed by a sigh of relief. In a frenzy, she updated her three remaining listings – the Belisle house included – and poked her way through every listing in the area to find a buyer who might be looking to move up (or down) and called those agents to recommend her listings. It was good for her. She began again to eat and breathe work, going into the office every day, talking on the phone. Setting goals.

Spring arrived unusually early, and it was felt everywhere in the city. The streets were busy again. People shucked coats too early and jackets came back, and late in the evening every bus stop had people shivering in their light wear, smiling against the cold, ready for the sun.

There was a message on her desk when she came in on Tuesday, in the childish handwriting of their new receptionist.

'She spelled "Mason" wrong,' Glenn commented to Elsie. 'She spelled it with an E. Is this another work-experience student from the high school?'

Elsie grunted and laughed. 'I think she's boss Paul's niece. Tread carefully. Who's Mason? Boyfriend I don't know about?' Glenn shot a look sideways at her. Elsie was paying no real attention to her; she was typing an ad on to the computer.

'Mason is Rebecca Mason, current vendor on 362 Belisle.'

Elsie nodded with mock respect. 'Aah, the grieving widow. And her lawyer?'

Glenn nodded absently. 'She wants to rent it. I'm supposed to check in regularly. I must admit I have been derelict in my duty.'

'Let her rent it. It's the proverbial white elephant. Must have a ghost or something, maybe even her husband. Maybe she should spend a night in the house. If she's alive in the morning, she can rent it.'

Glenn smiled. 'Well, we'll see,' she said. 'I just happen to have a showing there this morning. I'm on my way over to wait it out. I think I'll return Mrs Mason's call a little later. Wish me luck,' she said, tossing the message into the waste-paper basket between their two desks.

On her way out of the door, Elsie called, 'Luck.'

Glenn was early for her showing. The woman had called her out of the blue, having driven past the house on Sunday. She was house-shopping. She said it as though it were an activity of great fun, like a volleyball game, or a spending spree at the spa. *I was house-shopping!* Most of what she said on the phone sounded that way, falsely enthusiastic, like an outpatient in joy-therapy. *I'm house-shopping and happy about it!* Glenn did not hold a great deal of hope for the showing.

In the back of her car this time she'd brought a broom and dustpan and some rags from home. The last time she'd checked the house, it had begun to look a little shabby. The floor and window-sills had a winter's worth of dust, and while she hadn't seen any, she was concerned about mouse droppings. An empty house invited that sort of thing.

She carried her bag of rags and the broom into the house with her, juggling everything at the door, fumbling with the key. The snow was gone from the yard, and while there was yet to be any green on the hedge or trees, the day was sunny and that improved things a bit. The hedge had kept much of the worst of the winter's car exhaust from off the lower half of the house, unlike the neighbour's house, which was grey from the ground up nearly a metre, just under the window. It looked awful.

Once inside she leaned the broom against the door and looked up at the ceiling, as she always did when she came in. In the front hall it was marvellously high, all the way up to the first-floor landing. Positively cathedral-like.

The floor in front of the door bore the dirty snow imprints of previous visitors, but it was not bad. The dirt had dried to a powder and most of it would easily sweep away.

She was expecting a young, silly woman to come and look, very likely on a whim. But, really, it was the start of the season that had made her want to spruce things up. It was April. The days were getting longer and people were looking at houses once more. She felt good about it.

'I feel good about it,' she said, swiping the broom across the floor in front of the door. Dirt and dust flew up into the air, catching in the sunlight and hovering, falling softly to new places on the floor. She swept over footprints as best she could. They were small, a heeled shoe, and disappeared half-way down as the dirt came off on her way through the house. Most of the prints were in the dust that had settled on the floor. If there was time, she would swipe a rag over them. She looked at her watch. The woman would be there in just under an hour.

'There you are,' she said, cheerfully. 'A fresh start.'

The dining room and the living room produced the largest piles of dirt and when she was done with the lower floor, she swept all the piles into the dustpan and poured it into the empty bag she had brought. She decided she would have time to run around with the cloth. She looked again at her watch. Very quickly. She glanced around her. There were several months of dust settled on to window-sills. The small ledge above the fireplace (too small to be properly called a mantel) was grey where it was supposed to be white.

Bending down, she swept up the small pile of dirt in front of the fireplace. Turning her face away from it to keep it out of her nose, she saw something in the corner of the stove inset.

It was in shadow, so she got down on her knees and leaned in. Just as she did, it rolled out, but not far. It stopped just in reach. It was a small ball. A child's rubber ball. She picked it up.

The white stripe through the middle had faded away where it hadn't chipped, but she could still tell it was there, separating the red top from a blue bottom. She smiled. It was as familiar to her as her own childhood.

She squeezed it. It was rubber throughout, not hollow, like the ones you find now. She put it carefully on the mantel so that it wouldn't roll off. It sat patiently. She supposed a child had left it while his mother was looking at the house.

She poured the last of the piles into the bag and was just tucking everything away in the kitchen when there was a knock on the door. She was early. No time for the sills. *Shame.*

Before answering the door she looked around the room. The room looked back.

'Shipshape,' she whispered. The walls stood straight.

'Barbara Parkins?' Glenn asked. She had opened the door to a dumpy, middle-aged woman, with hair that needed cutting, in pants and a short coat.

'That's right. Are you Mrs Darnley?' Gone was the false enthusiasm. The woman spoke in a tired voice. Her eyes were red rimmed and underscored with dark half-moons. Glenn reached out her hand, after her initial surprise, and smiled.

'Please, call me Glenn,' she said, and stood aside for the woman to enter. She did, tentatively. She looked up, much the way Glenn did when she always walked in.

'Oh, my goodness!' she said. 'How on earth do you wash that ceiling?'

Glenn laughed, startled. No one had ever said anything like that in all her other showings. 'I haven't a clue,' she said. The two women looked at each other. Barbara Parkins tried a smile, but it didn't quite reach her eyes.

Been there, she thought flippantly.

'The floors have been sanded and refinished in the last two years,' Glenn said slowly, beginning her pitch. 'There have been renovations throughout. I'll point them out as we come to them.' She had to nudge the woman forward slightly. She seemed reluctant to take the lead. 'The living room, as you can see, has a lot of natural light. Lovely thing, a south-facing window. Very good for plants,' she said. The woman looked around, the corners of her mouth downturned. She seemed unfocused.

'Do you garden?' Glenn asked.

'I'm sorry, what's that?'

'I was just saying, this room is lovely for plants.'

Barbara Parkins smiled and nodded, adding an agreeable 'yes', to it, at the end of the nod, as though for a time she'd forgotten the word. 'What are they asking?'

'Well, the owners are motivated. The price has been reduced. They're asking $90,500.'

Barbara Parkins nodded. 'How many bedrooms?' she asked in the dining room.

'Three plus, as we say in the business,' Glenn said, with professional joviality. She felt alone in the room. 'That means simply that there are three bedrooms upstairs, and a small room under the stairs that could serve as a guest room, although it is very small. There's also an attic that is currently undeveloped. There is lots of room up there for whatever your needs are. Do you have children?' Glenn walked her into the kitchen and stood in the centre of it, to make it seem larger.

'I have one. A son. Petey. Only he doesn't like to be called Petey any more. I'm trying to remember to call him Peter.' She smiled ruefully.

'Well, then, there's ample room,' she said, dismissively. She opened her arms and pointed to the dishwasher and refrigerator, taking in the stove as well. 'There are four appliances. The fourth is a waste-disposal unit. And with a small table, you could eat in here, as well,' she said, and led Barbara to the back door. She opened it and moved aside so that the woman could look out. She did, dutifully.

'A nice, big backyard for your son to play in,' she said.

Barbara nodded and stared. And stared.

'Are you all right, Mrs Parkins?' Glenn asked.

Barbara turned her head jerkily to look at her, eyes wide, almost fearful. 'I'm fine,' she said quietly, turning her head back to the yard and staring out again. 'I have to find a place right away. My husband's left us. For another woman. I can't stay in that house another minute. I'll see the upstairs, please.'

Glenn had no idea what to say. 'That's terrible. I'm very sorry. I'm very sorry,' she repeated. She fumbled quickly for something better than that, toying with the idea of mentioning How, but it seemed somehow a betrayal to him, or to dignity. Instead she held out her hand for Barbara to go ahead.

On their way up the stairs, the woman's tone changed. She sounded cheerful when she said, 'It's very good to say it like that. Out loud. I've only said it once out loud. To my friend on the phone. It's good to say it,' she said, nodding brightly.

'Yes, it likely is,' Glenn said. 'The master bedroom is very large and roomy. It's L-shaped. Look at the lovely arched doorway. It reminds me of my childhood home in England,' she said, and thought, oddly, of the ball downstairs. 'There's a nice corner in here for reading, I've always thought.' She led Barbara around the edge of the wall, to where sunlight poured in from the small window.

'It's nice,' Barbara said, bobbing her head.

Glenn began the story of the tub being brought in through the wall with a crane. The woman was scarcely listening. They looked only briefly in the bathroom, and she never commented on the tub, to the point where Glenn almost wanted to point it out directly. *Look at the damn feet. It wants to eat you.*

The little blue room across the hall from the bath caught her attention. She clapped her hands together in delight, and Glenn smiled truly. It was a delightful little room.

'This is *perfect*!' she said. 'This is just perfect for my little boy! He'll love this room!' She walked in and across to the window, which overlooked the spacious backyard. Glenn repeated her statement about the yard. She was glad when the woman did not ask her about other children in the neighbourhood. 'There's a school less than two blocks from here,' she mentioned.

Barbara nodded, looking out the window. Then she suddenly spun round like a ballerina. 'I could paint clouds on the walls and ceilings! I just *love* the colour of these walls, like the sky!' she said.

'Do you paint?'

'I'm going to, I think. I'm not sure what I'm going to do, after all this is settled.' She looked at Glenn confessionally. 'I've never done anything. Wife and mother. That's what I am. Was.' She nodded, as though accepting that for the first time.

Glenn softened considerably. Her heart went out to the woman. Her eyes were puffy from crying. A small child, youngish woman. It would be so hard.

'There are lots and lots of things that you can do now. I think you should look at it as the start of a whole new life,' she said, cringing at the way she sounded like a women's magazine, or an ad for feminine protection. Barbara Parkins did not see it that way. She looked deeply, nakedly at Glenn, her brow furrowed in just the way it would be in a few months' time, permanently, if she did not take care.

'I know that. That's absolutely true.' She shrugged her shoulders, her arms hanging limply, impotently at her sides. 'I just have to get past this hump. Just get past this difficult part. Then everything will be all right,' she said. For a moment, Glenn was afraid she was going to cry. And she was reminded of her first tour through the house, that awful first day back to work. It occurred to her that that was a year earlier. She couldn't say it, couldn't tell this woman her story, this poor nakedly pained woman, who seemed an open wound.

So needy. Glenn leaned against the hallway wall. It was firm and cool, but not cold, in spite of the minimum of heat. She leaned her head against the doorframe in what she hoped was a casual posture, but was really to steady her. The woman's pain was making her tired. It was awful; draining.

She straightened up. There was an imperceptible nod of her head that needn't have been as subtle; the woman had faded out to somewhere.

She needs this house.

'I think they would accept eighty-nine thousand,' she

268

found herself saying, and it was a false brightness that came out of her mouth, this time.

Barbara Parkins stared past Glenn into the hallway. Glenn stepped out of the room and raised her arm to lead her to the last room in the house. Barbara stayed in the blue room. 'Shall we take a look at the other bedroom? I'll show you the attic after that. There's a sort of ladder that comes down on a pulley. It's really quite clever,' she babbled. There was no reaction from the woman.

'I guess I'll buy it,' Barbara said, sounding utterly exhausted, looking like she might just lie down in the middle of the room the colour of the sky and sleep. She stared down at the floor and raised her eyes when she was done speaking. She looked blankly as though she'd forgotten what they were talking about.

'I have a settlement,' she said quietly, and straightened her shoulders.

From downstairs there came a loud, hollow sound that echoed up the stairs, and both women started. They listened as another echo followed the first, and then another, each softer. In a moment, Glenn chuckled with recognition.

'The ball,' she said. Barbara looked blankly at her. Glenn smiled kindly. 'The rubber ball fell off the mantel. I guess it's pleased.'

The two smiled, met eyes. It was so.

Conditions of Decree

I

Barbara Parkins (or Staizer) leaned over the side of the tub in despair. The bulk of her bosom pressed painfully against the lip, her flesh cold from a damp line where splashing water had wet through her thin cotton blouse. From her right hand dangled a shiny new wrench. Beside her on the floor open to page six, 'What To Do With a Drippy Tap!', was a pamphlet from the hardware store where she'd bought the shiny new wrench and the less shiny but equally new washer. A little package of them, as though she would be needing a half-dozen more some time in the future. The pamphlet was called *Everyone's Guide to Simple Plumbing*, but was clearly marketed at women: a sturdy-looking blonde in overalls and a tool belt lay under a sink on the cover, and most of the title heads were *fun*! And everything ended in an exclamation mark! As though home repair for the desperate was just another Hollywood party!

She wanted to scream. She had been a half-hour getting the tap off (righty-tighty, *lefty*-loosy), only to find that the part in question was as pretty, shiny and new-looking as the washer she'd just bought to replace it. Did that matter?

The tap was in two pieces on the floor of the tub, near the drain. She had carefully placed the old washer – easily distinguishable from the new washer because it was *wet* – on the tank of the toilet, where it could be even more easily distinguished. The new one was in place. Her wrist was sore from trying to get the tap off and she was taking a breather.

Staizer. She was Barbara Staizer now, she supposed. Parkins was over. She hadn't actually decided yet to go back to her maiden name, it was nearly as tainted with bad baggage as her married name, and wished she could just pick some clean, fresh name to start over with. Something simple like Smith or Jones, or White or Brown.

It had been suspiciously easy to switch from her birth name to her married name. She remembered her astonishment at how easy it had been. All she had to do was present her marriage certificate and *voilà!* New person. Barbara Staizer became Barbara Parkins. What was that song?

Water from nowhere rolled out of the top of the tap and slid down the nozzle, dripping into the drain. The water line to the taps had been shut off (page two, 'Ready, set, repair!'). The water ran anyway, as though not subject to the law of physics.

'– *how that marriage licence works, on chamber MAIDS and hotel CLERKS!*' And on clerks in the Vital Statistics offices, also. Like a flash card, a badge.

Annie Get Your Gun? No. *Funny Girl.* Barbra Streisand. The wrench was heavy. Barbara Staizer-Parkins-Something-else-like-Brown picked up the tap from the tub and gingerly placed it over the nut and started wrenching. It was easier the second time. Righty-tighty.

She was pretty sure it wasn't as easy to go back to your maiden name, but that was one of the many things she would have to find out. Anyway, she wasn't even sure she would. She was just trying it on, mostly out of anger. Petey (Pe*ter*) was still Parkins and that was something to consider.

There was a minimum of mess to Simple Plumbing, and the tiny bit of water that had gotten around stayed mostly in the tub, or had been absorbed by her blouse. The sleeves were wet to the elbows, in spite of having been pulled up, and it was wet across her breasts. The house was a little cool and she suspected that it was poorly insulated, even though it had been renovated by the people who'd owned it last. She'd wondered more than once about those people in the last three days. It was a noisy house. Had they left it because of that?

For instance, the (damn) tub ran. Never when she was in the room, or even upstairs, although she had heard it the other night in the tentative place before sleep: it had woken her. It took just a moment to place the sound. Sitting up in bed, feet on floor, *up and at 'em*, she could hear it, muffled as though the bathroom door was closed, even though she could see it was open. It was water running from tap into tub, a medium flow, complete with splashing and the hollow sound of pipes in the wall clanging their work. It was a familiar sound, a background noise, the sound of Sunday nights after *Ed Sullivan* and *Bonanza*, familiar like winter wind rattling windows and the newspaper banging against the front door, the fridge coming on. There was no figuring it out: it was the tub, filling up with water. Then draining. And that was the worst part. She'd finally gotten up out of bed, barefoot on to spring-cold floor, and padded to the bathroom.

By the time she reached the doorway of the dark little

room, a trek of no more than four steps, she heard the distinct, unmistakable – no arguing, *I'm not a moron it is as familiar as rattling windows fridge coming on* – sound of the plug popping out of the drain, and the water running out. Clear as day.

She'd thought Petey was playing, of course. She'd said his name – in a whisper because it seemed the right thing to do with the dark and all – but he hadn't answered, and when she flicked the light switch beside the door, she looked first to his room. The light caught his smooth white face in sleep.

That's when her heart caught in her throat because obviously *there's someone in the house* but that lasted only a second because it was too late anyway, she'd turned the light on. *No escape lady, ha ha!* Someone in the house and he's taking a bath?

The bathroom, tiny as it was, was empty. So was the tub. Empty and dry. She thought it only looked dry, so she'd bent over it and run her hand along the bottom. Dry as a bone.

She spun round tensed and looked over her shoulder, only to see nothing. The house was quiet again: there was no hollow, muffled clang of pipes in the wall, no water draining out. She'd imagined it. It had been part of a dream.

Something had made the noise. It had to have been the tap. Although it was not the way it had been described in the pamphlet and the man at the hardware store had gone blank-faced as she'd explained it and hastily told her it was likely a leaky washer. He'd insisted, really, as she'd tried to explain. There had been no *dripping* sound, she'd explained, just the sound of water running and draining. (She hadn't gone so far as to explain the other noise, the one that precipitated the draining of the tub, because it sounded too preposterous, even to her, and she'd heard it, but right before the water *sounded* like it was draining, there had been the familiar and distinct sound of the plug popping out of the drain. Pop! And then drain; she hadn't brought it up.)

'It's most likely a washer, ma'am,' he'd said patiently, about one more question from a yawn or a sigh. 'It usually is.' She'd gone along with it because she didn't know, and while Elizabeth Staizer didn't raise any fools, she wasn't exactly Mrs Fixit, although she had once put together a yard composter from a kit. And there was no Mr Fixit any more.

And, insult to injury and poor repair skills, it turned out Elizabeth Staizer had raised at least one fool.

Barbara dried the wrench on a towel and left it on the back of the toilet. She tossed the old washer into the little wicker garbage basket beside the sink and put the pamphlet beside the wrench. She might need it again. Maybe some pipe would explode somewhere and really test her mettle. She went into the bedroom and changed her shirt, knowing full well the whole exercise had been a waste of time. There was nothing wrong with the washer she had replaced.

Before going downstairs for a cup of tea, she checked her face in the mirror of the little dresser she'd pinched from her mom's house for signs of crying. Her eyes were slightly red and puffy, but no worse than usual. She would rinse her face with cold water. That would take some of the swelling down and lessen the redness around her mouth, too. Petey would be home from school soon.

She didn't want him to know that she'd been sad today.

The tub was reflected in the mirror over the sink. Barbara did not keep her eyes closed long when she rinsed her face. She kept her feet tucked close under the pedestal sink, far away from the claws that held up the tub, her eyes fixed on the tub, its reflection white and cool in the mirror.

She had her tea in the living room. There were fewer boxes in there and less work to be done. The pictures that had to go up were stacked against the walls and she wasn't much of a knick-knack person. The bookshelves were up and two boxes of books were beside it, but that wasn't bad and she could have those put away before Petey got home. The TV and VCR were hooked up – correctly too, the illustrations in the owner's manual much easier to follow than the written directions – and the stereo had been up since their first day. The room looked terribly bare. She and Dennis had divided up much of the furniture, and she hadn't been very strident in those days. He had gotten most of the good things, when she thought about it. She did get the sofa – a lovely, creamy-coloured overstuffed soft thing, long enough to sleep on. He'd got the chair that matched, and the coffee table and one of the side tables. The side table that she'd taken had the stereo on it. Her cup of tea was on the floor at her feet. The décor was minimalist, to put a spin on it. The pictures would help. Time Marches On.

The pictures were currently an object of panic. She had tried to put one up in the hall on the way up the stairs that morning and had succeeded only in hammering a hole in the wall. The nail had loosened the drywall and fallen through. She hadn't attempted another. She would have to ask someone what to do. The pictures in their old house had just been hanging there. She had no idea how they'd got there, but she supposed that Dennis had put them up. She wondered if there was a guide called *Everyone's Guide to Hanging Pictures*, *Everyone's Guide to Hauling a Spare Bed Upstairs*, *Everyone's Guide to Unclogging the Gutter*. She bet there was. It was a world that needed a lot of home repair.

The floor creaked above her and she cast her eyes that way from under a cool washcloth, soothing away the puffiness around her eyes before the boy got home. It was a noisy house, full of creaks and bumps and draining tubs. The first night she had lain awake in bed, terrified, every bump someone breaking in, every creak someone's footfall. Petey had gone to her bed around midnight (after she'd spent the best part of the day putting his room together so that it was ready for him to sleep in). She crawled in with him about one, having put some of the kitchen together, towels in the bathroom so she could have a shower the next morning, and generally wandering around the strange house, poking her head into pitifully small closets and cubbies, running her hand over the smooth refinished surfaces, the new paint. The house smelled fresh and new, just built. The upstairs smelled like something else. Something chemical like fertilizer or that stuff you drag around your yard so that weeds won't grow. *Weed-Go*. She adjusted the cold cloth on her eyes and rested her head on the back of the sofa.

Petey would be home any minute. New school.

God, let it be okay. She really felt like crying again when she thought of her boy, alone in a new school. She didn't cry, but felt the sting of it behind the cloth. She'd cried herself out, maybe for that day. At least for that afternoon. Nights were harder. But for all the terrors of her day, they did not involve the staring eyes of three hundred new people. And he was *sensitive*.

As if in answer, there was a sudden, muffled *thump!* at the front door. Barbara pulled the cloth off her eyes and guiltily dropped it in a ball on the hidden side of the couch. She waited a moment, thinking it was Petey. The door was unlocked.

When nothing happened, she got up. Her heart jumped a little at the thought that maybe a neighbour was dropping by to say hello and welcome them, maybe a Welcome Wagon lady with all kinds of goodies and coupons and babysitting advice. Someone nice, and her age. Divorced would be an asset, but she would be willing to overlook an intact marriage. She put a smile on.

Her socked feet padded comfortably on the cool wood floor in the hall. She pushed her fringe back, damp from the cloth, and knew how she would look. She had put on a good twenty pounds over the last year and it was not kind on her. It was sloppy-fat and her frame was not large enough to hide anything, not even five pounds. Her lips pressed together and she frowned. There was momentary debate over opening the door at all.

Loneliness won out. Barbara fixed the smile, pushed her hair behind her ears and tugged her T-shirt – at least it was clean – down over her front, and pulled the door open, hoping she looked suburban, relaxed and only as unkempt as any new homeowner (*Oh, hello! Come in! Excuse me, but I've just been fixing a tap!*).

A gust of fresh air shuttled in through the open door, but the stoop was empty. She panicked, sticking her head out of the door – had she taken too long? There was no one on the path or on the street beyond the hedge at the end of the yard. Crossing her arms over her chest against the cool spring breeze, she stepped on to the stoop to get a better look and trod on something soft that gave. She lifted a foot and looked down simultaneously.

Her smile broadened into something real and she let out a little squeal of pleasure.

On the stoop (decidedly crushed by her foot) was a little yellow bouquet of buttercups. She bent over and scooped them up, letting go of a little groan at the sight of their stems, broken and flattened, bleeding green from having been stepped on. Two of the blossoms had been crushed as well. She bent her head and brought the flowers up to her nose, knowing already how they would smell, the wet way they would brush under her nose.

Do you like butter?

They were limp and battered as though having been carried a long way and Barbara, smiling, looked around again, scanning the street this time for a smaller neighbour, a child, maybe with her mother, coaxed into leaving the new family a hand-picked bouquet. Even when she walked down the path to the end of her yard, she still couldn't see anyone, big or small, who might have left such a delightful welcome on the step.

'Thank you!' she called out into the open street. She gave another glance around, but saw no one.

Maybe it will be all right, she thought. It was cold out. The buttercups were cold in her hands, the green juice bleeding on to her fingers. She knew from experience that it wouldn't come off easily, but would stay for an hour or so, until it wore off. Still smiling, she went inside, closing the door softly.

She dug around in kitchen boxes, finally coming up with a little blossom vase and put the flowers in water and placed them in the centre of the dining-room table where she could see them and be reminded every time she did that they weren't *really* alone, that there were people everywhere. Kind people.

Barbara stepped away and admired them for only a moment, and then Petey got home, his nose bloodied, his lip fat, and all the delight went out of the day.

Fat kid! Fat kid! Andy Devries and Marshall Hemp had taken off as soon as someone in the crowd had said, *He's hurt.* Pushing himself up off the hardened earth, spitting mud out of his mouth, Petey Parkins remembered what exactly had been said, it had been *shaddup the fat kid's hurt* and then Andy and Marshall had taken off.

Petey spat again and mud sputtered out with saliva, but instead of a good hard hawk on to the mud, something that might have salvaged some of his dignity, even just to him, the muddied spittle stayed mostly on his bottom lip. He swiped at it with the back of his hand, his mouth tender where his teeth had mashed into the tissue.

Fat kid.

He sniffled snot to the back of his throat. His nose was running. He'd cried. *Cried.* His face would be ridiculously red against his pale freckles and there would be more dirt, mixed with sweat, under his hairline. He could feel it running down his temples. There was nothing for him to wipe his nose with. He wore a white T-shirt, pulled out and over his pants to hide the large bulk of his belly. If he wiped it there, everyone would know. The snot tickled under his nose. Petey swiped at his eyes with the hand that wiped off the spit.

'Paul?'

He would have to use his fingers and then what? He couldn't bear to let it run into his mouth. The kids that had gotten off the bus to see the fight had mostly disappeared, bored now that it was over or scared they were going to get caught. They were all but gone.

'Paul?' Petey realized someone was talking to him. He flinched instinctively, cringing against whatever new horror was in the works. When none came, he answered. 'It's Pe*ter*,' he said, emphasizing out of habit the last syllable of his name. He said it that way nearly every minute to his mother, who still called him Petey. He told her and told her and told her that he was going to be Pe*ter* at the new school. At the old school he'd been Petey the Weenie.

'Oh,' said the kid. There was no taunt in the voice, but Petey stayed poised for it anyway. Alert. He spat again. He thought he might taste blood. Nothing came out that he could see. His lip hurt inside. He'd scraped his knee and palms landing from the first push – Andy Devries – while Marshall laughed but looked angry, and prepared for the next part, which was to kick *the fat kid's ass*. 'You okay? You're that new kid, right? You okay?'

Petey's nose was about to drip. He had no choice. He squeezed his nose with his fingers and pulled it away. He held his hand out in front of him, horrified. He walked a couple of steps to the edge of the sidewalk and wiped it on the grass there.

'Make it grow, eh?' Petey looked up at the kid talking. He was skinny and tall, older than Petey. He stared at him with rounded eyes and easy smile, and it took a second but Petey felt more than saw the blankness behind the eyes. The retard smiled at him, and when Petey didn't bite or snarl or try to punch him, he closed up the distance between them and patted Petey gently on the back.

The unexpected tenderness, or the fact that it was coming from a retard, stung his face and he felt the horrible taste of tears coming back. 'It's okay now, they took off,' the kid said smiling, nodding with deep under-standing. 'Andy's bad,' he added. 'He's a super*shit*.'

Petey nodded back, sort of, then bent over at the waist, leaning the full weight of his substantial upper body on his knees. His right knee throbbed, but he didn't favour it. Instead he let his head fall and the snot run out of his nose.

The kids at the old school had been used to his fatness. It had come on him gradually over his eight years. It had been a side issue. Instead he'd been a cry-baby. Petey the Weenie. If the kids from the new school saw him crying like a baby now, they'd figure it out. He hoped no one could see, hoped the moron couldn't or wouldn't tell, hoped the ground would start to shake and an earthquake would wipe out the whole snot-running city. And, of course, at the old school he'd had Jeremy. His best friend – his only friend, really – in the whole world.

An ache began like a black hole in his stomach at the thought of Jeremy and his friendly face, any friendly face, and the tears threatened then never to stop, to stay as long as the earth stood, long enough for another ice age, or another comet to hit the earth and destroy everything like it had when the dinosaurs lived there. He sobbed harder, feeling sorry for himself, sorry for familiar faces, even for the familiar assholes of the old school. The old taunts.

Fartin' Parkins. He hoped they didn't figure that one out.

Sideways glances on either side showed deserted, quiet streets. Far away he could hear the girls' field hockey team practising. Just him and the retard. Tears of sublime misery poured from him then and by only a hair he resisted just dropping to the ground and letting it rip, letting the tears swallow or kill him or just anything that would let him be dead.

'He's a shit, that Andy Devries,' the kid said. 'A shitty shit,' he added, and giggled. He repeated 'shit' another four times and seemed to get wrapped up in it. 'I have to go. You want me to come home with you?'

Just what he needed, to be walked home by the local retard – he stopped himself.

'Nah,' he said, standing up. He wiped his hand across his nose, wiped the mucus on his shirt, suddenly not caring who saw. 'Nah, I'm okay.'

'I better go. My mom yells.' The kid took off, running up the street, leaving Petey alone.

His house, their new house, was on Belisle Street, where the bus stopped at the end. It was almost four blocks from the corner and he realized with fresh horror that he didn't know what kids, if any, lived on Belisle, or if they were watching, waiting for him to walk by so they could toss a new taunt out at him, maybe more *hey fat kid*, or *whale boy* or something new like *fatass* or maybe they would just moo or oink when he walked by, hiding behind curtains, doors, fences, their parents still at work and no one home to stop them.

He sighed deeply and let it turn into a snuffle. He wiped again at his nose and it hurt too. His jeans were dirty. His mother would notice that, but first she'd see the snot on his T-shirt and be disgusted right up until she realized by looking at his (*fat*) face that he'd been crying. Then she would cry too. Or maybe she would just get that blank look and tell him quietly to go change. Then she'd disappear some place in the house and he wouldn't even be able to hear her.

Periodically he looked up at the houses, uncertain still which one was his. They were mostly the same on the block, old-fashioned but fixed up. Renovated. That's what theirs was, renovated. The ad had said, 'newly renovated'. His dad – before he left, of course, and stopped being his dad or (not so bad) *Your Father* had become *That Asshole, Your Father* – had renovated their basement for a year, adding walls and a bar and eighteen tiny little lights that recessed into the ceiling, running all along one side of the basement (he'd said they were 'a bitch to put in, just a *bitch*'. Whenever someone came over Petey's dad shuffled them down into the basement and gave them a drink from the bar and told them what a *bitch* the little lights had been to put in). Then he left it as though it had been the last order of business. It was as though once he finished the basement he had nothing else to do and so he left. Then his mom started crying and didn't stop for months. She didn't cry as much as she used to, but she still wasn't easy to pin down to one mood. Sometimes when Petey was still at his other school (not so bad) he would come home to find her sobbing in the living room looking through old photo albums like someone had died, the house quiet, breakfast dishes in the sink or even on the table still, the place smelling like cigarettes and coffee, her eyes puffed out and so red he could barely see them. Other days Time Marched On – that's what she said sometimes, like an announcement, 'Well, *time marches on*,' and she'd ruffle his hair, but it was okay, because even though he wasn't exactly sure what she meant, those were usually the best days.

On Time Marches On days, he might come home from school and she would be in her bedroom trying on every piece of clothing she owned, coming out to show him different outfits and asking him bizarre questions about colours and styles until he wanted to tell her, *Mom, Regis says to phone a friend*, but he never did. Those times her voice was on the edge of something scary that he didn't recognize but knew instinctively that he had to humour her or *else* – never knowing what the or-else was.

He crossed the street on to his block, the last one, and saw with mortification, that his mother had tied a huge, *HUGE* red bow to the front door, so that he would be able to find it amongst the other newly renovated old-fashioned houses. (On the other hand, it went quickly through his mind that if the bow was there, it meant at least she was *thinking* and that meant it might be a *Time Marches On* day, instead of a *That Asshole, Your Father* day, but it was quick and by rote and meaningless in the face of new torments such as Andy Devries and Marshall Hemp.) Without thinking about it, he swept his eyes stealthily around the block, searching for kids, any kids, even little ones, who might have seen. The streets were bare, the houses staring back. Of course, you couldn't see *in them*.

Petey ran past the four houses between him and home, the first plan of action to rip that bow off the door before someone saw (*Hey, fat kid! You get your house as a present?*).

Actually he didn't run, he scurried. Petey only ran when he was going to get beaten up. The rest of the time he scurried, like a bug, hoping not to be noticed.

He yanked the bow off, hearing a *riip!* with a certain amount of satisfaction, and then he pulled the door open. His mom looked up, a smile forming on her mouth, lips moving in a standard greeting, maybe *hi honey how was your day* or maybe *how was school sweetie*, but her whole face seemed to crash once she really looked at him and she leaped to her feet. Distantly, there was the sound of something turning over and clinking, like wine glasses in a toast.

'Oh, Pe-*tee*, ohmigod, oh, my poor baby, your *face* –' his mother cried when she saw him and crossed the floor in three long strides, dropping to her knees and pulling him into her body like a tiger, lungeing.

He let himself be pulled in. 'Pe*ter*,' he managed, before he burst into tears and succumbed completely to the rest of her mother-talk, soothing and hurtful at the same time, because she was crying too, and it was all his fault.

They went into the kitchen where his mom ran cold water over a dishcloth and held it softly to his lip asking him, without expecting his answer, if it felt better, if that helped and *there there*. Then they went to the little kitchen table where they'd eaten breakfast in the morning. He'd had Count Chocula cereal. So far they'd eaten breakfast and lunch in the little kitchen and dinner at the big table in the dining room. On their way to the table, his mom holding the cloth on his mouth, Petey noticed that a package of chicken was thawing on a plate on the counter.

He told her what had happened, but avoiding the things they said through pride and something like self-protection. She soothed and *aaahed* and poor-babied him until Petey began to calm down. There was a cross-over moment when his mother's voice began to fade, the words becoming sounds and when Petey's mind began to shift to other things soothing.

'I'm going to phone their mothers,' she said.

'Can I have some pudding?' he asked, just seconds before she finished closing her mouth on the last syllable. It had come out too sharply, too fast.

'What did you say their names were? You have to tell me their names again,' she said. 'I'm going to call them. This is a terrible thing to happen. You're a new boy in school. The *school*,' she all but spat out the word *school*, 'should have been watching out for you. Especially if they have such terrible boys there. I'll call the school, too.' She finished by picking up the cloth that Petey had let fall to the table. His lip had swollen to the point of feeling foreign against his teeth. His tongue couldn't stay away from it. The tenderest part was right in front of his chewing teeth.

'Mom?' he asked again. He couldn't repeat the whole question. Couldn't break the spell.

Barbara stared at him. She heard him. She chewed her own lip, the same place as Petey's sore spot. Her thinking look. Her eyes dragged away from him, to the counter where the microwave and its little green LCD clock were.

'It's almost supper time,' she said, her tone changing, carefully losing its animation.

There were no words, but no silence, between them. Petey's lip throbbed. He needed something in his mouth. He needed it to feel good in there, something creamy, sweet. Something that would take away the taste of the blood and snot. That was all.

'I'm hungry,' he said simply. His mouth hung open in his round face, bottom lip protruding, giving him a slightly moronic expression.

Barbara shut her eyes against him. Her arms crossed over her chest – her more ample chest than six months earlier. From inside, her chest tightened. The beginnings of panic rose not in her mind, but in her body. Her right leg began to shake and she raised her shoulders, tightening her neck muscles. She got up from the table. Tried to sound offhand.

'I'll have supper ready in a jiff, honey,' she said sweetly. 'You have to give me the names of those boys. I'm going to call their mothers. I mean it. This can't go unpunished.' But the initial anger had passed, and while she meant it, it came out sounding like filler. She knew that. Tasted it.

She pulled the big frying-pan out of a box on the floor. She opened the fridge door and grabbed the four potatoes that were left in the bag hastily bought the other night.

There was a can of peas in a box by the microwave. She plunked the frying-pan on to the stove and turned up the element to medium, then began shuffling through boxes for the oil. She ran across a can of mushroom soup. She would use it for a gravy. Petey liked that. That would be good. She found the can-opener and out of the corner of her eye, she saw Petey reach into the cupboard where she had laid out the treats the other night with almost tender consideration.

'No!' she said, too loud and firmly. In his chubby left hand he held a tiny, single-serving tin of pudding. Even as she said it, she looked at the little tin and thought, *Such a little bit, would it hurt?* and at the same time saw his chubby (not *fat* he was not *fat* he was growing) face and his chubby arms and his chubby little fist that gripped the tin with a force that made his knuckles white.

'Mom –' His round face twisted into an expression of pain and longing. He did not put the tin down.

She grabbed at the arm that held the tin and squeezed with more force than necessary, her brain crying, *He's just a little kid!*, but didn't stop and grabbed the tin with the other hand and started prising his fingers from it. All the while she kept her voice an octave too high, the words coming out clipped with the effort. 'Honey, I . . . said *no. Supper* . . . will be . . . *ready* . . . in fifteen minutes –' She prised the fingers, the body attached to them squirming with the effort to keep the can held tight. Sweat formed on his upper lip with the strain. Her fingers dug into his arm, into his fingers.

'Mom –' he said again, his voice pleading. His eyes squeezed shut.

He yanked on the arm with all his strength, causing

Barbara to marvel at how strong he'd gotten over the last year. With two hands, she managed to wrest the tin away from him, and in the final moment he made a grab for it and she pulled it away, behind her back, like a child. Her voice rose. 'I said *no!*' She breathed heavily. For a moment they stood in stasis, each heaving, Petey's eyes squinting with tears, arms reaching out, not to her but the pudding.

He crumpled to the floor and covered his face with his hands. He *needed* to have that pudding. *Needed* it. He wanted it. He let out a deep sob and began to wail, crying wordless sobs dragged from far inside. She stood helpless, watching him, her own eyes wide with her results.

His T-shirt tugged up at the sides and Barbara saw the big roll of his tummy over the top of his pants and how his T-shirt tugged up over his middle where the belly button had disappeared years ago, and how white his flesh was and would stay because he would not go without a shirt in the summer because he was fat. His freckled back shook. Round shoulders shook. Hands that seemed little and large at the same time covered his face so all that showed was his red hair.

She thought about what Dennis would say about this scene, so oft-repeated, especially in the last few months, and the look of disgust that would fill his face. The sound he would make, pointedly, at Barbara. *Look what you've done.* Dennis's contempt. She felt it as much as Petey must have over that last terrible year. *His terrible day, and now this.* She was, in that moment, so utterly, utterly sorry. For him. For his wanting, and his look and for herself.

'Petey,' she said. 'It's okay.' He didn't stop crying. He sobbed over her words. She couldn't raise her voice any further. She couldn't bring herself to cry, she was too tired.

'It's okay, honey,' she said. She stuck a finger in the little ring-tab on top of the pudding and pulled the lid off. She opened the drawer beside the stove and found a spoon. 'It's okay,' she said. By then he was looking up. His face was streaked with tears and dirt. The area around his mouth was red, his lip fat. Under his eyes were circles of shadow that she hadn't noticed.

'Here, baby,' she said. She filled the spoon with a mountain of pudding, rich and brown and dark and creamy. Chocolate. She squatted and held it out to him. He sat up, eyes round, red, wet. He opened his mouth like a baby bird. She spooned the chocolate in. 'Here you go,' she mumbled. Mother words. 'There you go.' He ate soundlessly, opening his mouth again after every swallow.

'It's okay.'

She spooned and fed, scraping the last of the chocolate out of the edges until the tin was streaked but mostly clean. Then she grabbed the lid from the counter and scraped the little remaining from that. 'There you go,' she said. When they were done she touched his hair and they smiled, defeated, at each other. Sad smiles.

'Supper will be ready in fifteen minutes,' she said, and stood up, as though nothing had happened. Then she turned back to the stove and had to take the pan off because it had gotten too hot. She started over again. In a moment she heard the TV come on. *The Simpsons* played out their particular dysfunction and the house

293

began, slowly, but by the first commercial, to sound normal again. Fifteen minutes later, when she ran across the empty tin on the counter, she tossed it into the recycling box without notice.

They had supper in the dining room.

Much, much later, Petey pawed through the bottom drawer of his dresser, through long underwear, big winter socks and less-loved pyjamas looking for his Hyper-Cat PJs. He found the bottoms and pulled them out, shoving back in the Montreal Canadiens pyjamas that came out with them. The top was harder to find, squished up by itself in the back corner. He stuffed everything as flat as he could and closed the drawer.

He told his mom what had happened after school, but he didn't tell her *all* of it. He didn't tell her about all the F-words that had been said as a precursor to the fight. He didn't tell her that he punched Andy first. He knew that was bad. It *had* been bad. He couldn't help it. Andy had *pushed his buttons*. All the kids had been looking, new kids. They all stared and wondered what he (new kid, fat kid) would do. *Why'd you come to our school, blubber belly?* That was what had done it. A full day of keeping his head down and hardly saying anything and feeling so bad and scared. A school full of Andy Devries and that had just *pushed his last button*. But it had started the fight.

His tongue found the raw place on his bottom lip and stroked it. It wasn't as fat as it had been and now only hurt when he touched it. His mom said she didn't think he'd get a shiner, but there was a little bruise on his cheek. He pulled off his T-shirt and put on his Hyper-Cat top. Hyper-Cat would kick Andy Devries' *ass*. Hyper-Cat would burn him with his eye lasers. Hyper-Cat, of course, would never have been in a fight in the first place, and not only because he could fly himself the hell out of there, but also because Hyper-Cat was a good guy and only fought back. He didn't start it. Petey sighed. He kicked off his jeans and scraped his socks off each foot using the other. He left his underwear on and pulled Hyper-Cat over his legs.

Hyper-Cat was on after school, right before supper, after *The Magic School Bus*, at home. Here he had to settle for the stupid show with the animals in balls. He hated that show. They still had *The Magic School Bus*, even though Petey was getting too old for it; he had watched it so long it was a comfort to him. He liked Ralphie. These pyjamas were his favourite because they were Hyper-Cat and because they were new, so they fitted him. He was growing like a weed. Everyone said so.

The TV was still on downstairs. There was nothing on, though. In a few minutes his mom would shut it off and come upstairs to tell him to brush his teeth, like he didn't know, and then she'd tuck him in. Since they'd moved into the house, she'd stayed upstairs with him for a while before he fell asleep, because it was a strange place. That was good. It *was* a strange place. He didn't like going to the bathroom. He had to go when she was upstairs. The feet on the tub were creepy. When he sat on the toilet, he made sure his feet were tucked under.

It hadn't been that bad tonight. His mom had been quieter than usual, but she was a little mad at him, maybe, because of the fight. The bad thing was, his dad didn't call. Petey hadn't talked to him since they moved in on the weekend and the last thing he'd said was that he would call and see how school went. Since it didn't go that good, maybe it was okay he didn't. The good thing was, Grandma Staizer didn't call either. His mom and her mom didn't get along too good. Sometimes his grandma Staizer said mean things. They didn't sound mean, just the words, but they were mean. (Sometimes when she told Petey how *big* he was getting, it sounded like how *fat* he was getting. He knew that.)

Petey and his mom had spent the night before their move at Grandma Staizer's. She hadn't let him call his best friend Jeremy – just to say goodbye again and hear his voice – and he'd been pissed off about that, although Petey could tell that his mother was hanging on by a thread, as she had even in good times, in her mother's house. Bugging her would have pushed her buttons. From upstairs after he was supposed to be sleeping, Petey heard the conversation that had been steeping all evening.

'How are you supposed to put things back together from four hours away?' Grandma Staizer asked.

'It's three hours, Ma. And it's over.'

'Nothing's ever really over, Barbara.'

'He's banging someone else, Mother. That makes it pretty over.' Petey didn't know what she meant by 'banging', but he knew from her tone and inflection that 'he' was his dad.

'You should watch your language, young lady. Anyway, how do you really know that? Did you catch him? Red-handed?'

'It wasn't his hand that was the problem, Ma.'

His grandma made a terrible sound in her throat at that and snapped, 'Your *mouth*, girl!'

It was quiet for a few minutes. Then Grandma Staizer said, 'You have to turn a blind eye. Men are men.'

'Oh, *Ma*.'

'All men do that sort of thing once in a while. You have to be patient. You're his wife.'

'Not any more. I am officially not his wife any more, Ma. I am divorced. It is over. Please, please, *please*, for my sake, let's let it go, okay? Let it go.' And for the hour or so it took Petey to fall asleep, she had. It was a good thing she never called.

He tongued his lip and wondered about asking for a snack. He and his mom had had fruit cocktail while they watched a show his mom liked, but he still felt hungry, for something good. He didn't really like fruit cocktail. He had wanted to say as much, but his mom wasn't going to hear it. He still wouldn't tell her the names of the boys at school (he told her he didn't know them) and she was at her *wits' end* over it. She said that the parents had to be *informed*. When she said it like that, Petey got an image of parents in suits around a big board table like on TV, and his mother standing at the front with charts and an overhead projector explaining, *So, as you see, your son beat the crap out of my son and that is unacceptable behaviour even though my son threw the first punch. Is everyone on the same page?* Then briefcases would snap shut and everyone would be on their way. He couldn't tell her. And there was no real way to explain to her that it was a different world on the playground and in the hallways. Bad kids beat the hell out of someone at lunch and morning recess and then went home after school and had a piece of chocolate cake and watched cartoons. Parenting was something parents did. Kids were bastards.

And he had to go back tomorrow.

The very thought of school tightened his belly and made it feel like there were cold rocks in it. His face pinched up and felt like it hurt, and not because of his lip, either. He guessed he would get his tomorrow. Probably not at recess. Probably after school. And then every day for a while until they got bored or forgot or soccer started. Scenarios of future poundings ran through Petey's mind. Andy Devries and Marshall Hemp were known quantities, not so much individuals in Petey's mind as types. There had been a kid at the old school, Gregory Johnston, a big, ugly kid with few friends, who had beaten Petey up. Not just Petey, but anyone smaller (but in the same grade – there were *rules*) or smarter or stupider – harder to find. He was another type. The Andys and Marshalls were different yet the same. Andy and Marshall were the kids who smiled and smart-mouthed the teachers to make them laugh and then got away with all kinds of things. They never got into trouble, or if they did, it was small trouble. They were different kids on the playground and inside the school. Inside the school it was all grins and winks and 'Thank you, Mrs Waddell'; on the playground it was *hey fat kid*. They had big smiles with white, even teeth and nice clothes and all the Pokémon trading cards and Nike running shoes. Teachers smiled back at them and never looked through them when they were asking a question. With those kids it was always 'Yes, Andy?' With other kids it was a glance and a glance away followed by a curt 'Yes?' Or if she was busy, it was 'What?'

Probably Gregory would pound Andy, but even if Andy pulverized Gregory, even if Andy started it,

Gregory would get into trouble. Those kinds of kids were always in trouble.

Anyway, in a fight between Gregory and Andy, Gregory, Petey decided, would win. But he would never go near Andy Devries. Andy Devries wasn't smaller or dumber or fat. He was smarter, but he was beautiful and that, for reasons Petey didn't even attempt to figure out but just accepted as the way things were, made him exempt.

Petey scooped up the clothes that he had dropped to the floor and stood a moment looking around with them in his arms. He couldn't remember where he was supposed to put them. At the other house the laundry hamper was in the bathroom, but this bathroom was too small. He thought maybe it was his mom's room. He started off in that direction.

Just before the door, he heard a small click. Not markedly, but unconsciously. It was enough for him to turn in reaction.

The little wooden door to the cubbyhole was swinging open, very slowly. He watched it, standing there, his arms full of his clothes from the day, the T-shirt with the grass and snot stains rolled into the middle, his jeans and socks a shell surrounding it.

The door swung fully open, right to the wall and stopped as if held there. Petey waited for the next logical thing to happen. *Something's coming out.* He did not think this pointedly, but assumed as much in the way a child of eight will follow things through to a literal conclusion. He waited, staring into the dark gape of the closet, so dark that the two boxes of toys (mostly kid stuff now) were buried in shadow. He couldn't even see them.

For a long time, nothing came out.

He heard it before he saw it. Coming from inside the shadows was the familiar sound of plastic wheels on bare floor, and while he stood there, a hot-wheels car (Corvette Stingray, his dad bought it for him, it was his *dream machine*) rolled through the cubbyhole doorway, across his bedroom floor and slid under the dresser, disappearing. He heard it gently hit the wall.

He recoiled for a second, belatedly startled, then worked through it easily. Petey was good at logic. Good at math. He was developing that kind of brain.

The door had swung open because the house had a lean. The car, loosed from the box (could have happened at any time), shifted with the motion of the door opening and rolled out. These things were not indexed in the thought, but assumed in one smooth motion of logic. Then dismissed.

Petey walked over to the wall and, shifting his load to free a hand, he snuck his fingers between that and the door and swung it back shut. He latched it with the old-fashioned latch that looked like the one he remembered being on the jam cupboard (which never had any jam in it but just stupid jars and Tupperware) at his grandma Parkins's old house. She was dead now. He snapped the latch shut, a good solid sound.

There was a brief moment of consideration and, against logical thought, Petey listened for sounds inside the closet. There were none. The door felt warm.

He took the clothes into his mom's room and found the hamper.

'Mom?' he called down the stairs when he was finished. 'I'm ready.'

*

Barbara sat on the stairs outside his room for a few minutes, just as she had when he was little, although back then there had been no stairs, and back then there would have been other sounds in the house: Dennis working on something in the basement, the intermittent sound of a power tool, the TV on, muffled curses coming from the little room off the bathroom after he'd gotten his computer and spent hours learning how it worked. It was quiet in this house.

Let tomorrow be better. She'd tucked him in and they'd read a comic book together. *Scooby-Doo.* They would have done better than that, but most of the books, his and hers (and some of Dennis's, but just the ones she liked, god knows he'd never miss a *book*), were still in boxes in the living room. He read a panel, then she read a panel and they'd read the thing together in that way. While he read, she watched his face, brows sometimes furrowing, puzzling out a word. He was not a great reader. He was better with numbers. Sometimes, if it was funny – he liked it when Scooby spoke with his distinctive lisp, and Barbara tried her best to imitate it – his face would open up with a smile and he would look so carefree and joyful, however briefly, forgetting everything, and Barbara would be amazed by his beauty. How did others not see it?

He'd been a beautiful baby, with soft pink skin that would take years to pale and freckle, and lovely golden hair that would turn red slowly. His cheeks had always been full, and she could remember pressing her cheek against his just to feel the pillow-fat softness. She'd left his hair long, long after she probably should have cut it and only did after Dennis insisted that he was starting to look like a girl. The curls were gone with that haircut and he had begun then to look like a boy, and by the time he was three or four, she realized for the first time that he was going to grow up and not be a baby for ever. That sort of thought had crept up on her every year. The one thing he had retained from babyhood was his long dark eyelashes, brown, not black, but thick and dark enough to pass as black. They were from Dennis. So was the weight.

She had pressed him after the comic book to tell her the names of the boys in the fight. He had explained that it would ruin his life if she called their parents and half-heartedly admitted that he had lost his temper.

They'd called him names. He wouldn't say what names, but she suspected well enough.

They talked about sticks and stones, brave, hard words for an eight-year-old to remember. Throughout the conversation, which got very quiet and introspective, she had remained upbeat and calm, but could feel her heart breaking, looking down at his round, beautiful face. His eyes had been downcast, his long lovely lashes shadowing his cheek, and had not looked at her until the end when he kissed her goodnight, smiling as he had when they'd read the comic book.

'Good night, sweetheart, I'll see you in my dreams.' She'd said it but didn't sing it, a joke. They'd used to sing it when he was little. He smiled, but didn't laugh. He was getting too old.

'Night, Mom.' He rolled over on to his side and she covered him. He looked back at her over his shoulder and said, 'You're going to stay up here for a while, right?'

'Yup. Going to put clothes away for a bit in my room, okay?'

''Kay.'

She smoothed the covers over him and brushed hair off his forehead. Looked at the bruise on his cheek. There had been incidents at his other school, but they had been rare. Kid stuff, Dennis claimed. She hoped this was just a one-time thing, some kind of initiation. Not every child could be popular and on top but she hoped to god, and anyone else who might be listening, that her child didn't end up on the bottom.

She snapped off the light.

'Love you,' she whispered into the dark. He heard her.

'Love you, too,' he muttered from under the covers.

Please leave him alone. She thought-prayed to whoever was listening that he needed a little extra help (because his mother might not be quite up to the job, just yet).

Barbara Parkins-Staizer? Not Parkins any more, but Staizer again, maybe, or maybe just the hyphen. It was hard to get used to either, neither sounded exactly right, and she still hadn't really, *really* decided to change, but was still sort of trying those changes on (out of anger). *This too shall pass.* That was what Debra had told her, anyway.

She folded the sweater in her lap and tucked it neatly into the middle drawer of her childhood dresser. She would keep that dresser in the closet, pushed to one side, and use the ample space on the other side to hang her few hangables. Not so many now – half, really. Dennis had got the big dresser in the divorce. She hadn't cared. He probably could have taken everything in the house and it would have been weeks before she had noticed.

She hadn't even seen him take it. He'd left a note. Near the end there, he'd taken to coming to the house when she was out and taking what he needed then and leaving a note in order to avoid the scenes that ranged between tearful acceptance and offers of friendship (always ending in tears of hysteria) to angry rages during which she might actually throw something – especially something he wanted. He himself was always the same, and it was still impossible for her to admit that his general feeling seemed to be one of relief.

He got the big dresser. She got the smaller, daintier bureau with the mirror – sort of good of him to leave that for her since she felt the need lately to look at herself all the time, just to make sure she was still there – and she'd pinched her childhood dresser from home. Her mother had shaken her head in disgust at that, the unsaid, *you had a husband and you let him go*. And then what? *Now you have no dresser?* Barbara smiled grimly.

She spent an hour putting things to rights in her bedroom. Her *own* room, something she hadn't had since she was a girl. She had done things her way.

Her bed had been pushed up against the wall, beside the window.

There was a pretty picture in her head of the girl: she was looking pensively out the window late at night, keeping watch. The first day in the house – when there were so many things to be done – she had gone upstairs to start on Petey's room (priorities: bathroom, Petey's room, kitchen), and glanced into her bedroom. Dropping the bag she had been carrying – towels – she went directly into it and pushed her bed frame up against the wall. It had to be moved out again to put the mattress on, but it had been a *moment*. My room. My bed. My window. There had been a sadness under the ferocity of the act, but she had chosen, briefly, bravely, to ignore it. She had her bed by the window.

She'd always wanted that, it touched some kind of childhood chord in her, but Dennis had been adamant about there being enough space between the bed and the window to get out in case of a fire.

'You want us to burn in our beds because we can't get out the window?' he'd said firmly. The thing was, both she and Petey had been small enough to crawl across the bed and get out the window. Only Dennis had been too large. Course, he was smaller now. That had been the thing. In the last six months before he finally left her, he'd been losing weight. He'd started working out, going to the gym, running in the morning before work, and she'd been pleased – *I was so stupid!* – and had dropped about thirty pounds. He'd lost more since. Not for her, like she'd foolishly believed. For the other one.

The other one. Nameless. She could pass her on the street and not know she had.

It was impossible to stop the process once it had begun, and there it was, the bad pain, the terrible pain, worse even than the reality of the situation she was currently in, the pain that she imagined was like a bone breaking, the first, nearly audible snap of PAIN, then the flooding over her of the real stuff, the real pain, visceral, whole body, complete.

She breathed deeply, tilting her head so that the tears would stay back. She felt the stinging in her nose first, and the full feeling of her face tightening. Her lips quivered for a second. She breathed and sat like that until she thought it would stop. It would stop.

Ancient history now. And no one cares.

She had a phone number. In the dark, disturbing days after she'd realized it, after checking the phone bills, she'd called. Again and again and a terrible, horrible voice (actually an ordinary voice, which was strangely worse, but she was not about to allow that thought, not yet but *it would come, it would come*) had answered every time. She'd fought the urge to speak, not hard because in the space between the last ring and the voice that answered there was every terror she felt, every fear, no anger at those moments, just terror, and in the stark face of it, she had nothing to say. What to say to the woman who has everything? She would hang up.

Another victory: she hadn't dialled the number in three weeks. By now it was probably changed. And, of course, there were no more phone bills to check.

Her room was almost done. She planned filmy lace curtains for the big window beside the bed where she could look (pensively) out at the moon. Her pretty picture. Her largest piece of art, Klimt's *The Kiss*, would go over on the far wall. It was romantic and moody and had lots of bright yellow in it, a good colour to wake up to. She might, when next spring rolled back around, paint the bedroom yellow. Bright, sunny. Not the yellow that was in the back bedroom (which would eventually be a sewing room–book room), but something *nice*. Whatever it was called, that colour was unsettling.

The sweaters put away, she gave the room a good look-around. Her bed seemed small in the large room, and as yet there was nothing to add to it except an ancient rocking chair that was ready for the dump but that she kept for sentimental reasons. She'd rocked Petey in that chair. She had her little dresser, daintier in the largish room than it had been in their cramped, smaller room at home, but other than that it looked a little vacant. A guest room with a permanent guest. It would be pretty with curtains and the big picture. A nice fat overstuffed chair, maybe, and a tea table. Next spring.

It was a good house. It had to be. She had spent the bulk of her settlement on it, and now it was hers without a mortgage. There was about twenty thousand dollars with which to start their new lives, hers and Petey's (Pe*ter*, she reminded herself). She wasn't absolutely sure, but she thought it was enough for about six months, and then she would have to work in earnest. Fifteen years of marriage had come to about $110,000, plus child-support.

Goddamn bastard shit Dennis hope you get herpes (not AIDS I need the child support ha ha).

Ancient history.

Barbara had just shut off the light in her room when she heard Petey's muffled voice, like shouting, saying something she didn't catch. She went to his door and looked in. 'Honey?'

His arm waved in the air above his head. '*Don't!*' It dropped and his elbow twitched up in a reactive gesture and he said something else, fiercely, unintelligible. He was sleeping. Talking in his sleep.

Barbara slipped into his room and knelt beside his bed, stroking his head. 'Ssssh . . .' she whispered. She soothed and stroked, whispering quietly, close to his face. He shifted on the bed. His little hands were clenched into fists, his face scrunched up, bottom lip jutting out because of his fat lip or some dreamt injury. 'Ssssh . . .'

Slowly his face lost its tightness and he settled down. She stroked his hair softly and stared at him intently, as if able to will away his troubled thoughts.

'Baby, ssssh . . .' She stayed there for a long time. Until every demon passed.

Those little bastards. Why was everyone such a bastard?

She made it as far as the top step outside his room before dropping down and sinking her head into her hands. What kind of place had she brought him to?

With an ear half cocked, just like when he was little, she listened for his breathing to get slow and regular, waited for sleep to truly take him – to a safer place. When he slept, just like he had as a toddler, he tucked a pudgy fist under his chin. His face would lose that look of concentrated confusion and relax. His lashes would lean gently on his cheeks. He would look like a baby, an angel.

God, at least let his dreams be nice.

A couple of years before, she would have called the parents. She wanted to; she wanted to call up the mothers of those children and scream into the phone, *What kind of animals are you raising?*, scream until she was hoarse and if she was a man, by god, she might have gone over there and thrown her weight around, see how they liked it. See how they liked to be the little one, the one on the dirty end of the stick.

He was just a little kid. How could people not see what a beautiful little boy he was?

Barbara had debated explaining their situation to

Petey's new school – in brief, of course, at least to his teacher and the principal. Explain Petey's silence, the expression of disbelief that he seemed to have on his face all the time, explain the little compulsions he had picked up over the last year, like eating without stopping, barely taking time to chew, that look he got on his face when he was doing it. Like a good mother, it had crossed her mind to explain, enlighten and, with hope, garner some compassion for her boy. The thought had crossed her mind and then disappeared in the –

In the what?

In the mess that had become her world. In the melting-pot of her brain, where all facts, initiatives and ideas came together to be about Dennis, the divorce, the pain of Barbara Parkins-Staizer. Petey had been lost in that mess for nearly a year.

She cried very quietly so that he wouldn't hear her, and she did this with practised skill, so second nature by then that this time she realized she hadn't even noticed that she had been crying at all. Once she did she cast a guilty glance towards his room and listened for a minute. His breathing was slow and easy. He was asleep. She smeared tears across her cheek and felt her nose running. She stood up on uncertain legs and stepped carefully down the stairs, not wanting to wake him up.

She needed to talk to someone. To hear a voice.

The phone at the bottom of the stairs was mute with accusation. Who would she call? She could call her mother, she could always call her mother. Barbara was lately of the opinion that her mother spent whole days thinking about the fool she had raised. But she'd also noticed Petey before Barbara had really given it a thought. *He's getting very fat, Barbara. What are you feeding him? Mother!* She didn't have to call her mother, she could hear her voice in her own head as clearly as if she was in the room. Hovering over her shoulder, shooting spiny comments at every move Barbara made, every decision, until everything she did became so filled with trepidation that she ceased to move altogether. And yet, her mother was often right; cruelly right.

You have to watch out for the boy now. He's without his father.

I know, Mother.

You could change that, Barbara.

No, I can't, Mother.

Men are men. They're all bastards. You have to turn a blind eye and take your licks.

He's gone, there's nothing I can do.

You're not a woman, Barbara.

She could call Debra. Debra was divorced. Successfully. Their friendship, since Barbara and Dennis's break-up, had changed course somehow, and they had both known it. Her shoulder, hardened by her own break-up, was no longer a place to cry. They could discuss clothes, clubs, movies, books, but nothing heavy. If Barbara tried to bring up a subject on the *verboten* list, Debra's eyes glazed over. She did not want to relive her own pain. Understandable.

The only other friend of any consequence she had was Gail, the neighbour from two doors down at the old house. Gail with 2.4 children, her husband in affable agreement to almost everything Gail said, her suburban life with blond kids, good kids (thin, *acceptable* kids), her dog, and unspoken judgements and pursed lips about the way the world had turned, and right in her own backyard!). Dennis still saw them, she knew. She supposed that he had gotten custody of Gail and Bob in the divorce. The temptation to ask (and the gleeful telling, probably) about Dennis would be worse than any tone Gail would take with her, and she *would* take a tone.

You're not a woman, Barbara.

Barbara walked past the phone, the hallway cold, the cold seeming to follow her into the kitchen. She would have a drink. There was a bottle of Canadian Club that Debra had given her for Christmas, about a month after Dennis had left. It had been a joke, to cheer her up. Debra's divorce was four years old already, long past the point of regret and pain and well into the realm of her own life. She was a good example of how things can go *right* after a divorce: her life was so wonderfully full and she was always laughing and running off somewhere with someone. 'Greener pastures and bigger dick,' was how Debra referred to divorce now, but it hadn't always been so, and Barbara, under the constraints of their current unspoken agreement, couldn't help but feel resentful for the hours of time she'd put in listening to Debra cry and rage. She also, regretfully, remembered her own smugness, which now looked so foolish and naïve, listening to the details, a Gail-like *tsk-tsk* carefully hidden under veils of sympathy. *Poor baby. Men are bastards.*

The bottle wasn't hard to find. The label had been replaced by one of those fake ones that you can produce on the computer; at the time (after a couple of belts at Debra's) it had seemed funny, but now was not funny in the least.

'Breakfast of Champions', and under that it had said, 'the broken heart's best friend'.

It was a little after, or before, breakfast, but she didn't think anyone would notice.

Barbara sipped her drink and opened boxes of books, shoving them indiscriminately on the shelf adjacent to the sofa. It would crowd the one corner of the room, but if she got a big chair or a love seat or something LARGE for the other corner, it would all balance out.

No ice. The whiskey was warm and sharp in her mouth and down her throat – *this too shall pass* – but the ice-cube trays were still buried in one of the many boxes yet to be unpacked in the kitchen. She supposed if she was going to take up drinking whiskey that she should also take up making ice cubes. For now they would stay buried. Too bad. She liked the sound of ice tinkling in a glass. It sounded *festive*.

She separated Petey's books from her own (and the ones of Dennis's she had taken because she liked them and because she *could*). The titles were all so familiar to her: *Charlotte's Web*, *Stuart Little*, *The Secret World of Og*, *Henry and Ribsy*; just before Dennis left she and Petey had finished reading the first in the Harry Potter series. It occurred to her that they hadn't read 'a long book' together since then. They had stuck to comic books and short, easy things. She couldn't really remember what they'd read.

She'd been in a fog. She would not be up for any mother-of-the-year awards. Not for a while, anyway. *This too shall pass.*

She'd always assumed, vaguely at least, that she would

have another child. They'd talked about it. But it was as though suddenly Petey was five and then he was seven and then, by the time he was eight, any desire for another child had been eclipsed by the slow disintegration of their marriage. If there had been two children, they might have been able to comfort each other during those first months after Dennis had left, but there had just been Petey. There had been nights when she hadn't been able to speak, and if she did, then it was to rage or cry. There had been many times when she'd cried while cooking supper, doing the dishes, laundry. *All day.* She'd broken down once in the middle of the grocery store, in the bread section, as she recalled, standing there, leaning against the cart, bawling like a baby, Petey looking at her, his round, freckled face white with – *embarrassment? Fear?* A lady had stopped and asked her if she was going to be all right and she'd blurted out that her husband had left them and that she was never going to be all right again. The woman had patted her shoulder or back or something tentative and then pushed her cart away as though it was catching. Petey just stood beside the cart, silent through the whole thing. After the woman walked away, he went to the shelf and picked up two loaves of bread. 'Two enough, Mom?' he'd asked, and she'd nodded and they moved on to Produce.

I'll make it up to him, all of it.

God knew he had enough on his plate. He was a big boy. The doctor said he would grow out of most of it, but that he might just be big. 'Like his dad,' Dr Poulin had said. Like his dad. Dennis had been on the heavy side when she met and married him, not something that had ever mattered to her, and when Petey inherited his weight, she hadn't thought about what it could mean for him. Red hair and freckles didn't help. And in a couple of years – if he was like Dennis – he was going to need glasses. She hoped that somewhere in the neighbourhood there was a Jeremy –

There was a *thump!* from upstairs, loud, like the sound of something (soft) falling over, and in her haste, Barbara jumped up and knocked over her drink on to the bare floor of the living room.

'Shit,' she said, out loud, looking upwards. Glancing at the mess her drink had made, she grimaced and went into the hall without turning on the light there. The stairs were dark, but she could see the faint light coming from the upstairs bathroom, the door half shut to cut the glare to his room. From the bottom of the stairs, she looked up and listened. It was quiet. All she could hear was the buzz of the clock in the hall. She stood still, hardly breathing, not wanting to make a sound and wake him, if something had fallen –

– and hadn't woken him. She listened intently. There was no further *thump!*, he did not call for her, and Barbara relaxed, diverted her attention back to the floor and the spilled drink. She leaned down and righted the glass. The smell of whiskey filled her nostrils and she wondered idly if it would score the varnish. On her way to get a cloth to wipe up the mess, something else caught her attention, again from upstairs.

Whatever she heard was enough to stop her. She paused between living room and dining room and figured she would just go up and have a peek. Petey was maybe having a nightmare. She remembered reading something once about young children sleepwalking during times of trauma and he wasn't yet used to the stairs.

In the pause between deciding, she heard a giggle. Then something else, not intelligible, but a word maybe. Very distinctly.

Barbara frowned, and went to the bottom of the stairs, one foot on the bottom step, listening. 'Petey?' It sounded loud in the dark hall. It was very quiet upstairs, the hush falling into a gap, like breath held.

Feet bare, padding across the floor, quick little steps (too little, she acknowledged before it was too late to take it back but that was *impossible*) across the floor upstairs. Barbara tightened, swallowed.

'Petey?' she said, and for the first time realized how dark it was up the stairs, in the hall, and how she couldn't see. There was silence up there again, but she was oddly reminded of slumber parties as a child, the little girls spread out over bedrooms (never at Elizabeth Staizer's house, no way) giggling in the dark, daring each other into darker rooms, down hallways, nasty tales of hooks for hands and prowlers in basements and in closets.

She took the stairs with soft steps.

'Petey?' she said louder, stronger, at the top of the stairs. *We're only fooling!* The light was on in the bathroom and she pushed the door open as she passed it, illuminating the hall and Petey's room, in a band, from the doorway to his bed, pushed against the far wall (by the window).

Party's over!

He slept. His covers were pulled under his arms, elbow tucked close to him, fist under chin, just as she'd left him. His face was still and relaxed.

She watched to see a smile appear, a suppressed giggle

released, *fooled ya! fooled ya!*, but none came. His lips were parted slightly, eyes still under pale lids. It was not fakery.

Barbara frowned. Her eyes darted around the room, indexing and marking off what might (or might not) have made the noise she'd heard. His comics were still piled as they had been when she put *Scooby-Doo* back on top; there was no laundry in a dark corner. Everything was in its place. She began to relax. *He hadn't heard it.* Hadn't woken up. She breathed deep and let it go. Smiled.

She went to him anyway, wanting to touch him, like saying good night, and there *was* something out of place. The closet door was open, pressed against the wall, wide.

Pulling the door closed, there was a brief moment when she glanced inside and thought, *It's so dark in there you can't see the back wall*, and marvelled at the fact before pushing the door shut, it fitting nicely, neatly into the frame, a satisfying sort of sound, pleasant, and latched it. She gave it a final push before turning back to Petey and (with her other hand) touched his shoulder, lightly. It seemed enough. *I heard it swing open, hit the wall. That was the thump.*

On her way out of the door, the thought crossed her mind that it had been closed when she had put Petey to bed, because she had thought about moving the untidy pile of comic books in there, to get them out of view. The door had been shut, and she had left it for morning. She gave the door a second glance. The latch may be loose. Houses move and settle over and over in the spring thaw. She dismissed it with a shrug. Out of the bedroom, she absently wiped her hand on her pants leg, the hand that had latched the little door.

It was only after ten. Even so, once downstairs she cleaned up her spilled drink and went to bed. She wanted to be upstairs.

Let his dreams be good. All our dreams.

Neither Petey nor Barbara woke up again that night.

From inside the closet, the sounds were muffled, as though taking place very far away. Remotely, as Barbara was dreaming about Dennis, and the hiding of things in desk drawers that could not be opened, the strains of *ollie ollie all-in free* penetrated only once, to be quickly lost in the dream sound of a computer's hum as she checked emails that she could not read, and her pace quickened because *Dennis is at the door! Dennis is at the door!* In the closet the game changed to a slow and eternal game of tag. Petey did not hear the cries, *You're it!* Because he too was far away, in a playground, surrounded.

Dreams covered the sleepy sounds of endless summer and the warm breeze was silent. If either of them noticed the sweet scent of tall grass, or felt the soft brush of dandelion fur under chins, it went unheeded in the upstairs of the house on Belisle. In places distant the sun shone at midday for ever.

Petey, more sensitive perhaps to the underscore of summer places, stirred first around three a.m. He shifted in his bed as, in his own dreams, the children on the playground scattered at the footfalls of a faceless principal in farmer's clothes. Behind the closet door, clouds gathered, the sun disappearing behind shadows. The sounds of play stopped. For a long time there was nothing, the sound that darkness makes.

Then, awful sounds under thunder.

2

Barbara got off her knees in the front hall with a groan, and surveyed her work. The floor was so bright and shiny, and more so now, after a good going-over with oil soap and a shammy. It had taken two hours, but the end result was gorgeous. The floor looked brand new, which, of course, it was. It was perfect now. And for a moment, there was slight panic inside her.

What now? There had been no plan for the rest of the morning. She had simply seen the small smudge at the doorway and decided to wash the hall floor. For two hours her mind had been deliciously blank in the repetitive motions and productive labour of housework, and now she was done. Little notions threatened.

Quickly, a list began forming in her head. There was plenty to do. The problem was that most of what had to be done were monstrous, horribly difficult things, enormous life choices that had to be made. Get a job, get a life, get over Dennis, stop thinking about the whore, don't call your mother, the world is not looking at you, plan for your retirement, figure out a budget, put Petey on a diet, make some friends –

It engulfed her. She decided, languidly almost, to wash the walls in the kitchen. She could use the oil soap. She thought it was okay to use on paint. She would read the label.

She got up with another groan (*oh god lose ten pounds*)

and with mincing, careful steps over her perfect floor –
thank god something can still work for me – she picked
up the bottle of oil soap from the living-room floor (*I
could do that next, big job*, she thought delightedly) and
read the back.

She read until she found what she was looking for,
painted surfaces and washable wallpaper. She twisted off
the cap and took a sniff, closing her eyes and enjoying
the soapy, clean smell of it – unnecessary, given that the
whole hall, and probably most of the house, smelled of
it. She'd been needing a lot of busy work.

It smells good. Some things are still good, she thought,
and raised her eyes to see a little girl standing in the
dining room. They stared at each other for a moment,
just a moment, and then the little girl smiled broadly,
revealing tiny, even white teeth.

It was impossible not to, and Barbara smiled back.
'Hello,' she said, kindly, not sure what else to say. She
flicked her eyes behind the girl looking for a mother, the
buttercup delivery of the previous week coming to mind.

'Hi,' the little girl said shyly. She shrugged her shoulders coyly and might have batted her eyes.

Barbara was charmed. She walked over and knelt close
in front of the child. 'And what's your name?'

The little girl blushed. 'Mariette,' she said.

'I'm Barbara. Does your mother know you're here?'
she asked, and looked again towards the back door,
wondering if a mother was indeed either waiting at the
door, or looking for her daughter.

'My mother's dead,' the child said, plainly.

Barbara was flustered, her face reddening. 'Oh dear,
I'm so sorry to hear that –' and all the emotion of her

morning climbed into her throat and hit her hard. She blinked away the too-familiar sting and stood up.

'Well, someone must be looking for you, dear,' she said. 'Do you live close by?' And she took a good look down at the little girl.

The child's hair was summer-blonde, the sort that would darken in time. It was long and, if tangled some, it looked to be clean. The ends curled up charmingly in a wave. She'd always wanted a little girl. This one was such a pretty little thing; she couldn't imagine her without a mother. So sad. She wore no coat and Barbara frowned, thinking how cool it had been that morning, although the day now warmed up by noon.

The little girl didn't answer her. Instead she said, 'I want your little boy,' in a voice so much like a baby, it too pulled at her.

Barbara turned away from the child, not trusting her emotions. She swallowed and fussed over the soap bottle, screwing the lid on tight and wiping the clean sides of it with her shammy, finally putting it with a swipe on the bookshelf against the wall. 'Oh,' she said. 'Well, Petey's at school. He's not home until after three thirty. You could come back then . . . would you like that? Would you like me to take you home?' Thinking, it would be so nice if Petey had made a friend in the neighbourhood – even if it was a little girl who had to be no more than four or five from the size of her – and she turned back to the child.

The child was gone.

'Mariette?' she called and walked into the living room, which was empty. She tried again. 'Mariette?' a little annoyed that someone would feel free just to wander around someone else's home – the thought poking through about the little girl's mother being dead and maybe she didn't –

Barbara walked all the way around the house. She did not see the little girl anywhere. The back door stood open and the screen door was loose, but she had left it open herself to air the house.

She shrugged and hoped the child was all right. And hoped that she would come back after school, and maybe (oh god please) bring a brother for Petey to play with.

At least there are kids in the neighbourhood, she thought. *I was starting to think we were going to be stuck in the house together for ever.*

By the last week of April, spring was waving its pale arm. The snow had been gone for weeks, but the weather had been unpredictable. The sun had been reluctant to make a commitment and so had hidden itself behind grey clouds and rain. *April showers bring May flowers* had worn out its welcome. On the first day that the field behind the school was declared dry *enough*, Petey's class had gym outside.

Grades four to six had Mr Casem for gym. He was an enormous man, towering over the littler kids, some of whom only came up to waist level. He coached the school teams with suppressed rage, his face apoplectically red the last half-hour of basketball and indoor hockey. In the winter he wore his silver whistle with a white T-shirt and grey sweatpants (there was a row of them hanging in his office off the gymnasium) and in warmer weather he wore grey sweat shorts and a white T-shirt, and the whistle. He was tall enough to look down on most of the teachers. He had a deep, manly voice and tended to shout things rather than say them, and it had been decided years before Petey ever got to Middleton School that it would be more appropriate for the classroom teachers to provide gym classes for the younger grades.

June Waddell, a larger, heavier woman in her early forties, taught gym with less enthusiasm than penmanship, but more than second-grade reading. She regularly forgot that Wednesdays were gym days and rarely had the appropriate clothing with her. On the days that she remembered, her gym clothes were a pair of brown athletic shorts from ten years earlier when, in a fit of early love, she had joined an aerobics class, and a T-shirt with cats or flowers on it. She almost never had a whistle. She yelled.

During morning recess in the staff room, she remembered fourth-period gym and groaned. Until she realized that, with the weather being so beautiful – and it was a beautiful day – she could take the children outside and play on the soccer field. 'Organized sport builds school spirit,' she said sarcastically to Nick Pearson, grade four teacher. 'And all I have to do is sweet-talk a whistle off Mr Frankenstein and *blow it*.' Nick had laughed and Mrs Waddell didn't so much sweet-talk Mr Casem as demand the whistle, but it was there around her neck at eleven fifteen when the kids were led out into the playground to play an hour's worth of soccer so she could fulfil her duty as a gym teacher for another week and spend her lunch hour typing a cover letter for a résumé she was sending to Washburn High School. She wanted to teach high-school English.

The children were lined up, and out of the line she pulled Betty Graham and Marshall Hemp as team captains and told them to choose teams.

The choosing went quickly in the beginning, the captains starting with their friends, and wound down once the friends were chosen. Marshall picked Andy Devries first, Betty picked Tiffany Winder (Tiffany *Wonder*). The picking and choosing went on for four rounds without interference. Mrs Waddell paid passing attention to the fact that Betty had chosen all girls in the initial rounds and Marshall all boys. She thought at first that it was interesting and something to mention to her women's group later in the week, a kind of pride-in-gender sort of thing, and quickly realized that she was probably setting the girls up for a fall.

'Betty, your next pick has to be a boy,' she said suddenly, just seconds before Betty was about to pick Linda Williams, her fifth-best friend. Betty groaned dramatically and looked to Mrs Waddell for mercy. The other girls looked to Betty for leadership, all eyes on her (another thing to mention to her women's group on Saturday).

'It's not fair to have just girls on your team,' she said, not adding that they would lose due to excessive gabbing and fretting on the field, not to mention – even at that age – the instinctive, and embarrassing, need to please the boys, which would make for very little passing or aggressing. Not something she would bring up at her women's group. Or maybe.

'Pick a boy,' she said firmly.

Sticking her chin out, which probably worked at home, did not work on Mrs Waddell. After agonizing for about an eighth of a second, Betty picked Teddy Markem. Mrs Waddell rolled her eyes at the typical choice. Teddy Markem was 'cute'.

Teddy Markem looked as though he had just heard about a terrible exotic disease he'd caught. He dragged his feet moving from the line-up to the 'girls' team' and stood about six feet away from the closest girl. Mrs Waddell ignored this. She made Marshall Hemp pick a girl. Bethany Sanders, who the girls didn't always like because she acted so 'big', whatever *that* meant. Mrs Waddell rolled her eyes again, but she thought it might have something to do with the fact that Bethany's mother and father were both doctors, never home, and it was taking its toll on her personality, in spite of the Gap-this and Reebok-that. She was going to be trouble one day.

Mrs Waddell let her mind wander some after that. In the meantime, Betty picked Lisa Cummings and Marshall picked Paul Timmons. And Betty picked Georgina Fritz out of desperation, because they were running out of girls. And boys.

'I *said* pick a *girl*, Marshall Hemp!'

'I *did*,' he protested, pointing at Bethany who looked utterly miserable and adorable in her low-rider (*god, they dress them like prostitutes!*) Levi's and pink T with the MTV logo splayed across what would one day be a bosom.

'Pick another one,' she said, through her teeth. She looked at the line-up. Four children were left: Todd Campbell, the new boy Peter Parkins, Benita Warins and Abby Morgan.

Marshall appeared to despair for a second, before

finally pointing vaguely in the direction of Abby, who wore glasses and whose parents were Jehovah's Witnesses. This was apparently better than Benita. Benita had wet her pants once in grade one, although June Waddell had no way of knowing this, and was for ever after known as Pee-pants Warins. She *smelled*, they said. She may have. Some children have a sort of pox on them that the faculty catches on to quickly, with or without knowing why. Schools are small towns. Except by very young teachers, these children are universally and unconsciously avoided. Their names are routinely forgotten, they are given average grades (if for no other reason than that their names are routinely forgotten) and their eyes are not met. If they are, they are met for only a second and then – unconsciously – dismissed.

'Marshall!' Mrs Waddell exclaimed. 'That's not the way you choose someone to play on your *team!*' She clapped her hands definitively. 'That's enough, then. Peter, Todd, you two are on Betty's team, and Benita, you're on Marshall's team. Let's play! Marshall, shirts! Let's go!' Shirts and skins were the colloquialism, but in the generation of co-ed teams, it meant shirts and not-shirts. The 'shirts' were vest-type things that fitted over the head and tied at the sides. This took some time for Marshall's team. Betty's team stood around waiting, the three boys huddling together, avoiding the girls. While Mrs Waddell handed out shirts, she heard Betty assigning positions.

'Way to hustle, Betty,' she called out, not really caring, but giving it the nod – one less thing for her to do. Betty would be centre (of course) and chose her best friend Tiffany Winder as right and her next-best friend Laurie

Perkins as left. The boys were defence. Linda Williams – ultimately chosen for Betty's team – was in goal. She said it was *easier*.

Indoor soccer was a winter favourite on those bad days when you had papers to mark and drycleaning to pick up and lessons to plan, and so there was little instruction required after the teams made their way on to the field.

Mrs Waddell blew the whistle and they ran in random directions, not one of them particularly athletically inclined, but with lots of dig.

'Guard your goalie, defence!' Mrs Waddell called out, hoping her voice sounded more enthusiastic than she felt. She hated team sports in the vague way of someone who had never played.

Within seconds of play, Andy Devries had the ball and was heading towards Linda Williams with a sure-footed grace that probably indicated an affinity for the game. He was closely trailed by Marshall and, surprisingly, Pee-pants.

'Benita! You're defence, get back in position,' she yelled. Todd Campbell, left defence for Betty's team, stood his ground, bending in a crouch, arms up slightly above his waist, ready to defend. On the other side, Peter the new boy, edged in uncomfortably, close to goal, just inside the perimeter. Linda Williams, clearly rethinking her decision to be in goal because it was 'easier', squealed desperately, hands covering her head, dashing arbitrarily from side to side across the six-foot goal, while team mates shouted instructions. 'Get over *there*, Linda!'

With the exception of Bethany Sanders in goal, the entire boys' team had followed the progress of the ball across the field, without any respect to boundaries or positions. Mrs Waddell sighed deeply. 'Mind your positions!' she called out, entirely unsure suddenly if that was the rule of the game. At least, she thought, Bethany had stayed in goal (and was now standing in the middle, uninterestedly postured with shoulders slumped, picking at a scab on her hand).

The defence players on Betty's team disappeared briefly, lost in the horde of the two teams. They bunched up in a battle for the ball, briefly, and Mrs Waddell lost sight of ball and key players in the squirming mass. 'Don't bunch up!' she called out, helpfully. She was ignored.

Players suddenly scattered in all directions and stopped. Play had stopped. Heads turned to look at Mrs Waddell and she blew her whistle and started towards the field when she saw a pile of kids wriggling there.

'Get off me! Get *off*!' someone was shouting from under the pile.

The 'pile' was actually the new boy and Todd Campbell, who wasn't in the pile exactly, but his leg was caught between the other two boys, the bottom half distinguishable only by his shirt. Andy Devries let go of a very bad swear and Mrs Waddell blanched, unable even to react before his arm swung out and caught Peter Parkins on the side of the head in a good, solid blow.

'Get the *fuck* off me, you *pig*!'

'Language, Andy!'

She blew her whistle again, sharply, and called out, 'That's enough, Andy Devries, that's *enough*!'

Peter had since rolled off the boy, and was now covering his head. Andy kept swinging, smooth, pleasant features twisted up in rage. Several blows had met their mark before Mrs Waddell managed her way on to the field and past the other kids, soccer now entirely forgotten, the ball resting a couple of feet away from the open net. Linda had left the goal and stood with Betty and Tiffany, all three girls with hands over their mouths, undecided between giggling and horror. Peter lay on the ground, curled up, covering the back of his head and as much of the sides as he could manage while Andy kept punching mindlessly, each sock punctuated with a grunt or a slur. Andy's neck was red, as though from a scratch. With involuntary dismay, Mrs Waddell noticed that Peter's shirt had pulled up over his belly. She had the urge to go and tug it down. Mud and dirt clung to his clothes and his flesh.

'Get off him, Andy! Andy, right now! That's enough!' she called as, sprinting to the site, she grabbed Andy's arm in mid-arc and pulled him recklessly to his feet. His face was tear-stained and he looked wide-eyed at her as though realizing suddenly where he was. She felt instant pity for him and let go of his arm.

'That's enough,' she said, with less force. She paused for a moment to make sure the worst had passed and bent over Peter, hand resting on the back of his head.

'Are you all right, Peter?' she said kindly. He did not change his position and she could feel him trembling under her hand. She rubbed his back and asked him again. The boy was crying. 'Can you stand up for me, dear?'

'Fat pig broke my collar-bone!' Andy screamed. There was a gasp from some girl or other.

June Waddell stood fiercely and stamped her foot. 'That's enough out of you, Mr Devries!'

'He *did*,' Andy muttered, rubbing his neck in the general direction of his collar-bone where a red mark had welted, but would fade within a half-hour.

Mrs Waddell bent over Peter again and rested her hand on his back. The boy continued crying, although it had slowed to sobs. He would not move his hands away from his head. A more sensitive teacher might have realized that the boy, hurt and embarrassed, was hiding. Mrs Waddell thought he was milking it and was losing patience. The period would be over before this was settled and she had no idea where to go from here. Mr Casem would have dragged Peter to his feet, made the boys shake on it and walked it off, but Mrs Waddell wasn't sure she could physically force Peter to his feet. He was a big boy.

She settled instead for patting his back and reverting to toddler techniques. She said (as quietly as possible) to Peter, 'Well, Peter, if you don't want to get up and resume the game, you'll just have to lie there while we play around you.' Then she stood up and said, 'What happened here?'

The children all spoke at once. She signalled for quiet, and got it, and asked Andy what happened. He said Peter leaped on him just as he was about to kick the ball into the goal. Marshall seconded this.

An odd silence descended. She looked over to the group of three girls who stood closest. Linda, who had been in goal, was most likely to have seen what happened.

'Linda, what happened?' Linda's face went red.

'I didn't see,' she said quietly, with as much conviction as possible, but clearly lying.

'Who *did* see?' she asked, with ominous patience.

Benita, perhaps out of outsider sympathy, put up her hand.

'Yes, Benita?'

'Andy kicked Peter in the leg and Peter fell on him,' she said.

'He tripped on the ball,' Todd said. Everyone looked at him and he blushed, and looked down. By this time Peter had stopped crying, but stayed on the ground as though he wished it would swallow him.

'That true, Andy?' she asked.

Andy refused to look at her, instead twisted his head sideways to shoot Todd Campbell a look to kill. She waited for him to answer and he didn't. The air on the playground was thick.

Finally, Marshall said, 'The new kid just whaled on him. He jumped him and grabbed him in the throat like he was going to kill him.'

With two different stories and a child she had not had time to measure up, there was only one thing left for June Waddell to do.

'Andy, Marshall, Benita, Peter – the office.' She walked over and nudged shoulders in the direction of the school. She blew her whistle, needlessly, since all the children were huddled around the action. 'The rest of you resume play. I will be right back and I want to see some hustle when I am!'

She marched the four children to the office, after grabbing Peter by the arm in an insistent manner and reminding him, in her best I'm-not-your-mother voice, to *get up*, adding that enough was enough.

*

Petey waited a long time before leaving school, hovering by the lunch room, wishing he had seventy-five cents to put in the snack machine. He forgot about crisps for long stretches of time, while he wondered whether Andy and Marshall were waiting for him outside, as they had threatened to do, or whether they had given up and left already. School let out at three thirty-five. When Petey finally decided to make the long walk down the hall to the back doors of the school, it was ten to four. It felt like he had been waiting for hours.

The hallways were empty by then; the school sounded hollow. Occasionally, sound from the gym could be heard echoing, kids yelling, the ball whacking against the wall, all of it garbled through the peculiar acoustics of the gym. As he passed the staff room he could hear movement inside, but that was all. The empty school had the bad feel of a hospital at night after all the visitors have left; it felt serious. They could talk all they wanted about how it was 'their' school; it was three fifty and Petey knew he wasn't supposed to be there.

The back doors were doubled, with a small foyer where the kids sometimes warmed up at recess until they were kicked out, mostly girls. He went through the first set of double doors and then peered out owlishly. His view of the playground was limited. He could see all the way to the back fence where the goal posts of his most recent disaster were. He could not, however, see far down the sidewalk that led to the school parking lot, where kids congregated after school, waiting for buses and parents to pick them up.

The rest of the day after the fight had been terrible.

They sat them apart in the office. The secretary had

been unsure as to who had been involved in what, but she sat Benita and Marshall together on a set of four chairs that faced the desk. She put Petey along the other wall where the teachers came to pick up their notes in the old pigeon-holed wall shelf. Teachers glanced over him sternly, setting their mouths to an automatic purse when they saw him sitting there, barely looking at the others because they weren't in their line of vision. The secretary sat Andy on the chair near her desk. She had frowned when she saw him and said, 'Andy Devries, what are you doing here? Not in trouble, I hope?' But he never answered, because Mrs Waddell was asking to see the principal in a disgusted-exhausted voice. After she disappeared into the inner office, the secretary frowned once more at Andy, and Andy passed it on to Petey.

He mouthed the words, *you're dead*. Marshall never said anything. He was preoccupied with keeping his whole body turned away from Benita, who was crying. You could hardly hear her crying and that sort of fascinated Petey, whose mother could do the same thing. Benita's face poured with tears but, except for her occasional snuffling, you couldn't tell she was crying.

The principal called them in one at a time, starting with Benita. Going first changed the course of her tears and she let out a cry that was loud and terrified. The secretary took pity on her, and said, 'It's *okay*, honey. He's not going to bite you.' They always said that.

When they were gone, Marshall sat up straight, saying in a whisper to Andy, 'She's going to pee her pants.' Andy snickered. They stopped when the secretary came back. She frowned at all of them.

Benita came out, no longer crying, but with a look of smugness on her tear-stained face. The secretary told her she should go back out to the field where the rest of the class was still in gym. 'Hurry, hurry,' she said. 'There's only ten minutes left in the period.'

Marshall went in next. He came out and was told to wait. The period was about to end.

Andy was still in the principal's office when the bell rang. Petey looked up at the clock. It was a quarter to twelve. Lunch would be starting. The thought of food reminded him that he was hungry, and the simple pleasure of eating created the most terrible self-pity inside him. His stomach rolled over with the sudden, remembered hunger and, as though to make up for lost time, rolled over a few more times, the last time very loudly. He looked over at the secretary to see if she'd heard but she hadn't. He put his hand on his belly and gave it a rub, trying to remember what his mom had put in his lunch.

Probably salami. Maybe a pudding. An apple, something like that. He had a dollar for milk, but he would probably buy a pop. Most of the kids did. He stopped thinking about his lunch because that might make him think about his mom, and he wanted her, and that would make him cry. Again.

He'd never been sent to the office before and he was scared. He felt scared mostly in his legs, which wanted to shake and did, at intervals. He was holding it in. When his legs got so scared they couldn't help it, he let them shake for a second and then changed his position on the chair so they would stop. His face felt doughy and soft. He could feel the stiff parts on his skin where the tears had dried, and he swiped at them, rubbing, so they would go away. He had to go to the bathroom.

Andy came out, looking white-faced but not crying. For a second, Petey looked at him thoughtlessly as a compatriot. The principal followed him out. Mr Hadley, whom Petey had only seen once before, the day he registered, was balding and small, but appeared much larger; whether it was the suit he wore, or his glasses, Petey would have been at odds to say. He had an angry look on his face, but it seemed fake. He led Andy by the shoulder around the long desk that divided the room in two and stopped him in front of Petey. Petey looked up, revealing his horror in his eyes, widened, for just a second. Then he shifted his eyes away from Andy and looked up at the principal.

'You boys shake on it,' he said firmly. For a moment Petey was confused, didn't know what he meant. Shake on it? Shake?

Andy rolled his neck away from Petey and made no confirming gesture.

'Stand up, Peter,' Mr Hadley commanded. Petey did. He was the same height as Andy, but much larger, visually. Mr Hadley sized the boys up and came to his own conclusions. 'Andrew,' he said. Andy stuck out his hand, his head turned away.

At last Petey understood. Shake. *Oh.* He stuck his hand out also and since Andy wasn't looking, he grabbed the boy's hand and pumped it once. His hand was warm in Petey's. He dropped it quickly.

'All right, then,' Mr Hadley said. He loosened his grip on Andy's shoulder and side-stepped towards Petey. He patted Petey and Andy on the shoulder. 'There you go.

Now you boys try to be friends. You're going to be in Middleton School a long time together,' he said. Neither boy commented. Petey was thinking that was it, that he could go. His heart began to slow down its relentless pulse. His legs felt shakier, as though something had been released. He really had to go to the bathroom.

'All right, Andy, off you go. Lunch room.' Andy swivelled and bolted out the door. Petey moved to go with him.

'Peter,' Mr Hadley said. He swept an arm in the direction of his office. 'Let's go,' he said. His voice had lost its pleasantness.

Deciding to chance it, Petey pushed the outer door open as quietly as it would, the mechanical click of metal-on-metal echoing in the space in the foyer. It sounded loud as a gun to Petey. He peeked around the door as he went through it. The schoolyard was deserted, the way it looked in summer. It would be summer soon, and then school would be out, but that was months away.

The parking lot was empty by then too, and he let the door close behind him.

It hadn't been that bad. He didn't get the strap or anything. Mr Hadley had talked to him about the importance of fitting in and making friends, that it was a new school and it was his job to fit in with the other students. There were no visible marks on his face or arms to show what Andy had done to him (unlike Andy, who had pointed to the fast-disappearing mark on his clavicle to shore up his defence that the new kid had attacked him). Andy had kicked him twice in the leg. The second time he'd tripped over the ball and had fallen into Andy, reaching out, and that was when he scratched his neck. It *was* an accident. (At first. After he fell on Andy and Andy started screaming *fatso* and *fat pig* Petey had grabbed him somewhere soft – he didn't know where, couldn't see – and pinched, digging his nails into him, but Andy wouldn't even discover that until later; Petey just knew he did it and it added to his shame and guilt.)

Andy and Marshall had told their sides of the story, each with their own particular twist on it. Petey would have no way of knowing what they had said, but the general impression given to Principal Hadley was that of a bully to be: a large, aggressive boy who didn't like Andy or Marshall personally.

It was fortunate for Petey that Hadley had been a very small child, and an equally small adult. He'd seen an Andy and a Marshall before.

Petey was given a stern talk on *fitting in* and *getting along* and through the whole thing he could tell that the principal was disgusted with him. He could tell by the way his eyes would shift from looking *at* Petey to looking very obviously away. Mr Hadley was a tidy, trim little man, in fact weighed the same as he had in high school, who also knew a thing or two about *fitting in* and *getting along* because he had been five foot six, 120 pounds in high school and *that* hadn't exactly made him a Big Man On Campus. He repeated some of that to Petey, leaving out the height and weight (just the fact about being the same). He told the boy to concentrate on his studies and, if he wanted to fit in, perhaps he could talk to the school nurse about a diet. To his credit, he was gentle on the last part, not saying diet but *programme of fitness*.

'Get involved in sports,' Mr Hadley, who had never been on a sports team, told him, and even as he said it, Petey's face and problem and situation were fading from his memory like the last few minutes of the day. He waved him out, wishing him luck, reminding him without finishing his sentence that his door was always open. What he said was, 'My door is always . . .' and then he just trailed off. But Petey knew what he meant.

Mr Hadley had said he would call his mom and explain. Petey wanted to ask him, *explain what?* but just couldn't bring himself to speak. The whole ten minutes in the principal's office, he hadn't uttered a word. He also hadn't been asked a direct question, or to explain his side of the story.

He crossed the empty parking lot mostly trying not to think. He didn't want to think about going home, or seeing his mom, or especially about school the next day. In last-period geography, Andy had caught his eye and said, 'Every day, fatso, *every day.*'

Instead of thinking, he imagined he was so tiny that he disappeared.

The principal had called around two, just as Barbara was dragging her ancient portable typewriter out of a nearly forgotten box in the attic and downstairs.

The attic gave her the creeps. Previous owners had made a half-hearted attempt to create a usable space out of it, insulating the roof and putting in a drop ceiling so that it resembled a room, albeit not for the particularly tall, the ceiling only about seven feet high. It had turned it into one large open space, but the low ceiling gave her a claustrophobic feeling. The walls remained unfinished, the drywall not white but grey. Along the far end were three huge oaken beams, likely planned to add character and colour to the room but which lay instead impotent and unused, waiting, somehow, on the floor. Boxes of lights to be hung were stacked with their wires spilling out like snakes. It was cold up there, although wads of insulation had been pressed between studs and the whole thing had been covered in plastic and drywall (it said in the papers). But the cold was there, like a message, as though something was caught unhappily between the plastic and the wall and needed attention.

There was a creeping feeling of something wanting to speak up there, metaphorically. A metaphor, that's what it was. Cheap walls, cheap intentions; life is cheap?

It somehow managed to look both modern and Gothic, the Gothic winning out atmospherically, in spite of the stack of cut drywall in the far corner, and the cheap, chipboard ceiling. The shadows spoke louder.

She was in and out as quickly as possible, and left the searched boxes open, the useless dreck of her lifetime spilling out on to the attic floor, once she'd found her typewriter.

The phone rang just as she was making her way down the stairs with the typewriter, which hadn't seen any action since college. She answered it on the third ring, brushing dust out of her hair frantically, thinking it to be cobwebs. (No matter how the attic looked, it seemed to be dark, and old like the loft in a barn or an old farmhouse, with bare wooden walls and beams exposed, creaking with things that hung suspended; there *seemed* to be spiders and rats and . . . nasty things.)

'Mrs Parkins, this is Richard Hadley from Middleton School. I'm Peter's principal.'

'Did something happen?' she said, alarmed. 'Is Petey all right?'

Mr Hadley cleared his throat. 'Well, there has been an incident,' he said, adding quickly that Petey was fine, but that he and two other boys had been sent to the office for fighting. He gave her the story in brief, calling it 'sport related', and adding that the fault seemed to have been both a misunderstanding and of equal blame. He stressed that there were no serious injuries, and reassured her that no one had been formally reprimanded, and that before they had left his office he'd made the boys involved shake hands.

'I thought, however, that you and I should talk about the incident, given that Peter is new to the school and the first few weeks are fairly critical in developing a niche,' he said.

Barbara, her back up, let it be heard in her voice: 'I'm not sure what you're saying.'

'Well, Peter has to find a way to fit in. To get along. Fighting in the first couple of weeks in school – and, according to one of the boys involved, this isn't his first incident – will build a certain kind of persona that we don't encourage . . .' He trailed off.

Barbara, confused, tried to muddle through what he had said. 'Are you implying that Petey is bullying?'

'All I'm saying, Mrs Parkins, is that we, as the school, and you, as the parent, have to take this incident as an opportunity to stress to Peter – is it *Peter* or *Petey* that he prefers?'

'Pe*ter*,' she said, reminding herself, quickly.

'That Peter makes the right choices regarding action. In short, we don't want him to develop a reputation for fighting, or for conflict on the playground.'

'I see. And did you make this same speech to the other boys' mothers?' Barbara frowned and held the telephone in a stiff grip.

'Peter is a new face in the school. My concern right now is for his educational experience as a whole. I want him – as I'm sure you do as well – to make his start at Middleton School a step in the right direction.' Then he added, like an afterthought, 'Have you ever considered a fitness programme for him?'

Barbara paused a long time, her face red with embarrassment for, and of, Petey. She pictured, briefly, the whole school turned against her boy. She was flustered.

'Mr Hadley, I would appreciate your calling the parents of the other boys involved. As for the other, that's none of your business. But it seems to me that because Peter is new at your school, then you should give him the benefit of the doubt. He's just a little boy,' she said, near tears. She took a deep breath and said, more softly, 'Petey's had a difficult year. A little compassion wouldn't hurt.' Then she hung up, afraid that if she didn't, she would start crying and make this whole thing something larger than it was. Creating memos and meetings at the school. She forgot to ask the names of the other boys, but wondered if they were the same boys from the other day, or if the whole school was populated with demons.

Barbara sat on the front step and waited for Petey to come home. It was just before four o'clock and the first really nice sunny day she could remember since moving in. Kids were just starting to come down the street, mostly teenagers. She saw few kids Petey's age.

A fitness programme.

Her blue Chevy station-wagon was parked across the street and kids disappeared behind it as they walked, emerging from the other side. The mid-size car looked smaller than it was compared to the mini-vans and SUVs that would be parked up and down the street after five o'clock. Right then it reigned supreme. She and Dennis had bought a Blazer several years earlier, but he'd got that, having claimed it pretty much as his own the day they'd brought it home. It had made sense at the time, of course, because he had done most of the driving, and also wanted the new vehicle for work. When she drove it was to take Petey somewhere or pick up groceries, or to go shopping. The cargo space in the station-wagon was better than the Blazer's. The station-wagon became 'hers', the Blazer 'his' (although both were in his name). She wished she had it now, so that at least her car would blend in the neighbourhood.

The neighbourhood appeared to be (*rife; riddled*) populated with families. Whether they were intact or blended she had no way of knowing, but she had pain-fully noted the absence of single moms waving goodbye to their children on the weekend, driving off in Daddy's car. She had noticed moms and dads working on the yard up and down the street last Saturday, cleaning garbage, raking fall and winter off the lawns, taking a break sitting on the front steps and porches. She'd been waved at a couple of times and once got a 'Welcome, neighbour,' from a woman walking across the street past her house, but the woman never stopped and Barbara did not see which house she had gone into, hadn't actually seen her since. So far no one had come over with a coffee cake or a handful of flyers or coupons or offers of babysitting. She was not offended by this, really: she knew people worked and neighbourhoods just weren't set up that way any more.

People were keeping their distance. Paranoid and self-serving as that thought was, it niggled at her like a sore tooth, something she couldn't help putting her tongue into from time to time. Even the children seemed to avoid walking past the house; they couldn't all live on the other side of the street, could they?

There's no daddy living there, Mommy.

Don't go there, that woman is divorced.

From the red front door, to her ageing car, to the daddyless front yard last weekend, everything about the Parkins house might appear different (although she was fairly sure that her five-year-old Chevy was worth more now than some of the cheap sports vehicles nosing their way up the street).

When these things went through her mind she couldn't help but think an equally unkind *they'll get theirs*, a suburban Cassandra in the middle of the calm. It surprised her, but she thought it just the same.

She was angry. The reason was less distinct than the emotion, and seemed to stem from all kinds of places inside her.

Fitness programme. She was really angry at that bastard principal, telling her her business. She had an image of him in her head, that wasn't far from right, a mealy little man, strutting around Middleton School. Maybe he would put Petey on probation until he lost a few pounds. Demote him or something. Bastard.

She was so angry. She needed to find a target for the anger before Petey got home. She was angry with Dennis for putting her there, for not being there to help her figure out what was wrong. To say something to Petey; to show a united front, not just to help him, but to show him that school wasn't the only place in the world. That he was special and loved. She couldn't do that all by herself. Dennis hadn't called in a week. What, exactly, was Petey supposed to make of that?

And me, I'm very angry with me. Shame shame; pull it together, girl.

Barbara was surprised at her feelings about Petey. They were a mix: of course, she was horrified that there had been another fight (of which she was sure he took the brunt) but that was enough. He couldn't go through school fighting. In that regard, as much as she hated to admit it, Mr Bastard Hadley was right. It was a new school and the things he did now would stick to him.

Last night she had promised he could call Jeremy back home. She was going to revoke that privilege (not for long, he could call tomorrow, but she wouldn't bring that up right away) as a means of showing him she meant business.

A Suburban passed the house, and the woman driving looked over at Barbara sitting on the steps. It pulled into a driveway about four houses up, on the other side. The first of the after-work arrivals. The two on either side of her didn't get home until six, sometimes later. Neither neighbour had children. She had caught a glimpse of the man on the west side. He was about fifty. Balding. She hadn't seen his wife, not really, just their other car driving away. Following the Suburban was a little Mazda. It belonged to the same house as the Suburban. She pictured the two of them kissing hello, surprised at being home so *early* together. They would cook supper together, maybe. And talk about their day. *What did they know about a day? She would tell them about a* day.

She tried to still some of the anger, the pointless, unnavigable anger inside her. Watching the neighbours wasn't helping.

She spotted Petey before he saw her.

He walked with his eyes peering at the sidewalk, looking up only occasionally, eyes swinging nervously from side to side and then down again. Her face, which had been stern, softened. Her heart went out to him and she got up off the bottom step and walked to the sidewalk to greet him.

'Hey,' she said. He looked up then, startled. He was so young. Dwarfed on the sidewalk, barren except for him and her. He was late.

'Hi,' he said. She opened her arm to catch him as he passed and she slipped it around his shoulders as the two of them walked up to the house.

She debated over what to say. She settled on, 'Got into a fight, huh?'

He shrugged. That coalesced all the unnavigable anger in her, for better or worse. Worse.

'Well, this is it, Peter Parkins.' She marched him into the living room. 'Sit,' she said, pointing to the sofa.

'Are you mad at me?' he asked, shocked.

'Mad at you? Mad? Yes, I'm mad. This is unacceptable. This is two fights in only a few days!' She stood above him, hands on hips, bending at the waist to emphasize her points. 'Do you think it's easy for me to start over? I have no one here helping me out! It's me and you. That's it, Petey. There's no one going to come and give us a hand here, we're on our own!' The anger spewed out of her, only partly directed at him.

Her voice got louder. 'We're supposed to be on the same side!' she shouted. 'You can't just go around fighting, the school calling me up in the middle of the damn day! I can't fix everything!' Petey stared at her in incomprehension. Briefly she noted his wide eyes, his slack mouth.

'I can't have this. We have to work together, that means you and me, both of us staying out of trouble, both of us trying to get along, both of us trying to make a go of things here, in our new life –'

'Mom –' he started, his voice quavering.

'Don't interrupt! You're grounded from calling Jeremy for two days, and I would like you to stay in your room until supper, got it?' Petey started to cry, and she softened some, but at the same time felt an irrational satisfaction. Her insides were shaking. She wanted to scream at him, wail at him until everything in the universe straightened out.

'Mom! Just let me tell you –' His face was red and he'd wrapped his arms around his middle as though for protection. He couldn't get the sentence out, but started bawling like a little kid (like a little kid falsely accused, the thought crossed her mind). Her heart went out to him and she was on the verge of crying again, too, and that brought up that *They'll get theirs* feeling of something giving. As though this situation was somehow going to be cathartic for both of them. Everyone needed a heads-up once in a while. This was his.

He's only eight. My god.

'I don't want to hear it. There is no excuse for all this fighting. You have to learn to get along. To fit in. Like I do. We both have to.' Shaking, worried that it was going to get worse, she strode away from him into the kitchen and whipped open the cupboard next to the fridge. She grabbed at the pudding cans there, the last two on the shelf, and then pulled a spoon out of the dish drainer beside the sink.

She went back into the living room, the break making her feel worse, somehow, her legs shaking with anger. Not at him. At this. Whatever 'this' was, it had less and less to do with Petey.

She shoved the cans at him, and the spoon, her face twisted into an angry shell. 'Go to your room till supper,' she said.

He stared at her, still crying. He opened his mouth to say something, but the look on her face made him stop. He took the puddings and the spoon and went upstairs.

Barbara collapsed on the sofa and cried.

He spooned pudding into his mouth, hardly tasting it over the salty tear taste, but letting the warm, soft feel of it fill his mouth for a second each time before swallowing. It felt good.

When the pudding filled the front of his mouth, he pressed his tongue into it until it spread out, over roof, over tongue, over teeth. He curled his tongue through it and then swallowed. It took about three seconds, and he did it every time. He was still crying a little, and every now and then he paused in his ritual to sniff. When his nose started to run he stopped completely (pleased because the break in the ritual meant that it would go on longer) and blew his nose. Then he started again.

God damn her.

He couldn't hear her crying. He was wrapped in his own misery so tightly that he was almost completely unaware of anything except the feel of the pudding in his mouth. It was chocolate.

He sat on his bed with his back to his closed door and contemplated his misery. His mom was so mad. She didn't even listen to him tell his side.

God damn her. Swearing was bad. So was she.

Petey was preternaturally aware of the second can of pudding on his dresser. Even as he emptied the tin he was eating, scraping the last bits from between the sides and the score on the bottom, he was aware of the other can. He licked the spoon clean and then traded the two, leaving the empty one on the dresser. The new tin opened with a satisfying *snick*. He licked the lid, dropping it on the bed when he was done.

He ate the second tin of pudding slower.

The window in his room overlooked the front yard. It was cracked open half-way, and he could hear the noise of the street. Traffic could be heard far away, on Macallum, the busy road where the grocery store was. Trees blocked his vision, but he could hear kids, not far, up the block. They would be playing road hockey. He knew that. They were older kids. He'd seen them. He squinted and tried to see them through the branches of the pine tree that dominated the front of the yard next to theirs. He thought he saw a stick in mid-air. The sun had dimmed behind a cloud and it looked more spring than summer. Probably it would rain. Wash out the field behind the school and no one would have to play soccer for a while. That would be good.

Then, out of the corner of his eye, he saw movement in his own yard. He looked into the corner, where the hedge turned. It was just budding, but even without the leaves it was thick.

Two children stood in the corner, looking up at him. He paused, spoon midway between tin and mouth, surprised.

His first thought was to duck out of sight. Not let them see him. But they were in the yard. His yard.

Instead, he shifted on to his knees and got closer to the window.

It was a little girl and a boy, the boy about his age. The girl was really little, like maybe four or five, coming up only to the boy's chest. He didn't recognize them from school or the block. He'd never seen them before. They were barefoot, their feet pale against the new sprouting grass. The little girl wore a dress that was too long for her and he couldn't make out the colour: it was like it was colourless, or grey even. The little girl raised her hand in a tentative wave. She was smiling.

Petey smiled back and raised his hand to wave back, the spoon coming up, vestiges of the last mouthful of pudding in ridges along its length.

The boy smiled back. He brought up his hand in what Petey thought was going to be a wave, but instead the boy gestured. *Over there.* He pointed to the other side of the yard. Petey looked. A grocery bag had blown up against the hedge and was held by sharp twigs, its edges fluttering. Garbage wrapped around the underside of the bushes. There was nothing there.

What?

When he looked back, the kids were gone.

He twisted his head to see as much of the hedge along the side of the house as was possible, but there was no sign of them. He opened his mouth to call them, trading glances between where the two had stood and where the boy had pointed. He stuck his head up close to the window, but they were gone.

They disappeared. He kept looking for them, twisting his head on his neck to see as far along the house as possible, but they were nowhere to be seen. They'd run away when he looked the other way.

Not enough time. His glance away from the hedge had been nothing, a shifting of his eyes.

They disappeared. Because they weren't there. His mind had played a trick. With unease, he turned away from the window. His eyes landed on his closed door.

He got up and opened it. He ate his pudding looking out into the hall, almost as if he was expecting to see something.

Barbara sat on the couch in the quiet living room for half an hour. She only cried for a few minutes, but the tears had served what the lashing-out at Petey had not: she had calmed down.

After several minutes of staring blankly out of the front window, looking barely out past the hedge, feeling both terrible and better, she got up. It was time to start supper.

The door to the goodie cupboard was still open. As

349

she went to shut it, mentally going over the preparations for dinner, she glanced inside.

What she saw: Kraft Dinner. Alphaghetti. Bugs 'n' Dirt. The space where the puddings had been was empty. A can of Pringles had been jammed into the back beside a jar of chocolate spread. Quik-drink mix. Kool-aid (with added sugar, no more measuring!). Even the tinned fruits were in syrup rather than juice.

She stared into the cupboard as though seeing the food for the first time. She reached in and pulled out a bag of Gummie Bears. The label said they were made with real fruit juice. The miniature boxes of juice also claimed (*claimed?*) to be made with real fruit. Weren't they? Weren't they *supposed* to be made of fruit? An opened bag on the bottom shelf spilled Reese's peanut-butter cups, only two left. When had she bought those? Saturday morning when she went for milk. Three mini-Oreo bags were missing, too, and those were supposed to be for lunches (but she didn't watch, did she?). The case of Coke she'd bought on Saturday was also nearly gone, and she'd bought those for herself. A bag of cookies had not been properly shut, and when she reached out to close it she found it empty. A whole *bag*! She hadn't had even one.

This was the form her mothering had taken.

Oh god I'm sorry I'm so sorry.

Barbara closed her eyes and pressed her forehead for a moment against the hard, cool edge of the pantry door, pressing until she could feel a mark forming. Her lips felt numb, her stomach/womb – something – full of stones. It lasted just a moment.

She could throw it away. Throw it out into the

garbage: that was what it was, after all. Junk. She could pull jars and bags and boxes and packets of sugar-laden, fat foods, useless but for the soothing quality of the fat as it rolled over your tongue and slid down your throat, kissing visceral boo-boos away when your mother was weeping in the bathroom with the door locked until supper. When your mother is sitting in her lawyer's office begging for some way to hurt *really hurt* your father. For when your mother stares at the wall for two hours, her mind a blank except for pain. Pain. Pain.

How many times had he come to her in the last year, when she sat in her fog. *Mom?* And she had looked up at him seeing not her son at all but Dennis's face. And how many times had she answered with, *I bought some ice cream would you like some?* How many trips to the grocery store had been for junk food? She herself had gained twenty pounds since that first horrible night that she'd learned about the affair. How many suppers had been canned spaghetti, Kraft Dinner, beans on toast with hot dogs, served singly because she had no appetite and it was easier to just open something for him? How many? How many nights had he eaten alone in the kitchen and where had she been? How many late nights had Barbara looked up from the television to find that a whole Sara Lee cake was gone? How many times had there been only half a cake to start with? How many times had she come across Petey in the kitchen, in front of the open fridge, spooning cake, ice cream, pudding into his mouth, a vague blank expression on his face, chewing incessantly . . . eyes half hooded in something akin to pleasure? Or maybe just a brief absence of pain.

Oh god. Fat kid they called him. Her fault.

She could throw it out.

Her eyes drifted away from the cupboard to the little window that looked out into the backyard. The tangles of bush and dead flowers that were there would bloom soon. There was a lot of work to be done in the yard. She could throw out all the junk, and they could start eating the right things. She could make Petey help her in the yard. They could go bike riding. She could talk him into Little League, or at least swimming lessons. She could start right that moment.

The kid had so few pleasures. *Cruel to be kind.*

Barbara closed the door on the pantry and started supper. Upstairs she heard water running into the tub, splashing as it hit what sounded like a half-full bath. A few seconds later the accustomed *pop!* of the plug, and the sound of water draining. She ignored it. They were having pork chops.

'Do any of the kids from school live on the street?'

Petey jumped. 'Huh?'

'Do any of the kids from school live here, on our street? Anyone you might like to invite over?' He stared at her, his forehead furrowed. She thought he was thinking about it. He was thinking about the kids he'd seen in the yard. He hadn't mentioned it to her. There had been little conversation.

Petey's grounding lasted only until supper time, and while she hadn't relented on calling Jeremy, she'd let him watch TV. He was watching *Sabrina the Teenage Witch*. It was a rerun. He hated it anyway.

'No,' he said slowly, after carefully judging her face,

deciding if she was trying to get him to tell her something. 'Nobody.'

In the dark of his bedroom, Petey dreamed.

Come play.

Peter stood at the edge of a wide field overgrown with witchgrass. It was summer, or at least the sun was high and bright: he could feel himself squinting against it, the corners of his eyes getting sore with the effort.

'Peter!' someone shouted. In the middle of the field a little girl waved. She smiled widely. The hand that waved held a bundle of grass that she had braided into a sheaf. *Come play!* she called. Other voices rang out. Singing? From behind the girl came an older boy. Peter shrank back, but the boy smiled and waved. *Come on!* he yelled. *You're missing it!*

He'd waved back, suddenly realizing he was smiling. They wanted him to join them. To come play. He started across the field, feeling the witchgrass slapping at his hands as he ran.

He topped a rise in the field and looked out over the expanse of grass. He felt like he could see for miles. The girl giggled and ran, waving him to follow. Behind her were other kids, all of them different ages. There was the older boy, maybe as old as twelve, and four other boys. There was only one girl, and she was about five. Her hair was wispy and soft like a baby's. Her dress reached to her knees and past, he couldn't really tell: the wind blew it every which way so that it never looked the same way twice.

Come play. Come play. The six of them formed a circle and chanted it. *Peter, come and play with us.*

He got over the rise and ran the rest of the way. The

circle broke to let him join in. The hands on either side of him were warm. On his left was the older boy, the leader of the group. 'We like you, Peter,' he said, and his voice was like singing.

They spun around in their circle, laughing when it made them dizzy.

The girl made a circlet of her braided witchgrass and put it over Peter's wrist. It was scratchy. 'If it itches, it means you love me,' she said coquettishly, although Peter didn't have a word for it. 'Does it itch?'

'Yes.'

'You can stay here for ever,' she said. He nodded happily. Yes. Yes.

They raced across the grass, the sting of it nice on his legs. He looked down at the grass, so tall, and wondered where they were, and saw that he wore his pyjamas and was embarrassed.

'It's okay,' one of the other boys said. *Ethan is his name*, Peter thought clearly. Ethan. He opened his arms as if to show Peter what he wore and Peter saw that his pants were too short and one knee was gone. It made Peter smile.

'Let's run!' The six of them ran together, collapsing in a pile.

'You can come all the time!' the little girl said. 'You can even bring your mama.'

The others nodded.

From far away there was a booming sound. The six children looked up when it sounded. They jumped up. Peter didn't.

'We have to go!' said the oldest boy, Jack. The girl was Mariette. They ran away.

Come back! he shouted. They turned and looked, but only waved. They were all smiling at him. They were disappearing into the distance while Peter lay in the deep grass, trying hard to follow them with his eyes because he could not move.

Your mother is calling you, he heard Mariette say, deep in his ear, even though she was a speck in the distance. *Your mama is calling.*

'Time to get up, Peter.'

He opened his eyes to morning and the smell of witchgrass in his bedroom.

There were three jobs in Monday's paper that Barbara thought she might have a shot at.

She took over one end of the long dining-room table, a fresh package of printer paper – she wasn't even sure they sold typing paper any more, but the twenty-year-old clerk had assured her that they were one and the same – opened next to her portable typewriter from college. Among the things stashed in the attic she had found a dried-up bottle of white-out, useless, and correct-it tape, also likely dried out, but she wasn't about to scour the city searching for antiquities. She would just have to be careful, and accurate.

Two of the ads were her 'safe bets': they were in childcare. At the very least, she could claim eight years' experience. Her work history over the last ten years was sketchy to non-existent. She didn't even have a résumé, résumés not being a necessary requirement in the volunteer sector. That was all she was going to have for previous experience, and she was smart enough to know how to play it up. She'd had some good volunteer positions, including an impressive year during which she (almost) single-handedly organized the 'Festival of Learning', a combination career-symposium-cum-adult-education-cum-elder-learning weekend at the community centre in their neighbourhood the year Petey turned three. She would see what she could make of that. The other job was slightly more interesting, a part-time secretarial position in a church office only a couple of blocks from the house. That would not only be more interesting than the day-cares, but also was close enough (and had boasted 'flexible hours') so that her own childcare requirements might be nil. It would be ironic if she had to hire childcare during the week so that she could care for other people's children, but she had to do something.

There was twenty thousand dollars in savings and another two thousand in checking. She had some mutual funds, and other small investments, and Petey's child support was just under five hundred dollars a month. All of it was adequate for now, but not for long. She had to get a start, some experience, so that she could move on. Work was good for a person.

The typewriter was a very old manual, and in addition to her poor, mostly forgotten manual skills, she noted with dismay how old-fashioned and small the letters were, as made by the keys. The secretarial ad had suggested that a knowledge of computers was an asset, but not essential. She hoped that meant she didn't have to have a home computer to qualify. While she wasn't exactly computer illiterate, she had rarely used theirs when she'd had the opportunity. Dennis had got the computer.

Does he have a jewellery box, personal drawer, something like that? The morning after Dennis had left, after Petey had gone to school so that he wouldn't see his dad walking out with a suitcase and have to explain, Barbara got on the phone to Debra, hysterical by then, having watched Dennis leave without so much as a backward glance. In fact, his very walk to the car had seemed . . . jaunty.

Right from the start Deb had insisted there was another woman. Barbara, smug and foolish, had claimed vehemently that he would never do that, bolstered with a petulant, and in retrospect, naïve *I would know*.

She underscored her name on the résumé and decided after the fact that she should have centred it. She yanked the paper out and carefully added another sheet, beautiful, clean, white and centred and underscored her name; then she centred her address, 362 Belisle Street. It looked strange and unfamiliar on the page.

There had been nothing in his drawer or in the little wooden box that Barbara had given him for Christmas around the time Petey was four. Debra stayed on the phone and coached her through the little pieces of paper, the search through the jacket pockets of his suits, his shoeboxes on the floor in the back of the closet, and made her shake books from his side of the bed table. She was astounded at the variety of hiding places Debra came up with, and began, by osmosis almost, to feel suspicious herself. She would never have thought to look in his books. What a tremendous hiding place they would have made. But there had been nothing.

What else has he got that's only his, that only he uses?
She filled in her education, excluding her dates of

graduation, a moot point since she had added her date and year of birth. She toyed with the idea of starting over again, putting her vitals (other than the pertinent like her address) at the end of the résumé, after she'd dazzled them with her abilities.

What else has he got that's only his, that only he uses?

Debra had walked her through the downstairs, more coat pockets, old briefcases, his knapsack that he took to the gym; when she told her to look inside his winter boots, she drew the line, feeling that Debra – her friend – *wanted* her to find something incriminating when there was nothing. After an hour on the phone, an hour of sticking her hand into the most absurd places, growing more and more suspicious, more and more frightened – as much as by what she was doing as what she was looking for – she finally got off the phone, pleading an appointment and offering the promise that she would call a lawyer, 'just to see'.

What else has he got that's only his, that only he uses?

The ad for the day-care closest to the house on Belisle had said that electronically transmitted applications were acceptable before the fourteenth. Email.

Dennis was an LPP guy: little pieces of paper. There had been dozens of them found in her search through his things. None of them had any meaning for her, all pertaining, she suspected, to work: indecipherable things that said, '110 bcu. 120', and appointment notes, all men's names, likely work-related since they were all daytime hours. Debra was disappointed each time they found one.

She'd been a computer widow one long year, when Petey was about six. Dennis had bought a brand new computer 'for the family' that Christmas and was enamoured. He'd spent hours every evening after Christmas playing with it, and when the initial thrill abated, he continued to use it religiously, for work, she assumed, and had taught both her and Petey some basic uses. Petey played computer games, becoming easily bored with the Step 1–2–3 to Grade Two! types of games that Dennis bought for him. Slowly, over the year, it became Dennis's toy.

Barbara tried to jot down some notes on her work experience on a piece of the printer paper beside the typewriter. She got lost several times. She started again.

The password had been easy enough to find: Dennis was an LPP guy. It was written on a Post-it tucked on the bottom of the keyboard. That hadn't exactly been detective work. She had seen him do it. She'd asked him what it was.

The password got her into the programs. On the bottom of the computer screen there was a little symbol of a letter. She only vaguely understood the concept of email, had certainly never sent one and didn't know the mechanics of how it worked, even, but it really was point-and-click – who'd have thought? – and from there it was easy enough to decipher in-box from out-box and so on. It took a little longer to figure out 'sent'.

The pen was still in her hand, but by then Barbara was staring off into space, her face slack with remembered disbelief and the hurt. The terrible hurt. Real physical pain. A bone breaking. She'd curled up into a ball, clutching her stomach in very real pain on the floor of the office and let out a wail. Without warning, everything she had eaten the night before and that morning, mostly nothing, a piece of toast and a couple of sips of coffee, came rushing up and she vomited right there on the spot, some of the vomit hitting her hand, warm and horribly wet. The taste of it in her mouth forced her up off the floor and into the bathroom. She rinsed her mouth and bent over the toilet and threw up again. Off and on, for an hour, until her sides hurt, her throat burned, and her jaw ached from being forced open so wide, so often.

She pressed her eyes tightly shut, trying desperately to get the memory out of her head. Finally she curled her hands into fists and closed them so hard for so long that it became distracting. Did it until it hurt. That helped.

Ancient history.

She wrote two sentences about organizing the Festival of Learning, and then gave up. Just for a little while she would do something else. It would all fade in a half-hour or so, she knew from experience. She wondered, ironically, if she could add 'effective knowledge of electronic mailing', to her special skills. Wouldn't that be a kicker?

It was several hours before she sat back down at the typewriter and worked on her résumé in earnest, putting behind her the memories of what was ancient history. In between she cleaned her house.

The sun was bright again, for several days in a row. It poured in through the windows on the south side of the house, lighting the hall and making even the bathroom, with its menacing and mysterious tub, seem benign. She flung open the windows in all the rooms and let spring-summer inside. It cheered her considerably.

When she was downstairs collecting her dust mop, she put on a CD. Dusty Springfield. She sang along.

Even the sad songs were okay, buffered as they were by her own ignorance of the lyrics and the whole first floor.

Petey had left the empty tins of pudding on his dresser, along with the spoon. Otherwise, his room was tidy, if (probably) dirty. She moved everything out of the way for her mop, pushing the dresser away from the wall and retrieving two mismatched socks and a Matchbox car, before dusting behind it. Motes of dust flew everywhere, in spite of the spray of oil soap she gave her mop. She rolled up his little rug and left it in the hall for later shaking. Under his bed there were a number of books and two empty wrappers from the peanut-butter cups, and pyjama bottoms that she had thought were in the wash. She stepped on a piece of Lego, shrieking with pain when it dug into her arch. Lego was deadly. All in all, she was in a good mood.

She would get one of the jobs, of that she was certain. She hoped for the secretarial thing, but would take the childcare work. If nothing panned out – a pointless exercise in futility, that sort of thinking – she would apply for a cashier's job at any number of the stores just blocks from the Belisle house. She felt like there were (suddenly) endless options.

The worst parts done, under the bed, behind, under the dresser, she turned her attention to the rest of the floor and gave it a once-over, pausing now and then to rub at something with the cloth she kept with her for tougher marks. She would have to come back for two: a dust-coated splash of what looked to be dried apple juice and an unidentified blue mark that scraped off – partly, with her thumbnail.

Barbara was just on her way to the bathroom, for a

sturdier cloth and some chemical elbow grease, when she saw yet another mark on the floor that hadn't been swept away with the mop, noticeable only with the sun shining on it. She backed up a step or two and tried finding it again. When she did, she knelt down for a better look. It was alongside the cubbyhole door.

It was a footprint. That in itself wasn't strange – she had found a footprint beside the apple-juice mark, but it had apparently been covered in a sock at the time – except that this footprint was substantially smaller than the sock print. She looked closely at it, putting her hand down beside it, wondering if it was some sort of optical illusion. But no, it was small. It was smaller than the length of her hand, practically a toddler's footprint. And complete. She could count all five toes.

She looked at it for a long time.

Eventually she shrugged. She hadn't washed all the floors when they'd moved in. Obviously a small child had looked at the house with its parents before Barbara and Petey. She/he had left their mark. (She just hoped they hadn't stepped in pee or something disgusting before they'd done it, the nasty germs that might have been left.)

She got up off the floor and went and got a cloth. She rubbed the mark away easily. She finished her dusting of the floor and, for no good reason at all, was reminded of the night she heard Petey sleepwalking.

The footprint had been facing outward. As though leaving the closet.

My mother's dead.

That's terrible.

By the time she was once again ready to work on her résumé – *no bad thoughts allowed!* – she was feeling pumped and in control. The upstairs sparkled. If she finished the résumé in time, she could stop at the copier's, get several made and be back in time to do the same for the downstairs. Dusty Springfield was on her third tour when she sat back down to the typewriter.

Everything was going to be fine.

There are no alleyways all the length of Belisle Street; it is one of the few distinctions of the neighbourhood. Instead of an alley, Belisle and its backyard sister, Harrod, are separated by a copse of birch trees that have been standing for as long as anyone can remember. Most of the houses have back gardens, whether planned or the very opposite. A great many of the homeowners over the years have put up fences that run the length of their property, protection against the small animals that make the mini-forest their home. A narrow path has been beaten down from the time of the first child to live there, and so the 'back way' is passable, but only on foot. Branches and the unpredictable undergrowth have made even bike riding inadvisable. Every few years a neighbour gets up a petition to turn the back way into a real alley, wanting to park his car and bring in his groceries in anonymity. So far, they have all given up. Cars are parked in driveways or on the street; garbage and recycling is toted out front, deliveries, moving vans and guests all enter and exit through the front street; neighbours with a tendency towards embarrassment have learned to ask for paper instead of plastic.

There was a good four feet on the east side of the

house, between it and the hedge. When Petey got home from school, he looked anxiously towards the side of the house, as though expecting to see something there, then ran up the steps and inside. It was a cool place, he bet. He hadn't spent any time exploring the yard, at all.

He dumped his backpack on the floor. He listened for his mom, and, after a second or two of hearing the unfamiliar *tap tap tap*, he poked his head around the archway between the hall and the living room and saw her at the end of the dining-room table, pecking away at the keys of her little typewriter, her forehead crunched in concentration.

She heard him. 'Hey, baby,' she said, distractedly.

'Hi.'

'I'm just typing up my résumé, I'll be done in a couple of minutes. How was school? School okay?'

Petey mumbled something that she didn't catch and she looked up quickly, and he could almost see her doing a quick assessment in her head. Clothes unsoiled, face clean of dirt and tears, no pinched look (no more than usual), and she smiled swiftly, and bent her head back over the keyboard. She resumed her awkward pecking until the carriage bell rang. She wiggled her shoulders and glanced back at him once more with a satisfied smile.

'I might just get this right,' she said.

'I'm going out in the yard, 'kay?' he said.

'Okay. Don't go far. Dinner in an hour or so.'

The pecking started again, just as Petey closed the door.

It was still nice out, although the sun had been hidden behind clouds for most of the afternoon and it looked like it might rain. Petey pulled his jacket down over his belly – it was getting too small, but he didn't want to say anything to his mom because mostly it was getting too small in the *front*, and that was about being a *husky kid* and he didn't want to talk about it – and stepped off the small stoop, standing on the sidewalk for a heartbeat, as though establishing his presence. He took a deep, manufactured breath, then ducked his head covertly and headed towards the side of the house.

The grass was just starting to turn green. The sidewalk went around the other side of the house to the backyard, so there was no path between the east side of the house and the sidewalk. Petey took big steps as though wanting to disturb the earth as little as possible. It was different at the side of the house, though. It was narrow and dark between the hedge and the house. The house next door had only one window along that side, at the top. Petey's house didn't have any windows on the west side of the house, and for a little bit that fascinated him. The houses all looked so much the same he hadn't considered that they might be different. His mom's room, the biggest in the house, had a window on the east side. He could see it – although not *in* it, he was too close to the house – if he looked up from where he stood. Maybe the neighbours' house had an opposite layout? He compared the two houses in the most casual way, a thoughtful, responsible expression on his face, a look of casual curiosity. Then he got to business.

It was nice and private with the hedge.

Petey bent down in a crouch, resting on his heels, mindful that the ground was wet. The hedge hadn't grown through yet, but was so old and thick and tangled with branches that he had to squint and tilt his head to see clearly through to the other yard. In a month, the hedge would be green and thick with little pale yellow flowers. They'd had one just like it at their old house. He even knew how it would smell. He and Jeremy used to eat the buds when they were small. They tasted sweet.

He looked over to the back corner of the garden, of which he had a perfect view, where he had seen the two children yesterday.

A big rock was directly in the path between the house and the hedge. He gave it a push until it turned over. A fat slug, grey and wet-looking, was stuck to the bottom. He nudged it with his finger. It gave slightly like a bogey, but didn't move. He rolled it over with his finger and it complied. It left behind a smear of bogey-like stuff. He wrinkled his nose. He was a beetle man.

He looked over to the corner of the garden.

The slug woke up enough to move its body in a rippling motion. Petey knew that it wasn't moving but heating itself up. He prodded it gently with his finger. There was no reaction. He peered at the ground, broken and raw, where the rock had pulled loose. There were no bugs yet, but a number of little white tubular things were scattered in the black dirt. Larvae. They were probably beetles.

As if predetermined, he reached out and grasped the rock slowly, his eyes turning up at the same time, in one fluid motion. In a preternaturally slow movement, he pulled the rock back into place and found his mark in the backyard.

And they were there.

Two of them. The little girl and the boy about his

own age. They were barefoot. The little girl wore a dress that was too long for her and you couldn't tell what colour it was.

'*Come and play,*' the boy said. If the girl had said it, Petey might have hesitated. But because it was the boy (and somehow, because they were barefoot) he went.

He stood up on legs that had decided at the last minute to shake. He walked the length of the house, a child's natural suspicion apparent in his posture, eagerness and curiosity on his face. He jumped over the rock, and then over some brush and debris from previous years, previous owners, and in the seconds it took to go the length of the house, the two children had disappeared behind the trees and brush that grew randomly along the back garden.

'Hey!' Petey said, but he felt like he'd shouted it and was embarrassed. The words were absorbed into the trees, the garden, the air.

He heard the little girl giggle. They were in the garden, hiding.

It was a tangle of overgrowth and perennials. It was thick. While he wouldn't have estimated its size, it was well over eight feet deep. Large backyards (and the lack of an alleyway) were a feature that only this neighbourhood could boast. The only feature. He couldn't see the children through it.

When he was at the edge of the garden, hesitating, he called another trepidatious 'Hey!', half expecting at any moment to be pelted with dirt, rocks, epithets.

Hey fat kid. He stood with his hands in the pockets of his (too small in front) jacket, and waited for it.

The little girl poked her head through the brush and

waved. *Come play*. She giggled. She laughed. Her whole posture was laughter, even when not a sound came out of her mouth. Her skin was white, and so was her hair. The boy – and Petey thought he might be her brother, for no reason at all – was fair too.

He ran through the small opening between the garden in their yard and the back way, made by boys just his age over the years, and found them.

When Barbara finally looked up from her typewriter she was shocked to see that it was already after five o'clock. It had taken nearly two hours to type three letters and her résumé. She hoped they didn't give her a typing test. Did they still do such things?

There had been no word from Petey. He was still outside.

She got up from the dining-room table and allowed herself a great stretch. On the floor beside her chair there were a half-dozen balled-up pieces of paper. Probably not a great ratio, but the three letters and her résumé were absolutely error-free. She shuffled through each again, marvelling at the tidiness of the pages and the facts of her life written, literally, in black and white. It didn't seem to amount to much. She piled the pages beside the type-writer and picked up the little balls from the floor. Cradled in her blouse, they looked like snowballs.

Tomorrow she would go to the library and make copies of the résumé, pick up envelopes and then deliver all three by hand. Maybe she would get an interview on the spot. She would wear her yellow suit, the one she'd bought for Dennis's cousin's wedding, about two months before he left her.

Don't start. Instead, she wondered if it would still fit.

She started supper, expecting Petey to come through the door at any moment. She cooked efficiently and by rote, one ear half cocked for the sound of the door.

They were having spaghetti. With a practised motion, she pulled a frying-pan out of the bottom drawer of the stove and plunked it on a burner. Oil went in, and after a suitable waiting period of a nanosecond inspired by the notion that it was already after five, she put the meat in the oil and cut up an onion.

The onion went into the frying-pan with the meat. Its smell filled the kitchen in a good way and she realized she was hungry. She picked up the garlic, and peeled it, the smell sharp in her nose – *oh geez I'm hungry Petey must be starv*– wondering then, where was he?

In the yard. Did he say he was playing in the yard?

Garlic peeled but still in her hand, she pulled open the heavy back door and peered through the dirty glass of the screen door. Just as she was going to push it open and call for him, Petey came bursting through the tangled mess of the garden, boughs and limbs grabbing at his jacket. He stumbled at the edge, into the dirt and scrambled up again. Alarmed, hand on the door, she would have jumped out screaming for him, but he was laughing. His broad face was split in an open-mouthed laugh, and he looked behind him, twisting his neck and shoulders just once before getting on to the grass and stopping. He crouched, hands on knees, and breathed heavily from his run. He faced the bush.

She watched, smiling, with him, for whoever it was who chased him.

No one came out after him. Petey dropped to the

grass on his back. Dead leaves and twigs clung to his jacket and jeans. He tugged down the front of his jacket, but his T-shirt had pulled up and she could see the white flesh of his stomach. *That jacket's too short.* It had lasted only one season. Boys grow.

He lay on his back on the grass a moment, then rolled on to his side, his body facing the house. Still smiling, his cheeks red from the fresh air and exertion, he steadied himself with a hand pressed to the ground.

Still no one had come out of the garden. *He's playing by himself.* The thought made her suddenly very sad, the laughter false, an attempt at cheering himself up, maybe. Playing alone. Her heart sinking, she decided she would let him phone Jeremy that night after supper.

Hand on the small, cold handle of the screen door, she was about to push it open, when she saw, but did not hear, Petey say something. Into the air.

His lips moved, eyes focused on something in front of him. He jutted out his chin, exposing the soft flesh of his neck.

Do you like butter?

As quickly as he'd done it, he tucked his chin fully into his jacket as though something had tickled him. Then he ran two fingers under there and looked at them as though expecting to see something.

Do you like butter?

'PETEY!' Barbara pushed open the screen door and called him, her voice near a screech. He looked startled and sat up, glancing just once to his side. A guilty look might have crossed over briefly.

'What?'

'Time to come in,' she said, voice shaking. 'Supper time.'

He scrambled up on his feet then, joyfully she thought (not the least bit embarrassed), and ran to the back door, not looking back again, exactly, but slightly turning his head in that direction in a way that disturbed her even more than what she thought she might have seen.

She held the door open and he squeezed past her. 'What's for supper?' he demanded, dropping his jacket to the floor and kicking off his running shoes. One landed at the narrow wooden door to the Murphy bedroom.

'Pick up your jacket, pick up your shoes,' she said. She pulled the screen door shut and closed the heavy wooden door. She locked it, and looked once more out of the window. The backyard was empty.

'What's for supper?' Petey poked his head over the stove and lifted the lid, looking at her inquiringly. 'Spaghetti?' he asked hopefully.

Barbara crossed her arms over her chest, chilled from the open door. 'Yup,' she said.

Petey gave a whoop of delight and ran into the living room. In a moment she heard the TV prattling.

Shaken, she lifted the lid and poked at the hamburger meat browning. She turned up the element. The garlic. It was still in her hand. It was warm. She put it on the counter and began chopping it into small pieces to put in the presser.

For just a split second, she thought she'd seen something.

Just as Petey looked at his fingers, he had half glanced beside him. So had Barbara.

Trick of the light.

When he'd glanced beside him, like a single frame of film in a movie, there had been a flash of something.

Beside him there had been a little girl. (Not *a* little girl; *the* little girl. *My mother's dead.*) She'd been holding a buttercup.

Trick of the light. For the first time since their first night in the house, the house that had begun to feel like home felt strange.

Over dinner, she asked him. 'Who were you playing with outside?' She kept her voice cheerful.

He didn't look up from his spaghetti. 'No one.'

'Oh,' she said. 'I thought I heard kids.'

Petey shrugged.

'You were playing by yourself? All that time?'

He looked at her sideways, under the cover of his thick lashes; a sly look, her mother might have said. He didn't answer right away, the hesitation equally suspicious. 'Uh-huh.'

He slurped a long piece of spaghetti into his mouth, the sauce splashing off it around his mouth. 'Petey, don't do that, you'll get it on my papers.' The typewriter and her stack of letters and the résumé sat undisturbed at the end of the table.

'Want me to move them?' he asked, looking up finally.

'No. Just don't eat like a little piggy.'

''Kay.'

Barbara didn't press him and he seemed preoccupied much of dinner. She told him about her job prospects and rambled on about what she would do if she got a job, about whether or not he would be home alone and, finally, what she was probably going to wear. His responses were monosyllabic.

'Are you okay, honey? You seem awfully quiet. Maybe there's something you want to talk about?'

He shook his head. 'No.'

'You're not saying anything, though.'

'I just said something,' he said indignantly. Barbara sighed and gave up.

'Can I phone Jeremy tonight? Is my punishment over?' he said suddenly, animated for the first time since coming inside.

Even trying to listen and not listen at the same time, Barbara only heard half of the conversation. It was typical. After the initial awkward hellos and stiff how-are-yous, they made noises and laughed and made more mouth noises. Jeremy must have started on some kind of team because Petey said, 'Did you score?' and listened without saying anything for a long time while, she supposed, Jeremy regaled him with a story. Once everything sounded normal, Barbara's mind wandered away from the conversation. The television was still on and she cleared the table half listening to the news, half listening to the conversation, the words filtered through her mother's radar, listening mostly to the emotions behind them. Jeremy seemed to do most of the talking, Petey answering him in much the way he'd answered Barbara at supper, with one word, or commented, *Oh, yeah?* There was a lot of giggling and (hand covering the phone) secret messages passed – likely on Jeremy's side as well – and more mouth/animal noises.

The call was long-distance and after Petey had been talking for a half-hour she went into the hall. He was sitting on the bottom stair, with the phone cord curled around the banister.

'No *way*,' he said into the phone. There was a garbled answer on the other end.

He repeated, 'No *way*.' It went on for another five *no ways* before she got his attention. He looked up at her, wide-eyed, and covered the mouthpiece with his hand. 'I'm talking on the phone,' he stressed, in a remarkable imitation of her. She rolled her eyes, smiling. She tapped her watch and gave him five fingers.

'*Okay*,' he said. Then he said, into the phone, '*Way*,' and there were hilarious giggles.

She watched television from the dining-room table while she packed up her papers and typewriter, finally looking at her watch again. Five minutes was *way* up. What the hell could two eight-year-olds talk about for so long?

Just before the hall she heard, '– yeah, a couple.' Then silence. There had been a change in his voice. It was neither defensive nor matter-of-fact, but somewhere between. He said, 'Around here.' And 'They're really great,' between silences. Her heart thumped a little in her chest. He was talking about kids and there was just enough fuel in the air for her to believe that he was talking about friends. From school?

'– this guy and his sister. When can you come and sleep over?' he asked, and it sounded to Barbara like a subject change.

Then Petey volunteered Barbara to pick Jeremy up for the big sleep-over and she went into the hall. 'Petey, five minutes are up. Say goodbye to Jeremy.' And she stood waiting for him to do it.

'Can you pick Jeremy up, so he can sleep over?'

'I'm sure I can. But we'll talk about it later.' He whooped and repeated what she said into the phone; then he asked her again, *when?*, but she eyed him menacingly and the commiseration sounded like it was about to start and Barbara was losing patience.

'Enough, Petey. It's bathtime.' And he hung up, reluctantly, with a whispered, 'I'll talk her into it.'

And he tried, all the way up the stairs. She reminded him that he would see Jeremy very soon, when he went to visit his dad in their old city. Petey snorted. 'Dad's never going to come get me,' and it stung. She knew she should defend Dennis, it was in every child-of-divorce book available, but she found she couldn't. He had called only once since they had moved in, and then not a word. She supposed he thought he was giving them time to settle in and whatever else he could convince himself of, but he still hadn't called and it was hard to explain that away to a little kid. Instead, what she said was, 'You want bubbles with that?' in her best McDonald's voice.

'No,' was his answer.

She sent Petey to his room to pick out pyjamas and strip down. He surprised her by closing the door to his room to do it. He was getting private. He was about that age.

The tub was gleaming and white in the false light of the bathroom bulb. Its claws dug into the floor, looking as though they had sprung outward with her approach. Silly.

Boldly she grabbed the plug – an old friend by now, she'd examined it for any sort of fault that might cause it to plug and unplug itself, in her weaker moments –

and pushed it firmly into the hole. Then she turned the hot tap on, full blast, and while the tub filled she got a clean towel for Petey and laid out shampoo and soap for him.

He came out with his robe on, tied at the middle in a huge bow. She smiled, amused.

'You ready, Hef?'

'Huh?' he said, flashing her a rude look, understanding, if not the joke, the intent.

'Never mind, pile in. You want me to go?'

He bent over and checked out the claws on the feet of the tub. 'They look real, hey?'

'But they're not. How about I do something in the yellow room while you bath? Would that be best?'

He stood in front of the tub, robe still intact as if waiting for her to leave. 'Uh-uh. That's okay. Go downstairs, okay? I'll have my bath and tell you when I'm done.' He looked behind her, into his room.

She followed his gaze. There was nothing there. 'You forget something?'

He shook his head. ''Kay, go now, Mom. Okay?'

'You don't want me to wash your hair? Do your back? Rotate your tyres?'

'*No*.' He sounded annoyed and she frowned.

'Okay, okay, okay – I'm going. Call me if you need anything.' And she shut the door behind her as she went.

Petey hurried through his bath, giving only casual consideration to the big angry feet on the bottom of the tub. There was something bad about the tub and Petey knew and accepted that in the way that no adult would have, or would even have understood. He washed his hair, not pausing to make it into a soapy crown the way he usually did. Instead, he soaped up and lay on his back, swishing his head back and forth to rinse it good. He lingered just a second, enjoying the warm water that he sloshed over his tummy and tried to fit himself in such a way that his whole body was under water at the same time and found he could no longer do that. He was too tall. That made him smile. He would be nine, next birthday. He sat up and pushed the hair out of his eyes. The floating white mountains of soap were destroyed by giant hands and feet, but not all of them. He was in a hurry.

The sooner he was done with his bath, the sooner he could get back into his room. He was sure they would come. Maybe all of them.

They had a secret. They had promised they would tell him.

Soon.

3

Barbara was checking her lipstick in the little mirror in the living room when the phone rang. She pursed her lips and debated answering it. She was ready to head out. It had been a terribly busy morning. First she'd had to drag Petey out of bed. Then she'd quickly dressed and run down to the library and copied her résumé (six copies . . . too optimistic?) and each of the letters, for her records. Then she'd come home, typed the addresses and attentions on envelopes and carefully, with the reverence due a minor god, she folded each letter and résumé and sealed them in the proper envelopes. Then she had a shower and put on her second-nicest outfit – she'd decided to save the pretty suit for the actual interviews, assuming she wouldn't get interviews today – and she was ready to go.

The answering-machine was not yet hooked up. She needed a battery for the clock, which she would pick up on her way home, so that if she did get any calls about the jobs and she was *in the yard at the store in the can* she wouldn't miss it. But it was not hooked up yet, and the phone jangled at her.

It could be school. Petey hurt or in a fight. She answered it on the fifth ring.

'I was starting to think you weren't home.' His voice was so familiar, so very familiar, that it actually took a second for her to place it, as though it was gauzy, behind a curtain. *Barbara Parkins, do you remember* this *voice from* your *past?* Barbara froze speechless.

'Barbara? It's Dennis,' he said.

'Hullo.' Her face felt stiff and doughy at the same time. Her cheeks felt cold as though the phrase *the colour drained from her face* wasn't a cliché at all, but happening then, to her.

'So, uh, how are you?' She swallowed before answering. Her voice sounded weak.

'I'm fine.' *I don't care how you are. Got herpes yet?*

There was a pause at the other end as though he was as uncomfortable (impossible) as she was. In a strange way, she wanted him to speak, to hear his voice again.

'Petey's at school,' she said.

'I know that.' He was calling from his office: in the background she could hear the clatter of the open room. She heard him close a door – his – and then it was quieter. 'I'm actually calling to talk to you.'

Her heart did a little flip, even as she pushed it down. It was not about *that*, but her stomach ignored her and got hard, acidy.

'Oh,' was all she managed.

He cleared his throat. 'This isn't . . . easy for me. At all. I want you to know that.' His voice softened and she wondered, *Is he talking about the divorce ohmigod?* and then he sniffed and cleared his throat again.

'Are you crying?' she asked suddenly.

He laughed. 'No. Got a little cold coming on, I think. Went skiing of all things, last weekend. My ass hurts, too.' He laughed again.

She gave her head a shake. *Skiing?* He'd never taken her skiing. She felt suddenly tired, as if his voice had the power to drain her of all her energy and good intentions. 'What do you want, Dennis? You didn't call to tell me you went skiing, did you?' She couldn't keep the sarcasm out of her voice. If he had wanted her back, she supposed he wouldn't now. It was all moot anyway. She hated him. His voice was draining her. She hoped he died from his cold. Hoped it escalated into a venereal disease.

There was a long pause during which she had time to think more vile things of him. She searched her mind as to what he wanted and assumed that it was either to cut off her alimony or child support or to see Petey on the weekend.

'I don't know how –' and then, in the space before he said that it was much, much more than that, in her gut she knew it was going to be something LARGE, whether it was the breath he took next or the stiff sound behind his bluff.

'I'm getting married.' And then an explosion from somewhere internal complete with flashing, blinding light behind her eyes, squeezed shut tight, she couldn't breathe, couldn't, wouldn't speak (*what to say?*) and pain, never well-buried, came. Her face hurt, a sting like a wasp, her nose stopped up and she had to open her mouth to let air inside, it didn't come in and she wanted to gasp –

'Are you okay?'

She didn't answer, couldn't think of a single word to say. Her lip started to quiver and her eyes filled with tears and she was angry and scared. Everything hurt and she still couldn't breathe. Finally, she gasped at the air, and it sounded like a deep, annoyed breath. She believed that.

'Barb?'

'Remarried,' she said, finally.

'Yes, well –'

Tears ran down her cheeks. *I'll have to redo my makeup.* One dangled from her chin and dripped on to the collar of her blouse.

'Well, I don't know. Say something,' he said weakly.

You're a dirty lying asshole bastard I hope you rot in hell I hope your bitch is barren I hope you get cancer Aids herpes mono –

'Is it her?' It came out cracked, fearful.

'Her who?' he said, but she knew from his voice that they both knew *her who*, and that it was.

'I have to go.' She pulled the phone from her ear and was about to slam it down when she heard him yell, 'Wait! I need to ask you something else . . .'

Too weak to refuse, too weak-stupid to give up hope, *ha ha just kidding let's get back together,* she put the phone slowly back up to her ear.

She made a sound into the mouthpiece. It was all she could do.

'I want Petey to come this weekend. I'll come and get him. I want him to meet Phyllis. I know this is short notice, but I know he'll want to come and, I mean, let's be adult about this. It's time. You know what I mean?'

Her name was Phyllis. All this time I didn't even know her name.

'Phyllis,' she said.

Dennis sounded relieved, maybe just to hear his beloved's name. 'Yeah, that's right. Phyllis is her name. You'll really like her – I do want us to be okay with this, Barb –' he said more, but Barbara never heard it. She hung up the phone and bounded up the stairs, trying to run, to run away from the phone, in a blind panic. Not blind. She made it as far as half-way up and then collapsed in a heap, sobbing, screaming, wailing her pain out to the house, the wails and sobs bouncing off the walls and coming back to her. She was blasted with the sound of her own pain.

For nearly an hour she stayed like that, until the wails subsided into sobs.

Once, under the stairs, from in the Murphy bedroom, her wail was echoed with another scream, one of a different kind of pain. Wrapped in a shroud, a veil of tears, she heard nothing. Not the scream and not the low, single bar of music that played right after. She also didn't hear the little patter of footsteps in the room above her. Or the creak of a rope scraping against a beam in the attic.

She didn't hear any of it. She was a wall of pain and nothing broke through.

Once a week in the afternoon, Mr Casem, the big gym teacher whose voice sounded mad even when he wasn't, taught Good Health to June Waddell's grade three class. During this period, Mrs Waddell would retire to the staff room to mark papers and complain about grade three. Her most recent application to the high school had been rejected and Mr Waddell was not thrilled with the prospect of his wife either spending a year away from him in another city to teach grade anything after eight, or with uprooting himself and moving somewhere for a job of hers.

Mr Waddell was a senior city clerk in the water

department, who never brought his work home with him (and who secretly believed there was no difference between teaching grade three and teaching grade eleven). June's complaints were a frequent feature of their dinner conversations and, lately, a frequent source of friction after dinner. He was sick of hearing about it – not sick enough to pack up and move, but sick enough to tell her as much. And she found herself pouring her heart out to the new kid, with the appropriate name of 'Miss Trainer'.

'I must have explained it a dozen times now,' she said, not really on the verge of tears but thinking she should be, so screwing up her face. 'Grade three is *Dick and Jane* and *More Dick*. I want to teach *English*, literature. Not English as a first language.' She waited for Miss Trainer to laugh; that remark had got a big laugh at her women's group.

Miss Trainer, however, nodded sympathetically. 'Men can be so difficult,' she said. Miss Trainer herself had never been involved with a man, and had no inclination in that arena. She was a woman's woman in the strictest sense. She'd had a lover who had been straight for a while, though, and most of her relationship information had come from that source. Men *were* difficult, as far as she had heard.

Good Health covered a small range of topics, strictly monitored by the public-health system. This drove Mr Casem crazy. He was allowed to tell the kids to 'take their vitamins', but not which vitamins (except for vitamin C, which was somehow exempt); he was allowed to talk about hygiene, but not mental or moral hygiene, or genital hygiene; he was allowed to talk about food, but not specifically processed food, fast food (except in a very general way) or fashionable 'health food'. He could not tell the children to eat oat bran or yogurt *specifically* for good health, only in general terms of having a well-balanced diet. He could not address poverty – except when referring to countries less fortunate – or professional health care (except to say 'visit your dentist/ doctor for regular check-ups'); he was not allowed to discuss specific health-care issues (except smoking and drugs) that contribute to poor health, like pollution (except in general terms, i.e., *pollution is bad*). He most certainly could not talk about any of the hot-button issues: cancer, abortion, teen pregnancy, large chemical companies, the pharmaceutical industry, or alternative health (apart from vitamin C).

This put Mr Casem at a disadvantage. It was part of his contract that the physical-education teacher actually teach a subject other than physical education. The obvious subject was 'health'. Mr Casem was a man of few words at the best of times, most of those shouted or grunted, either positively or negatively, and his early days of teaching – of wanting to guide very young children into the joyous world of organized sport and team building – were fast fading. And he hated teaching Good Health. He was forever in search of a subject that didn't limit him to actual parts of the body, but which generated lively discussion so that he only had to moderate. His fall-back subject matter was always 'physical fitness'. Whether he noticed or not, the kids got a lively discussion on physical fitness nearly every other week.

'This week, our topic is fitness, a mind and body experience,' he began, quite pleased with his intro. He had come up with the 'mind and body experience' the night before. His wife had liked it. He spoke in a neutral tone, emphasizing phrases rather than points. The kids sat in alert positions, eyes front, backs straight, waiting for any deviation of character to signal an explosion. Mr Casem's temper was legendary. Mostly born of myth.

'Physical fitness is a gift we give our bodies. Your body is your temple, I think that's even in the Bible somewhere, it is your responsibility to keep it in top working condition. There are many ways to do that,' he said. And with that he turned towards the blackboard. It was the one pleasure of Good Health. He wrote: STAM-INA, ENERGY, APPEARANCE, STRENGTH, in large block letters across the top of the board where the chalk rarely visited and the paint was still dark as pitch. When he was done, he faced the children dramatically, brow glowering with the seriousness of the subject.

'Stamina!' he yelled out. The kids jumped. 'When we work out regularly, we are able to withstand the rigours of physical extremes, whether they are a hockey game in overtime, or getting lost on your bike after a long ride into the city.' The children's eyes widened with the possibilities that that presented. 'You must exercise regularly and to the ends of your stamina in order to BUILD stamina!'

'Energy!' he shouted again. Energy was a gift from the exercise gods.

Strength was gained on the playing-field and off with regular, rigorous exercise.

'Appearance! Appearance is improved with regular exercise,' he intoned. 'You won't be fat and flabby and pasty and breathing heavily when you exercise regularly!'

Although Mr Casem avoided looking directly at Petey, a number of the kids around him glanced and snickered silently. Andy Devries, who was seated two rows over from Petey and closer to the front, poked his buddy Marshall and pointed.

'No one wants to be a loser,' he said, more softly. He then proceeded to give examples about how each of the four topics improved the other areas of life, mind and emotion. It boiled down to: if you were strong, attractive, had an acceptable amount of stamina and energy, your self-esteem bubbled over and you were a guaranteed Big Man On Campus.

'And everyone wants that, right, girls?' he asked, and added a wink. From Mrs Waddell's desk he took a brown manila folder and withdrew a sheaf of papers. He counted the rows of desks.

'Okay, get out your pencil crayons.' He handed a bunch of papers to each row. 'Each row represents a food group, with the last row representing foods that are poison . . . or, er, not exactly poison but not belonging to the other groups, certainly,' he said. 'Colour 'em up and we'll discuss them when you're done. Oh, and don't forget that there is such a thing as blue cheese.' The class giggled politely and Mr Casem looked relieved, either because it was a quiet time for him or because they had laughed. The room sounded like shuffling papers for a while and then there was silence except for the scratch of pencils on paper.

Petey took a photocopied picture of a cow from the girl who sat in front of him. His row was meat. He chose a black pencil crayon and drew irregular circles on its body until it looked like a Dalmatian.

He had not listened to much of what Mr Casem had been saying. His notebook was open in front of him, and at the top, in his neat, small printing were the words, 'Good Health'. Underneath that was a fair rendition of the field from his dream.

It was a flat, front view that tapered off into a fine perspective drawing of a hill in the distance. He had added little bunches of witchgrass and crabgrass, surrounding clusters of tiny buttercups. He didn't draw the sun, but when he looked at the picture he could see the blue sky and the wisps of clouds. It represented a complicated bunch of emotions to him. Each was felt, one on top of another, until they measured out into one conglomerate of meaning: *summer*. No school, lunch in the yard, endless days, good smells. The picture was pretty good. He tilted his head and appraised it. There was stuff missing. The kids weren't there. He didn't think he could draw kids. Just looking at it made him want to be there.

He discarded the black pencil and coloured the sky blue in his own picture instead. He made the buttercups a bright yellow and was just starting into the grass (a rich green: it took a moment to choose, but he finally settled on 'grass green', after debating between it and 'moss green') when Mr Casem passed his desk.

'What's your name?' he asked sternly.

Petey looked up and stiffened. His face went red. 'Peter.'

'Peter *Who*?'

'Peter Parkins.' He snapped Peter's notebook up off the desk. The hand-out picture fell gently to the floor.

'Up,' he said. He pointed to the front of the class.

Petey stared up at him pathetically hoping he didn't really mean it. 'Up! Up! Up!' he shouted, and the shout echoed in the room. Petey jumped up out of his desk knocking his knee on the edge. Mr Casem put a firm hand on his shoulder and nearly pushed him to the front of the class, which had gone silent and was holding its breath interestedly, terribly grateful it wasn't them and, in their way, very sorry for Petey.

Mr Casem's face was mottled with red, especially his ears, and Petey could see that he held his jaw stiff, teeth clenched.

'Mr Parkins has coloured his picture and wants to share it with us,' he said. He jabbed the notebook at Petey. 'Go ahead,' he said. Petey looked down at the floor and couldn't look up.

'Mr Parkins,' he said pointedly.

Petey felt a hitch in his chest. He wanted to cry but held it in. He was afraid. Everyone was staring. Through the windows on the north side, he could see the sun shining on the playground. The school shadow stretched out to touch the first set of goal posts.

Mr Casem grabbed the notebook and held it out to the class.

'Here's Peter's food group,' he said sarcastically. 'Maybe he could tell us what it is. Mr Parkins?'

'It's a field,' Petey said quietly. Mr Casem made him repeat it.

'Oh, yes, I see,' he said, looking down at it. 'Here is the grass, and the sky and these little yellow things are . . . what?'

'Buttercups.'

'Buttercups. This is cow food. Not people food. Can

388

you explain to me why you're not doing the assignment?' He spun Petey round so that they were facing. The class watched, still breathless, eyes wide. Somewhere there was a murmur of something that might have been words. Mr Casem blew up. He pointed to the class, his face crimson.

'DO NOT SPEAK WHEN I AM SPEAKING,' he shouted. Benita started to cry. He only glanced at her and grabbed Petey by his shoulder, getting close to his face.

'Why are you drawing pictures when I gave an assignment?'

Petey's face pinched in pain and horror. He muttered, 'I'm sorry,' which Mr Casem didn't seem to hear. He was so angry. He shook him lightly, just once, but behind it Petey could feel the anger.

'Is this what you eat at home? Hmmm? Is it?' Petey shook his head, no. 'Then what is it doing in this classroom?'

'Nothing.' Petey lost the battle and tears rolled down his cheeks. His face was as red as Mr Casem's.

In a moment Mr Casem realized he'd gone too far and had somehow to regain control of the situation. Distantly, he could hear a little girl crying.

'All right then, go back to your seat and colour the assignment, do you hear me?' Unable to speak, Petey nodded. Mr Casem gave him a little nudge towards his row. He straightened up, his face red and angry, his eyes narrowed. 'No more slacking. Colour those pictures and then we'll discuss the food groups,' he said, lowering his voice. The kids bent maniacally over their pictures and coloured, desperate to stay in the lines. Benita sniffed, and another little girl did too, on the edge of tears.

Petey flopped into his chair, squeezing his eyes shut tight against the room. He tried to think of his mom, or the field, and nothing would come to him. The room felt like it was going to blow up. He leaned over in his seat, afraid to get up, and fished the picture of the cow off the floor. He coloured his oddly shaped circles black. When the tip broke from the force of his pressure, he used brown. He coloured the eyes blue. He made everything else brown.

Mr Casem never called on him during the discussion, and Petey never raised his hand.

He took off at lunchtime, not telling anyone.

Todd Campbell came up to him at the lockers and told him Casem was an asshole, and saying he bet he got fired if Petey told his mom. By recess, the story would be all over the school. And next week he would have Casem again, for Good Health. He took his lunch out of his locker like the other kids but instead of turning at the gym or the multi-purpose room where most of the kids ate their lunch, he just walked out of the back doors. No one stopped him or even noticed.

He took the long way, skirting the route that would walk him west to Belisle, and instead went further to where the busy street started. It was lunchtime and the streets were packed with people. No one noticed the little boy without his jacket, cheeks burned red, eyes puffed out from crying and from holding it in. He was cool in his T-shirt, but it was nice in the sun. He wished he was lying in the field. He wished he was dreaming.

He had not yet deliberately associated the two children in the yard with the kids in his dream. He had actually avoided thinking about it, in the way that children can compartmentalize things that are too complicated to figure out. He knew and didn't know. He didn't care.

A lady bumped into him and apologized. 'Aren't you cold, sweetheart?' she said, frowning and smiling.

'No, thank you,' he answered politely.

She looked at her watch. 'Oh, you'd better hurry along. Lunch is almost over.' And she patted him on the head.

He thought of his mom. She would be mad. They would know at school that he was gone and then they would phone her. He thought of his room and was suddenly very tired. Maybe if he went home, his mom would let him go to his room (with a pudding) and sleep. He sighed deeply and walked to the end of the street, turning to go home, trying to debate in his head whether to tell his mom about Mr Casem or not. She would be mad at somebody.

Barbara had taken off her jacket and blouse and lay on the bed in her bra and skirt. In a strange way she was okay, she felt terribly exhausted and depleted, but okay. She wondered if she was in some kind of shock. She wanted to disappear. But she wouldn't; she never did.

She tried closing her eyes, but when she did, the conversation rolled over and over in her head as though on a loop. *Then he said . . . then I said*. When she couldn't stand it any more she opened her eyes and stared at the ceiling.

Around her, the house shifted like a child in its seat.

The tub filled slowly with water and she listened to it in a way she hadn't before. The tap ran – the sound muffled as though the door was closed – into a tub half filled already with water. She could hear it splash. It was pleasant. The sound of soaking in warm scent, smothered in a quiet feeling. Something scraped rhythmically across a wooden beam above her head. Very faintly, she could hear music playing, something old.

The water from the tap stopped running. She waited, poised for the sound of the plug popping out and the draining. A beat went by. And another. Her ears sharpened for it.

What she heard instead was water lapping up against the secondary drain, a hollow *clug clug*, rhythmic; like waves.

She sat up, a torporish fog like a shell around her. The mattress creaked with the shift in weight and the sound, for a second, was lost. She sat on the edge of the bed and tried to recapture it.

From downstairs an old ballad droned, Ruth Etting or maybe Bessie Smith, something dreamy and sad, the recording tinny. She preferred show tunes.

Who's Ruth Etting?

It was only a moment before it faded into far away and she could hear (feel) the sound of warm water lapping over flesh, washing up the front of the tub just high enough occasionally to swamp over the small silver cover and make that *clugging* sound, not unlike the drain. The other sounds of the house melted way as she focused.

The tub was full, this time. But, of course, that couldn't be. Unless that had been covered at the end of *Everyone's Guide to Simple Plumbing*; perhaps there was a section at the back. 'Really Really Bad Drains!' or 'Haunted Tubs!'

Barbara got up off the bed, a host of tempestuous

images and thoughts running through her mind. She remembered the look on Dennis's face when he had first seen Petey, his eyes wide with wonder and so much love; she remembered the dress she had worn to meet his parents, the first car they'd had (*isn't there something he uses that no one else does?*), packing her own suitcase once after a fight long before Petey was born, then sitting childlike and quiet on the bed while Dennis unpacked her case with great care, and put it all back in the drawers; the realtor who had showed them this house, telling her mother Dennis had left, trying to get the mattress for the spare bed up the stairs alone, her father's hand on her back when she rode her bicycle. Her father dying. Her mother braiding her hair. The restaurant Dennis always took clients to.

Her legs felt weak. Her vision was tunnelled. She wondered if she was dreaming.

The sun had gone behind a cloud. The hall had dimmed, the sun usually coming through the window in Petey's room now darkened in shadow. It was cold in the hall. The floor was cold on her feet. Steam, equally cold so that it puckered her flesh, poured from the bathroom. She entered and looked into the tub.

The water was red. Red water had seeped up and stained the sides of the tub, curdling along the soap line. Red water sloshed up in rhythm, washing over the secondary drain *clug clug clug*. Toes stuck up through the red water, the deep, rich colour hiding whatever else lay beneath.

Her eyes followed the toes, the natural line formed by memory. *Elementary, dear Watson. Where there's toes, there's fire.*

A man lay in the tub. His head lolled over on to his shoulder, bent slightly forward, blocking his chest. Water lapped around his middle, the black hairs of his stomach and chest poking through the murky water, torso bobbing freely with the motion of his body.

She bent forward and looked at his face. His eyes were closed as though sleeping. The expression on his face was serene.

He's at peace.

His hands floated by his sides. Deep gouges ran along the length of his arms, two rows on each arm. The flesh was curled at the cleave, the inside purple in the red water.

'You had enough,' she whispered, not really sure if she had said it or not. But knowing it was true.

The water was inviting. Warm water lapping over exhausted flesh. *A bath is a lovely thing. You could lie in one for ever.* She smiled sadly. There was a scraping sound on the tile and she glanced down to see the claws on the feet of the tub clench and relax.

Barbara stood motionless, calmly, her hands clasped demurely in front of her in a sort of reverence for the overwhelming, seductive feeling of peace in the little steamy-cold room. She did not know how long she stood there, mind blank in a sort of echo of tranquillity. Long enough to feel chilled.

And then she found herself, alone, in an empty bathroom.

She blinked and shook her head. The tub was empty and dry, and white and pristine as the day she bought the house. She shuddered. *Awful thing*, she thought. She waited a moment, expectantly, for the tub to begin its pop and drain, and it didn't.

The room was soundless.

Why was I in here? Something niggled, but would not come.

Downstairs, the front door opened and she jumped.

Dennis's face and all that she knew (all that was over) loomed. Pain, her most visceral friend, threatened to bring her down and she swayed, her mouth opening in a groan that was silent, and all the while downstairs there was the sound of her other man, home. For him she had to be okay.

Never.

On unsteady legs, she made her way down the stairs. Her son looked up to her, his beautiful wide green eyes peering up, mouth pursed, forehead crunched in an expression of dismay.

The stairs were warm where the sun poured in through the tall narrow windows beside the door. She paused ever so briefly on one spot and let the heat soak into her cold feet. Petey didn't seem to notice her pausing. He was staring at her.

'What are you doing home?' she said, her voice flattened.

'You don't have a top on,' he said. Barbara looked down. She was in her bra. Her skirt was wrinkled and twisted to one side. Her pantyhose sagged at the knee. She came down the stairs, took her sweater off the hook by the door and put it on. As she turned to face him, Petey grabbed her around her middle and hugged her hard. She knelt and put her arms around him, feeling his weight, his heat, his clinging. They stayed like that for a minute.

'What happened?' she asked, saying the words into his neck. He smelled like outdoors, fresh.

'School's over,' he said shortly.

She made a sound of affirmation in her throat. They parted and she stood, running her hand through his thick red hair. It had lost its baby softness a long time ago, and was just hair now, but her fingers felt the baby he had been. He hadn't been bald like most babies. And from the start, his hair had been red. Like Dennis's. Dennis's mother had told her that when Dennis was born he looked like a matchstick, so red was his hair and so white his body.

Scattered on the floor were her three letters. She stooped and picked them up, clutching the sweater around her. She held them. 'Are you hungry?'

'Yeah,' Petey said. 'I have my lunch.' He had the brown bag in his hand. She nodded. The two of them walked to the kitchen. On the way through the living room, Barbara dropped the letters on to the sofa. They were crushed and bent. She would have to redo them.

'What do you want?' she asked him, pulling open, by accident or design, the treat cupboard. Petey hesitated. Choose food, of a sort.

'Kraft Dinner?' She closed the treat cupboard and found the cupboard where such things were kept in untidy piles, bags of macaroni, spaghetti, jars and cans of spaghetti sauce and tomatoes, all things that didn't readily stack or row neatly. She pawed around until she found a lonely package of Kraft Dinner in the back, and took it down.

Barbara went through the motions of making lunch, pulling out pots and lids and adding things in a way that seemed precisely timed, and yet were only false images of cooking.

Petey sat at the table and watched her. He hadn't seen her like this in a long time – not since they had left the old house. He wondered if he should tell her what had happened.

'Petey, I have something to tell you,' she said. A rational voice somewhere lost inside her told her sternly (a voice surprisingly like her mother's) that now was not the time.

'What?'

She stirred the pot on the stove needlessly. Kraft Dinner didn't stick. It didn't do anything. You could probably leave it on the counter next to a pot and it would cook itself without error. She stirred, staring into the murky water. Now and then a tiny little yellow log would bob up to the top.

With her back to him, she told him that his father had called from work.

'He's going to get married,' she said. And swallowed. Saying it was better than she'd thought it would be. The words sounded as though they had been said very far away from her, and by another person.

When Petey didn't respond, she finally turned and looked at him. Their eyes met. His face looked drawn and old, his cheeks slack. He blinked and she wondered if he understood, but didn't have the energy to explain it.

'He wants you to come to his house this weekend and meet her, his new . . . wife.'

His lips formed the words, *new wife*, without sound. 'Is she my mother, too?'

Barbara shook her head. 'I'm your mom and he's your dad. She'll be his wife, is all.' It came out blankly, but properly, like all the books said it should. There was no inflection. It all felt blank. And sleepy. Her stomach was heavy like lead. She explained that he would probably call back tonight and talk to Petey. She rambled for a moment about how he could see Jeremy and maybe some of his other old friends. While she rambled, upstairs a plug popped out of the drain and water ran out through pipes. If she noticed, she did not acknowledge.

Petey's eyes went up to the ceiling and then down to her again. 'If he wants a wife why doesn't he just marry you again?' he asked.

The macaroni fattened and grew creamy. She turned off the element and pulled the pot off. The rings were red with heat and she felt it distantly through the opening of the sweater. She had the incomprehensible urge to press her hand on it.

'We're divorced,' she said simply, the voice belonging to someone else.

While Barbara put the last bits together for the lunch, Petey ate his sandwich at the table. He took bites without deliberation, not tasting them, the bread and meat pressing together between his tongue and the roof of his mouth feeling like cardboard. He had a hard time chewing, couldn't seem to move the food around in his mouth. Barbara brought him a plate of orange noodles and they sat together at the little table, holding their forks. Barbara pushed hers around the plate. Petey shoved forkful after forkful into his mouth and swallowed, methodically.

'I ran away from school,' Petey blurted. Then burst into tears.

*

Petey went to his room.

Barbara cleaned up the kitchen and when that was done, sat down at the end of the dining-room table, her typewriter in front of her. She rolled a fresh envelope into the carriage and it sat there. She didn't want to do it. Felt too tired. She thought about how nice a long, long bath would feel. She sat there and stared, listening to the music that filtered around the house without a distinct origin. Time went by. At one point she heard her son laugh. Once in a while there were too many footsteps, for so few people in the house.

There's something wrong with this house. And she smiled, cruelly.

Petey had gone up to his room after looking through the kitchen window for a long time. They weren't in the yard. They were waiting for him upstairs.

He sat on his bed for a minute or two and they didn't come. He thought he could hear them. He knew where they were.

He got off the bed and went slowly to the little cupboard door cut down from what had been a huge, tall board, once the door to a large barn. The bottom half had been cut into a little round door. What had happened to the rest of it, he didn't know. There were lots of boards from the barn in the bedroom. The window was trimmed with it, and the baseboards had once been the horizontal slabs for the horse stall. If he looked, he could find a gouged piece where a horse had chewed and chewed. The boards had all been deeply stained and varnished, but you could still see the marks and bores where machinery had run into walls, where chains had hung and eroded into the wood, where scratches had been made.

He pressed his thumb on the little latch and it made a nice click when it opened. A gratifying sound. He pulled the door open until it was adjacent to the wall and left it there. Inside it was black as pitch; black as night. In spite of the sun streaming in through his window, none penetrated the darkness of the cubbyhole. He listened, hoping to hear them, but it was silent.

His heart pounding because he didn't really, *really* want to do it, he ducked his head and walked into the blackness.

The retarded kid who had been nice that first afternoon at the bus stop when Andy and Marshall had beaten him up had the same recess time as Petey's class. His name was Kevin. After a while Petey had got used to him following him around. Kevin couldn't find Petey at lunch. He had seen him that morning, but not at lunch. Then not at recess.

Eventually someone took note. Kevin asked Mrs Waddell if Peter had a dentist's appointment. He'd had one himself not long ago (to him: it had in fact been months before, but had hurt – like a *bugger* – and he remembered it well; he was preoccupied with dental appointments after that). Mrs Waddell hadn't answered with much more than a negative throat sound. She was watching the little kids. She hated playground duty.

The very things that worked against Petey with the children worked in his favour with the adults: he was not an attractive child, and did not stand out as a student, because he was new and had yet to make any sort of an impression whether with good work or bad. When a teacher looked out over the sea of faces, their eyes skidded over him, pausing only on kids like Bethany Sanders, who had curling blonde hair and saucer-sized blue eyes and wore a different dress every day, or even Brad Genner, who had pleasant features, smooth white teeth and an easy smile and was very smart. Or Andy Devries and Marshall Hemp, who were troublemakers with soft, clean brown hair and easy smiles and quips that were mean and funny, comments that were repeated later in the staff room with guilty snickers and chuckles hidden behind hands with remarks like *oh, my* and *What will he be like in ten years?* But the eyes just swept past boys like Petey. Pe*ter*.

She had noticed that the new kid wasn't around after lunch, but the thought kept slipping in and out of her consciousness, like the hum of a refrigerator or the drone of a lawn-mower on a Saturday afternoon in June. Kevin said he thought Peter had run away from school, telling Mrs Waddell at afternoon recess, but Kevin was one of those kids the adults listened to only half-way, and as soon as he disappeared and the discomfort of having him near her subsided, Mrs Waddell forgot whatever it was he had said, only to remember an hour later, during grammar. At lunchtime she'd taken a look around the play yard and finally asked Andy Devries, of all people, if he knew where the new kid was. Andy spat before answering, and she chastised him for it, but later when she was talking to Tina Klassen about the missing new kid, she mentioned Andy spitting and remarked that he looked just like his father when he did it, and Tina Klassen knew just what she meant and they both *cluck-clucked* like

401

old ladies, but secretly the image they carried in their heads about Andy Devries's father was sexual in nature, his maleness a topic of exchanged looks at every parent–teacher night. He was a looker, that one, and the kid was going to be just like him.

They called his house and told his mother that he hadn't been in school after recess that day. Barbara had listened to the teacher on the phone, calling at two o'clock in the afternoon, her forehead lined with a sort of distant anger.

'You noticed he wasn't there *when*?' she asked.

The teacher had fumbled then, attempting to cover tracks of some distance. It boiled down to, he ran off at recess. Mrs Waddell not offering the information that she really didn't know when he'd gone. For all she knew, it might have been morning recess, except by then she'd heard what had happened with the gym teacher (and she was *appalled*, make no mistake about that, but these things happened and they have to be handled carefully; it was an unfortunate situation, an *accident*). Mrs Waddell considered herself quite accurately *intuitive* and did not feel at all *concerned* about the boy's whereabouts. While she did not explain why (people were so grounded in earth properties they missed the whole wide *other* world around them), she did tell Mrs Parkins that the school – taking some liberty there – was not concerned.

'We have found that children who have not yet found their *niche* often *act out* in these sorts of ways. He is very likely just waiting until after school is out to come home,' Mrs Waddell said reasonably.

'My son is not at school,' Barbara said, with deadly calm into the phone. 'You don't know where he is.

You have called me at two o'clock in the afternoon –' She paused to think. 'What kind of a school are you operating, Mrs Waddell?' There was a patient, long-suffering sigh at the other end of the line and that made Barbara angry. Mrs Waddell (while dreaming of teaching grades eight through twelve) had taken a child-psychology course at night, and waited patiently (*one of those mothers*) for Barbara to vent her (perfectly *understandable*, although unproductive and *unreasonable*) dismay.

'This is an unfortunate turn of events, Mrs Parkins –'

'Don't call me that,' said Barbara, suddenly. 'I'm Barbara Staizer now.'

There was a brief pause, during which June Waddell summed up the situation and allowed herself an unseen smile of self-satisfaction. So it was like *that*. 'Mrs Staizer, my apologies. Peter will likely show up there after school as though he's been in school all day. It happens. When he arrives home –'

'For your information, Mrs Waddell, my son has been home since lunchtime. He left school at lunchtime. He has been missing from your care since *lunchtime*. And he will not be returning to your school.' And she hung up.

Endless summer.

They played tag for the longest time. Petey fell exhausted into the heap with the others, all of them out of breath. *I tagged you, Mariette*, Ethan said.

Mariette answered, *I'm too tired*. Lying on her back, she rolled over and tagged Petey's arm. Her fingers were warm. *You're it*, she giggled. Petey rolled over and tagged Alan. Alan poked Berk with his toe. They were all it. Everybody was it.

You should bring your mother here, Mariette said. *She could have fun with us.* She twirled a bit of foxtail above her face, dipping it close to her nose, to tickle it. When she did it to Peter, he felt like sneezing.

She wouldn't, he said.

Why not?

Petey felt the grass on his back and stared up at the sky. The sun didn't hurt his eyes too bad if he squinted. It did eventually and he turned his head to the side, staring off into the distance. Far away, he could see the hill. It was nothing more than a bump on the horizon. It seemed to Petey that they had just climbed it.

Why not? Mariette repeated the question, and Petey heard it like the first time.

My mom is always sad, he said.

She'd be happy here.

I don't think so. I don't think she can be. He said it and it was the first time he'd thought it. But he knew instantly that it was true and that he had known it all along. His face screwed up in a frown. He scratched a sweaty, itchy part of his back. The grass itched. It was too hot. He was uncomfortable and fidgeted. Mariette raised herself up on one elbow and tucked the foxtail under Peter's chin. Her eyes were as blue as the sky, as though Petey were looking right through her eyes, and seeing the sky.

The sky through Mariette's eyes grew dark and grey.

We don't have a momma. Mariette tickled him. He stared at her eyes, thinking something was wrong with the colour and then realized it was just the sky, growing cloudy.

Then Ethan stood above him and dropped a baseball on to his tummy. It didn't hurt. It rolled off him silently on to the sweet grass of the field.

Let's play ball, Ethan said. *You pitch.* No teams, just hitting and catching and throwing. Every now and then, Peter looked off into the distance. The hill was further away every time.

Barbara hummed an old song, now stuck in her head.

And he will not be returning to your school. She would keep him home with her. They would do something else. Have school at home. She would teach him. They would stay in the house together.

She felt a sort of relief. It was over. All the anxiety about school and bullies and fitting in and fitness programmes and trying to squeeze a (fat) square peg into a round hole, and the empty hours between eight thirty and three thirty. Over.

She wondered if Petey had heard her on the phone, but all was silent upstairs. The reasons for which she did not explore. He was all right up there. She was sure of it. Everything was going to be all right. Briefly, she stood beside the phone, fighting a moment. Call the school? Make some sort of statement, and send him back, or just let things go? The receiver was still warm from her hand. The phone itself was indifferent, neither inspiring nor rejecting her. It sat.

Barbara went into the kitchen and got a spoon out of the dish drainer and a pudding from the treat cupboard, for Petey.

She mounted the stairs tiredly. A bath would be nice. Peaceful.

It was very quiet upstairs. The afternoon sun had lowered in the sky and it streamed in through Petey's window, flooding across the floor into the bathroom. It was so bright and pretty. The odd smell from the yellow room was generally worse when the upstairs warmed with the heat of the day, but she was used to it; it had become background noise. She hadn't quite put her finger on it. It smelled of swimming-pools and locker rooms. A disinfectant, but more specific than that – and it could hardly be a disinfectant. She was a Vim girl.

'Peter?' she said, into the still air. He didn't answer. Barbara poked her head into his bedroom. There was a comic on his rumpled bed, but it had been there all day. She bent at the waist and looked under the bed. Dust bunnies.

The cubbyhole door was open. She stepped inside the room to close it. The sun had rested on the dark varnish all day and the door was warm. The sun glinted off a blemish in the wood and it caught her eye. She looked a little closer, seeing a pattern. A row of words running down the side of the door. She'd never noticed it before. Squinting, she got closer.

The varnish had been laid on thick and the wood gleamed. She had to open the door wider to get the sun off it to see what they said. Years had worn the wood down and it was hard to make out. The stain made it better.

She could read only a couple of them: *Ethan, Marianne*? *Bert*, maybe. There were three or four others there. Names. Her finger traced the letters of the others, or tried to. They were too faint. The letters were even and well drawn as though carved or chiselled into the wood.

Her grandfather had chiselled the family name Staizer into a bench that he kept in the backyard. It looked like that. Strange she had never noticed before. She wondered if Peter had seen them.

'Peter?' she said again. He wasn't upstairs.

It bothered her and she wasn't sure why. Cool air seemed to breeze out of the cubbyhole and the inside was as dark as ever, in spite of the light in the room. She could make out the outline of a box of toys, but nothing more. She knew the wood in the bedroom had been salvaged from somewhere – she'd assumed a junk yard or something like that – and it was disconcerting to think that it was from somewhere less anonymous. She straightened up. She had enough to (not) think about. Giving the room a last glance, she saw nothing that indicated Peter had even come upstairs.

He's somewhere in the house, anyway. Maybe in the yard. She put the pudding and the spoon on his dresser where he would see it when he walked in, and left the room, the door to the cubbyhole standing open, the names just visible if you looked, in the sun.

She ran a warm bath. Peaceful.

It was Peter's favourite.

All seven of them ran up the side of the hill, fast as they could. At the top, they dropped to the ground and rolled back down, earth, grass, wild field flowers, rushing past them loud in their ears, brush catching and sticking to their hair and clothes. At the bottom when they finally stopped, they were dizzy. They stood up on confused legs and stumbled around until the dizziness was controllable, then did it all again. The last time Peter rolled to a stop, he rested there, lying on his back looking up at the cloudless sky.

George stopped too, where he fell.

Hal banged into Peter and rolled over him. Then there was a mass of them, seven of them including Peter, lying on their backs. For a while all Peter could hear was breathing.

Do you go to school? Peter asked them.

Mariette giggled. *It's summer.*

It's spring, Peter said.

It's summer. No school in the summer. Peter tried to think of what he was supposed to say next, but it was too hard with the sun hot on his front and his eyes closed. Every now and then a breeze, warm and soft, blew over him and it felt like a sigh. Like a dream. He tried to remember when he'd come and couldn't. Thinking felt like slogging through water.

It's always summer, Ethan said. They played red rover with a red ball.

Barbara dropped a bath bead into the warm water, running her hand around the edges to swirl the scent around. She gave the door a push, hearing it close. The pantyhose fell on to the sweater with her panties. She slipped into the tub, heat flooding over her. Sweat formed on her upper lip.

The tub dominated the little bathroom and getting into it gave her a new perspective on the space. She'd only showered until then, the tub having been a source of anxiety. It felt different now. The water so warm and lovely. The scent of lilac drifted above her, filling the room. She pulled the shower curtain half-way around the tub in case Petey needed to come in. The curtain diffused the light and made the air inside the tub steamy and the light soft. She lay back and closed her eyes.

Her breathing became shallow and regular as she relaxed.

I'm getting married. The pain hit like new, his voice on the phone saying it. The familiar voice that used to say love words to her. It repeated itself in her head like a schoolyard taunt. How could he? She still felt married to him.

If he wants a wife why doesn't he just marry you again? What had she told him? She couldn't remember. In spite of knowing about the reasons for his leaving, Barbara had been, still even after the divorce, entirely unprepared for *I'm getting married.*

She wanted to curl up into a little ball. Instead she lay on her back, still, feeling her heart pounding and the sting of tears in her eyes and nose. Her face felt hard like her stomach. She forced herself to breathe deeply. She ran her arms up her sides in a gesture of soothing, then let them drop into the water and float.

She could imagine doing it.

The razor up the arm, from wrist to elbow. It would sting if you did it fast. Hurt more if you did it slowly, if you were afraid. It would hurt more when the water got inside the wound. If you kept your eyes closed, it would hurt less. If you didn't see it.

It would sting. Then it would be warm. You might feel a rush of heat leaving your body. The force of your own heart – pumping fast because you were afraid – pushing your life out into the water. It would feel hotter than the bath: like when you peed. The heat would be different, not encased in your flesh.

There would be fear. Last-minute regret, maybe. But peace would come before your skin became cold and you got so tired – she thought that was what would happen, you would fall asleep, feeling peace, the warmth of your own blood lapping over your legs and arms, taking you away.

She could imagine doing it. Her eyes closed and she drifted somewhere between waking and sleep, arms dangling, floating, gently at her sides. She let herself feel the peace. As her face softened and relaxed, she looked like she was smiling.

Mariette wore a crown of wild daisies. She danced.

The boys stood around. Each had a stem of wheatgrass dangling from his mouth. They bounced when they chewed. Petey said it tasted green. After talking about it, they decided that things could taste green. Or red. But not blue.

All of the boys had braided tails of sweetgrass hanging from their back pockets. Berk had lost his. They had played a game of tail-tag with elaborate rules and out-of-bounds. It had taken most of the game to explain the rules. Their time-outs were long and involved. It was a game for summer afternoons.

It *did* taste green to Peter. He spat out bits of grass every so often, but his lips felt stiff and distant. All his reflexes required thought. It was hot and easy just to sit and stare at the sky or to walk and feel the waves of grass under his hands.

Far off in the distance was the other hill. Sometimes

he could see a building. Sometimes he couldn't. But it was the nature of the place that he always forgot to ask.

This time he almost remembered. When the clouds came.

Ethan, Berk, George, Hal, Jack, Lonnie and Mariette looked fretfully up at the sky all together. Clouds advanced over the sun and darkened it.

Everyone grew silent when the clouds came. Ethan stood up when it was dark enough to be menacing rain. Summer disappeared and in its place a grim midwinter evening. The wind picked up.

We have to go, he said. The others stood. They fell into line, one behind the other, by age, not height. Peter knew Berk was older, and George, who was taller, shifted in behind him.

You have to go home now, Peter, Ethan said. He was the oldest. More than twelve. He was a beautiful, strapping boy, with an expression that was sombre most of the time. He organized the games. Peter wanted to tell him no, that he wanted to stay. That they should come back, but by then they were going. Already.

Don't go, Peter said instead. He said it into the wind. They didn't hear him. They didn't look back. He called it out again, cupping his hands around his mouth. *Don't go!*

Mariette looked back at him. Her eyes were round, white against her tan. She raised a tiny hand and pulled the daisy crown from her head. She dropped it to the ground. She tried a little smile and a wave to Peter.

Don't go. They disappeared quickly, as though every time he blinked they were further away until they were nearly at the building in the distance.

He shouldn't follow them.

Let me come. He tried to call it out. He shouldn't go there, to the hill. Not sure why, just shouldn't. Seven blond heads faded beyond the hill, in turn. Just before she fell behind the rise, with the building dark in front of her, Mariette looked back. Her lips moved. She was a great distance away, but Peter heard her in his head.

Make your mom come.

Then they were gone. He stood up on tiptoe, straining to see where they went. He thought he could see blond heads by the building. And in an instant he knew that the building was the Barn.

The Barn shifted and changed in his view, moving further away, then appearing again as it had. He couldn't see far enough over the hill. He couldn't see the children.

On his toes, he squinted and strained, shifting this way and that to keep his balance. He would get a tantalizing look and then it would fade.

The wind grew fierce, the sky black with huge thunderclouds. Dust from the fields blew over his face and he squeezed his eyes shut against it. It scraped his skin and he turned his back. The wind whipped through his clothes and the first *BOOM!* crash of thunder made him scream and that was when he wanted out. He clamped his hands to his ears just as another *BOOM!* shook his body, and then the air he sucked into his lungs in great heaves of panic and fear was different; stuffy and airless.

Petey was in his room. He was *back*.

The little door to the cupboard was closed, latched. Without wondering how that could be, Petey reached out from his place on the floor and opened it wide.

The cubbyhole's inside door stared at him, what he wanted to see, with its scroll of names at just about eye level and much more readable than they had seemed before. The end of Lonnie was cut off, so that it looked like 'Lonn'. The edges of the first letters on all the names except Jack's had been rubbed off – maybe by a hundred fingers opening and shutting the door.

It made Petey happy to see the names.

The floor in front of the cubbyhole was cold and he got up. He thought he could smell flower stems crushed on his fingers. The green juice of the long stems of wheatgrass was still in his mouth.

Wasn't it?

He sat down on his bed. Blinking, he tried to decide what was real. He leaned one hand on the bed. Felt it give. Felt the smooth texture of the sheets under his hand. Sun, like in the field, poured in through his window, but it was low.

He latched the cubbyhole door. He was tired (from playing)? His bed was rumpled. There was a confused moment of desperation when he wasn't sure, couldn't tell, didn't dare to decide one way or the other, each conclusion having its own horrible, bad ends (*But was I? Could I really have been? Gone there? Did I? Pleasepleaseplease let there be a there*).

He cocked an ear and listened to the house.

Far away, a sound that might have been thunder.

'Mom?' he said, down the stairs. He'd found the pudding and eaten it. He didn't know what time it was. It seemed late. The house was quiet.

Behind him, the bathroom door opened. 'I'm here,

honey,' his mom said. She was pink and sweaty in a robe. From behind her, smoky steam billowed and settled with the motion of the door opening and closing. Her hair was dry, but pushed back over her forehead.

'Oh,' he said. 'What time is it?' They met eyes. Met secrets. Both frowned, sizing up. Barbara smiled, a long, loving smile that was sleepy and happy at the same time. Petey grinned back.

'I don't know. Are you hungry?'

'I guess.'

Barbara swayed into her room to get dressed. From the top of the stairs Petey listened to drawers open and close lazily and then he went down.

She had fallen asleep in the tub. According to the clock on the dresser it was after six. Was that possible?

Three hours? She shook her head, and felt the urge to stretch, not from stiffness, which she should have felt if she had indeed lain in the tub for three hours, but because she felt languid and like a cat after a nap.

The water was still warm when she'd come out. There were snatches of alarm at such behaviour, it didn't seem right to sleep, unknowingly, for three hours! A child wandering around the empty house, alone. She tried to work up a head of steam over it, but found she just couldn't. She felt rested.

And she'd had the loveliest dream.

By the time they had dinner, *I Love Lucy* was on cable, and Barbara decided they could eat in front of the TV. She'd asked Peter where he'd been. He told her he'd been outside, playing. He said it very quietly, very quickly, and she didn't believe him.

They had beans and wieners. Petey poured ketchup over his.

I Love Lucy was the one where Lucy and Ethel decide to live together so Fred and Desi live together, in an attempt to be single once more. Each imagines the other to be having a fabulous time. Really, they miss their spouses. Havoc ensues.

She tried to watch. The beans were soggy in her mouth and she couldn't eat them. She waited for the phone to ring. For Dennis to call. The warm, languid feeling that she'd carried for so long after her soak was all but used up. Anxiety was a breathing thing, waiting just below the surface, waiting for the phone.

Desi and Fred dress up for a night on the town and pretend they're having the time of their lives. Television took the high road every time. The fifties, if you went by television, seemed so innocent and bereft of complication. It was all long-finned cars, and waitresses on roller skates and beehive hairdos.

No one had affairs, got pregnant in high school, took drugs or came home drunk. It was a golden time. Lucy was endearingly well-meaning and funny, but never inopportune or irritating; Desi was ignorant and demanding and endearing, but never overbearing. Wise fathers and homey mothers, children who sparkled and said amusing things. It hadn't really been. Fathers in the fifties probably walked out on their wives and children, too; it just didn't fit the sitcom format.

Music up. Mother sits crying at the kitchen table. Boy, eight, bounds in at the back door, heading for refrigerator. Sees mother crying. *What is it, Mother?*

Oh dear, your father's left us. He has another woman.

Break to commercial for razor blades and rope.

Petey said suddenly, into her thoughts (guilty), 'What are dreams for?'

She started and the laugh track sounded. 'What kind of dreams?' she said carefully. 'Like day-dreams?'

'When you go to sleep and dream,' he said matter-of-factly.

'I'm not sure. Are you having bad dreams?'

'No,' he said, almost fiercely. 'I *like* my dreams.'

And the phone rang. Barbara's heart clenched. 'You go ahead, honey. I think it's your dad.' It rang three more times while Petey looked at her for a reaction and got up and answered.

Of course she listened.

Petey's end was all yups and nopes. And an *okay*. There had been one fake-enthusiastic *oh, yeah?* He must have said there was a surprise. The call did not go on long.

'He's coming to get me Friday,' Petey said. He sat on the couch beside his mom. He leaned into her and she put her arms around him, resting her chin on his head. Like they used to.

'That'll be fun. You haven't seen him in a long time.'

'I guess.' It felt like a deadline.

Lucy made the crowd laugh. It roared up and fell, in a wave.

4

Petey lay awake in bed. He'd gone up on his own after watching *I Dream of Jeannie* with his mom, which was a totally dumb show but Jeannie was pretty. His mom had gone into the kitchen during a commercial and had come back out with a candy bar for him and a drink with ice for herself. The ice tinkled in the glass. He went upstairs and put on his pyjamas and afterwards she came upstairs and they read together. When she kissed him good night she tasted like whiskey. It was unnerving.

His dad didn't tell him about getting married. He said, 'I have a surprise for you this weekend. I hope you're going to like it.' But first he asked him if he'd talked to his mother that day. That was how he said it: 'Did you talk to your *mother* today?' Petey had said yeah. He asked him if she'd said anything.

''Bout what?' he said. He knew what he was doing. His dad's voice sounded familiar and unfamiliar at the same time, and there was a hollow sound at the other end, as though he was very far away. After that he said *never mind* and then said he had a surprise for him. Petey knew what the surprise was.

If his dad got a new wife was she his other mother, or what? Jeremy's parents weren't divorced. Neither were Bobby and Angela's parents, the kids who used to live next door. He used to sort of know a girl whose mom had a new husband or something, but he thought the old one had died. She was at his old school. Not that he'd asked her anything.

If his dad got a new wife, what was his mom? His other wife? He had two wives, then. He wasn't nice to his mom any more anyway, so maybe she didn't really care. Maybe she was just mad. She was something, but he couldn't quite put his finger on it. Like she had a curtain up over her or something.

He didn't want to go to his dad's. Not if he had to meet some stupid woman and call her Mom. He sort of wanted to see his dad. Mostly he wanted to see Jeremy. *What if he teases me about my stomach in front of his new wife?* That would be worse than school. He wondered if his mom meant it about him not having to go back there. He had wanted to ask her all night, but was scared. She would probably make him go back. You *had* to go to school.

He wished it was summer.

The thoughts went round and round. There seemed to be no safe place in his head to go.

Sleep took a long time to come.

Barbara stumbled up the stairs a little in her cups. She'd had two drinks, straight whiskey, with ice, thinking it would be enough to keep her in the numb state that she'd had most of the day. Shock, likely. It was the same kind of apathy she'd felt in the first few days after Dennis had left. She pulled off her clothes and got into her oldest, softest nightie, the whiskey already making her mouth taste bad and her head pound. She crawled into her bed by the window and lay on her back.

Whatever pleasant effects the whiskey had promoted disappeared when the heaviness of reality rolled over her.

Dennis gone. For good, for real, for ever.

Petey fat and persecuted.

Long for-evers twisted in front of her, new horrors likely ahead, all of it to be faced alone. Alone. The worst word in the world. After *fat*.

And then dreams.

Petey's with us, Mrs Parkins.

She tried to tell them that it wasn't Parkins any more, that it was *Staizer*, but they disappeared as quickly as they had come, their blond heads bobbing up and down, reminding her sweetly of clean white rabbits, and instead of *Staizer* coming out, she laughed out loud. It was returned by them. It was so pretty here. Sky and field seemed to go on endlessly, the air and breeze warm and soft. There was laughter. Among them – although she couldn't separate his voice from the others, but somehow just *knew* – was Petey's laugh, hearty and real. She grinned hard enough that she thought her face would hurt later if she kept on. She could feel it, her cheeks puffing out from it, the sting in the corners from being held broadly.

In the dream the smile stretched across her teeth and it did hurt. It was a hard smile.

But it was right.

Barbara woke two hours later.

The house shook, rocked with the sound of explosion.

She sat up, crouching against the sound of it, and fumbled out of bed. She clamped her hands over her ears. It sounded like the earth was breaking in two. She ran out of her room calling, '*Petey! Petey!*' In the confusion and noise, she didn't turn on the light. The room was black dark, not even the street-lamp seemed to be on.

Her eyes adjusted and she stumbled into Peter's room, her head pounding either from the *BOOM BOOM BOOM* that vibrated the floor, or from the whiskey.

He wasn't in his bed. Panicked, she swung around, squinting into the dark, bending and searching. *Was he hiding, afraid?*

'PETER!' She tried to scream over the sound. She could hardly hear her own voice. She looked under the bed. Ran across into the bathroom. He wasn't in there. The sound came from everywhere, with no discernible position, just as loud in the hall and bathroom as in her room and Petey's room. She ran down the stairs, calling his name.

She flung open the front door, expecting to see neighbours out. The street itself was lit with lamps, an orange glow blanketing the yard and road. The houses were blank, windows dark; she could see no one on front steps or sidewalk. She checked the kitchen, the living room, behind the sofa.

It's a dream. This happens in dreams.

That calmed her. *Petey's upstairs in bed I'll wake up in a moment or start something else*, and swung around the banister pole, the panic not as easy to lose as the knowledge that it was a dream was to accept.

Half-way up the stairs she fell and knocked her knee. Pain shot up her leg. She clutched it and moaned, unable to hear her own voice. Where was the sound coming from? She limped up the rest of the stairs. She had to find Peter.

'Peter!' she shouted, straining her throat, making it burn. She called and called, terror replacing panic, and still the booming sounded, echoing through the house, through her body. She looked into her room – *maybe he came in here when he couldn't find me hear me.*

'PETER!' she screeched. She swung round in the hall and went back into his room.

And the booming stopped.

Silence was heavy and thick after the cacophony. It, too, seemed to echo. She collapsed on Petey's bed, body still shaking and vibrating as though she was in a part of the house still roaring.

'Petey,' she said into the dark. Her voice was a croak, broken and shrill.

Murmurs made her look up and the room was filled with the children. They watched her with big round eyes, the whites glowing in the black room. A little girl, *why it's Mariette: she hadn't left, after all* and behind her, boys. They were blond and handsome. Her mouth opened and she leaned away.

– *dream dream dream* –

'Peter's with us, Mrs Parkins,' said the little girl. She reached out her hand. Barbara looked down; it was grubby and plump, a child's hand. 'Peter doesn't want to go to school,' she said, apologetically. 'He wants to play with us.'

The tallest boy moved forward through the others and placed a hand on the little girl's shoulder. 'He wants to stay,' he said.

'I'm dreaming,' Barbara mumbled. The boy grinned appealingly.

The little girl took Barbara's limp hand from her lap.

Her little hand was sun-warm. She was gentle. 'Our mama died,' the little girl said. 'It's nice where we are. It's summer. Peter likes it. No school in summer.' Barbara stared down at the tiny pink hand in hers. It felt so real. So warm.

'We want you to come too,' she said simply. She tugged on Barbara's hand. 'Come.'

The tall boy said, 'Yeah. It's nice.'

Then the room was empty. The cubbyhole door stood open. Barbara buried her face in her hands, rubbing hard. *Wake up!* Any moment she would wake up in her own bed and this would fade.

Petey's with us, Mrs Parkins.

'Mom?'

Barbara pulled her hands away from her face and saw Petey, flushed, dressed, in front of the cubbyhole. She opened her arms to him. He ran to her and folded himself into her arms, his body vibrant and more than awake, alive. He smelled fresh like summer. He let her cling to him for a moment and then pulled away. He grabbed her hands and tugged. His were warm like Mariette's.

'Come on, Mom. Come with me.' He pulled her to standing. He pulled her to the cubbyhole door.

She stopped. 'No.'

'It's wonderful. It's nice. You'll like it.' He pulled her.

Light shone through the little door. Bright sunlight, midsummer afternoon. The smell of wild flowers and tall grass wafted over her on a breeze. Beyond the door an endless field of green, dotted with colour. Not too far away were seven little blond heads, still; waiting.

She looked at Petey, his eyes pleading. 'You'll *like* it.' His eyes sparkled with an unfamiliar expression, something she rarely saw. He looked happy. She glanced back through the bedroom door. The bathroom was dark, forbidding. Downstairs music played. Out on the streets there was no one.

With Peter holding her hand, Barbara ducked her head under the doorframe.

She sat on the downside of the hill, playing her hands over the long grass. Every once in a while she could see the sun glint off something bright and she knew it was blond heads. Among them was a red head, somewhere, and that alone made her smile.

It was all so pretty. She scanned the horizon. For miles, as far as her eyes could see, it was meadow. Far, far in the distance, she could see something dark on the edge of the earth, a building or a silo, or something country-fitting. She strained for a better focus but it seemed to shift in her vision. She could only hold her attention on it for a moment before it was lost. *Like trying to read in a dream*, she thought.

But this is a dream. She smiled. It wasn't a dream. It was a dream. It would be perfect, but for her eyes drawn back time and again to the dark spot on the horizon. Whatever it was, it was a *bad part* and it was best not to look. It was far away and from where she sat, *far far away* from the dark spot on the horizon, she could hear the children, Petey with them. Peter. Here he was *Peter*.

When their voices became too distant, she frowned. She stood up and tried to see or hear them better and it was lost, their voices fading in and out of the air that never seemed to move and yet was alive with breeze and scent. The building was closer. The hill was suddenly behind her. She took this in with the panicked calm of a dream.

This is a dream, she reminded herself.

The children shouldn't play so close to the barn, their father doesn't like it. Yes, it was a barn. How could she not have known that?

Children! she called. *Don't go near the barn!* Dennis would be angry. She had to call them back. She cupped her hands around her mouth.

Come back!

Beside her, clear as a bell, clearer even than her own voice had been in her own ears, one of the children said, *We can't come back because it's time. We have to go now.*

She nodded without even glancing beside her. She understood. *It was time.* Petey/Peter would have to come home now. *Peter will have to come home*, she repeated, dream-firm.

She saw the line of children walking into the barn. *Petey!* she called, without answer. She strained to see his red hair in the line of children and, like the barn itself, her focus kept shifting. She called again and again, her throat aching with it, her lips dry with the effort.

The sun was dropping. Grey clouds blew in from somewhere else and covered the sky. *It might rain.* That didn't matter. *This is a dream. Petey's not coming because it is a dream.* Her dream-heart began to pound with fear every time the big dark barn came into focus, and the grey clouds seemed to rush around her like a storm about to start, a terrible storm with gusts of wind and cracking lightning and earth-moving shakes of thunder. *Bad storm coming. PETEY!* Terror rose in her throat even as she screamed it out, calling her son, willing him to answer, fearing great doom and horror if he didn't, even though *this is a dream*.

Great booms sounded from the direction of the barn and Barbara screamed, for the first time hearing herself do it, screaming one long keel of horror. The booming was thunder, great cracks of it, shaking the earth under her and the children were gone – not one blond head could be seen. Not one red head.

She dream-ran, the barn coming closer. As she crested the hill, she saw the children, in a line, from oldest to youngest. Ethan was first.

A man, tall and swarthy, dark, stood at the door, cradling a rifle. He called Ethan into the barn. She couldn't hear the words, but she knew he told him *There's a surprise*; he motioned the other children to stay where they were. They'd all get a surprise.

BOOM!

Over and over the children walked into the barn. Barbara was nearly there. Petey was second to last. The man came out again and called to Peter as though he were his own son, child of the dead mother. No one to care for them. Too many mouths.

PETER! NO! The man turned and saw her, and turned away as though it were of little meaning. She ran on dream legs, slogging through grass as though it were the deepest lake. Peter disappeared into the barn.

She ran down the hill, moving faster with dream logic and gravity. The man came out of the barn. The sky was dark with thunderclouds and the air smelled of ozone and smoke.

Mariette looked over her shoulder sadly at Barbara. Barbara threw her hands up and screamed, *NO!* The man shouldered his rifle and shot the little girl. Mariette flew up into the air, arms spread wide, she hovered a moment, silhouetted against the sky, and then fell, dream slow, to the ground. She lay still.

Barbara ran to her, dropped to her knees beside her. The front of the little girl's faded cotton dress was red with blood. The man lowered his gun and turned his back, began walking away. Then he disappeared. They were dead, all of them.

Their father had shot them. She staggered to her feet and lurched in the direction of the barn. Behind her, the child spoke.

'It's all right,' she said, her tiny voice a lilt. The sky began to clear. Half-way between the barn and the little girl, Barbara stopped and turned. Mariette was standing. The blood on her dress faded. She spun, arms out, smiling. Dancing.

Out of the barn came the others, groggy, grinning. Each of them touched her. They called her Mama. Petey came out. He hugged her and joined the children, who by then were making their way up the hill.

Barbara followed them. She was their mother. Mariette and Peter dropped back and waited for her, grabbing her hands.

'Let's run,' Mariette sang. They did. They ran over the hill and down the other side. It was a beautiful day, endless summer, and Peter's laugh echoed across the hill.

Dennis arrived to pick up Petey on Friday night, only to find the house empty. He waited for several hours before calling Barbara's mother and then, finally, the police.

A search of the house turned up a note. The note, in

Barbara's handwriting, stated that she and Petey had run away. They would not be coming back. They could do what they wished with their things.

There was an investigation. Dennis was closely watched. He had a perfect alibi. The days before their disappearance he had been, consistently, in the company of employees, or publicly with his fiancée. He was investigated, none the less.

Barbara and Petey never turned up. Eventually, the house was cleared. Elizabeth Staizer asked Dennis, of all people, to sell the house for her. She didn't know a darn thing about houses.

Glenn

Bad penny.

Glenn smiled wryly into her cellphone, listening with only half an ear since the (fated) first description of her soon-to-be new – *falling into your lap, Glenn!* – listing. The woman on the other end of the line was an acquaintance from How's days of teaching. She struggled to remember even what the woman looked like, and could remember, despite being told in the introduction, only her first name. Dee-Dee.

Dee-Dee had taught with Howard, years before. She'd retired before he had, even.

Imagine the course life takes. A twist, a turn and then –

Back where you started. It was downright amusing, she thought. If the whole thing just wasn't too perfect.

'– and I thought right away of you!' she said graciously into the phone. Glenn's smile was pasted on. It all seemed too pat.

A house on Belisle. *Do you know Belisle?* Dee-Dee had asked, quite innocently, and Glenn's mouth had pursed to answer quickly, some sort of comfortable non-remark about having had a listing on Belisle previously, but she had stopped short of saying anything.

'You must know it,' Dee-Dee had continued. 'It's not terribly far from downtown,' and she had launched into a virtual register of streets leading up to Belisle, all very familiar.

'It's just a lovely old place. There's two floors and an attic – I think it needs work still – but there's three bedrooms, and a massive living room. Fireplace. It's really a very good-looking house, you know. Dennis would be so glad to get it off his plate, if you know what I mean –'

Dennis? Glenn struggled but remembered no Dennis, horrified suddenly that she might be losing her memory. She remembered only the brightly brittle woman, a woman so pained that there almost appeared to be sound when she moved, her movements harsh and sudden, as though provoked only by necessity and circulation. *Poor thing*, she'd thought then.

The wrong house, Glenn thought suddenly, and for reasons felt somewhere in the pit of her belly, like a wrong step not taken, she sighed with relief. Not the same house. Couldn't be.

'Dennis?' she asked politely. It wasn't the same house. Not the same.

'Dennis Parkins. He's an old friend of mine. Well, his mother is an old friend, anyway. It was – I think, and I don't want to gossip – his ex-wife's house. I have no idea what is going on, so don't ask. But, for whatever reason, and he didn't say, he's selling the house. There's nothing wrong with it, but she's taken off, I guess. Poof. Gone. Took her – and *his* – son with her. Bad divorce, I'm thinking. Anyway, all of that is none of my business. All I know is that his mother remembered that I had sold my place – do you remember the old place on Kennedy? Good god, Glenn, when the hell was that? Fifteen years ago – I love my place on Washington. Never leave. But anyway, Gladys remembered you – of all things! –'

Dee-Dee rambled on and so did Glenn.

The house.

Bad penny, you, she thought but not altogether unfondly. *It can't be.*

'It's in the 300 block,' Dee-Dee said, interrupting herself. 'Do you think you can take it on?'

Of course it was the same house exactly.

It was all so unlikely, so serendipitous, that she didn't even bother mentioning it to anyone at the office. Elsie asked her what was new twice, and Glenn, a secret on pale lips, said nothing.

She listed it on the multiple listings site, and quietly put an ad into their regular section of the Sunday paper, and nothing more. No one noticed.

For two weeks she didn't bring it up to prospective buyers, although it seemed always there in her thoughts, a secret, a shadow, a knowing of something not quite tainted, not quite bad, but by then something . . . *fated* with undertones that she did not care to examine. Glenn drove by, peeking behind half-lids, but never once stopped in.

Stop calling me Shirley, went the old joke. *Stop calling me, surely,* she heard.

When she did think of the house, unbidden, she thought of the terrible fragility of that woman, her determined brightness followed always by the vague, frightened look of the lost. She did, Glenn admitted, have the look of someone who would choose escape.

She's taken off, I guess.

Very likely. The ex-husband, then, the one who had given her the settlement (that was what she had said, wasn't it? *I have a settlement,* as a way of explanation

433

about buying the house at all, as though saying, *I have a coupon*), was the vendor on the listing and Glenn sometimes felt like a conspirator on the wrong side of the ideology.

Very little of it mattered, she realized, although did not admit, in the face of other, more pressing, distractions.

If they were together at the office, at the appropriate time, Elsie and Glenn would have lunch together. Glenn picked at hers and Elsie frowned and watched her sideways.

'You're a rake, Glenn Darnley,' she said with a sniff one day. 'Are you on a diet? Did you meet someone? 'Cause it's not flattering, you know. To lose too much weight.'

'I've not lost much,' she said, with what she hoped was conviction. Like her, the conviction was thin.

Elsie shrugged. 'You should get it checked. Maybe you have a tapeworm or something. I would kill for a tapeworm,' she sighed, forking lasagne into her mouth. 'You lost a bit, girl.'

The two of them took very early lunches (for very different reasons). Glenn did not eat breakfast any longer, her stomach being too delicate and tender to contemplate food at an hour before ten, and Elsie because she really couldn't wait between meals. If she noticed Glenn fading by the time it was just after one, she didn't mention it. Almost without fail, Glenn was not in the office in the afternoons. Without telling anyone, she would go home in the early afternoon and sleep. Sometimes she slept for several hours, sleeping through her phone, her pager, her fax, waking to a list of client calls and offers that she couldn't get up the stomach for, literally, lunch having coiled its way through her stomach into her intestines, or worse.

It's fine, she told herself.

Lunch is a bad penny, ha ha. Turning up.

She slept through entire afternoons, only dreaming occasionally. When she dreamed, it was pleasant; as fitting, she dreamed of houses. Rooms of yellow, blue. Flowers bloomed in yards. Summer breezes blew through musical rooms.

Always, Glenn considered new clients. By rote, she went through lists of needs and wants and the property on Belisle sometimes seemed appropriate.

There were no takers throughout the summer. Whatever charms the house held for its previous owners and for Glenn herself remained masked, replaced by a silence and neutrality that did nothing for its appeal. Once or twice, with carefully selected viewers, Glenn tried to drum up enthusiasm for the very things that had always appealed to her in the house: with flash and drama she pulled down the little bed in the room under the stairs; she ran a hand up the shiny banister and pointed out the tin ceilings and the sweetness of the little blue room. She told the story of the tub coming through the window, and opened and closed the specially fitted, arched door in the master bedroom, it seemed mostly, to deaf ears and blind eyes.

Around August, she gave up, and decided that, for good or bad, the house was going to be her personal white elephant; she also gave up understanding why.

Dennis Parkins, the ersatz vendor, perhaps waiting to get all of his 'settlement' back out of the house, refused to budge on the asking. The grass grew up around the hedge and no rain through July kept the house covered in a fine layer of dust. It began to absorb the character of 'the abandoned house' so popular in teen movies. One nearly expected shadowy figures to walk past blind windows.

She did not drive by at night. At night she slept. Sometimes the house, like a bad penny, would turn up in dreams.

You're not helping. Not one little bit, she would think to herself. Always, the house stared back silently.

Who, me?

Richie Bramley was the sort of handsome that had an undertone of manipulation to it. When he smiled – a bright, broad, toothy smile – it was the smile of a boy who knows he can get what he wants, if he can only charm his companion. In this way, it was impossible not to like him. In repose, when the smile faded without the scrutiny of the person he was trying hard to charm, he took on a vulnerable quality that had the same effect. Glenn was thoroughly taken.

She took him on a tour of the usual places, mostly multiple listings of the sort that every single man or woman was looking for. Small, easy, carefree homes with no maintenance and maybe no memories? He stared ahead out of the window of the car, his lovely, full-lipped mouth turned slightly down at the corners, not in anger, but more like sadness, or exhaustion. Dark half-moons clouded the underside of his eyes. He did not elaborate, but mentioned a teenaged son and that he was moving from a rather larger home to something smaller, and Glenn assumed – as with most of her single clients – that there was a break-up or divorce in his past. Glancing sideways at him, she decided he looked very sad.

There was something wrong with everything that she showed him. As much as she inwardly sighed, with each wasted mile on her car ticking away slowly at her 6 per cent on houses that were beneath her, she understood. With some clients, you could practically hear a *click* when they walked into a place that would be right for them. Some people, of course, clicked with everything. Everyone clicked with something. Whether they bought it or not was another story, but Richie did not seem comfortable in any of the small, characterless homes that she pulled him through.

His reasons were equally unspecific. And after several hours, he had the good nature to be apologetic about it. He ran his fingers through his hair and chuckled.

'I guess I'm not sure exactly what I want. I just want something . . .' and he trailed off, as though he had nothing further to add. Glenn waited, but still had the feeling that she was cutting him off.

'I have something you might like,' she said carefully, keeping her eyes on the road – even though she didn't really have to at that point. At some time in the drive between homes her body had gone into a kind of autopilot. The familiar street names whizzed by: Cranston, Gibbons, Lane Drive.

She hadn't even known she was going to say it.

'It's a lovely place on Belisle,' she said.

The sun had come out and shone on the front of the house with the golden light of late day. A recent rain had brightened the exterior. Windows shone back, hiding secrets coyly, like long lashes.

'Just lovely,' she said. She watched his face in profile as he stared out the window of the car at the big house she had inexplicably brought him to. He grinned. *Too big*, he said. *Too much.*

He, of course, couldn't hear the *click*. Richie Bramley, she realized, was looking for the house on Belisle.

And maybe, it was looking for him.

Stop calling me, surely. She smiled.

The Drunkard's Child

I

The kitchen was full of empty boxes, stacked in a crazy pile. Some had been neatly opened up and folded flat; these were shoved in behind the too-large table, pushed next to the back wall of the house. The girls had folded them in the afternoon, before the beer began in earnest. The stack threatened to fall over with every passing guest that came afterwards. The unpacking was over, but the party was just getting started. It had seemed like a good idea at two in the afternoon with his buddies, and their girls (who did most of the unpacking, truth be told, like little steam engines, they were) had been running up and downstairs in a fury of industriousness, all the enthusiasm of new starts in every sip of coffee, every bizarre discovery in one of the boxes, *Hey! You guys! Richie has hockey sheets! Bwahhhhh!* and later, the sweet escape of liquor.

The party was getting too big. Richie grabbed another beer from the fridge and caught sight of a pretty girl out of the corner of his eye. He didn't know her. There was also a guy he didn't know smoking a cigarette next to his mother's ancient, maybe antique, buffet. The ash end of the cigarette was long and ready to fall. There were a half-dozen beer bottles on the buffet that he could have tapped the ash into, but the guy was just stood there, jabbering away, gesturing sometimes, with his cigarette and its long ash. Richie stared, fascinated. He was very stoned. And getting pretty drunk. But pretty drunk wasn't bad.

He took a long, kindly swallow of the beer in his hand, not very cold, but good, it tasted *good*. It tasted like a party. He liked a party. Parties were *fun*. A person deserved a little fun after moving. He took another (kindly) swallow of the beer and felt around in his shirt pocket for his smokes. They weren't there.

The pretty-girl-he-didn't-know looked a little young, maybe mid-twenties. Young for his crowd. He found his smokes on the counter and pulled one out. There were only three left. He frowned. Was he smoking that much? He was trying to cut down. *Aah, it's a party.*

'Bay-beee!' Steve walked into the kitchen and pulled open the fridge door peering in. 'Uh-oh . . . time for another run. Who's okay to drive?'

'I saw Jimmy standing up.' Richie laughed, the drawn-out guffaw of a drunk. 'Myself, I'm a little over the limit,' he added, needlessly. It was getting hard to focus. He would have to watch it: it was a delicate balance between drunk and *pretty* drunk. *(Gotta maintain. Aaah, it's a party.)*

Steve pulled out a beer and twisted off the cap. 'This isn't even cold.' Frowning, he opened the fridge, grabbed a mittful of beers and put them into the freezer. 'That'll do it,' he said cheerfully. 'Don't forget those are in there, buddy.'

'You put 'em there. You remember,' Richie slurred.

Steve swallowed beer. 'Well, what d'ya think? 'Nother beer run, or kick everybody out? Your place, your call.'

'Who's that girl?' Richie nodded into the dining room. The guy with the cigarette didn't have it any more. In a back part of his brain, Richie hoped it was in one of the empties on the buffet. The other part of his brain was focused on the girl.

'Who?' Steve said, without looking. Richie gestured again. Steve shrugged.

'Dunno. I think she came with Roger and them. Roger and them? That right? Roger and *they*? What is it, writer-boy?'

'Correct usage would be *"them guys what come with Roger"*. Or alternatively, *"Who the fuck cares?"*'

Steve howled.

Richie watched as the girl swung her blonde hair. Through the archway into the kitchen she spotted him looking. He was just sober enough to grin and wink. She checked him out coyly. He was just drunk enough to buy the coyness.

Steve watched the exchange and then, *oddly*, yelled, 'Jenniferrrrr! Baby. Ass. In. Here. *Now!*' He smiled broadly and Jennifer (his Jennifer) pushed through the crowd into the kitchen, somehow filling the room with her . . . Richie struggled with the word. With her . . . *lifeness*, he decided. He grinned at his own bad word.

She smelled fresh from the outside air. Her cheeks were pink in the soft light of the kitchen. She opened her arms and hugged Steve with affection. It was genuine. 'Steve! How're you doing?' she said, easily. She did everything easily.

Richie grinned. Over his shoulder she locked eyes with him, then blinked away.

'Grand, just grand. Haven't seen you in a while. You're scarce. You're rare. You're damn near endangered in these parts.' They let go, and Steve opened the freezer and grabbed her one of the cold beers in there.

In the interim she said hello to Richie. 'How are you, bud?' she said. Her voice was a little tighter, a little more formal, in spite of the familiarity. *Bud? Since when am I 'bud'?*

'Can't complain,' he said, garnering all his resources so that he did not slur his words. *Have to watch it.* 'This is my housewarming. This is my *house*.'

She looked around, taking in the stacks of boxes at the door and then the crowd that spilled from the living room into the dining room. The noise was a drone of unintelligible conversation. 'So I heard,' she said. 'I ran into Wendy and Lois at the bar, they said they were on their way here. Housewarming . . . nice place. Maybe I could get a tour later,' she finished.

Steve gallantly opened her beer and handed it to her. He felt the change in the air and pecked her cheek. 'I'm going to go find Bev. Just about time to call it a night for me. Not a bad idea,' he said, cuffing the air in front of Richie and nodding meaningfully.

Richie smacked his cheek back lightly, and with affection. 'Yeah? Kick 'em out, then,' he said, just barely. Steve laughed and disappeared into the crowd in the dining room, swallowed up, whole.

Jennifer was watching him over the delicate sip she took from the bottle. Over her shoulder the little blonde had stopped looking at him. He avoided looking too hard at Jen. *My Jen. No, not my Jen.*

'So,' she said. 'How's the new book coming?'

'Coming right along,' he lied brightly.

She nodded, raised her eyebrows. 'Good for you. How's RJ?'

At the mention of his son, there was a sobering click

inside him that he did not appreciate. He furrowed his brow at Jen, resenting her. 'Great. How's the *boyfriend*? Is that who you were at the bar with?'

'Yes, and he's fine, thank you, employed and everything,' she said, pointedly.

'Did you bring him here?'

She shook her head. 'Sent him home.' They looked at Richie's floor for a moment, his new floor in his new home.

Richie grinned at the floor, remembering. 'With a lick and promise?' he said. Their old thing.

She laughed shyly. 'No. Just "goodbye". We're kind of casual now.'

'You're blushing,' he said, forgetting the boyfriend in light of circumstance. Light of her face.

'You're drunk,' she said, but affectionately.

Their eyes met again and held for a second longer. He wanted to reach out and touch her hair or her shoulder or something, and realized it wasn't lust. He just wanted to touch her. All the beer he'd drunk throughout the day rolled over in his stomach and he felt suddenly very drunk, and tired. Maybe even tired of being drunk, if that was possible. Maybe bad, like he wanted to fold himself into a foetal position at her feet. He forced a grin on his face and drained the beer in his hand.

'How's the Job?' he said, meaningfully, and hurtfully, making her sigh. Whatever moment might have come next disappeared. Richie was grateful and didn't listen to her answer, instead peered over her shoulder and tried to catch a glimpse of the other girl, who had disappeared. He leaned over too far accidentally and swayed, catching himself.

She said quietly, 'I thought you quit drinking.'

'I said I was going to drink "no *more*",' he said, flippantly, slurring the R in drink. 'Also, no *less*.' He pointed at her, swaying a little too close.

'Okay. Well, it was nice to see you again,' she said sarcastically. 'As always.'

'Come on, Jen. At least gimme a hug.' And he plunked his empty bottle down on the counter and reached around her, engulfing her. He squeezed her warmly for a moment, and felt that click that he hated so much, that nakedness. She hugged him back, sincerely, and he felt her relax into him. Their bodies were familiar to each other, as familiar as the dance of emotions, the anger-love, the accusatory words. Her breasts pushed into his chest. Her hair smelled like outside and the skin of her shoulder was warm and soft under his chin until he couldn't stand her closeness, his nakedness. His hands slipped down her back and groped her ass, one cheek in each hand and he squeezed.

She pushed him away. 'Same old Rich,' she said, sadly. She wandered off into the party, leaving him alone in the kitchen, a grin pasted over lips that wanted to sneer. It was the *sadly* that did it.

He found the blonde. The living room was packed with people, most of whom he knew only casually. Steve had left with Bev. The clock that was propped on the mantel at a crazy angle said it was after one. He was getting anxious for the party to break up. He was still drunk, but had started nursing a beer instead of guzzling them. He was feeling a little sick. He would feel worse in the morning if he wasn't careful. He was tired. Dubs was in the corner telling dirty jokes to a bunch that had come over from the bar. Richie wandered over. 'Hey,' he said.

Dubs shook his hand, wrist style, and said, 'Nice place,' before continuing with the story.

Richie waited for the punchline of the joke he'd heard already that day, before telling the group that it was time to call it a night. 'I got my kid coming in the morning,' he said. The crowd from the bar went quiet at the mention of real life.

The blonde was over by the buffet again. Someone had rummaged through his cupboards and found a box of crackers. She and some other girl were eating them. Richie sauntered over as best he could. 'Hello,' he said, keeping focused on the words in his mouth. His eyes were at half-mast, mostly from being tired. 'How do you like my house, and who are you?'

She smiled sweetly. 'Ashley,' she said, widening her eyes appealingly. 'Is this your house?' It was a lie, and he could tell, but he let her have it.

'It's my *new* house,' he said. He realized it, then. He'd hardly thought about it. He'd bought a fucken house. 'I'm Richie Bramley,' he said, and then, gesturing grandly and nearly knocking over a beer bottle on the buffet, he added, 'And this is my house.'

She introduced her friend and Richie didn't hear the friend's name, but he chatted with her politely in a bid to confuse the blonde and nudge her interest up a notch. It worked mostly because the girl was a girl. Jen wouldn't have fallen for that. When Andy started telling him a story about her dog, he leaned in especially close and listened with what he hoped was an intent expression. Because the stereo was loud, he was able to lean in with

447

his head tilted downwards, listening, allowing his eyes to rest on her breasts. They were nice little round ones. When she moved her arms in the story, they jiggled happily.

Like a bowl full of jelly, he thought. *Two bowls*. And then he giggled. The story wasn't funny, though. And she said, punching him lightly on the arm (first contact), 'What's so funny about that?' But, of course, he hadn't been listening and could think of no plausible answer.

'I'm sorry, darlin',' he said, standing up straight and looking into her large brown eyes. A brown-eyed blonde. Very nice. 'I was just thinking about how you are as cute as a little bunny,' he said, stealing – mostly for himself – a line from a movie. 'And that made me laugh.' Her eyes blinked a little slower than they should have and he realized (gleefully) that she was a little drunk. It made him bold. He reached an arm around her waist and pulled her into him. There was a nice curve to her, between ass and waist. Quickly he wondered, guiltily, if Jen was still at the party and dismissed it on impulse. *Fuck it; not my Jen.*

She laughed, let him hold her a second too long before squirming away without much force. He reached for her again, but only lightly – he didn't want to scare away the little bunny – and whispered in her ear, *You are very hot*. She smiled and giggled and did not try to get away.

He let her talk. Slowly, around them, the party broke up, disappeared. Dubs wandered over to say goodbye and remind him about the football game. 'Around two,' he said. 'You bringing RJ?' and Richie went blank. *RJ?* Looked confused.

Shit. Richard Junior. RJ. 'Yeah,' he said, recovering

quickly, letting go of the girl and assuming a serious expression for the moment. 'Around two. See ya, buddy,' he said, and they shook hands again.

Dubs checked out the girl with an unreadable expression and from somewhere near the door his wife called him and hollered a goodbye to Richie. 'Happy housewarming,' she sing-songed.

Richie raised a hand. 'Thanks, Brenda. See ya!'

The door slammed and it was suddenly quiet, the room empty, and Richie and the girl (Amber? Angie?) were standing too close together. She stared at him openly, a knowing expression on her face.

' 'Nother beer?' She shook her head. She did not move away. He reached around and pulled her to him again and smiled close to her face before putting his mouth on hers. She tasted like cigarettes and gum. She made a sound in her throat and kissed back, and between them heat spread.

'Wanna see the house?' he asked, low, everything suddenly different. She nodded, and put her beer down.

She was bent backwards over the edge of the bed. Richie had pushed her T-shirt and her bra up over her breasts and her nipples were poked up at him, hard and red in the dark room. Her jeans were unbuttoned at the waist, but not off. He buried his face between her breasts, pushing them together against his cheeks, hands full. She pressed her pelvis against his. His hard-on pressed against the tab of his zipper. They were silent except for the noises made in their throats.

He rubbed her nipples with his thumbs and she squirmed under him. He kissed her mouth and pulled his lips over her chin and neck and over the fabric of her shirt and on to her chest, finding breasts and, at the same time, tugging up her T-shirt. She raised her arms, and they paused long enough to take her shirt off. He pulled his off and it was flesh on flesh. Her body was warm, she was fleshy and firm, not skinny like so many girls.

'Take these off,' she breathed, tugging at the waistband of his pants. He stood up and undid his jeans and pulled them down over his legs, stepping out of them in a much-practised motion. His cock pressed up against the front of his underwear and she sat up and pulled them down. They slid on their own over his thighs to the floor. She put her mouth on him and he put his head back, sucking in breath. He pulled her closer, hands on her shoulders.

He pushed her away and grabbed her around the buttocks, lifting her up on to the bed, scrambling after her. He laughed joyfully and laid himself across her, parting her legs with one of his. He nuzzled his face into her neck and ran his other hand over her body, which was warm and soft and flat-bellied and *different*.

'Mmmm, *mmmm*,' he said, enthusiastically, smiling broadly, digging himself into her with mouth, hands, knees. She caught his mood and giggled back. He stroked her to silence and her breath was catching, so he leaned over her and pushed himself between her legs, the end of his cock finding the beginning of her and he was beyond thought by then.

'I really loved your last book,' she breathed into his ear.

There was a beat of time and she did not notice before he pushed himself into her and dropped himself over her, his weight held partly on his elbows, his mouth at her ear. He pressed into her again.

'Oh, baby,' he moaned. *'So did I.'*

Richie was drunk enough to sleep poorly. He lapsed in and out of dreams. Once, between sobriety and sleep, he thought he heard someone in the house. A door, far away, opened and closed and shod footsteps echoed down a hall. Without opening his eyes, he mumbled in half sleep, *Who's there?* and slept again. He dreamed then that he had left the stereo on and it played softly through the house.

He opened his eyes painfully to sunlight streaming right in his face. His first thought was *Fuck I gotta move this bed* just before noticing the lump on the mattress beside him and remembering the night before. He grinned. Ashley. No, Amber. *Ashley.* He squinted back against the sun streaming in from the window that faced the front of the house and raised his head slightly to look around for the clock. His head pounded painfully with a hangover. He spotted the clock on his weight bench in the corner. It was just after eight a.m. He dropped his head to the pillow and let it pound. He took stock. Stomach wasn't too bad. Couple of aspirins would take care of the head. *Not that bad. Had worse*, he thought. *Had worse last week, ha ha*. He looked over at the lump, which was all he could see given that it was covered with a sheet and blanket and facing away. The lump was lying on its side and a delicious-looking curve was in the middle. It was a very attractive-looking lump. He took stock a second time to see if he could get the juices going for a nice warm goodbye, but his thirty-five-year-old hung-over body did not seem compliant with the old Richie Bramley regulations. He touched himself as an incentive, but his head pounded and it started to seem like a lot of trouble, so he reached over and shook the lump. *Ashley*.

Ashley stirred, made an aggressive sound, and he paused for second to let it sink in. Then he shook her again, gently. She rolled over, eyes closed, and readjusted herself.

Her face was young, unlined, lips soft and plump in sleep. She was quite pretty, so no real errors in judgement had been made. He hadn't drunk that much. That was good. *Good for me*. He was trying to keep it manageable.

'Ashley,' he said, sing-songy. 'Asshhh-leee.' She pulled her arm out of the sheet and he caught a glimpse of her breasts, but remained unmoved. The spirit willing and all that. It was a moment more before she opened her eyes. There was a brief panic in her eyes, and then her expression softened. 'Hi,' she said sleepily.

'Hi.' She closed her eyes again and he put his hand on her shoulder. 'Hey,' he said. 'Hey, you gotta get up. You gotta go, baby.'

'Huh?' She opened her eyes again, keeping one shut, focusing on him. 'What time is it?'

'After eight.' He kept his hand on her shoulder. She snuggled in close to him and he was annoyed. It wasn't what he wanted. 'Hey,' he repeated, a little louder, 'you gotta go, honey. My kid's coming.'

'Mmmm,' she answered, snuggling in. 'I looove kids.'

Horror at the thought of her being there when RJ showed prompted him. He sat up and looked apprehensively around the room, as if seeing it for the first time.

His clothes were in a pile beside the bed. At the foot were a pair of red nylon panties.

He stood up, naked, and his head pounded newly with the surge of blood. He closed his eyes against the pain. He wandered out of the bedroom, calling behind him, 'Rise and shine, baby,' and made his way to the can.

He lifted the seat of the toilet and began a long piss. On the wall behind the toilet, one of his buddies had tacked a *New Yorker* cartoon. It showed a ragged-looking man holding up a sign beside a busy street. 'Will write for food,' the sign said. He stared at it throughout his piss.

Getting Ashley out and on her way proved to be harder than he'd thought. They ended up having another go at it and by the time she left it was nine. He locked the door after waving goodbye to her, and climbed back up the stairs feeling like shit.

The locked door bought him a couple of minutes when he woke up after ten to the sound of someone pounding on it. He jumped out of bed, knowing full well who it was. He threw on jeans and the shirt he had had on the night before. As an afterthought, he grabbed his ball cap and threw it on his head, taking the stairs two at a time. Before going back to sleep, he'd dropped a couple of aspirins, which had apparently had their work cut out for them: his head pounded with every step.

'Coming!' he yelled, from midway down the stairs.

Richie twisted the deadbolt open and threw open the door. Janis had her lips pursed. Behind her, Rick Jr, their thirteen-year-old son, stood awkwardly, half staring at the steps, half looking up at his father.

'Heeeey! Come on in, how's my boy?' Janis came in and RJ came in with his bag, grinning shyly. He swung it a little, tossing it towards the stairs. It landed half on and half off the bottom stair with a *thlumpf!*

'Hi, Dad,' he said.

Richie tugged on his ball cap, a nervous gesture that Janis caught. 'I hope your Game Boy's not in there,' she said.

'It didn't break.'

She shook her head and sighed. 'We wake you up?' she asked Richie.

'No, *oh, no*. I was upstairs in the attic – new office. Pounding keys,' he lied.

She nodded and looked around. Then she peeked round the corner of the hall into the living room. Richie followed her gaze. The living room was littered with empty beer bottles. On the floor beside the sofa was an ashtray overflowing with butts. The only one in the house. There were dirty glasses and spills here and there. The floor had ashes from cigarettes too far away from the ashtray or an empty bottle, and the stereo was surrounded by CDs and their empty cases.

'Party last night?' Janis said.

'Ah, just Steve and Dubs, Bev, Rob, those guys. Helped me unpack. Went kinda late so I left it all, caught some Zs, you know,' he said. His face reddened, and she crossed her arms over her chest and nodded disbelievingly.

They stood awkwardly without speaking for a beat of a few seconds, long enough for Richie to notice that the house smelled of beer and cigarettes.

'Well, I'm taking off,' Janis said, pulling her coat

around herself. She pecked RJ on the cheek. 'Hey, not too late, right?' And she looked meaningfully at Richie, before giving him a friendly kiss on his cheek.

'Not too late,' he said, winking.

'He's got math homework that's not done. You're going to drop him off at school in the morning, right?' She used the same tone with Richie that she used when talking to her son.

'Absolutely. You don't want a tour of the new Casa Bramley?'

Janis leaned forward far enough to take another peek into the living room. 'I'll wait until you're settled in,' she said. She opened the door and said, 'Love you, RJ, be good, and I'll see you tomorrow. And we're back on our regular schedule next week, right, Rich?' He walked to the door and waved goodbye, then shut it and gave it a little push.

Father and son grinned at each other. 'Hey, give your dad a hug,' he said, when the door was shut. It was clumsy, a cross between a pat on the shoulder and a hug. RJ was getting so big, was as tall as his father, but without the breadth.

Richie opened his arms dramatically. 'I bid you welcome to Casa Bramley, the soon-to-be-heritage home of the great Bramley clan. This fine hotel has several options for a distinguished visitor such as yourself: you can toss it on the couch down here,' he said, waving one arm like a product model, but with a manly little bow, 'or you can sleep in my bed with me – no snoring, no stealing covers, no growing any bigger overnight – or *check it out*.' He nodded for RJ to follow him and the two of them slipped down the hall to where the house opened up into the back door mudroom. He pointed to a small door nestled into the space under the stairs.

'Behold,' he said, and he flung open the door, reached in and flicked on a light. Ricky Junior peered in. Under the stairs was a tiny empty room. He looked at his dad.

'Sleep on the floor?'

'Ahhh,' Richie said, waving a finger. 'Many would believe that. But I give to you the secrets of the dark cave of Casa Bramley, soon-to-be-heritage, yadda yadda yadda –' and he stepped inside and pulled from out of the wall a hidden bed, about the size of a small double.

It sprang out and hit the floor with the sound of springs and metal squeals. The thin mattress bounced and settled in the middle.

'Wow!'

Richie grinned. 'Cool, huh? The futon fit perfectly,' he said, smoothing down a lump that had formed in the centre. 'It's bending a bit in the middle. We'll just keep it down until I can get a proper mattress for one of these things. I just wanted it up there so I could show you.'

'This is so cool!' RJ said. He came in and pushed down on the bed, checking it out. 'Is it safe? It looks kinda . . . old and stuff.'

'It is old. Came with the house, the house is old. But me and Wendy and Dubs and them were all on it yesterday. I was going to set the futon up in one of the upstairs bedrooms, but I figured you might like this better.' He smiled, his grin hurting his face, with delight that he had made his son happy. 'Go ahead, try her out.'

RJ pulled himself up to the high bed with his hands, tentatively at first. When the whole thing didn't collapse, he crawled closer to the middle and lay down, staring up at the ceiling. Staring back down at him was the bare hanging bulb.

'That light sucks,' he said, squinting, shielding his eyes with his hand.

'Problem solved. We'll put the table I used to have beside the couch in the other place and put it beside the bed with a lamp. We can use my old desk lamp. I'll get a good one for in here if you like. This can be your room,' he said, ingenuously.

'*Cool*,' RJ said.

They set RJ's things in the room and found a lamp and the little table. It came barely up to the mattress, but would serve as a temporary measure. Richie showed his son through the rest of the house, avoiding the living room, dining room, kitchen except for a quick look, once he caught Rick's interest in the remains of the party, strewn about like fat brown bombs.

'Wow, you guys sure drank a lot of beer,' the boy said, impressed, when they were in the kitchen. Beside the refrigerator, half-heartedly stacked and lying about, were endless cases of beer, all empty.

'Lotta people,' Richie said shortly and steered the boy upstairs.

He loved the tub, said it was *cool*, especially the feet, but he'd rather shower. He said it seemed kind of weird that a bathtub would have something like that on the bottom. 'It looks so . . . violent,' he said.

Richie was impressed. He shrugged, though, while they looked. He frowned. 'If I was writing it,' he started, fading off the way he sometimes did, 'I would say that having the feet of a vicious animal on the bottom of the tub would be symbolic of protection. A person's naked when they're bathing, right? You're at your most vulnerable when you're naked. No place to hang your sidearm.' He nudged RJ and they chuckled. 'So the feet of the thing, in a way, would be symbolic. I bet it's from Roman times or something like that, all that symbolism.'

RJ looked at his father, impressed. It was gratifying and Richie felt better than he had all morning; all weekend. 'Come and see my office,' he said. 'It's upstairs.'

RJ liked the pull-down ladder from the attic. Richie showed him the pulleys and explained how it worked. The two of them examined the mechanism, RJ pulling it up and down, from the hallway, while they watched it work.

'I like stuff like that,' RJ said, blushing.

Richie gave him a sidelong look, tilting his head. He himself was not always handy with a tool; he would be surprised if his son was. 'Yah?' he said. 'You like carpenter stuff, is that what you mean?'

RJ shook his head, blushing furiously then. 'The pulleys,' he said, watching how it moved. 'I like seeing how things are put together. Big things. How the weight of that ladder and the hatch are held up by those little spools. It's cool.' He shrugged, and then said casually, but with a touch of importance, 'I'm going to be an engineer.'

Richie raised his eyebrows. It was the first he had heard of that. 'Oh, yeah? Not a writer like your old man?' As RJ had been growing up, Richie had paid careful attention to the work he brought home from school, and any indication that he had some of what his father had in his fingers. The boy was smart enough, and papers and essays, lately, had good, solid word-usage, but little of the flair that Richie remembered enjoying in school.

RJ shrugged, embarrassed. 'Mom says it's a good job.'

Richie nodded and shrugged, allowing that it was. If he thought about it, and he had been trying very hard not to lately, writing and publishing was no place for a loved one. *Will build bridge for food*, would not cut it as a *New Yorker* cartoon.

He pulled the ladder back down so that it was propped against the floor of the upstairs hall. Above them yawned the black hole of the attic. 'Let's go up, see the place. It's dark, it's dingy, you have to fumble around to the desk to turn on the light – I'm using a desk lamp – and I had to run power from the wall all the way from the front of the house, so there's cords –' From downstairs, he heard the phone ring. RJ was just stepping on to the ladder.

'I'm going to grab that, you go on up.' And he ran down the stairs to get the phone, catching it on the fourth ring.

'Hey,' he breathed into the phone. Too much smoking.

'It's me, Richie.' *Jennifer. Not-his-jen any more.*

Jennifer. Party. Last night. *Asshole.* His head ached again and he realized he needed more aspirins. He carried the portable phone into the kitchen with him and started opening cupboards. 'Hey,' he repeated. 'What's up?'

He heard her clear her throat and for a moment her neck and its length came into his mind's eye with an ache much worse than the one in his head. He closed the cupboard he'd opened and checked another. He looked in cupboards while she talked.

'I just got thinking about you. Sorry I was rude last night,' she said, drawing it out as though not sorry at all, but wanting amends to be made. 'What you do is none of my business.'

'You weren't. I was –' *an asshole* ' – rude. Anyway, I'm sorry. Wasn't a nice way to say hello again. How are you doing? Or did you already tell me?' He laughed nervously. From upstairs he heard footsteps creaking: RJ was wandering around up there.

She didn't laugh. There was a pause and then she said, 'I thought you quit.'

Drinking was their issue, if they had to put a finger on it. There were many, many, *many* other issues, but they all somehow came to be about him drinking. It annoyed the hell out of him. It wasn't like he was a drunk. He drank too much on occasion. That was it. The end. All there was to it, and if he was alone in being the only one who drank too much *on occasion*, then he would absolutely, without a doubt, quit.

'Is that why you called?' he asked, his face scrunching up in an annoyed frown. 'To be my mother? I can't talk, RJ's here.' But he did not say goodbye or hang up. He listened.

'How's the kiddo doing?' she asked, with affection.

'He's going to be an engineer,' Richie said wryly.

'Good plan. Unions, partnerships, development grants –'

He cut her off. 'I'll be sure to have him talk to you. So, what's going on? The boyfriend out of town, or something?' He was not forgiving her easily. Another issue.

'You just looked shitty last night. I got thinking about it, thought I'd call.'

He found the bottle of aspirins behind a rack of coffee mugs in the last cupboard. He pulled it out and yanked the cap off fiercely, hurting his finger. He mouthed the word *fuck* and shook four pills out of the bottle. They would make his ears ring later, but they would take care of the headache. He grabbed one of the coffee mugs and filled it with water from the tap. He downed it, and with a mouthful of water, answered her, so that it came out slightly garbled. 'I looked shitty. Nice. You gained five pounds.'

'I *know* when I've gained five pounds. I look *fab-u-lous*, thank you very much.' She laughed. 'I don't mean shitty that way. I mean, you looked . . . off. Like you've been thinking too much about all the wrong things. I just thought I'd call and see if you wanted to get together and . . .' She trailed off and they were paused together on the phone.

Richie's mind clicked away at possibilities, *hey anything to get you in bed*, or *it's true I need to be made love to heh heh* – and the smooth sway of her back as it yielded to the curve of her backside and the time when they went to the beach in the middle of March and dumped their clothes and went for a very fast swim. Some guy drove up when they were coming out of the water, completely naked and freezing, and he was just getting out of his truck. He took one look and jumped back in and fired out of the lot. He smiled, remembering that.

As if she'd felt him smile or heard it, she said, '*What?*'

'I was thinking about that time at Black Lake.'

She snorted into the phone and he knew exactly how her breath would smell. 'So I was thinking dinner on Tuesday,' she offered. 'Okay?'

He nodded. 'Okay. You wanna go out or should I impress you?'

'Impress me,' she said softly. From upstairs, he heard the knock of feet on the floor and the sound of the ladder swinging up on its pulleys. It went up and then down again. Then again.

'I'll say hi to Engineer Bob for you,' he said. Feet on the stairs.

'Give him my love. See you Tuesday around seven,' she said, and they hung up.

Richie kept himself to two beers through the game at Dubs'. With him and RJ there were six of them: Dubs, Steve, Brad, and Rob. No wives or girlfriends, but Brenda had made trays of goodies before she went off wherever she'd gone. There were sandwiches and cheese and salami and bags of chips with dip made from onion-soup mix and sour cream, and beer.

'You know, when Brenda made sandwiches for Mikey's christening, she cut the crusts off,' Steve said, pointedly. 'How come she left them on for us?'

'You're not worth the extra effort, Stevie,' Brad said, stuffing half a sandwich into his mouth. 'Try that, RJ,' he said to Rick Jr.

'If your mouth's as big as your dad's it should be *nooo* problem,' Rob snorted.

It was like that all afternoon, with smart remarks and insults of the sort Richie knew that at least Janis tried to teach RJ not to use. He watched RJ watching the action and soaking it all in. He smiled at most of it, but there was sometimes a look of confusion on his face. The guys managed to keep their language decent for the most part, except during crucial moments of yardage, penalties and touch-downs. RJ laughed when someone swore. He seemed to find *fuckme* most amusing. Steve already had a kid, but Bev and Dubs were so far childless (which Steve never failed to point out, assuming in a falsely sympathetic tone that there was something wrong with Dubs' dick: *Get that thing to work, yet?*) so his language was more colourful than most.

It went uncommented on until he lost out on his point spread and sang loudly, a series of about ten *fuckme fuckme fuckme*s and then everyone jumped on him at once.

'Sorry,' he said, laughing. 'RJ, don't listen to me. I have a mouth like a truck driver. When your mom was dating your dad she used to charge me a dollar for every F-word,' he laughed. 'I think I still owe her about a hundred bucks.'

RJ looked stunned. 'My mom dated my dad?' That stopped all conversation in the room for a beat and then everyone laughed.

Richie picked up the ball, putting a hand on his heart and saying, with mock sincerity, 'Believe it or not, your mom and I were once an item. Many years ago. You are what we have to show for our deep love.' He laughed, too.

'That's so gross,' RJ said, recoiling comically. Everyone laughed.

It was a good day.

RJ was still hungry on the way home, in spite of everything they'd eaten at Dubs' place, so they stopped and picked up a pizza and ate it in the kitchen, the least offensive room in the house. Richie moved beer bottles off the table and the two of them ate right out of the box.

'So if you and Mom dated, and you had me, how come you never got married?'

'Mom never talked to you about that?' RJ shook his head. Richie shrugged easily. 'We were young – well, not that young, I guess. But we weren't the best couple. I think we knew that if we got married, it would have been the long way around the inevitable. I mean divorce, you know. So we cut our losses and decided to have you and raise you together, and now we're best friends – I count on your mom for a lot, you know – and so everything worked out great.'

RJ considered this and nodded. 'A lot of my friends' parents are divorced,' he said.

'There you go.'

'Are you going to marry Jennifer?' he asked. There was a pained pause that RJ didn't notice, but it filled the air in Richie's lungs and made him realize how much he couldn't share with the kid. He wasn't sure, at that moment, if he had even mentioned their break-up, and guessed he must have, but that RJ didn't understand about those things. He skipped over it awkwardly.

'Don't you have homework? It's after nine. Your mom would kill me if she knew that I was feeding you pizza at nine o'clock at night, school the next morning, after hanging around with filthy guys who swear and gamble and then asking you to do your homework. She would have my *balls* –' he said dramatically. RJ laughed so hard at that, red-faced and half embarrassed, that he spat pizza out in self-defence.

Richie grinned, self-satisfied. *Nothing like a dick joke to change the subject.*

He set his son up in the room under the stairs, getting sheets on the bed and letting him do his homework in there, giving him until ten. 'Then lights out, no joking, RJ. I'll be checking.'

''Kay,' he said, and Richie closed the door on the image of his son, who managed somehow to look like a baby in his big-boy pyjamas, his hair falling softly over his forehead, and at the same time, a man-to-be.

The vision in his living room was less wholesome.

Everywhere he looked there were beer bottles. He could smell flat, sweet beer and the stale air of cigarette smoke. Every surface had a layer of filth on it. Someone had obviously spilled something and then stepped in it; with the light shining on the floor from the overhead lamp, he could see the dried puddle and the dust bunnies it had gathered during the day, and the outline of a shoeprint just outside the puddle. There was a smear of ash on his green sofa, which was no great shakes to begin with, and he bent over it, brushing the ash away, hoping it wasn't burned. It wasn't. The ashtray was at his feet and he kicked it, spilling butts and ash all over the floor.

He closed his eyes against it and wanted nothing more than to hit the sack and leave it all for the fairies.

Instead he bent down and started picking up butts, putting them into the ashtray.

Penance. He carried it into the kitchen, collecting a couple of empties on the way. He dumped the contents of the ashtray into the garbage can and stuck the empties into a case. He grabbed another case to take into the

465

living room and inside it was an orphaned bottle, still full. Its brothers and sisters were either empty or in the freezer. He pulled it out and opened the freezer to put it in.

Inside, the bright, bald light sparkled off a dozen or so full, cold beers.

Would make it go faster. Behind the beer was a big bottle of ketchup, and a carton of orange juice. Take-out containers were on the shelf underneath and in all it was a pathetic sight, although he reminded himself that he'd just moved in and – *cut a guy some slack!* – he hadn't gone shopping yet. The little light in the fridge glowed amber through the glass. *The colour of love. See the world through amber glasses. Beer goggles.*

His hand shook as he set the beer bottle on the shelf. It knocked into another and glass on glass tinkled invitingly. Richie swallowed. *I don't even want one.*

He took a beer out and twisted off the cap. It sounded like wet evil and music; Satan and the love of a good woman. Smelled like vomit and a headache.

For Chrissakes, it's just one. Cut a guy some slack. Drinking no more; also no less.

Sweet escape and, aaah, it's a party.

He raised it to his mouth and took a swallow.

It did make it go faster, as though that were the price for the beer itself. He dragged himself through the first one, drinking it slow, making it last. He was only half-way through it when he heard the light switched off in RJ's room. By the time the living room looked habitable again, he was on his second. That one didn't last half as long. He put Nilsson on the stereo and dug on that, feeling the beginnings of a nice buzz. Before starting on the dining room, he sat on the couch and lit a smoke, dragging deeply, thinking only once about the smell wafting into the bedroom where his son was sleeping. There was a mild twinge of guilt, deeply ingrained and complicated and thick, that had little to do with smoking and everything to do with the kind of father he was on the whole, that in some kind of inner defence disappeared without much notice, as though it were an animal so large as to be impossible to contain. The only real defence against that creature was to close your eyes against it and pretend it wasn't there; that and another beer.

It was during the third beer that he started thinking about hitting the computer. Before he was too drunk to write anything. The very thought of writing invited back the animal (*must be kept at bay*) and made him tired. Richie tried to remember the last time he'd worked on the book and came up with Friday night. What had he written? Maybe half a page. He'd sat for hours at the computer, drinking water and trying to make sense of a useless second act. He'd been working on the second act of his fourth book for nearly six months and was no further ahead than he had been at the beginning. He never, ever, not even in jest or to himself in the small hours of the naked morning, used the word *blocked*. He was not blocked. Sometimes he allowed himself to believe it was simply an unwritable book and then his futile attempts to produce something were draped in nobility. His plot was too complicated. There were too many elements to be dealt with easily. There were some moments of brilliance and some amazing scenes of utter grace and beauty that he had no idea where inside him they might have come from. Those moments kept it alive. And maybe that was it: maybe he was keeping something alive that was better off dead. Thinking it gave him a surge of some kind of protective instinct not dissimilar from the way he sometimes felt about RJ. He felt that, however briefly then. *I can write this bitch. Whatever works.*

So, he made a small, feeble attempt, mostly for himself. He put on his ball cap. He wrote in a ball cap. Way back in the middle of his life, it was kind of a trademark around his buddies. When he had the ball cap on, his head was up his ass. They were proud of him.

He realized that no one at Dubs' had asked him how the book was going.

Five years between books is a long time.

He got up off the couch and started on the dining room. It made him think of Ashley and (*oh god forbid*) before that thought was allowed to turn pleasant in his head, he thought of everyone seeing him picking her up that way. Right after Jennifer had been there. Right after she left. Then he thought about the stupid things he'd said and done. Fucking around with Jen. At some point in the night he'd called over to Wellington's, the bar they always drank at, all of them, and told Matt the bartender to pass the word about the party.

What the fuck was I thinking? He'd told Rob he wouldn't mind fucking Lois. Lois was Rob's wife. He'd sent Gord Kimble out for beer and then, like an asshole, called him *sucker* when he asked for money after coming back. Gord Kimble hadn't worked in a year. He was living with his ex-wife on unemployment insurance.

He dragged on the smoke and put it out in the ashtray

that he'd emptied but hadn't washed. It was coated in thick black ashes. Beside the ashtray on the filthy, sticky coffee table was the pack of cigarettes from the night before.

I stole those smokes. He'd run out and he'd seen the pack on the table in the living room when he'd changed the CD. He'd just picked it up and walked away with it, feeling clever. Richie drained the beer, went into the kitchen and put the bottle in one of the cases. He stacked them neatly, the full ones on the bottom. He stared at the pile. They'd been drinking all day, hadn't they? Or had it just been him?

His insides felt like they were curling up, away from his flesh, as though trying to get away, or make themselves small.

I'm not an alcoholic. Any thought, real or pretended, of writing slipped away, buried under the ugly, bare words. A heavy grey blanket of shit settled over him and then began what he knew very well would be a long, arduous trip through a self-loathing so palpable and strong that he sometimes thought it was a part of his body, like his nervous system, carried along on his pulse.

I'm not.

As if to prove it, he reached into the fridge and opened another beer. To help him sleep.

Richie woke up in the living room on the sofa. The room was bright, the light above him still on. *Passed out.* On the coffee table in front of him were (and he sized this up with apprehension) three empty bottles. He did the math in his head and decided that he had fallen asleep because he was tired. He breathed. He sat up and stretched.

The clock was still perched at the wrong angle on the little shelf over the fireplace. It was after one already. He had to be up early to drive RJ to school in the morning. He noticed then, for the first time, that three or four beer bottles had been tucked into the open fireplace, hidden earlier because of the shadow. He got up and stretched again, bone weary, his headache back and his stomach a little weak. He bent over and stuck his fingers into the necks of the bottles and grabbed all four with both hands. He gathered the bottles on the table into his arms and he had all eight. An abundance of riches.

Aaah, it was a party.

He stood up straight, his back sore from (passing out) sleeping on the couch, and bent backwards to stretch it and from upstairs came a familiar but unplaceable sound. He stopped and listened, holding his body in that awkward position and tilting his head towards the ceiling.

Tapping. Regular tapping sounds, quietly from upstairs. Tap tap tap.

Obviously, a tap dancer, ba-boom-ba!

It stopped. He listened intently for it to start up again, and when it didn't, he shrugged and lost interest immediately. Could have been anything, a mouse, the house settling, termites; whatever it had been, he was in no position to care at that moment in time. He took the bottles into the kitchen and put them on the counter. He was going to leave them there – *I'll deal with it in the morning* – but they looked so bad, he put them in the cases.

On his way through the hall, the tapping started again. He ignored it until he got to the foot of the stairs and then it was so close that the familiar sound ceased to be theoretical, and it occurred to him what it was.

The computer keys. He looked up the stairs.

'RJ?' he called up. The tapping stopped. He listened, trying just to listen, but probabilities confronted him because he was a writer; a paranoid, self-loathing, drunken writer.

He woke up and saw me passed out sleeping on the couch and got pissed off went upstairs writing me a note about my parenting or just pissing me off playing his fucken computer game –

'Ricky!' he called up, more forcefully and started up the stairs. The tapping had quit (*of course it had he heard me coming*). 'RJ!'

The ladder was down, the hallway lights were on. Richie stalked towards it, frowning; how the hell was he supposed to deal with this now?

And smaller yet: would RJ tell his mom that he found his dad on the sofa in a –

Richie climbed the ladder.

It was dark in the attic, the desk lamp was not on. It took a moment for his eyes to adjust to the darkness. Even once they did, he could hardly see past the hatch. The only light in the room came from the glow of the computer screen.

'RJ?' he said, more quietly, because the space seemed to demand it. The room was utterly silent. Underlying the silence was the friendly purr of his laptop. No one sat in his chair, the outline of which had begun to come clear. If Rick Junior was in the attic, he was hiding. He glanced around at the deep, unrelenting blackness that constituted the attic. Hiding?

That seemed improbable.

Plot change: the kid's asleep, there are mice in your attic, and you are a paranoid son-of-a-bitch who drinks too much (but is not an alcoholic) and you left your computer on, idiot.

With a sigh he heaved himself up into the attic and over to his desk, navigating by the light of the screen. Leaving the computer on was an improbability that flew in and out of his weary brain, and he did not pursue it. He was too tired.

He did, however, read the words on the screen.

Little legs little arms little heads little necks sweet flesh inside

He read it twice over, believing he'd gotten it wrong the first time and that it was something he'd written while fucking around buying time. But it couldn't be placed in his head. Gooseflesh grew on his arms and the hairs on the back of his neck stood up sharply because he could swear – *blackout* – that when he read it, he heard a voice in his head reading it back. It wasn't his own.

'Dad?'

He jumped, nearly knocking over the chair behind him. He looked over his shoulder, a most terrible feeling surrounding him, the feeling of spiders dropping on your shoulder, mice running across your face in sleep, something breathing in the dark.

'I'm up here!' he called, and the sound of his own voice, so loud in the dark, frightened him. He flipped on the desk lamp, and light flooded around him in a circle. It was not much better, casting shadows where anything could be (breathing).

'Dad?' RJ's voice was sleepy-sounding.

'I'm coming,' he called, and that time it was better. He didn't bother with technical details, he shut the

computer off, happy enough to see the screen go dangerously black. When it was gone he shut the lid and
managed, only with the greatest trepidation, to shut out
the light.

'I don't feel good,' RJ said. He was waiting for him in
the hallway, wearing only his pyjama shirt and a pair of
underwear.

'What's wrong? You wanna throw up?'

The boy shook his head. 'I wanna sleep in your room,'
he said, apologetically.

Richie gestured with his chin. 'Go ahead. I'm going
to the can. Don't hog the covers,' he said, trying to make
his voice light. It didn't quite come out that way.

2

There was a morning rush that neither Richie nor RJ was used to yet in the new house. Game Boy, hat, PJs were all left behind. Breakfast was toast (no milk for cereal) and warm juice from leftover juice boxes – picked up at the convenience store and used as a mixer by someone at the party, but he didn't tell RJ that – and Richie hadn't reprogrammed the stereo to get the settings right for the radio, so they had to listen to crappy shit.

After dropping RJ off at school, Richie came home to get in a full day's work at the computer. Passing by the little bedroom under the stairs, he noticed that the light was still on, the bed was still down and sheets and blankets had been left in a pile at the foot of the bed, where RJ had no doubt kicked them the night before.

He went in, pulled off the blanket and folded it. Once folded he didn't know what to do with it; there was no dresser or desk or table, except for the little one beside the bed with the lamp on it. He tossed it into the corner.

Richie debated taking the sheets off, but instead just straightened them out. A lump of something stuck up under the top sheet at the foot of the bed. He pulled the sheet back. The lump was RJ's pyjama bottoms, crumpled into a ball.

The night before he'd gotten into Richie's bed with

just a pair of underwear. He'd gone to bed in pyjamas, though.

Plot twist.

Richie grinned sheepishly, almost shyly, unfurling the bottoms and seeing the tell-tale stain in the middle. He blushed in spite of himself and shook his head, realizing why the boy hadn't felt well and why he'd gone to sleep with his old man. Wet dream. Probably it scared the shit out of him.

That's it now, boy. It owns you.

Still grinning, he pulled off the sheets without further inspection and tossed everything into a pile on the floor. He'd call it laundry and not mention it to RJ unless he brought it up. He shut off the light and closed the door to the room. It shut smoothly, without creaking, in spite of its age and position under the stairs. He found that remarkable. He looked up at the large light fixture on the ceiling in the hall in wonderment. The house, so huge, and he was alone in it.

'I think it's a little big for me,' he'd said to the realtor.

She stared off into the space up the stairs with a small smile on her lips. 'It's a lovely house,' she said.

It was, of course. But he still wondered why he'd bought it.

Richie grabbed the paper from the porch and stood in the hallway glancing over the headlines. Municipal gas prices were going up. The annual pageant of lights was scheduled for a week following. A girl from the west end was still missing. He scanned that article and then fumbled through the rest of the paper for the crossword, pulling it out and dropping the rest on the floor. *Maid'll get it.* When he got a maid. *Jen's coming tomorrow.* The thought, running quickly through his head, left him feeling light, easy. She had that way about her.

He poured himself another cup of coffee and made his way upstairs. He got his ball cap from his bedroom and stuck it on his head.

And so began the ritual that was, for him, as old as his firstborn.

In the attic, he turned on the computer and pulled up his file, chapter twelve, *The Copernicus Tale*. He stared alternately at the last few words on the screen and at the crossword in his lap. When things felt right, he began.

The realtor had shown him at least a dozen houses before taking him to the property on Belisle. Mostly they'd looked at small, two-bedroom bungalows, almost to a number without character or remark. She'd pumped him repeatedly on what exactly it was he was looking for.

A fresh start. But he couldn't tell her that. Something without Jennifer's smell in it. Something without the reek of too much drinking. Something without the option of failure. But he couldn't tell her that either. So he had said, 'At least two bedrooms, possibly three, so I can have an office, and appliances.' And there was an image in his head of the sort that only a fresh start can instigate, of a trouble-free, alcohol-free life, tossing a football around the yard on a sunny Sunday afternoon with his kid. 'And a yard,' he added.

He had a price range, but it was vague. He had some money cached away and had made a small profit on the sale of his house. Between price range and qualifications, they could have looked at about a hundred houses within the city limits.

'Close to downtown is better,' he'd told her, flashing her the smile that had melted a million female hearts and at least one book reviewer. It hadn't necessarily worked on Mrs Darnley, however, because she began to sigh when she pulled up in front of each new showing, each little different from the other.

Then she drove him, on a whim, she said later, to the house on Belisle.

'It's too big,' he said.

'Well, we're already here,' she'd countered. 'It's a lovely house.' He'd believed as soon as they were inside the front door that she had brought him to her own white elephant, the one house that a realtor couldn't unload. The sheer size of the place made him think of heating bills and plumbing problems, but she pointed out that there was only one bathroom. 'It looks much larger than it really is,' she'd told him. And that was when they'd both looked up at the huge chandelier in the front hall.

He didn't think so.

They looked at the downstairs first, the appliances, the large front window, the shining, redone wood floors, the *working* fireplace! (She'd given him a saucy wink with that and he had blushed, the images in his own head more likely much worse than the wholesome, romantic pictures in hers.) They'd opened the back door and looked out into the yard, with its tangle of dead plants that gave it such a Gothic look. She pointed out the privacy offered by a roadless back lane. No real lane at all, she'd explained, just a path.

By the time they got to the room with the Murphy bed, he was catching some of her enthusiasm. When they were crouched on the floor in the bathroom looking behind the toilet at the new pipes and at the bestial feet of the tub-that-had-been-bought-at-auction, it was more of a tour and less of a showing.

Only once had he faltered. The two of them were in the enormous master bedroom with its odd L-shape, looking out to the hallway through the door.

'The door has been replaced; they had to have it specially cut to fit the archway,' she'd told him, and he immediately thought, *Jen'll love that it looks like something from a fairy tale* – and then he remembered that *there is no Jen no fairy tale and this is a fresh start*. His heart jumped into his throat and all the fun had gone out of looking at this house, and every other house and every fresh start that might possibly be waiting out there for him.

The realtor had been looking at him, though, gauging his reaction and she said then, 'There's a kind of energy here. I cringe when I think that, but sometimes I can feel it. I'm always happy to show this house.'

And a beat later he felt it flood over him. There was an energy there. It had felt fresh, like a bracing gust of wind.

He hadn't regretted it. He had, even before moving in, fallen in love with the place, in a way that he might never have articulated, in spite of the fact that he articulated nearly everything, maybe not always in speech but certainly at some point or other, to himself, in his head, where the words resided. He did not think in terms of *I love this house* but more like there was sometimes a lightness of step that he hadn't felt in a while, the feeling that a blank page could give him when he was revved, or the way the delete button could be if he had worked poorly. The place made him feel like there were options. And they weren't all bad.

It had surprised him when he chose the attic to work in, although not entirely. Attics had that writerly feel to them; a room of one's own, if you were a man, would be an attic. The top of the house, command position. The dark, too, had appealed to him somewhat. In the dark there were fewer distractions. No windows to gaze out of and see grass to cut, trees to trim, cars driving by going somewhere (for a drink). No lives to distract him.

Of the other options, the Murphy room was too small and the little bedroom was too blue (although he liked the little cubbyhole, it reminded him of the cubby they'd had in his grandmother's house when he was a boy, he used to go inside there with a flashlight and read Tarzan books, strictly forbidden by his mother for their feral quality). The yellow room had some kind of smell in it that was both musty and alive, like decay. Mrs Darnley hadn't mentioned it, hadn't said much about that room at all, but he had noticed it off and on since he'd moved in, and certainly during his search for a 'place'. The attic it had been.

He had yet to get his desk up there. The guys had declared him insane for even suggesting that it would fit up there. One day they would get together and take it apart and then reassemble it in the attic. He was using a small side table until they got the desk apart, with his desk lamp and his portable computer on top; there was no room for notes but, then, he was far enough along in the book that he rarely sat around doodling any longer.

He did his ritualistic crossword in his lap. The coffee cup and ashtray sat almost on top of the mouse, and while he knew that was an accident waiting to happen, so far it had not.

He felt good about it. The work would be good. If nothing else, he really felt like it would *be*.

The crossword lay unfinished on the floor at his feet where he had dropped it when he felt ready to write, and it lay equally abandoned and at-the-ready, in case he needed it to escape the very real horrors of the next line, the next paragraph, the next scene, the dreaded blank page. It sat there, abandoned, for much of the morning.

Richie fell into the zone around ten thirty.

His fingers moved almost without thought, skating over keys rapidly and then slowly, and then pausing, the sound like an uncertain soldier with an automatic weapon. The attic grew slowly warmer, and light beads of sweat gathered on his forehead. At some point he paused and pulled off his sweatshirt, sitting in the dark in a T-shirt and his jeans. He smoked only twice. Both times the cigarette burned down in the saucer that served as an ashtray. It was going very well. Smoothly.

He wrote without interruption, internally or externally, until twelve thirty when he hit a snag and the rapid tapping of his fingers paused for too long, and broke whatever spell it was that he fell into when he did.

The line read, *what did they look like?* as spoken by his protagonist, thirteen-year-old Porter. The pause inside would not leave. Richie tried to get back into the page, his body leaning forward, shoulders hunched, eyes focused, a short, hard line that would one day be permanent etched between his brows. His breathing was shallow, and in spite of his focus, he was preter-naturally aware of himself, his body and his sur-roundings while being at the same time utterly lost in his own words.

What did they look like?

They were aliens. Spacemen. Bad ones, coming in the dark of night and standing sentinel at the foot of the bed, rousing their victim from a sound sleep and taking them off into the most terrible of all unknowns. (He had a thing he said to people when they asked him what he was writing about. He said it was *alien meets boy; alien loses boy; boy tells the world*. Ha ha. A typical Richie Bramley tale of the unknown.)

What *did* they look like? He knew, of course: it was a matter of making the description both accurate according to the tabloid tales and somehow more fearsome than that which had been massively consumed.

It was there that he fumbled and dropped the ball. He glanced at the little clock on the computer and saw the time and thought, *Not bad*. Four pages. Single-spaced, about two thousand words. Keepers, for the most part. Not bad at all.

He stared ineffectually for a moment or two at the last few words he'd written, then pushed back his chair from the table and leaned down to pick up the crossword. Sometimes all he needed was a little distance. As he leaned down, he saw something out of the corner of his eye. Movement. A flash of light; not light exactly, but maybe reflected light. Fluid.

He snapped his head to the left, and stared into the dark.

There was nothing there. It was so dark, he thought,

like a sudden realization. The darkness filtered in, through the space that was Richie's thoughts. He smelled raw wood, the dry scent of plasterboard, the dust, but saw almost nothing.

And then:

Little legs little arms little heads little necks sweet flesh inside

His shoulders went tight and beads of sweat on the back of his neck felt suddenly cold. He swallowed. Grinned. He hadn't written it. Could have been anyone, though – there hadn't been a lock on the attic hatch and, god knew, his friends were just the sort to write scurrilous, offensive child pornography on his computer. Funny stuff. Steve, Dubs, Brad, could have been anyone. Thing was, it hadn't been saved so that let him out. God knew he saved every puerile, infantile, fractious thing he wrote, like gold from his fingertips, no matter the subject matter; he was an inveterate saver, having had a computer since the days before time. He could look back on a past with function keys and five-and-a-quarter-inch disks, and when booting up your computer meant a whole series of commands and disturbing messages (*bad command or file name*).

He peered into the dark, not yet frightened but with the interest of someone who has spotted a *spider mouse rat* (something *awful*) and looks to see, knowing it is not there. The grin felt stiff and unreal on his face and, in lieu of anything else, he spoke into the dark.

'Wasn't me.' His voice sounded flat and small. Instead of whatever he hoped to achieve, he had a terrible (puerile) thought that he had just told the *ghosts monsters beasties* his exact position. Rule number one: must not wake the monsters. That was why you didn't close doors, flush toilets or turn lights on at night. It was why you kept your feet off the floor when you slept, tucking them under the blankets; that was why you kept the closet closed the bedroom door slightly ajar a way out an escape.

The grin broadened and became real. He chuckled in his throat, and that sounded better in the dark (like a whistle or a song monsters ghosts haunts beasties *hate* that). He sat up with the crossword and turned his attention to finding the pencil – under the computer – and poised it above the *other work* and it was *one with an axe* and just as Richie was about to add it to the puzzle, he smelled the oily, acrid smell of something badly burned. Pork roast, Sundays, too much beer. He curled his nose up against it. Slowly it retreated. The oily reek remained in his nostrils, melting into his throat. Burnt barbecue.

And the dark felt very close. He tightened.

It occurred to him, for no reason at all, that things moved behind him.

The small light beside the computer, perched precariously on the table, lit up only as far as his leg would reach, if he stretched it out into the gulf between him and the opposite wall.

There was a small window, no more than a foot circular on the east side of the attic (something he thought he might take care of before winter he thought it would probably get pretty fucken cold up there no sense adding to the problem) that cast nothing more than a feeble glow on to the floor directly under it. The rest of the place was dark.

He could not shake the feeling that things moved in the dark. *But they didn't.*

Richie stared, eyes straining to make something out, and could see nothing. Not even shadows looked back at him. Darkness was deep, separated only by the feeble glow of the lamp and screen. Dark and light cut sharply. From nowhere came Longfellow. How did it go? Something between dark and daylight.

(Comes pause in the day's occupation/that is known as the children's hour)

Only the light from his small lamp and the screen of the computer were visible. He could not so much as see a beam overhead.

Young Porter waited on the page (*for the children's hour?*) on the screen in front of him. *What did they look like?* He stared blankly at the words there, reading nothing, terribly aware instead of the dark.

(Things move)

Richie stood up deliberately, his chair scuttling out behind him only a short way, the small castors catching on a bit of the unfinished plywood floor and stopping. The noise of it was good. Unlike his voice, it filled the room. Sounded loud and solid.

A break was what he needed. And a spotlight to hang from the ceiling, for safety's sake, if not for the dark. He'd spooked himself, obviously, with his own material. *Has to be a good sign, right?* He'd have a little lunch, then pick it up in the afternoon.

He descended the ladder until his head was all that poked out into the attic. At floor level, the room looked less large, the dark less surrounding. The hall was cool under him and he jumped from the ladder into the light.

Richie had two good solid days of writing behind him by the time he started seriously planning his attack. Not attack, exactly: more like a conquering, a storm on the citadel that was Jennifer.

He felt, entirely, like he was back. Not just back, but *back*. Two years of horror sometimes sat on his back like some kind of medieval deformity, impeding not only the navigation of his future, but the single steps themselves. A weight, heavy and shameful, sometimes even visible to him. When he looked at himself in the mirror he could see the weight in his eyes, and when a night of bad drinking was behind him, he could see it in the hollows of his cheeks, in the slouch of his shoulders, the hang of his arms by his side. For the first time, it felt like some of that might be lifting.

Two good days at the computer was all it really took. There was nothing (and he really meant nothing, not the kid not the girl not a straight-up bourbon and a good reason to drink it not a good book not food when he was hungry water when he was thirsty, *nothing*) like the feeling after writing a good bit of work. Suns shone; he could feel his own heart beating, his own pulse running, he could feel himself, alive and *pleased*. Pleased was better, somehow, than happy. Happy implied a flipside, one he had spent far too much of the last two years visiting. Pleased was spiritual, and entirely belonging to him.

And Jen was coming.

He was Rajah of the Kingdom of All Right.

Richie quit work (eight pages, six hours an excellent, *excellent* take for a day bringing the two-day total up to *drumroll* seventeen fucking pages and about three scenes shy of a chapter) around three and went to the grocery store. He picked up steaks, fresh, small red potatoes from California, which he was going to roast slowly in a tin of consommé just the way his mother used to, and a bag o' salad (no way to screw up a salad why not let them do it?). Groceries bought, he stopped at the dollar store and picked up twenty tiny scented candles having only a moment of doubt – was it gauche to burn scented candles with the heady aromas of a spectacular (steak was her favourite) dinner cooking? – but bought them anyway. She loved shit like candles and little dishes of dead plants that smelled nothing like they had in life and those stupid rings that were scented that he had been forever knocking off lamps when he turned them on – he didn't buy any of those, although he was tempted and then decided it seemed like too much: he wasn't going to buy too much. Probably the flowers he picked up at the florist were about three stems on their way to being too much, but he didn't care by then. After the florist he spent a whopping fourteen dollars on a chocolate torte thing that was bound to enter an entire leap for mankind into *too much*.

He didn't care. He was happy. Not happy. He was pleased, and that was better.

And Jen was coming.

At home, he started the potatoes in the roaster Jen had left behind (that he had kept for sentimental reasons: she often cooked a roast on Saturday night and they would have Steve, Dubs, Brad and their women over and the six, eight, ten of them would sit around after smoke dope drink beers play cards rent a movie and trash it those were the old days); most of the other stuff that she had left behind had been burned in an impromptu ceremony on a very bad, very drunken night last summer. When she asked for some of those things, he said she was mistaken.

A point of contention, but a small one. After they were married and had a couple more kids, he would tell her what he'd done and they would *laaauuuuuggghh*.

He moved the little kitchen table from the kitchen into the dining room, and it filled the space nicely, made it cosy; his mother's buffet in the background made the space look somehow real. He covered the table with his only tablecloth, a gift from the same mother. The folds in the cloth stuck up untidily, but Richie didn't notice. He put the flowers in a large pickle jar that would have to serve as a vase, but first soaked the label off so it wouldn't be too telling. Probably she would think it was charming. It would be, if he was writing it.

Around the house he distributed candles, all twenty, in their new little glass holders. He started to feel silly around candle fifteen. *Too much.* (She would think it was charming; he would, if he was writing it.) He solved that problem by putting the last five in the bedroom, with wistful anticipation.

Ohhhh, she would say, her mouth a perfect red circle. He knew how she would taste. Sweet, like gum. Her cheeks would redden and she would smile, the half-way-up-her-cheek smile that she mostly smiled in their moments of love. He remembered it. He would see her breasts by candlelight again and later he would tell her of his plans for a soft, thick rug for in front of the *working!* fireplace so that he could see her naked by firelight.

The house began to fill with the smell of the roast potatoes. He looked at his watch. He would turn them down some.

Downstairs, in final preparation, he carefully put the single bottle of red wine that he had debated purchasing in the middle of the table, the corkscrew beside it like a waiting tongue.

The debate outside the liquor store had been hell.

Drinking was their (his) issue.

How could you have a romantic dinner without a bottle of wine? It was in all the books. All the movies. *All your movies.* It was no big deal. A bottle of wine. It wasn't like he was going to buy a great big amber bottle of whiskey and down it in shots. It wasn't like he had sixteen cases of empties by the back door (he had taken them back). It didn't mean anything.

He decided to get the wine and then it would look like he could have a couple of glasses and stop. It would be telling, for her. It would show her. I can drink socially.

Can you?

The bottle looked somehow right on the table, with the plates and the silverware and the napkins he'd bought that afternoon with the candles.

He grinned. Too much, of course. And, he thought, she'd love it. If he was writing it, she would.

RJ called at five thirty, just home from school, to say hi and talk in excited tones about some science project that he had been assigned that Richie could not relate to, but he could definitely get into the sound of his kid happy. Maybe the kid was even *pleased*. He thought of explaining the difference between the two to RJ, but decided to keep that nugget to himself. Instead, when RJ asked him what he was doing, he mentioned casually that Jennifer was coming for dinner.

'Oh, yeah?' RJ said, interested. 'Are you getting back together with her?'

Richie tried to keep his heart from thumping, even just hearing it, and played it cool. Just like he would later, playing down the candles, the wine, the bloody tablecloth. The closer it got to Jen, the more too *much* it all seemed. He grinned into the phone, in spite of himself. 'It's just dinner. We're friends. You know how it is,' he said, and quickly changed the subject. 'How's your mom?'

Then RJ launched into a completely beautiful adolescent rant about an ongoing debate on a new bedtime. He felt too old to have a bedtime, and his mother had countered that if he was given free rein he would stay up all night. Richie said he would talk to her, the grin never leaving his face.

Then she was there.

The door opened with a blast of cold air from outside. It was snowing, big fat flakes coming down, looking Christmassy and nice. She shook it from herself, her cheeks pink with the cold, her even white teeth showing through her smiling mouth, and Richie resisted, barely, the urge to grab her, take her in his arms and keep her.

'It got so cold!' she said, laughing.

'Looks nice. When did it start snowing?' he said formally, grinning, happy (*pleased* like a Rajah overlooking the Kingdom of All Right). She smiled warmly at him and told him all about traffic and city drivers and trucks downtown.

She shook off her coat and handed him a narrow brown-paper bag with wine inside.

'Oh, you brought wine,' he said, surprised. So much for the debate. 'I bought some this afternoon.'

She shrugged happily. 'Well, keep it for another day,' she said, and inside, he whirled. Another day.

He took her coat and hung it on the hooks on the wall. She stomped her feet and laughed, telling him he was going to have to wash the floor tomorrow. He laughed too. The hall felt warm and he could smell the snow off her boots and her coat. The little drops of melted snow sparkled under the hall light. He was cool.

'Steaks are going on the 'cue in a minute,' he said.

She breathed deeply, 'Smells good in here. Roast potatoes like Mom used to make?'

He grinned. 'You know me so well,' he said, sarcastically.

They walked into the living room together and Jennifer stopped to look around.

He'd lit all the candles (*fifteen* candles) and set the dimmer on so they glowed and danced against the mostly unadorned walls. The dishes on the table sparkled with the glasses, and cutlery, the pickle jar. It looked, even to him, even if he wasn't writing it, charming. Romantic.

She turned slowly to look at him, his face beaming just a beat longer, as he took in her expression, her face naked of pretence or politeness. She was not smiling. Her head tilted apologetically to the side and she said, 'Oh, Richie.'

Oh, Richie. With no ability to control it, his face just fell, and then it, too, was naked. She closed her eyes a second, not a blink, really, and then smiled. Sadly?

'What were you thinking?' she said softly. Her shoulders drooped.

He swallowed. Tried to pick up the ball. He walked over to the mantel and blew out two of the candles there. 'I wasn't thinking nothing.'

'It looks very romantic in here,' she said, a prod. 'We should probably talk about this.' Her voice had dropped sombrely, the way it used to. Better than anything else she did, he recognized that tone (and hated it – *we should talk we need to talk let's talk about this*): he never came out good in those conversations.

No romance.

'So I jumped the gun, big deal,' he said. He walked briskly into the dining room and began opening the bottle of wine he had bought. He wanted a drink. And he guessed he could bloody well have one now. No one here to impress.

'I'll have some too,' she said.

'Did you think I was opening it just for me?' he sneered. He yanked on the cork less than delicately and the pop sounded loud. He smelled the mouth of the bottle. He'd heard once that if a wine bottle popped too loudly, the wine would be bad. It smelled good to him. Good old grapes.

Jennifer walked slowly into the dining room, hands in the front pockets of her jeans. 'Of course not,' she said. 'Just . . . making conversation. Are you okay about this? Should I go?'

He looked up from pouring the wine expertly

into glasses. 'I'm fine,' he said, annoyed. 'So I lit a few candles for atmosphere. Big deal. I don't know what I was thinking, so don't ask me. I'm going to throw the steaks on, you're medium-well, right?' he said, as though he didn't remember, and smiled a bright, beaming, nearly painful-to-produce smile to soften the edge in his voice.

'That's right,' she said, as if buying that.

She followed him to the back door and stood framed in it while he dropped steaks on the barbecue, its newly filled canister of propane grey against the soft white snow that had fallen around it. She talked incessantly about mundane matters, what friends were doing, her job, the new place she'd moved into, her mother. She asked about RJ and he told her about bedtime. She suggested a compromise of trying out a new no-bedtime rule and seeing how he managed his time. He said that was a good suggestion and he would mention it to Janis. She asked about Janis. He responded, and slowly, painfully, most of the moment passed.

Oh, Richie.

The steak had been good, and the potatoes came out nicely roasted on the outside, soft and white on the inside; the salad was salad. Richie barely tasted any of it.

The cosy, warm, intimate feeling he had expected for the evening was completely unaccounted for, replaced instead by a growing feeling of mortification. Jennifer kept up a steady stream of small-talk, newsy bits about work and common friends, what she was doing to her apartment and nonsense about the house (with fake intimate – *friend* – moments stuck in for good measure, like a mother talking to a child: 'You should put the Picasso over the fireplace, don't you think?').

The food had gone down because he'd chewed and swallowed. He'd nodded at her statements and laughed at her small jokes and added his own here and there, but at the core of it was that mortification, that horrible, beyond-embarrassed feeling, that was growing in him, even as he tried to ignore it. As it grew, he seemed to feel it physically. Hotly.

It was just hot in the house. While coffee brewed and filled the dining room with its benign smell, they swirled their wine in their glasses and looked around the room at everything but each other. The news seemed spent.

It was too hot. *It's not the heat it's the humiliation ha ha.* Richie slipped off his carefully chosen sweater and sat at the table in his T-shirt, his face flaming, although hopefully she couldn't see that in the glow of the stupid candles. He stood up and grabbed his sweater, tossing it towards the couch and hitting his mark. He turned up the lights in the dining room with the dimmer switch. Jennifer did not remark on it.

The coffee pot made its last gasping burps before quitting and Richie, who did not feel like coffee at all unless it was coffee-flavoured vodka, poured the rest of the wine into his glass, stopping just before the bottle was empty and gesturing with it to Jennifer.

'No thanks, I have to drive,' she said primly.

Fuck you. When she looked away, he made a mocking face at her. *No thanks I have to drive.* A small, too small, voice inside told him to cool it. Watch it. Don't be stupid.

Fuck you too.

'Coffee?' he offered Jennifer, his voice controlled, pleasant.

'Yes, thank you,' she said, almost gratefully. He went into the kitchen to pour her a cup. She took it with milk and sugar. Just a touch of sugar. She dipped her spoon into the coffee, just at the tip, and then dipped the wet end into the sugar, that was how much she took. Just enough to take the edge off, she would explain. It used to drive him crazy, the little brown lumps in the sugar bowl. He did it for her, though. Carefully. Stirred it. He pulled himself together. Some of the growing anger was pushed down. *Just because today wasn't the day didn't mean it wasn't coming.* He'd just jumped the gun, was all. Probably scared her. Too much, too fast. He understood that. He stirred her coffee, staring into it, moving the spoon gently around the mug.

From the dining room, she called, 'I'm so glad to hear you're working again,' and he stiffened.

Slowly, a sneer grew on his face. *She was glad he was working again?*

The two points in his head, Jennifer and work, separated by what he would likely think of – given a chance – as his soul smashed together inside him, crushing him. How dare she even assume to think about him and his *work*?

How dare she? *I'm so glad to hear you're working again.* Condescension. Pity. Maybe pity. *Oh I'm so glad to hear that you can still work even without me in your life poor baby.* His teeth gritted together and a vein in his jaw throbbed. He felt the wine in his head. It felt mushy and vague, angry. He realized that through dinner Jennifer had only had one glass of wine and he had drunk the rest.

Not the rest, there was still a nearly full glass on the table. *How dare she?* A nearly empty glass on the table. *How dare she?*

He gritted his teeth and tried to get straight. His good work over the last two days felt tainted. *It's not. Calm down.* Little voices inside. *Settle it. Get straight.*

Through teeth still mostly gritted he called back, 'Thanks.' And then he took her her coffee. And sat down with his wine. But with every intention of sipping it. She looked hopefully at him, her eyes wide, over the lip of her coffee cup, and he softened. He felt like an asshole.

So he said, 'The work's good.' And kept his smile stiffly on his face.

She nodded brightly. 'I'm so glad to hear that. I was worried when I saw you Saturday night. I know from the guys that you haven't been writing.'

He pressed his lips together. *It's not the heat . . .* 'So you guys just sit around talking about poor old Richie?' he said, shaking his head.

'Of course not! Nobody *said* anything –'

He raised his hand and rubbed his face. 'Don't . . . let's not go . . . there. I don't want to talk about this. Let's talk about you. Painful subjects about you,' he spat. 'How about that boyfriend? He know you're here? He doesn't care if you go visit the ex?'

She looked down, stared at the table. Her eyes filled with tears and her chin wobbled and he felt like an ass again.

'Hey –' he said, with a sigh.

'Richie –' she started, and he saw an opportunity in her face, and he shifted his chair around and got close beside her.

'Hey,' he repeated, and put his arms around her. 'Hey.'

She shook her head, no, and moved only a little away from him, so he got closer, inching his chair awkwardly on the shining wood floor. She let out a sob and allowed him to hold her, leaning into him with equal awkwardness, her head and shoulders ending up somewhere near his heart.

'Hey,' he said dumbly.

'Richie, I have to tell you something –' and she cried.

He buried his face in her hair, the smell of her scalp close and familiar, like one of those memories from childhood that hit you when you feel bad and vulnerable. He pressed his face into her and ran his hands gently over her back, into her hair, along her shoulders. He ran his fingers up her spine, feeling and remembering each knob of bone. She was warm beneath her sweater. He longed to put his hands up under it and feel her skin; it was not lust, but her; he wanted to feel her. 'It's okay,' he breathed into her hair.

She shook her head again, and began pulling away. He let her. He wanted to see her face. When she cried, her nose got red and her lips quivered. He wanted to see it.

He was distracted by her and hardly noticed that she was still shaking her head, *no*. And when she stood up and moved away from the table, he stood up too, and followed her. She was still crying. He thought of a Kleenex, but the only thing he had was toilet paper, all the way upstairs in the bathroom – glancing through his mind quickly on another level was the option of getting her upstairs for tissue and then leading her into the bedroom and making love to her but he let go of it (remembering to think *asshole* but not really feeling it) and ran into the kitchen, grabbed the roll of paper towel by the sink and brought it to her. She took the whole roll, laughing oddly, and pulled off a sheet. She blew her nose, but kept crying.

'What's wrong? What's going on?' he asked gently. Some boyfriend trouble. If he was writing it, the boyfriend was history, she couldn't forget him, but was afraid, was it right? She would hurt the other guy, gentle creature that she was, she couldn't face that, but couldn't live without –

'He asked me to marry him and I think –' She sobbed hard into the towel. 'I don't know what to say –' she said, and buried her face in her hands. Her shoulders shook and Richie stared. 'I'm so sorry, Richie, I'm so sorry,' she repeated several times, not taking her hands off her face.

He stared, incapable of saying anything. The room was filled with the sound of her crying, more softly now, and it occurred to him to ask her why the hell she was crying. It occurred to him to ask her to repeat what she'd said, he'd heard it wrong – *on Saturday you were cooling it off*. It occurred to him to ask her to die. To get lost. To *fuck* off.

'I thought you were taking a break,' he said, stupidly. It sounded flat. He was flat. He was one-dimensional. A stick man.

She nodded. 'He came over Sunday night. He said he didn't –' She wiped her eyes on the towel, looking up for the first time, although not at Richie yet. She looked at the opposite wall, something in the tone of his voice making her feel safe.

'Didn't what?' he screamed.

'Don't *yell* at me!'

They stood, separated by a room and a host of options. Neither spoke. Richie's mind tried to grasp *Jennifer's marrying someone they said she would it was a joke how could she marry someone she was his what the hell do I say* –

He had no idea what to say, but they both stood there, motionless and dumb, and before he could stop it, he asked the last question he wanted the answer to, tried to stop himself and still asked it anyway.

'Are you going to marry him?'

Jennifer wiped her nose needlessly. She stared at the floor, and said nothing. His eyes widened and he raised an eyebrow, willing her to answer. But she didn't.

She was.

'Well,' he said, softly, 'congratulations.' Then he laughed.

She looked sharply at him. 'I haven't *decided*,' she screamed at him.

When he finally moved, his body responded as though on a five-second delay. He spun round too fast, his head light, and went and got his glass of wine. His heart thudded in his chest, but it was dull, like an ache. 'Well, let me make it easy for you. I don't care what you do. That's what you wanted me to say, right? You wanted me to say it was okay. It is. I don't care.'

He sat at the table and glared at her, tried to pretend it wasn't a glare. She looked around the room, the candles burning, the flowers.

He shook his head. 'I wanted to get laid,' he said. 'Pardon me.'

She closed her eyes and sighed heavily, put-upon; that sound was also familiar, the patented Jennifer's-had-enough sound. Fucken princess. 'Don't do this,' she said. *Took the words right out of my mouth.*

He downed the wine in his glass. He stood up and went into the kitchen and came back with the bottle Jennifer had brought. He opened it with the same jerking motions with which he had opened the first. 'So when's the happy day?' he snarled. 'Am I invited?' She wiped her nose again with the paper towel and then went to the hall. 'Come back. Let's toast the *union*.'

Jennifer crossed her arms over her chest and stood framed in the doorway between the hall and the living room. She screamed at him, her body leaning towards him.

'*I didn't want it to be this way! I wanted to talk to you about it! This is my life!*'

Richie poured himself another glass.

'Go ahead, drink until it hurts. Or doesn't hurt,' she said, evilly. He did not respond.

'I'm sorry,' she said, starting to cry again.

'Just fuck off.'

Stick your sorry.

That would be 'sorrow', Mr Bramley.

Oh, pardon.

She grabbed at her coat and it stuck on the hook. She tugged angrily at it, her pretty face contorting in a sneer. 'I knew it would be like this. *I knew it.* Never mind,' she said. She shook her head and pulled her coat down. The zipper clacked on the floor.

'Don't scratch my floor,' he said petulantly, from behind a fog. Rajah looking down on the Kingdom of All Right.

'Another pleasant evening with Richie Bramley, author of nothing but his own demise,' she snarled back. It had the distinct flavour of a speech written some time before and practised. He knew these speeches well. And in this honour he raised his glass to her in *salud* but by then she didn't see it, because she was tearing open the door and slamming it hard, leaving behind her a whirl of snowflakes, big and fat and white and happy. They danced into the hall and descended, elegantly to the floor.

Richie drank.

It was a dangerous sort of drinking, filled with abandon, no holds barred, untethered, unfettered and completely (for a change) justified. There would be no stops.

He stared at the wine bottle. The bottle she'd brought. *Well, let it bring me pleasure. And it will. And it was good, so sayeth Lord Richie Bramley, Rajah of the Kingdom of All Right.* It was a Merlot. She had a fondness for Merlots, in the way that a passenger has a fondness for a Mercedes. *She had no idea, not a grand clue of the pleasures made possible by a decent Merlot. She might know a decent Merlot, but she wouldn't know decent drunk if she stepped on it, ha ha.*

Richie had watched the door for a good half-hour after she'd slammed it shut, expecting (not really but expecting) her to come back through it again, and tell him once more, *I'm sorry I know how difficult this is for you I know how difficult you are and I love you anyway I know how difficult*. But, of course, she didn't. He did not so much give up on it as forget to watch after a while. There were other things going on.

He stared at the dishes on the table. He felt that humiliation. He let the candles burn, enjoying the horror of their witness. *Ha ha you thought you were going to get the girl did you we have seen all the love and we knew all along ha ha*. He rewrote every line he said in his head. By the time the third glass of the second bottle of wine was drunk, he didn't come off quite so bad.

So many things he could have said.

Simple. *What do you want to do?* Because even three sheets to the wind he knew, *knew*, that that was the crux of the matter, and the right thing to say. So simple. But he had instead baited her with anger and then got the spatter back.

In his head as written by Richie Bramley, master of the supernatural and all things paranormal, he said all the right things.

The dishes, he felt, stared back at him, smugly. *We knew, too*. He sometimes buried his head in his hands and cried. Drops on the tablecloth, the crisp, sharp folds still visible, were testament to it. It went unnoticed by him.

There are four glasses in a bottle of wine. (Unless you get the jug, and no one gets the jug after age thirty.) And Richie poured the final glass, licking the last drip as it dangled on the mouth of the throat of the bottle. The last glass of anything – if you notice – is a depressing and downright loathsome thing. His first taste of it was a sip.

He piled a plate on top of another. He picked up cutlery and put that on the plates. It was a mess. The kitchen was still full of dishes and pots and pans, because in spite of having cooked a simple meal, he had seemed to require numerous and sundry appliances. They were scattered everywhere.

He hid from himself his need to hurt. And he piled dishes. He thought about Porter. Or tried to. The boy in the story. The story, at that point, was too far away from him to make even a small dent in his head.

She could come back. He could call her tomorrow. Don't do it. Come back to me. I'll fix it. I'll do it all. Everything. In a burst of condolence – whether to him or to her he didn't analyse – he thought he would quit drinking. He stumbled into the kitchen, glass in one hand, dishes in the other and made that vow. I'll quit.

I will. Tomorrow I will. If you come back. If you come back and stay.

But the feeling in his head was an old and familiar friend that he needed. The only consolation he got came out of the bottle, the only time he could make things completely right (or not matter) was with the bottle. *If you could bottle that feeling – and thank god someone did.*

He put the dishes in the sink. He put water in the roaster – her roaster – to soak off the remnants of potato that had stuck there. It was tossed into the sink also, where it stood at an awkward angle, the water all on one side. He tried to prop it up on a glass and it fell. He wandered around the kitchen, back between stove and sink a couple of times, and called it done. He downed the last of his wine.

The glass was empty. And something niggled at him. *Enough.*

Even as he argued, a lesser part of his brain whispering

truths, Richie walked deliberately over to the far corner of the last cupboard under the sink and opened it. Amidst the bottles of cleanser and dish soap was a gleaming, shining example of the American go-to attitude that he liked. A contingency plan.

He reached out for the (half) bottle of bourbon (half) hidden behind a rag and a bottle of Javex. *Aha.*

Hello. And how did you get there?

It flashed through his mind. The trip to the liquor store. The standing endlessly in the wine aisle, finding, choosing, reading, just the right wine to bring her back. To tell her, I'm okay now. A benign wine. A wine of the casual drinker. A wine for all seasons. He wandered through the wines of Italy, France, America, South Africa, Spain, Canada, way to the back, where there was no wine. *Ran out of wine.* The bourbon had been in his hand, almost as a before-thought, and then he picked a nice light, woody South African because it seemed arbitrary and just the sort of thing a non-totally-casual-drinker might choose because of its political value.

The bourbon had come along just for the ride. And now it gleamed with possibilities.

Enough.

Go to bed. Write like hell tomorrow. Be –

He pulled it out and turned the cap before he had a glass or a decision at hand.

On the couch, much later, he ruminated and came up with *it just wasn't really worth it*. His heart was gone. History. Toast. No more heart. She had taken it with her. He stared unfocused into the dark of the living room (the candles had long since burned away) and thought that it (most of it) was over. She wasn't going to come back. Not to him. Not to that. To this. And somewhere in the rumination came the scent of something bad.

It took a long time to get there.

He became aware, first, of his nose tingling. He smoked intermittently, *smoking too much nose hurts*, but realized in a sleepy part of his brain that it wasn't smoke he smelled, but something burning.

It grew until it bothered him. His house on fire. *It would just be like that, for sure.*

Bitch.

The highball glass on the coffee table swirled and doubled but looked nearly empty no matter what the view. Richie leaned over and filled it to the half-way mark (half-full), slopping bourbon down the side and on to the table.

The smell lingered, getting inside him. He tasted it in his throat. It was bad, like something gone over, tyres burning, the dump. Decay. He frowned and stood up, wobbling, nearly falling back down on to the couch again, and then, grabbing his glass, he sniffed the air. It was hard to tell where it was coming from.

He squinted into the dark room looking for smoke. He couldn't see anything, although, he realized, he could see two of the nothing that he saw. This made him giggle. He stumbled past the couch, hitting his shin on the coffee table without noticing.

He walked first towards the kitchen, the most obvious place in the house for a fire. The smell was less noticeable in there. He tried to remember if he had shut off the barbecue after the steaks were done, but remembered that he hadn't been drunk then. Not then. Just now. *And*

I am most definitely drunk now. He walked to the back door and, after a couple of futile passes, pulled it open and peeked outside. No smoke. No obvious flame. Just the smell of steak.

The faint smell of meat cooked earlier was nostalgic and accusing. He hadn't meant it. None of it. Drunken regret overwhelmed him for a moment before anger took its place. He had meant well; it just hadn't come out that way.

He was misunderstood. Always had been.

Nobody knows what it's like to be me, he thought with boozy self-pity.

He stared out into the dark wishing he was seeing it through someone else's (sober) eyes, squinting, trying to focus. All he could really see was the dark. A metaphor for my life, he thought, with equal parts pity and clarity.

Fuck it.

He backed up and closed the door, forgetting entirely why he had opened it in the first place until he was assaulted, the moment the door closed on the fresh air, with the acrid smell of something burning. It seemed almost to be coming from behind him, thicker there in the hall than it had been in the kitchen or the living room.

Funnelling down the stairs.

Still holding his drink, he wandered down the hall and looked up the dark stairwell. Upstairs in his room, the candles would still be burning. One might have fallen over, lit something man-made, something made of chemicals, synthesized from nature, getting it right in every way except the way it smelled when it burned. A shirt; a sheet; there were no curtains as yet in the bedroom. There was a little rug on the far side of the bed by the window.

Very logical. Or maybe, by then, the candles would have burned out. Given up.

He climbed the stairs, pausing at the bottom only a moment to sip his drink.

The bathroom light had been left on for Jennifer, in case she had to go there in the planned interim between dinner and retiring to the candlelit bedroom. Richie's bedroom door was closed; he thought maybe the flickering candlelight, spotted on her way up to relieve herself, might have seemed presumptuous.

The smell was very strong at the bottom of the stairs. He jogged his way up, taking the stairs two at a time, one hand on the rail, his drink splashing dangerously against the sides of the glass. The light from the bathroom pooled in the hall outside the door.

At the top of the stairs he flicked a switch and the upstairs hall sconces came on.

The hatch to the attic was open, the ladder down. Like an invitation.

He looked to his bedroom door, still closed, and back to the attic hatch. He stared at it, blinking once, a long, restive blink.

I closed that.

Without giving it further thought, he reached over (not taking his eyes from the hatch and the ladder, *just hanging there . . . yoo hoo! Up here!*) and turned the knob to his bedroom, pushing the door open.

It was dark in there. No glow from the lit candles.

Dragging his eyes from the hatch with both drunken

and cautionary slowness (*Yoo hoo! Up here!*), he poked his head into the bedroom and sniffed deeply. There was a smell, but it was waxy and familiar; like a burned match. Sulphury. He flicked on the light. He saw the small glass candle-holder, purchased just that afternoon, on the edge of the dresser closest to the window. It was burned down, and the sides of the glass were murky and grey with the residue of the candle. He looked over to the bedside table and saw a virtual replica of the first. He stepped inside the bedroom, just two steps further, and glanced over towards the side of the bed. He couldn't smell the smell of synthetic fibres smouldering; he counted off his five little candle-holders that had made their way, foolishly, upstairs and nothing was tipped or dripping.

He hadn't expected it to be. The hatch was open and the ladder down. *Yoo hoo.*

After all, he wrote this stuff. He smiled gamely and closed the bedroom door after himself.

Under the hatch, he stared up into the dark yawn of the attic. He tried to work up a bit of adrenaline and found himself too drunk. He tried to find the drama inside – of course there was nothing up there, obviously he had simply not shut the attic hatch after working that day, but it was an opportunity none the less to be his reader for just a moment – but he was too drunk. He stood instead under the hatch and sniffed.

The smell was definitely up there. It would be electrical. The smart thing to do was to go back downstairs and turn off the breaker that served the attic. Bad wiring. Old house. Very expensive. The odour of whatever was burning did not smell electrical: missing was that sharp, plastic smell of the coatings burning. This particular smell was somehow animal, like pork, gone-over pork, burned too long on a barbecue; but it had a rubbery smell, like tyres. It was biting, painful in his nose, especially so close. Synthetics did that. If it was the insulation, he was fucked.

He climbed the ladder. If there was a fire, he might just throw himself on it.

The drink in his hand presented a problem, but he climbed without addressing it. Two steps up he heard the hum of his computer, such an intimate and comfortable sound that he hardly noticed it at first. Not until he reached the top stair and the light from the screen, facing the hatch, met him. Facing the wrong way. Facing the hatch.

The lid to the tiny portable was half closed (half empty), directing the light towards the opposite wall. The screen inside, just visible, was white. Like a page. His word-processing program produced a blank white page to write on, just like the greats of old: Hemingway and his notebooks; Fitzgerald at the typewriter; Plath and her pages of baggage.

All around the computer was black. It was the only light, casting a weak glow around the table it sat on, so that he could just see the edge, and the floor underneath it. Fruitlessly, he glanced around the attic at floor level. The light that filtered up through the hatch pooled around the opening in the floor, but not far. He would turn on the desk lamp. He could flash it around the room, like a club. See what there was to see.

Richie took one more sip of his drink before resting it on the floor by the hatch and pulling himself up. With a bit of a struggle, he stood into blackness. He strained into the dark. The room was silent. It stank up there, for sure, but the smell seemed suddenly old, a hangover, yesterday's meat.

He reached over and pulled up the lid on the computer.

The screen was blank except for a few words in the middle, as though laid out. He squinted to read, but it was too small.

Four lines. Like a poem.

(little arms little legs)

> *sweet pain does it hurt does it hurt*
> *is it exquisite taste it*
> *does it please you*
> *does it hurt you let it hurt let it eat you eat it up*

He stared and read it again, trying to make sense of the words all running together, and he lost himself in them, finally finding the drama. The back of his neck tightened. His mouth was dry and he tasted the old smell of burning (*meat*) rubber and synthetics. And he looked up into the dark.

Out of the corner of his eye, a flash of white. He spun that way, staring madly into the dark, one hand lightly on the edge of the lid to his computer.

'*Hey!*' he called.

Nothing answered back but the dark. He stared a long time into it, waiting for something to show itself.

Wondering.

The wonder touched some basic, primal place inside him that it might not have reached in the harsh light of sobriety. In sobriety, he might have (*eat it up*) freaked out, slammed the hatch door, called it heebie-jeebies, left it alone. Calmed himself and maybe (until nightfall) laughed it off.

In his drunken half-numb, half-open state, he allowed the wonder. The fear, prickly, felt good.

'What is this?' he asked of the dark. He swallowed on a dry mouth. His skin woke up, sobering him slightly, but not enough. 'What is this?' he repeated, very softly.

Something like a shadow flickered to his right, grey and indefinite. Richie squinted, focusing with difficulty. The light from the computer glowed beside him.

A man stepped closer, out of the dark, and stared back. Richie shrieked. Stood frozen, open-mouthed.

The man smiled softly, sadly, kindly, and Richie saw him distinctly, his grey, watery eyes, white face topped with whiter hair, neck wrinkled and long, poking out of a white collar; the rest of him was dark. Long: he wore something long, like a cloak. The man was very tall and slender, like a tree, his tremendous age and height making him seem firmly rooted.

The edges of the man wavered, features shivered. The nose, long and sleek, grew bulbous and mottled with red. The eyes darkened, became shot through with red veins. The great height that he had first seen shrank. The girth widened. His old man looked into Richie's eyes with a kind of longing that Richie felt through the fog of drink.

'Dad?' The old man smiled. He raised a hand in a practised gesture, and one Richie remembered with complications. In the raised hand was a glass. Amber liquid sloshed. His father did not speak, but Richie heard it in his head: *Salud*. Glass was not raised to lips (as it would have been, *Salud*, to his brothers and his mother, his mother's face a mask, smile plastered thinly, that would be early in the evening; as the night wore on, the *saluds* would be fewer and finally they would be gone and the old man would just sit at the table leaning closer and closer to his glass, silent except for the unintelligible mumbling and the clink of the glass on the table, the gurgle of bourbon or whiskey into the glass, the splash of bourbon or whiskey into the glass all of it repeated repeatedly, his mother's mask stiff and angry by bedtime and the reek of another burned dinner in the oven kept warm because his father didn't like to eat at night when he was pouring a few, *salud*). But the smile stayed there, on his lips, also a practised motion. The old man's facial expression changed only with the slackening of his muscles as the night wore on. The smile was one of acquiescence, *I mean no harm. Don't mean it a bit.*

The glass caught light from somewhere and sparkled. Richie stared into the face of his father, dead nearly fifteen years, victim of his own submission, not to his mother but the glass, and felt longing for him. The *salud* of early evening, the Saturday mornings when he was *feeling a little rough today little man* and they would slip out, the four of them, for bacon and eggs and coffee *hot and black please* while his mother slept or fumed behind the closed door of the big bedroom.

'Dad?' Richie whispered, afraid that his voice would frighten him off break some spell and he would be without him. It sounded like a sob.

The figure wavered and Richie's father was gone.

In his place was the tall man. He smiled broadly,

dragging it out over large grey teeth, his lips stretching uncomfortably over them, their wrinkles smoothing out and appearing in his cheeks. The smile was broad and pleased. The smile of the Rajah.

His lips did not move but, as with his dad, Richie heard him.

Do you hurt?

He looked down to the computer screen with just the corner of his eye. The words on the screen sat passively, like little soldiers, waiting. *At your go.*

does it hurt you let it hurt let it eat you eat it up

(eat it up)

Richie looked back at the man. 'No,' he said.

The old man smiled. And faded into the black.

Then the moaning began. Low, at first, high-pitched like animal wails, the howls of pain from something young. Richie strained to see the place where the man had been, but the sound was everywhere in the room; he swung his head round. Everywhere seemed to be movement.

He backed up to the hatch, something flew by him, hands outstretched, flashing past in a split second. Under the low growls of pain and fear were soft sobs, hiccuping sobs. It rose to a cacophony and he pressed his hands over his ears. He stumbled backwards, one foot hitting his glass and sending it falling down the hatch. He heard it break on the bare floor. He followed it, tripping first on the edge, catching himself on the ladder and then, in haste, missing the last step and toppling down to the floor of the hall, where it was bright and cool. He hit the floor right knee first and pain shot up through his leg and into his hip and he groaned, throwing his head back. He brought his knee up and cradled it.

He rocked, briskly rubbing his kneecap. Broken glass sparkled in the hall light. *Dad*. Drunk even when he was dead. Drinking. His version of heaven. Richie's knee ached and he wondered if it was bleeding. He looked up through the dark hole of the attic. His head throbbed with the beginnings of a headache. The hall smelled of bourbon. Like his dad. *Salud*.

Silence fell down around him. The only sound audible was the hum from his computer, still on, and he listened to it.

He sat that way for a minute, then stood up and hobbled, limping, to his bedroom. He pushed open the door and fell on to the bed, leaving all the lights on downstairs, the light on in the hall, the computer on upstairs, and the music on downstairs, although he didn't remember it playing before. Not since Jen left.

Let it play. Leave the lights. Let the neighbours think there's a party going on.

Salud.

Just before sleep and alcohol claimed him for the night he thought *the DTs. Bad really bad Bramley*.

(do you hurt)

3

Rare November sunshine streamed through the tall windows that Mia Tia was famous for, and glanced off the china and glasses. The sun was so bright, reflecting as it did off the fresh, thin layer of snow outside, that it made some places in the restaurant hard to look at. It was too bright, and Glenn Darnley could feel the beginnings of a headache. A tension headache. A bright patch of sun on the floor seemed to dull and fade the carpet, and she tried to make out the pattern. She didn't feel dizzy exactly, but things were swimming around inside her. She dared not look at her plate.

She took a sip of wine from her glass and it did not help, might, in fact, have made the nausea worse. She closed her eyes and breathed deeply in an attempt to stave it off.

'Glenn?'

She was having lunch with Gavin and Helen, their treat, a fact that had not gone unremarked upon when Gavin saw what she'd ordered. *For Chrissakes, Glenny, have a steak! It's my treat!* On the plate in front of her was a small, unadorned salad and a piece of grilled fish – no sauce. Between the two was a small pile of roast potatoes coated in some sort of Creole batter that Gavin had insisted was ambrosia and that she *must* try. He'd piled a half-dozen on her plate and teased her about watching her figure. She had meant to counter with a remark upon his growing waistline, and would have, if she hadn't believed deeply and sincerely that if she opened her mouth all that she had thus far eaten and drunk would come sailing up and on to his medium-rare steak and potato ambrosia.

'Are you all right, dear?' Helen asked. Glenn opened her eyes to Helen's soft brown ones, frowning in concern. 'You're just pale as the tablecloth,' she said.

Glenn pressed a hand to her cheek and smiled wanly. 'I'm fine. A little indigestion, I'm afraid.'

'From what?' Gavin bellowed. 'There's nothing on your goddamn plate!'

She shrugged gently. 'I'm afraid I might have an ulcer,' she said. 'I just can't eat the things I used to. If you don't mind –' Glenn pulled her purse into her lap from the floor and rummaged through it for her antacids. She put two into her mouth discreetly and chewed. 'There. Better in a flash,' she said, without conviction. Lately, the antacids had not helped. She chewed the thick chalky tablets and kept her smile firm.

Helen stared her down, kindly. 'I've never heard of someone going pale from heartburn,' she said.

Glenn swallowed the rest of the tablets and they left her mouth coated and dry. Awful things. She picked up her white wine and sipped.

It occurred to her very suddenly that it was not going to stay down. She grabbed her napkin, muttered an *excuse me* through it and moved very quickly to the ladies'.

She flushed the toilet a second time and wiped her mouth again with the napkin from the table. It was fouled with vomit and saliva. She grimaced, folded it into itself and stepped out of the stall, mortified, unsure as to whether she had ever vomited in a public rest room before in the whole course of her life. *Who says life stops at fifty?*

Helen was waiting for her. 'Are you all right now?' she asked. She handed Glenn her purse, left at the table.

Glenn nodded, taking it. She put it down beside the sink and turned the water on, letting it run cold.

'I don't suppose you're pregnant?' Helen asked wryly, while Glenn rinsed her face and mouth with cold water from the tap. The rest room was empty except for the two of them. Her mouth tasted terrible; like tinned peas, or something equally distasteful.

'I don't think so. Unless I've been sleeping more deeply than usual.'

Helen did not smile. 'Has this been going on long?'

It wasn't the first time that Glenn had vomited after eating, but it was not information that she was about to share. Not even with Helen. Maybe with How, if he had been there. Thinking of him made her feel worse. 'I've likely got some sort of bug,' she said.

'Well, let me tell you what I've noticed,' Helen said. 'You have lost about ten or more pounds since the fall. I saw you in your yellow dress at the broker's luncheon and then in that same dress at Thanksgiving. It hung on you like a hanger at Thanksgiving.'

'Isn't that good?' she said, trying to sound light. She rinsed the napkin under warm water and then patted her face with it. She looked at herself in the mirror. She was pale.

'You pop Tums like they're breath mints. You never

eat any more. My god, Glenn! Even Gavin noticed. Are you sick or what?'

The two women locked eyes. Glenn shook her head. 'I'm sure I'm fine.'

Helen pressed her lips together. Then she opened her mouth and stuck out her tongue just a little way. She pressed her teeth into it.

Glenn frowned. 'What on earth are you doing?' she said.

Helen did not smile. 'I'm biting my tongue. Please go to the doctor.' And with that she left the room.

Glenn opened her purse and took out her comb. She fixed her hair and reapplied makeup, which improved her colour. Her stomach felt awful. There was an ache, almost omnipresent, but after vomiting it always felt hot, like a wound broken open and not healing well. There was a hardness there that she could feel only from the inside; she had tried on numerous evenings to feel something by pressing down on her abdomen – fingers searching, terrified and vainly, for a lump, a tumour, a place where the pain was worse than everywhere else.

Rarely could she eat anything any more of any significance. She kept her meals very small, these days, and very, very bland. She had tried buttermilk, her mother's remedy for upset stomach, and for a while that had seemed to help. Certainly an ulcer was not out of the question: her mother and an aunt had both suffered from ulcers in their lifetimes, and had given up eating their own famous pickled eggs due to it. Horrible things: of all things to give up, pickled eggs seemed a choice preordained.

She put lipstick on her mouth and patted the excess

on to a piece of tissue that she pulled from her purse. She looked much better. Except for the hollows around her eyes and the slackness in her cheeks.

Twelve pounds, it had been. Maybe more by now. She hadn't been on a scale in two weeks, but the weight seemed to be falling off with an alarming regularity.

Very bad sign, weight loss. Diabetes. She'd had a cousin with diabetes, she thought. She had fuzzy memories of surreptitious blood tests in the home of a distant aunt, and the adults whispering concern.

Course, diabetes didn't make you throw up, did it? Glenn patted her hair, still fashionably short, and smoothed the front of her blouse over an unfamiliarly flat belly. The weight had come off so quickly she had yet to get used to it. She looked pretty good still. She supposed, eventually, she would look worse. She didn't have a thin frame. She needed a little meat on her large bones. That was what made the weight loss seem so alarming to a tiny, delicate thing like Helen. It was the big bones jutting through the fine fabrics Glenn wore. She pushed open the door to the ladies' and felt suddenly as though the whole restaurant would be watching her. As though they had known.

She's sick, you know. Poor thing. Her husband died last year. But, of course, no one was watching, except Helen, who still had a slightly suspicious look on her face, the sort reserved for mothers. Gavin was chewing, and had another bite of steak on deck. He smiled happily at her, sauce on his outer lip. Her stomach flopped.

No appetite, either. She would have to stop lunching with others.

4

Richie woke to the phone ringing. He opened his eyes to sunshine, blazing through the uncurtained window, and flinched against it. His head thudded with a tremendous headache, a monstrous headache, a headache of epic proportions. *In the corner, introducing Richie Bramley, the lightweight champion of medium-sized publishers everywhere! And in this corner! Ladies and gentlemen, the Headache! This will be a day for infamy! No contest whatsoever!*

The phone jangled sharply into his very bones. He willed it to stop ringing. Briefly some of the night came back to him – the argument with Jen. Remorse hit him worse than the headache. But it was not as long-lasting.

He yanked himself out of bed, grimacing against the pounding in his head *Excedrin Headache #568 the one where the guy kills himself* and ran down the stairs grabbing the phone on the ring.

Mouth full of snakes, he said, 'Hello.'

'Dad?' RJ seemed to scream it into the phone.

His head pounded and his stomach felt queasy. He hadn't thrown up after a night of drinking in about three years. He would get a sign for the bathroom '900 Vomit Free Days' if he kept it down.

'What's up, RJ?' he said, tiredly, pained.

'Are you okay? You sound sick or something.'

'I'm fine. What's up?' Razors stabbed his temples. Rock rolled in his stomach. Bits and pieces of the things he had said came back. *I don't care what you do. I just wanted to get laid.* And the never to be forgotten, *Just fuck off.*

'I need you to pick me up from the Science Centre tonight. We're out at three and me and Jason are going there to use the library for the science project. Mom's got a late meeting and she can't do it, and if I take the bus, I have to walk about four miles and, anyway, I have to be back by six for my math tutor. Okay?'

Richie felt like his brain was maybe swollen. It felt like it was pressing against the front of his skull. The voice on the phone cut through it like a rock through a window, and yet he was strangely outside it. As though he was still drunk. He tried to think how much sleep he'd had. 'What time is it?' he said.

'It's eight ten,' RJ told him.

Eight ten? He couldn't have crashed until three or more. He couldn't remember. He'd drunk a lot. *Ladies and gentlemen, that was the Understatement of the Day, heard right here at Richie Bramley's House of Drunk A Lot! You heard it here –*

'Okay?' RJ repeated. 'Pick me up around five? Is that good?'

Richie just wanted to crawl back into bed. Maybe to lie there and die. He'd take a couple of aspirins, maybe some orange juice. Alcohol strips the body of vitamin C.

'Yeah. Five o'clock,' he said.

'Did I wake you up?'

'Yeah,' he said. 'Late night.' Guilt flooded over him then, the horror of chatting to his little boy with a hangover the size of a horse. The spectre of death standing beside him, poking him with his stick. *Na na na boo boo.*

'Oh, sorry,' RJ said. ''Kay, I'll see you later, Dad. 'Bye.'

And he hung up and the dial tone was somehow that much worse in his ear and Richie put the phone down, standing on weak, unreliable legs. His body felt like it desperately wanted to shake, but the effort was too much. He stood there for a moment, then stumbled to the front door and opened it, allowing frigid nearly-December air to rush over him until he was chilled. It smelled good and cool, and distracting. When he shut the door he felt like a piece of shit again.

What am I doing to myself?

He walked into the kitchen on shaking legs and opened the fridge and got a glass of orange juice. He found the aspirins in the cupboard and swallowed four. He stood there a moment, leaning against the counter, and thought, *That's not so bad, maybe I'll just stay up now.* Then the juice hit the stomach and rumbled threats, and he closed his eyes and pressed his forehead against the cool front of the cupboard door and wanted to die.

He went slowly and painfully back to bed.

When Richie woke up for the second time that day, he was feeling better but still rough. He wandered downstairs and checked out the clock on the mantel. It was after noon. He'd slept most of the day away, and what he thought about first was the book. He wondered, painfully, if he had lost the momentum he had built up over the previous two days, and castigated himself. The headache was better, but present, and he felt foggy and tired. And contrite.

While coffee brewed he did a quick damage-control

assessment and decided there was little he could do except maybe shift some karma around by putting in a day's work at the computer and making it count. He could call Jen, but he didn't think she'd want to hear from him just yet. He would give it a couple of days: a couple of days would soften the things he'd said, *Just fuck off* and *just wanted to get laid*, and give her some perspective on maybe how *he* felt, having bullshit news like that piled on him. It was a bitchy, princessy thing to do: *Oh Richie I'm so sorry I'm getting married but I want your* approval *so I won't feel like the shit I really am.*

He went to the front door to get the paper. He'd play with the crossword as usual and go on up to work on the book. Maybe later he'd go for a walk. The fresh air would clear his head.

Richie pulled open the front door and lying at his feet was a small cardboard box with an envelope taped to the top. A light dusting of snow covered it. He bent down and picked it up, shaking the snow off. 'Richie' was written across the middle of the envelope in Jennifer's handwriting. The box was taped shut.

He stared at it for a minute, and then looked up the street for her car. There were no cars other than his parked on the street and, in any case, no footprints on the path, just a fine layer of new snow. He nodded, knowing this was not good (*maybe I shouldn't open it it could be a bomb, ha ha*) and reached around and casually got the paper from the mailbox. He took both inside.

He poured himself a cup of coffee first, preternaturally aware of the box under his arms, as though it were a live thing, writhing with some kind of malice. The kitchen was still full of dishes stacked haphazardly from the night before. The table was in the dining room, still covered with the tablecloth his mother had given him, although the wrinkled folds were a little less prominent. It was stained here and there with drops of red wine. Two empty bottles sat on top. The bottle of bourbon – half empty, in true alcoholic fashion – was in the living room, uncapped.

He took everything, coffee, paper, small box, with him to the table in the dining room, two sides of him arguing as to what was in the box. What the letter said. Apology? I'm coming back, here's a present? Dead flowers and a cryptic note, maybe. The box went to the other side of the table and Richie pretended to read the paper. He wouldn't give her the satisfaction of eagerness.

His resolve lasted no more than a second or two. He pulled the envelope off the box and opened it.

There was no greeting. It said, 'Here are the few things left from "us". I would like back my roaster, my pink sweater that you stole, and the ring my grandfather gave you for Christmas last year. It is a family heirloom and I don't think you should have it. I would appreciate your dropping these things off at Karen's, then we won't have to see each other.' And it was unsigned.

Could be from anyone, ha ha.

His heart fell into his stomach. His stomach went hard and cold. His face twisted into a pained look that stiffened his cheeks, but made his mouth feel weak and shaky, as though he was going to cry.

He opened the box. *Shit.* First thing he saw was the little black velvet box, and he didn't have to open it to know what was inside. Two years earlier (after, ha ha, how *ironic*) a huge fight about his drinking, he had bought her a promise ring, a little delicate thing with a small diamond, worth nothing at all to a jeweller. The tiny rock, he'd written in the card that went with the ring, was supposed to be the 'seed' from which his promises would grow. *Ha ha.* She'd been moved to tears. He took out the box and opened it, hoping it would be empty. It wasn't. The ring was firmly inside the fine velvet slot. He closed it and looked uncaringly at the other things. A ring of keys from the old place. His gold chain from the eighties that he'd given her to wear. His Mets T-shirt, rolled up and shoved into the corner. His single pair of cufflinks (which *she* had stolen); a card to him from his brother in LA. And that was it.

Could be from anyone.

He leaned his head on one hand and covered his face with the other. His headache returned and his heart pounded. For a second he thought he wasn't going to be able to breathe. His eyes hurt. They wanted, he knew, to cry.

No. He'd take the pain. He'd earned it. It was his.

(eat it up does it hurt)

Richie's head shot up out of his hands and looked at the ceiling. The old man. Had he dreamed it? Does it hurt? he'd said. Does it hurt? Something had been on the computer. A poem. Hurting.

He swallowed, his mouth dry. He took a gulp of hot coffee.

Eat it up sweet pain, something like that. Written on the computer. And his father, his dad, standing there in the middle of the room, raising a glass to his son. *Salud.* Like a warning.

The room felt small and close. His eyes glanced at the bottle of bourbon (half empty) on the living-room table and, just looking at it, he could taste the bitter, sharp smell of it. He'd been very, very drunk. A bad drunk.

He'd dreamed it, of course. It was so symbolic. Dreamed it or hallucinated the whole thing. Some alcohol could do that to you. (And if he hallucinated, how far away was his first blackout?)

At the edges of his mind, various realities, epiphanies threatened, poking into the sides of his consciousness like little wasps. Blankly, he moved them away.

I'm going to have to watch my drinking, he thought. On the heels of that was the announcer, proclaiming the Second Understatement of the Day. He ignored it and piled the few things into the box, stuffed the letter – *could be from anyone ha ha* – into the box on top and closed it. It got shoved on to the buffet where it was lost among other stuff, the junk and miscellany of everyday life, letters, bills, keys, piles of change and books. You could hardly make it out with all the other stuff.

Richie opened the paper to the crossword and poured himself a fresh cup of coffee. He would get upstairs and then everything would be fine. A good day at the computer was all he needed. All he ever needed. And pretty much all he hadn't fucked up yet that day.

Before going up, he grabbed the spotlight from the toolbox at the back door. Encased in the bright yellow cage was a 120-watt bulb. It cast light for miles. He took it with him to the attic.

All the way up he felt defeated and he hadn't even started.

Richie stared unproductively at the screen for a good two hours. The crossword puzzle was on the small table where his mouse normally sat, completed; he'd read Ann Landers, his horoscope and, out of desperation, an article about Cher. There was a review about a jazz compilation that he thought sounded pretty good, but if he was honest, he might have said the same thing about a review of *The Monkees: A Retrospective*. He'd smoked a pile of cigarettes and finished his coffee.

He wrote a page that wasn't bad, but had been hard in coming with at least as many words deleted as kept. Around two he decided he needed a break, something in his stomach and another couple of aspirins to stave off the headache that was coming back, a bad one, that he could feel niggling at the back of his neck, that probably had less to do with his hangover (still in good standing) than the bad morning. So he gave up and went downstairs, toying with the idea of walking downtown, a little fresh air, and boxing up a pile of Jennifer's shit and sending it to her. See how she liked it. Maybe he'd save that particular thrill for her wedding day. Just thinking the words sent fresh pain into his chest and the headache he had hoped to ward off banged into his skull.

It was after two and he still felt like shit.

He poured himself more coffee and made a sandwich out of leftover steak, saturating the bread with mustard on one side and ketchup on the other. He cut the steak as thin as possible and the smell turned his stomach slightly, but he had to get something into it. There was nothing else unless he wanted RJ's cereal, or peanut butter. Neither seemed a compelling prospect so he took the steak sandwich into the dining room and pulled out the rest of the paper.

The first story was about the missing girl. She'd been

found. Underneath the large article was the headline, 'Manhunt Begins'. He scanned the top article first. The girl had been found. The paper was vague, but it seemed that *most* of her was found. 'Portions of the body, as reported by officers at the scene, were said to have been "removed". While no specifics have been released, a source indicated that fleshy sections of the girl's body were missing from the scene, having been removed with a precision that mostly ruled out animal or natural decomposition.'

Christ. Richie put his sandwich down and read the rest of the story.

The article recapped the girl's last known movements, the story about studying at a friend's place, and quoted an uncle about the family's reaction.

The two articles seemed horribly out of place among the other stories on the front page, one about bank rates falling, and a recycling project.

The sandwich was not sitting nicely in his stomach (what the hell was the guy doing with parts of the girl's *body*?) and his head was pounding anew. He pushed it further away because the smell was getting to him. He closed his eyes against the pain in his head and just tried to breathe quietly and evenly.

You know what you need?

Everything, in the space of one day, seemed to have gotten away from him. The day before – the trip to town – had been full and easy and *good*. Rajah of the Kingdom of All Right.

You know what you need?

His body ached to sleep, or just to lie down and be still. He wished the same for his mind. *Just wanted to get laid. Just fuck off.* There was no way he could lie down then and hope to have a nap. His head would spin with the folly of his death-wish.

The demon liquor.

You know what you need?

Richie carried the remains of his sandwich into the kitchen and took a couple more aspirins. If he took too many more, his ears would start to – *you know what you need?* – ring. He rinsed the glass, which had only held water, and dried it carefully on the tea-towel hanging off the handle of the fridge. It caught the overhead light and sparkled. *Déjà vu.*

You know what you need? Without thought Richie wandered into the living room, his gait casual and at the same time completely deliberate. At the sofa he leaned over and picked up the bottle (half empty) of bourbon and poured himself one.

A nip of the dog that bit me. It was awful going down. And instantly soothing and warm, like the voice of an old friend on the phone.

He went upstairs to the attic, feeling suddenly like he was making a terrible compromise and feeling very, very comfortable with that. At the bottom of the stairs in the hall, he turned on the answering-machine, hardly noticing that in his other hand, as he worked the controls on the little box, was the bottle of bourbon. Amber liquid sloshed in the bottle, cheerfully, all the way up the stairs.

Things went much better once the compromise had been reached. Richie sipped at a glass of bourbon and wrote the end of the bedroom scene with Porter. He got Porter and his grandfather out at the site where the old man had seen the spaceship and back in the car where they sat at the edge of the road in the shadow of the old man's most haunted past. They talked about Porter's parents. Porter cried.

It went well. It read fast and the road scene foreshadowed a scene that would come much later in the book. Richie wrote through the first glass of bourbon, hardly noticing when his hand poured the second. He sipped it, the friendly feeling flowing through him and covering up the mistakes of the day before like a blanket covering a corpse. *Nothing to see here, folks. Just go on home.* That reminded him uncomfortably about the girl, and he gave his head a shake. What the hell was the guy doing with *parts* of her? Souvenirs.

Somewhere between the second and third filling of the glass, his typing began to degenerate. He made lots of typos, which forced him to go back and fix them in order to make sense of what he was writing. The ideas were good, though. Good strong ideas. He had just needed to relax.

And relaxed he was. The effect of the bourbon, once the initial buzz had moved up a notch, made him sleepy enough to have a nap. He checked the time on the computer. It was just after four by then, and that gave him lots of time to have a nap and still get some more work done that night. Just after four he decided to do that, planning to sleep no more than an hour then maybe a bite downtown and then back at it. And nothing more to drink.

He'd get serious. It was going well. The spell was broken.

*

He woke to the phone ringing, slowly opening his eyes in the dark room and remembering something, something that just touched the edges of memory, but something bad and like *déjà vu* all over again. The machine picked it up before he could even think about getting out of bed to grab it. For a second he thought it was morning again, and the phone was ringing, waking him up. His head was still sore.

Janis's voice screamed up the stairwell on the machine. '*WHERE THE FUCK WERE YOU?*' He sat up in bed and in the dark saw his clock radio. It was six thirty p.m. Had to be evening. 'You call me back, you bastard. Fuck, *Richie . . .*' and it trailed off, a mixture of disappointment and disgust.

It was the dial tone that brought it to him. Janis must have hung up then, and the machine continued to record, the annoying high-pitched sound of the dial tone coming up the stairs and it, too, was –

RJ. He was supposed to pick up RJ.

He sprang out of bed and ran down the stairs. At the bottom he was paralysed with indecision. Should he put on his coat and just drive down there and get him? Was he still waiting? What time was he supposed to pick him up? He fucked up something, because Janis was pissed off. Five. He was supposed to pick him up at five. Was he supposed to pick him up at five? *Shit.*

Richie picked up the phone and dialled Janis, and tried to think of a lie.

In the end, he hadn't been able to. He had been left with somewhat of the truth: he told her he'd worked really late the night before, then got at it early in the morning and had simply fallen asleep. Two lies and a truth. He hung up, dejected and mortified by his own behaviour. Janis had wrung him out. RJ had waited a full hour outside in the cold, turned down a ride from Jason's mother, then started to worry that something terrible had happened to his father. Finally he called Janis on her cellphone *during her meeting* and told her that Richie hadn't shown up. Then Janis had worried. She *cut her meeting short*, and they had driven the route home that Richie would have taken – all the way to his house – and saw the lights out and his car outside on the street. She had contemplated going in and *killing* him, but RJ was upset and she just took him home. He'd missed his math tutor, and that was thirty-five dollars she'd have to pay anyway (*and no way am I paying it, buddy, that particular bill is yours*, she'd said). What the fuck was he thinking?

'Were you drinking?' she asked, in the tone of voice that was a curious mixture of concern and disgust.

He'd answered, quickly, with utter indignation, 'Of course not!' horrified even as he answered her that she would have the nerve (the *nerve*) to ask and that she'd been right. He might have been drinking. He had *not* been drunk.

In all, Richie had managed to say two other things. He'd asked to speak to RJ, and Janis told him RJ was too mad at him to talk. And then he'd said, stupidly, 'He has a math tutor?' in a vain attempt to distract her from the conversation.

To that Janis had said, 'What kind of a father are you hoping to be, Richie? What kind?' And then she hung up.

He sat on the couch. His kid. Jen. The book that wouldn't be. He thought horrible thoughts of himself, the sort of thoughts that ended with no realization outside killing himself for the sake of society and the people he loved. They threatened to drown him. Thoughts went round and round in his head.

So he would have a drink. Just one. He needed one. No one would deny that.

He had brought the bottle of bourbon down to the dining room. With the two empty wine bottles and the dust and crumbs from the night before, it was not a pretty picture. The bottle did not have much more than a drink or two left in it, maybe three shots. When the hell had that happened?

The drinking fairies are at it again, obviously. Terrible hosebags, those fairies. Drink all your beer, drink all your wine, drink all your brown pop and then make you sleep right through picking your kid up after school. Expensive little buggers, too. Represented on the table at that very moment was nearly thirty dollars in liquor – even if, technically, it hadn't all been his money. But there was thirty bucks, pissed away. Not to mention (technically) a hundred-dollar promise ring and the possible earnings from the last two days, add that to the fact that his kid might never again cut his lawn for free, you were looking at a few dollars.

Terrible prospect for a guy with so few to spare (ironically, previously due to the drinking fairies; insidious little bastards, when you gave it any thought at all).

One drink never hurt anyone. Sometimes you *need* a drink. That's what it was there for. Medicinal purposes.

You could even say a guy *earned* a drink, because what was that warm and fuzzy feeling if not some sort of reward for the piss-poor fucked-over world that you have to wake up to every morning of your life?

He'd make it all right with RJ. Like no other father in the history of the world ever forgot to pick a kid up after some kind of school thing.

He'd make it all right with Jennifer. Give up. Get a nice wedding present. Bygones and all that.

He'd make it all right with Janis.

He'd make it all right with his agent. Write a fucken book already.

He'd make it all right with . . .

Well, the list could just go on and on.

He understood, perfectly and clearly, deeply and profoundly, that he could not have a drink. Not one, he could never, ever have just one, and he could not have a drink then. It would be wrong, in the grand scheme of things, cosmically and karmically, it would be wrong. He also understood that the reason it was cosmically and karmically wrong was because it was (gentlemen of the jury) absolutely the one thing that could be traced back to every fucked-up moment of his life. The drinking fairies did it, absolutely, if not directly then certainly through a chain (such as today) of events that led right back to their little lairs, buried deep in the chasms of Richie Bramley himself, host of hosts.

I am not an alcoholic, he thought, frightened, the word so dark and large in his head that it bore no looking at, no indulgence. A scream in uniform. *Of course not. I might* (might) *have a drinking* problem. *Not an alcoholic.* On the heels of that thought came an equally disturbing, petulant one, *If I'm not an alcoholic then I can have one lousy drink. Just one.*

He stepped forward, legs weak and grasped the throat of the bottle. His hand shook. He carried it into the kitchen.

Glasses dried upturned on the draining board by the sink. Glasses in the cupboards. Richie realized that he had a lot of glasses. Mugs, he had a half-dozen. He had a six-piece setting from his mother. The cutlery was a jumble of cast-offs from god knew where, but he had two sets of highball glasses and any number of short, fat Rob Roys. He had wine glasses, beer mugs, shot glasses, shooter glasses, and even a set of Martini glasses that had come with a shaker one Christmas from Steve or Dubs or Brad or someone. When in doubt, get Bramley a bottle. And ice-cube trays. He had to have four in the freezer at all times, at all times full. He was meticulous about filling ice-cube trays. He might forget to pick the kid up from school, but you never had to go for ice at Bramley's.

His hand still gripped the throat of the Wild Turkey bottle. He stared at the bottle, taking in the label, as familiar as most of the faces of his friends.

He raised the bottle, hand shaking, and resolutely dumped the rest of it down the sink drain, the heady, metallic smell of it flooding over him, turning his stomach at the same time that it made him yearn to taste it. He rinsed the sink. The bottle was left beside the draining board.

His hands still shook, and the act had not made him feel strong or even better, as an action sometimes can. Instead it made him feel vulnerable and exposed to whatever evils the rest of the night could or would lay on him. For them, he would be sober. Edges would be sharp and dangerous.

Thinking about RJ did not help. Deeply, so deeply inside that he didn't feel any need to acknowledge it was a small seed of petulant anger towards the child, his child. *See what you made me do.*

Richie went upstairs to the attic, hoping to salvage whatever he could from the rest of the day.

Glenn Darnley wiped her mouth with a piece of tissue paper from her place in front of the toilet in her house. She knelt on the cold tiled floor thinking how dirty it probably was, even as she heaved a third time, fruitlessly, and spat the foul bile out of her mouth into the toilet where it joined the remnants of half a toasted bagel and some weak tea. The other half of the bagel waited in the kitchen for her and she didn't think they'd be seeing each other for the rest of the evening. Maybe she would sip some tea, but she felt perfectly awful and it was time to admit that.

She stood up on weak legs and dropped the tissue into the bowl and flushed. The smell of her vomit, stirred up by the action of the water, swirled up around her nose and threatened her stomach in a whole other way, but she managed not to gag. Not that anything more could possibly come up: everything she had consumed that day was gone. She leaned over the sink and ran water over a cloth. She rinsed her mouth.

It was the flu, or some other bug that was always circling the globe at that time of the year, the change in weather: the dropping of the barometer, or some such nonsense, had lowered her usually stoic resistance to bugs and now she was paying for it. Likely she should have been in bed a week before, when this had all begun in earnest.

There were lots of bugs around.

Of course, something else bothered her. Things she hardly wanted to think about. Like the weight loss. A dress that had fitted nicely two months earlier was now hanging loosely. Her stomach had been, for almost a year, weak and uneasy. The pharmacist at her local drugstore had teased her about putting Tums on a tab. And she had no fever, no aches, no other flu symptoms. Nothing common.

But there were lots of bugs going around. At any given moment you could find a variation on a flu bug. She'd simply been fighting the good fight and was finally conceding. A prescription of antibiotics and this would be a memory.

Glenn changed into warm pyjamas and turned the heat up in the house a notch. Without bothering to clear up the few things in the kitchen, she brought her cool, weak tea into the bedroom with her and thought to read a moment, but instead fell quickly into exhaustion and put out the light. The flu didn't last long; she would indulge herself with a very early night and be up and about in time for her doctor's appointment in the morning. That was very important to her.

She would not wander sick and vulnerable into the surgery. She would go in straight-shouldered, straight up. And whatever it was he would have to say, that's how she would hear it.

*

Richie called it a night early, too. He had sat up in the attic, staring blankly at his computer for what seemed like a very long time, typing the odd sentence here and there when he could focus his mind on it, but for the most part, he ran over interminably in his head the disarray of his life.

Everything had been there, ready for him to seize and control. And he had done that, in the beginning. He had started off with some pretty major disadvantages – although not necessarily disadvantages within his chosen profession: sometimes a bad childhood can be a writer's best friend and most constant muse – but he had moved aside the obstacles of a falsely middle-class existence and risen above it. For a while. He had taken the meagre tools of youth and built them into something grander than he had thought himself capable of, in the dark, lonely nights of childhood, lying in bed listening to the fighting from the kitchen, the old man drunk in his chair, his mother screaming well-earned obscenities at him, the old man mostly silent through her tirades, his only contribution to it all a sort of background noise, a shuffle to the refrigerator for another beer, a shuffle to the bedroom for another pack of smokes, the occasional, heartfelt *'You're absolutely right.'* His mother's tears. The clunk of bottle or glass on table. The squeal of the sofa springs with his father's weight.

On those mornings when the kids woke up, they would find their father on the sofa, their mother in her room, all remnants of the night before erased, his mother sometimes waking up in the middle of the night to clean up whatever mess his father had made in the last extremities of drunkenness: vomit on the bathroom floor, urine stains on the kitchen chair, spilled whiskey/bourbon/beer on the table; if nothing else, there were the tell-tale ghostly rings on the table from overflowing glasses of good cheer. *Salud*.

I am not my father.

For a while he had taken all of that, the misdirected anger at his mother, the clearly directed anger at his father, and focused it elsewhere. The energy that he did not (for a while) expend in destruction he had put into the building of something. He wrote.

Harder to lose were the secrets. The going to school and sitting in class, the ringing of his mother's hysterical voice in his head, and pretending they were like everyone else. The 'did you watch blah-blah last night?' questions from peers, when his mother had, months earlier, thrown a full bottle of whiskey through the front of the television, teeth bared like a frenzied animal, face red, veins on her forehead near to popping, a vicious, accurate arc of her arm in full swing, aimed not at the television at all but at their father, sitting passively in the chair in front of it, his eyes glassed over, body slumped – a viciously accurate throw with a vital force that would, in all likelihood, have killed him. *I don't watch TV*, he would tell them.

His mother came to school events when necessary. She wore her hat, her gloves, her hair in place, her dress a little behind the times, but worn with dignity, like an eccentric who had found her style and elected to keep it, rather than because the old man had lost his job and money was tight. Richie didn't participate in school things after a while, but his little brothers did. His mother went to those. No one asked about his father, and information was never volunteered.

The secrets were hardest. No talking about his family. No talking about what went on in the darkened living room starting soon after the six o'clock news, no talking about what went on in the kitchen later, when television was dull and the tension in the house made it impossible to watch. No talking.

No one asked. That made Richie skittish. How could there not be questions when he came to school so tired from waking up in the middle of the night to something smashing against the outside wall of his bedroom? How could no one ask when none of the Bramley kids brought lunch, or went home for lunch? He always thought it was because they knew, as though the dysfunction of his family was somewhere written on him, a telling expression or way of walking. All the Bramley boys and no one talked.

After a certain age, no one went home any longer either. They went to friends' houses, to the arena, to hang out in front of the 7–11.

For years it was like that, and then it stopped, very suddenly.

He came home from school the year he was fifteen and his mother was sitting at the kitchen table with her sister. She looked drawn. The night before had been a long one. He noticed nothing. (Except for the fact that his auntie Elsie was there at the table: a new face around the Bramley household was rare enough, but hers was a familiar enough face for it to escape the immediate attention of a fifteen-year-old.)

His mother stood up when he walked in. She cleared her throat, began to sit down, then stopped. Richie was just about to say *where's Da* – when she cut him off.

'Your father has died,' she said, flatly. She stood there, her arms snaking out just a few inches in front of her as though she knew there was something she was supposed to do right then but couldn't quite remember what it was, it being something she was not entirely motivated to do.

Richie stared without hearing for the longest time. The house got quiet enough in that blank space waiting for the next thing to be said, and he heard his aunt sob. Upstairs he thought he heard one of the boys (probably Robbie, he was the youngest) cry out.

His face started to squeeze in, feeling tight, and he felt like he couldn't move. He tried to think of what to ask, but amidst the dozens of questions was the absence of any order in which to put them. He settled eventually on 'What?', the universal question.

His mother strode towards him then, remembering suddenly what it was she was supposed to do, and she reached out for him, her face tear-stained (how had he not seen that? it was a state of being for her, tear-stains) and contorted into an expression of pain. *Not for him*, he thought. *Not for Dad*. He instinctively stepped back from her, anger taking him up.

'What happened? *What happened to him*? Did you kill him?'

Elsie gasped, and his mother wept, covering her face with her own outstretched arms.

'*Richie . . .*' she started, without energy.

Then Jimmy and Robbie came downstairs, Robbie standing on the bottom landing, his eyes red from crying, and Jimmy jumped down the last two, his expression pure unadulterated anger, hands bunched into fists, and he got right in Richie's face, his whole body tensed and leaning into his brother, and he screeched, in a perfect imitation of his mother's posture and inflection, 'Don't you *dare* say anything to my mother! He killed himself! *Dad killed himself*!' And his mother shrieked in horror and pain and reached out then to Jimmy – *Jimmy don't* – grabbing him and trying to turn him into her body and not Richie's, and Jimmy took a vague swing – not at her or at Richie, just a swing in general – and it clipped the edge of the broken TV and suddenly Robbie was screaming and crying and Elsie was saying something no one was listening to and the four of them gathered into a rough circle and cried together. The sounds were primal and complex, a perfect chaos of unspent, un-spoken, undirected emotions, most of which were a back-log that only then found expression.

Richie fell into the moment of remembering with perfect clarity everything about the rest of that day. The silence broken only by sounds that were mostly unfamiliar. The quiet click of pots on counter as Elsie fixed them supper, his mother drained of energy, but also of the anger that usually began around supper (*salud*), no matter how good the day. The sobs of Robbie, so little still, he seemed, sitting on Dad's side of the couch, curled up like a kitten, just staring into the air and crying quietly once in a while. Richie had felt for him; but he had not gone to him. His mother would get up and wander around the house, as though at a perfect loss for some-thing to do (something to be angry about) but she wandered anyway, like an out-patient, eyes taking in her children, going to them, touching heads, then, as if forgetting what she was supposed to be doing and suddenly remembering, going to the phone, where the boys would hear her uncharacteristically soft voice explaining what had happened to someone at the other end of the line.

He'd hanged himself, anchoring the rope to the upstairs railing then using the landing as his jumping-off point. It was more than a week before Richie had thought to ask, and years later he would wonder if finding that out was what made a writer of him, truly. He hadn't thought about the *how*. It hadn't occurred to him that the old man hadn't just somehow *willed* himself to die that day. Finding out the *how* gave him a whole new perspective on his dad. To hang himself in that way would have required a certain amount of planning. It wasn't immediately obvious. It would take Richie years to realize that fact. There were moments growing up after that when he just assumed that it was the sort of thing adults knew by some kind of osmosis, like the fact that you had to file taxes before 30 April, or the mechanics of sex, or how to pick a good steak.

Richie took it so much further than just that one fact. Further than just knowing *how* he did it. For a while he became nearly obsessed with it, imagining it in detail. The way the rope was tied, how it held his weight. The drop, straight down, from the upstairs railing was a height of about twelve feet, and his body would have swung wildly, away from the stairs and then back again. At the last moment, had his dad grappled with the closeness of the stairs? Did his legs scramble and pump in a last-minute effort to gain purchase?

Every day for the previous week? month? year? did he walk down those stairs and think, *There, that's where I'm going to tie it; there, that's where I'll be when she finds me.* Did it make him sad to think it? Had he tested the integrity of the railing before he tied the rope?

There, that's where I'll be when she finds me.

His mother had come home from work and found him hanging. The front door, through which she came, opened directly on to the stairwell. His feet, dangling (maybe still moving), were what she would have seen, his body still swaying with its weight and the force of the act. What she had thought or seen remained her memory alone. Richie had never tried to get her to talk about it, and she had never volunteered anything. He didn't even know if the old man had been drunk at the time.

What he had asked her was *why*.

'Your father was a troubled man who *drank*,' had been her curt and final answer. A troubled man.

Richie had tried, in the days that came after, to find a hook to hang the whole thing on. He could remember nothing. The old man had been drunk, his mother angry. There was nothing that stood out as a final straw. No shouted ultimatums that had not been shouted before. No penetrating threats. No unusual violence. When Richie had left for school that morning, his dad had been sleeping on the couch, on his back. The living room had smelled of booze and cigarettes. His mother had already left for work. The house was quiet and dark in the way it always was in the early morning. Breakfast bowls were left on the kitchen table, half filled with milk, cereal floating desultorily and forgotten, sharing space with a nearly empty bottle of whiskey. Richie had left that morning, his mind on other things, lost to him now. He hadn't said goodbye to the old man, partly because he was sleeping and partly because he never did. The funeral was a closed-casket affair.

A troubled man and a drunk.

Richie digested the memory and let it go. He read the last line he'd written on the computer, in all its ragged, meaningless glory: *Porter stood up from the desk and wandered out of the room.* Richie didn't even have a room to send him to. He sighed deeply and closed the document, shutting down his computer for the night. It had been a long one, and he was dead on his feet, in spite of the nap.

Were you drinking? His cheeks reddened and stung him. He and Janis had never, ever discussed drinking, his or anyone's, as far as he remembered. What did it mean, that she had asked him that?

The image of his mother, her face when looking at his father while he sat at the kitchen table *salud* in the drinks between affable and drunk. Her face curled up into a sneer when she thought one of the kids was looking. Bramley family secrets.

Richie closed the lid on his computer after it went unflinchingly dark and realized, for the first time that night, how quiet it was in the attic, in the house. It was an odd, full sort of quiet, where it seemed there were voices held in stasis, tongues bitten, breaths held. He gazed into the dark. He stared that way until he felt uneasy and then he climbed down the ladder, leaving the little light on beside the computer. He closed the hatchway, all the way, remembering that first day, when RJ had liked the motion so much. Bad hangover.

He wanted a drink, of course. Something to take the edge off.

He crawled naked into bed, wanting the drink, and thinking about not having it. Not having one for the rest of his life. A lifetime of sobriety. All the sharp edges of life staying in the same crisp focus that they were in at that moment, with nothing ever there to take the sting out of a day. The thought of never having another drink overwhelmed him.

Fear, plain and simple, a basic fear, overtook him. *Never.* And another thing came into focus, flippantly.

Maybe that's why Dad killed himself, he began to think, *ha ha*, trying to lighten the moment, but as soon as the thought was present, it took hold and he had to abandon it.

It seemed, in that moment, like the truth.

Richie fell into a troubled sleep. His dreams were filled with young men, RJ running up and down a set of stairs, his brother Jimmy, not as the man he was now but as a boy, standing in the kitchen of the new house, a drink in his hand, explaining to the half-circle of faceless men around him that he never said *salud* before downing another one. It was bad juju. Then he said *bottoms up* and finished the drink in his hand. In the dream Richie kept trying to play a drinking game, the one where you knock a bottle cap off a bottle of beer, but he never got to shoot because RJ kept calling him, running up and down the stairs, *I'm going to be an engineer commeer Dad!* He kept going back and forth between RJ and the game, wanting only to taste the beer that was sitting on the table, so cold that droplets had formed on the outside of the bottle. It would taste sweet and cold. Someone spilled a drink and it dripped with agonizing slowness off the edge of a table –

He woke up, hearing the dripping. He opened his eyes in his room, not very dark with the moon shining in through the window. At first he assumed he was still in the throes of the dream. It had been a good dream. Richie turned over on to his side and closed his eyes again and wriggled down into the bed, under the covers, the new placement on the sheets cool and fresh-feeling –

And, from somewhere, water dripped.

This time he raised his head a little, listening. Distinctly, there was the unmistakable *plink* of water into a tub, high-pitched and resonant. A tap dripping, but not leaking because the *plinks* were far apart. He wriggled in once more and tried to ignore it.

Plink.

He could almost see the ripples the little drop would send across the body of water it fell into. He got up. Through the half-closed bathroom door came a crack of bright light as though he'd left it on. He pushed the door open.

Steam filled the room. It rushed out in little puffs through the open door, hot and damp, swirling like smoke or clouds. It swam over his naked body warming and making him cold when it swept past, away from him. He couldn't make out anything in the room. He peered through the steam, his heart beginning to pound. He was still dreaming. It was his dream. In a moment RJ would spring up the stairs –

Plink.

A big fat drop of water fell from the tap to the tub and echoed.

Richie went inside.

The steam was too thick to see through. The room

was wet and sticky, his feet stepped into small puddles of water near the tub. He waved his hands through it, and they were barely visible, thick as fog. *Could cut it with a knife*, he thought, and with that thought he made out the taps at the far end of the bathtub. He leaned against the side wall, arching himself over the expanse of the enormous tub and reached through the steam to the tap, twisting the left one, the hot-water tap. It was off, but he twisted it hard and as he did the steam rose up and through the door, clearing the air enough for the red, red water in the bathtub to come clear.

A hand floated serenely, bobbing lightly in the water. The wrist was cut. A long gash running the width of the wrist, its edges curled up –

He screamed and backed away, his hip hitting the sink and he whirled around and caught himself in the mirror, a tall, dark-haired man who looked just like his father. He locked eyes with his image. Behind him, the room had cleared. There was no steam. He looked down at the tub, which was dry and empty, the bottom glossy. There was no red water, no hand floating (serenely).

He covered his face with his hands and rubbed. He opened them again and the same bathroom stared back. The toilet seat was up; the *New Yorker* cartoon was taped on the wall above it, the towel was askew.

The floor was cold and dry under his bare feet. He deliberately relaxed his shoulders, the first faint whiff of perspiration under his arms reaching his nose. Fear sweat. He glanced over his shoulder at the big tub. Empty, dry.

His eyes followed the soft curve of its bottomside

down to the taloned feet beneath, and a bad dream seemed all the more likely. On his way out he dragged his palm over the underside of the faucet. It came out dry. The tap hadn't even been dripping. He shrugged *it seemed so real*, and just inside the door, he stepped in a small puddle of water. He paused hardly a heartbeat. He left the light on and closed the door, firmly, not taking his hand from the knob until he heard the tongue snap securely into the groove. And he went back to bed.

Drifting off, the awful image of the floating hand came back to him. Only it didn't seem quite so awful. It had floated easily. Serenely. Peacefully, as though in a world without edges.

Glenn woke up in the middle of night, disoriented. It was dark in the bedroom and she had no idea what time it was. Time, lately, had been very elastic. She had taken to napping whenever the mood was upon her, as much out of concern as the lack of energy to fight it. She opened her eyes and fumbled around in bed (*weak, I am so weak*) until she had turned her body enough to see the clock on the night stand. It was three a.m. She got up.

Glenn weighed herself. In robe and slippers over yoga pants and a casual T-shirt, she had expected to see another couple of pounds missing from her body. She was horrified when she read her new weight. Glenn weighed 110 pounds. She hadn't weighed that since she was married, and then only briefly.

Standing in front of the bathroom mirror, she dropped the robe and slipped off her T-shirt. She tugged off the light cotton pants and stood there in brassière and underpants and took stock. Her cheeks were hollow.

Her hair hung limp and full. There seemed to be no colour anywhere on her: she was colourless, thin, and drawn. She was ill.

At first, she panicked. A string of commands ran through her head. *Must force myself to eat something; have to get some weight back on first thing, pitter patter; fresh air, very important too, I should have a walk every night, build up an appetite. I'll have to get back into a regular sleep pattern I don't know which way is up I'm all hours –*

She pulled her robe on over her underwear and sank down on the closed lid of the loo, exhausted, having been out of bed only a minute.

She felt that she had to eat something. She was wasting away. The thought of eating made the now-constant burn in her stomach seem worse and the quandary presented itself like the punchline of an old joke.

Ah, now there's the rub. Ba-boom.

She made herself some tea, and sipped it slowly, trying very hard to feel normal, to feel like she used to feel. The tea stayed down, and she added a cracker to it, telling herself that it was baby steps she had to take at a time like this, and went over some of the circumstances of her life. Imagined a different sort of life, with a different man, or maybe just children with the same man, a large family, even. A loud, larger life.

The pieces didn't fit and she took instead to remembering the days of the life that she had had. She and How on the boat. She and How on trips. The summer barbecues. How bent over crosswords. School plays and school parades and school parties. How dressing up for Hallowe'en and the time he frightened the little girl across the lane, who was no longer a little girl, but now a junior in college. Men that she had dated in college. How's old roommate Terry.

In the middle of the night before Glenn's test results, she sat at her island in her quiet kitchen, going over very nearly every minute of her life, smiling, remembering, getting lost in it, sipping tea and enjoying it more than any other cup of tea she'd ever had because somehow it managed to stay put.

5

Richie had an unsettled night, dream after bad dream. He'd woken twice after the dream about the bathroom, both times because of something bad in his sleep. He'd dreamed that he was in an old house, with the wallpaper peeling off the walls right as he stood there watching. In the dream he knew that the house was on fire, but he was powerless to stop it. Another dream, closer to morning, had him on a train, a boxcar like a hobo. He was trying to write in a journal, but no ink would come out of the pen and he was deciding, even as he wrote, where a good place to jump off would be. The landscape outside the train doors whizzed by unidentified. Sometimes it was buildings and sometimes just grass and trees. He was trying desperately to make something out, shaking his pen and watching outside. He had to find just the right place to jump. To jump to die.

He woke just after eight, still tired, feeling as though he hadn't slept at all, but got up anyway; it seemed a better prospect than more dreams. And he needed a piss. It was still dark outside, a thin indigo light just starting on the horizon, and Richie flicked the bedroom light on, squinting against it. His head felt heavy, like the first early-warning signs of a headache. The unnatural brightness did nothing for that. The hall was dark and cool. Cold air seemed to pour from the little blue bedroom across the hall from the master bedroom, where Richie's skis and skates, old records and the rest of the detritus of everyday life were stored. Air seemed to blow freely, cold, through that room and when he reached over to pull the door shut he noted that the closet door in the bedroom was wide open. He thought the cold air might have been coming from there.

Have to get that insulated or something. He pulled the bedroom door closed and turned to face the bathroom. He really needed to go.

He turned the knob and opened the bathroom door, light flooding the room – *perfectly normal*. He straightened up and went inside, pissing hard and happily. It seemed to go on for hours.

Richie had spent most of the day trying to squeeze words out. His heart wasn't in it. There was something indefinably wrong with the way he was feeling, and while he fought it off for most of the day, it was like the headache that had begun in the morning, or rather, hadn't begun in the morning. All day, the fuzzy, half-way headache had sat at the back of his neck, like a threatening cloud, but had never really prospered. He felt, instead, dull and unable to concentrate, restless in a way he sometimes got, when there was something bad going on, but nothing he could fix. It was as if he was depressed.

I need a drink is all.

He abandoned work around three and went to the grocery store for a few things. He walked, thinking the fresh air might clear his head, but by the time he got home, nothing seemed different. It had been hard enough to work up the head of steam to get himself out of the house.

He passed the liquor store twice and did not go in.

At home the little red light on the answering-machine blinked. He pressed play; he had one message. From Dubs.

'Where the hell you been? Hey, Richie, I'm coming over tonight . . . I'll bring beer. If you want a movie or something call me back. Call me back anyway. I'm coming around seven. See ya.'

Richie perked up at the word 'beer.' He looked over at the clock – it was just after four. Three hours till Dubs came. Time to eat and shower.

His mood lifted. All he needed was a drink. *A couple of beers with Dubs, just to take away the bad shit. That's all.*

I am not my father.

It was late enough to give RJ a call. But he didn't. Instead, he put away the groceries in the kitchen and thought maybe he'd call him later. The kid had just got home from school. Probably wanted to watch some tube, eat the fridge empty, phone girls and smoke cigarettes. He didn't want his old man phoning him. He'd call him later, closer to dinner.

When Janis was home and able to run interference.

He made a sandwich and sat at the dining-room table to eat it, the table still covered with the excesses of the other night, petulant reminders of where he'd gone wrong, and steadfast harbingers, counting off the days since his last drink. *Forgive me, Father, for I am sober now two days; it has been two days since my last drink.*

The house seemed to sit around him, quiet and waiting, while he ate his meagre supper and glanced now and then at the clock, a lover awaiting a love. The air was heavy with waiting. Once he thought he heard something upstairs, in the attic. The sound of something heavy hitting the floor and being dragged. He looked up without moving his head and pretended concern that the lamp had fallen over, perched as it was on the too-little table.

He had decided he would move his writing shit to the table in the dining room. Maybe he'd get another table for the kitchen. The dining room felt . . . sane. The sound of dragging stopped briefly and resumed. Stopped. He sat stiffly at the table, ignoring it (*lamp, mice*), and wished Dubs was there already.

Richie read the rest of the paper. Then he went up to have a shower, hesitating a second before going into the bathroom, giving himself the creeps and thinking at the same time, with a jocularity he did not feel, *something bloody wrong with this house*, thinking it even as he entered the perfectly normal bathroom and stepped into the perfectly normal shower.

Glenn drove from the doctor's office with dry eyes and a stiff back. If her hands shook, who would deny her that? It was snowing. The sky was grey, but seemed bright. It had been snowing off and on, now, for two days, the wet, easy snow that was not threatening or too cold, but just pretty and new, novel, like the first days of December before Christmas is a chore to be completed but not yet an event to be enjoyed. The calm before, if not the storm then something large.

Really, she thought, it reminded her in some way of spring.

Because of the snow, cars were moving slower, more cautiously than usual. Lines of them waited at every stop and, as often as not, you sat through two lights at the busier sections before crossing an intersection. It was all right. It was pretty out; it was pretty to see. She felt like everything was intensely human and frail, and might disappear altogether if she didn't take a good, kind, personal look. And so she did. She looked at buses and postboxes and fire hydrants and dogs; the fronts of buildings, carved and ornate, some, and others glass and flat, reflecting the flakes as they fell, creating the illusion of more life than was really there, but appreciably so.

All of it, each flake and stone, was lovely.

I am Glenn's Oesophagus.

In the earlier days of their marriage, before health had become a regular topic of conversation around the dinner table, and long before either she or Howard had even begun to think in terms of Their Health, *Reader's Digest* magazine (the world's most-read magazine!) used to run a regular feature about a fellow named Joe and his general body parts. *I am Joe's Liver. I am Joe's Pancreas.* It had struck Howard as the most amusing thing written for the very longest time, and was the punchline to as many jokes as he could fit in in an evening.

You'd told a lot of jokes, How. Most of them bad, you know.

Now, Miss Glenn, a joke is very much in the eye of the beholder.

Poor Joe, the subject of the articles, was abused in every which way in the Darnley household. If Glenn couldn't find a match for a sock on laundry day, she might find it pinned to the message board in the kitchen, neatly, like a bug on display, with its own little placard: *I am Joe's Sock*. Steaks (after a glass of wine) were Joe's left flank. Glenn had a nubbly sweater that How had never taken to, and he referred to it as 'Joe's skin condition' whenever she wore it.

You were such a card. I should have dealt with you.

Sitting parked in her car, outside 366 Belisle Street, just two doors down from her former listing, Glenn smiled, remembering. It faded.

I am Glenn's Oesophagus. And I might be in deep trouble.

She'd eaten at Topper's, a very reliable restaurant not far from downtown (she'd driven with near deliberation to Topper's, on the exact route she would need to take to bring her easily, *without* deliberation to Belisle; she did this unthinkingly, naturally, as though it were a plan). The soup of the day had been chicken noodle, a singularly inoffensive soup, highly recommended by the elderly and sage everywhere for whatever ails you. She'd ordered it without guile, and on the side a plain order of brown toast, no butter. A harmless lunch by any stretch of the imagination, and she felt buffered yet still by the good faith in her medication. Her only trepidation at all had been the thought of joining the rolls of people required to medicate before activity. It was such an *old* thing. But it was bound to happen.

Chicken soup and its prescriptive powers notwithstanding, the whole deal was sitting precariously close to her oesophagus, ready and willing to come up. Glenn held it down by will, and a carefully orchestrated plan of swallowing.

She stared at 362 Belisle, in all its falling-down beauty, and what she saw comforted her. There was a dignity there, a towering survival that calmed her. But she cried anyway, maybe without noticing, certainly without caring.

Well, we know it's not an ulcer.

She smoothed down the front of her dress, over her unfamiliarly flat belly, fingers running over rib bones she hadn't felt in years. Too many years, really.

She swallowed hard and realized lunch was not going to stay. She opened the car door, leaned out and vomited on to the street. Undigested chicken soup and the few bites of toast came rushing up and out, the sound echoing on the bright, empty street. Still leaning out she found a tissue in her coat pocket and used it to wipe her mouth. She gagged once more, but nothing came of it: everything had already come up. It looked terrible, there on the road, warm from her body and soaking into the snow. It looked exactly like what it was.

I'll be able to eat anything I want and not get fat, she thought flippantly. *Nothing would take.* She leaned her head back against the rest a moment and began to feel better. When she turned her head sideways, she could see the house. That helped.

Hello, house.

The owner's car, Richard Bramley was his name, was parked directly in front, covered in snow. Buried in snow. It looked as though it hadn't moved in days. A nice young man. She hoped – everything was all right.

Maybe he's out of town.

The thought didn't linger. She gazed affectionately up at the house. It gazed down, in turn, benevolently back at her. Snow had begun to layer delightfully over the barren, sharp branches of the caragana bush, making it look distinctly different from all the other ways she had seen it.

Now I have seen you in every season, she thought. *I'll just rest here a moment.* She had not entirely figured out what to do, but sitting in the shadow of the house seemed to give her peace. And so she did.

Dubs showed up about a quarter past seven and he would never have known by the casual way that Richie had answered the door that the previous fifteen minutes had been spent pacing and looking at the clock. Richie, by then, was rabid for a drink. The very thought had made his mouth salivate and it frightened him.

At seven, he had called RJ, carefully planning the call to correspond with Dubs' arrival so that if the conversation was tense he could get off the phone with the excuse that Dubs was at the door.

Janis had answered. He chatted inane small-talk with her for a moment, Christmas plans (too soon to know) and the snow. Her mother and work. Mentioned the book was going well (lie) when she didn't ask. Then he asked for RJ. 'So lemme talk to the boy,' he had said cheerfully. He listened to her put the phone down. She'd said he was in the basement on the computer. He heard the squeal of the basement door open. He heard her voice, muffled by distance. Then there was a long pause while something else happened. Richie waited, chewing his thumbnail, looking at the clock, the door, the clock, glancing out the window for Dubs' truck.

It was Janis who came back to the phone. She sounded apologetic. 'Richie, he says he'll call you back.'

'I got company coming. I could talk to him tomorrow. Is everything okay?'

She paused. 'He's still a little mad at you.'

'For Chrissakes, was it really that big a deal?' he

said, angrily. 'Am I the first parent in history to miss a deadline?'

She sighed, heavily. 'Well, I'm still a little mad at you too,' she said. 'He's thirteen. He's mad at everything. I think he's embarrassed a little bit. He stood out there waiting, he figures the world looked at him, and it scared him. He thought you were hurt in an accident. You're going to have to wait on this. By the weekend he'll have forgotten the whole thing. Just let it go, okay? I gotta run. Say hi to Dubs for me.' And she hung up.

No big deal, he thought, but guilt rose in him, the connection between sleeping through the afternoon when he was supposed to be picking up his kid, and the fact that it was because he'd been drinking, and the way his heart was pounding in anticipation of drinking again.

I have a drinking problem. The weight of the statement overwhelmed the guilt completely, the sheer blackness of thinking that something *had to be done*. A problem had to be fixed. The overwhelming, multi-faceted issue of drinking and quitting and repairing the damage that had probably, surely, been done in the whole course of his life threatened to topple every other thought in his head. The ruined relationship with Jen, which she would attribute entirely to his drinking (never once thinking about her superior attitude or nagging or any number of other things that might have contributed to his *drinking*); the stupid, nasty things he'd said and done bolstered by drunkenness over the last few years; the four years it had taken him even to come up with an idea for a book and the fact that it was both lame and not even really being written; the weekends he'd spent hung-over during his kid's visits, the times he'd waited for RJ to go to bed so he could pop a few caps –

It all threatened to overwhelm him, in the minutes before Dubs showed up at his door with a twelve for a night of fellowship, and it all boiled down to one thought (in his favour): surely if he had a drinking problem, a buddy of his wouldn't be showing up at the door with a case. Surely not.

Doom shrouded him, a small feeling in his belly that if he didn't do something right now, he would be on a different path altogether, and that the moment for thinking and doing was right there – right *there* at hand – and it was like opportunity knocking or shouting, a moment such as the sort he might give a character, like an epiphany.

Character shoots up in bed. *Aha.*

Character stops in the middle of a thought and remembers, *aha*!

Character stands poised above a precipice and jumps.

Richie pushed all thoughts from his mind. As if on cue, just the way he might have written it, Dubs knocked on the door and let himself in.

'Hey!' he said. Dangling from his right hand was a twelve-pack.

'Hey,' Richie said, smiling, casually. 'How're you doing?' With equal casualness, he said, 'Here, lemme put that in the fridge.' And he took the box of beer from his friend while Dubs pulled off his boots and hung up his coat. He said things, Richie heard them and responded to them, they were the customary greetings of a friend, the how-are-yous, the what's-ups, things that were heard and answered without labour or consideration, but Richie did it outside himself, hearing just the intonation and rise and fall of Dubs' familiar voice, for by then he was in the kitchen, pulling out bottles that gleamed amber in the light and putting them on the nearly empty shelf in the fridge, their shape and weight comforting in his hand, the pounding of his heart slowing and being comforted, the shape and weight and necessary strength behind the act of twisting off the cap, the smell of the hops as he brought the bottle to his lips like balm, a bit of good news, a meditation, a prayer, a break in the storm. He answered Dubs, without once hearing him.

'You want a beer?' he called from the kitchen, the taste of it in his mouth, the cool earthy taste still in his throat, his lips still damp from it. He licked them.

'You having one?' Dubs called.

Richie drank from his bottle. 'Does a bear shit in the woods?' he called back. He twisted the cap off a bottle for Dubs and took it to him. It was snowing outside, big fat flakes that said goodbye truly and inexorably to November and ushered in the long Midwestern winter. They toasted it, and drank.

Salud.

The beer was nearly gone by ten so they called Steve at home and told him to come over and to bring beer.

Steve came over and about an hour later they called Brad and he wasn't doing anything. Everyone brought something to drink. Richie laughed with his friend, throwing his head back in long, cold swallows and felt good – *if I had a drinking problem would my friends drink with me?* Someone phoned Rob but he wouldn't come and Richie, already loaded or half-way there, got on the phone and berated him, loudly calling him a pussy and a wuss. He laughed at this, hardly noticing that, at the other end, Rob said not much at all, and that all around him the room was pretty quiet too, but by then he was off the phone, hanging up on his friend of fifteen years with 'Stay home, then, fucking wimp.'

He helped himself to another beer, also not noticing just yet that the number of full ones no longer exceeded the number of empties and that it wasn't even eleven o'clock. Dubs was feeling no pain, but the other two had hardly arrived. Brad wanted to play cards, maybe a little poker, and they got out the cards, but Richie had trouble keeping his mind on the game. He folded on nearly every hand, the reds and blacks swimming into each other, the nines and sixes looking alike until he suggested that all he was good for was a round of *go fish* because he was seeing double anyway. This got a small laugh.

Richie stood at the open fridge around midnight and there were only two beers left. Brad had only brought a six. He swayed in front of the fridge, leaning on the door, staring unfocused at the two bottles left and called into the dining room, 'Hey, someone's gotta go for beer!'

He felt in his pocket for cash and pulled out a twenty. He hit the doorway between the kitchen and dining room and held it out. 'Who's going for beer?' he asked. 'I'm not good to drive.' He laughed. It earned him a guffaw from Dubs (also not really good to drive) and chuckles from the others. Brad looked over his cards and said he had to get going. He had a shitload of things to do in the morning.

Steve tossed his cards down, folding. 'Yeah,' he said, 'stretching, 'I gotta take off too. We're heading out tomorrow night with Al and Karen.' He offered Dubs a ride home. Dubs burped in acceptance.

'You guys are taking off? Where's the party spirit?' Richie said, too loudly.

Brad patted him on the shoulder on his way into the kitchen, 'Buddy, you got enough party spirit for all of us!' They got up from the table and lit smokes and started winding things up. Steve and Dubs got their coats on at the door.

'If you're taking off, run by the off-licence and get me some more beer, how about?' he said, trying to sound casual; his voice was high and too loud.

'Go to bed, Bramley,' Steve said.

The door opened and snow swirled in, reminding Richie of the night Jennifer had come over. Terrible night. Had it really been just a few days earlier?

Dubs gave him the Boy Scout salute. 'Later,' he said.

'*Salud*,' Richie said, in another place.

Brad yelled goodbyes from the sofa in the living room. He smoked a cigarette, reflectively.

Richie came in and said, 'You leaving too?'

'Not yet. Any beer left?'

The sarcasm was lost on Richie. 'Go get me some more beer when you go, okay?'

'What's left?'

Richie shrugged, not wanting to say. Brad went into the kitchen and opened the fridge. Richie heard the sound of the bottle rattling on the slatted metal shelf in the fridge.

'You want one?' Brad called from there.

'Yeah,' he said, thinking, *Last one. Sad*.

Brad opened it for him. 'I ran into Karen yesterday,'

he said pointedly. Richie blinked slowly. He raised the bottle to his mouth. He did not respond.

Brad continued, 'She told me about Jen coming over.'

Richie shrugged. 'Me and Jen are no more. Jen and me no more. She's getting married.' For no reason, this struck him as amusing and he laughed. 'It's cool,' he added softly, more to himself than to Brad. He stared off into space.

'You really okay with that?'

He shrugged again. 'Fuck it,' he said. He leaned over, his centre of balance shifting too far forward and he caught himself on the coffee table. He laughed. He fished around in the package of cigarettes on the table, pulled one out, and lit it.

'Karen said Jen feels really bad about it. I guess she was here and it went kind of badly. She seems to think you're killing yourself,' he said, seriously, softening it, lightening it, with a snort of disbelief that he didn't really feel.

'She wants to be a princess,' Richie said, getting pissed off. 'And there's only room for one princess in a relationship.' He dragged out 'relationship' sarcastically. 'And I'm it, in ours.' He laughed. 'I don't want to talk about this.'

Brad shrugged. Then, 'I think we should.'

'What?'

He took a deep breath and said, a little louder than he should have, but not cruelly, 'You're a bit of a drunk, Bramley. You gotta nip that shit in the bud. You don't want to wake up ten years from now and wish you had, right?'

Richie stared at him, incredulously. He sputtered for

a minute, his mind, fuzzy with drinks, unable to grasp even one of the four or five indignant responses that were always at the ready; and equally unable to assimilate his indignation with the sudden naked, terrified feeling he had. 'What the fuck do you –' was the best he could come up with.

Brad stood up and raised a hand in surrender. 'Okay, okay – I'm outa my element here. Just a friend, okay? Spirit intended and all that.' He started towards the door.

Richie, cheeks burning, heart thumping, stomach rolling, pain starting, just sat on the couch and said nothing more. He clutched the beer tighter in his hand, the glass getting warm around his fingers.

Brad put his coat on in the silence. He poked his head around the door and said, with genuine regret, 'Hey, look, it's none of my business, okay? But let's hook up this week. We'll go get something to eat and you can tell me what an asshole I am. Okay?'

Richie nodded.

''Kay? Rich?'

'Yeah,' Richie said. 'See ya.' Brad said goodbye and the door opened and closed, cold air rushing over Richie refreshingly for a moment, and then it was gone. And he was alone. Brad's beer, left on the table, unfinished, was nearly full.

Least he left me his beer.

Richie finished his own beer, then took Brad's bottle upstairs with him, fully intending to get into bed and (die) go to sleep. *Fucking friends. Like they don't get pissed up every weekend.* The thought stopped there, but if he had been in the state of mind where a thought could be sustained, he might have added, *They used to get pissed up every weekend but they don't any more*. Kids, jobs, school, women, each additional element to their lives had reduced the amount of socializing they did. Each element had raised the quality of their entertainment, until those weekend piss-ups had dwindled down to once a month. Maybe twice. The guys got together and maybe a couple of them got out of hand, but someone would have to drive, someone had to work in the morning, someone had a life to deal with the next day and didn't want to do it kneeling in front of a toilet.

It was just him. But he was not in the state of mind to take that thought to the next level. Not consciously.

He intended to get into bed, but on his way to the can for a piss, he noticed that the ladder and hatch were open, yawning, awaiting him.

Richie snorted, seeing it, his focus blurry-eyed and weak. He raised the bottle to the open mouth of the attic and said, '*Salud*,' and nodded. 'First, a piss.' He stumbled into the bathroom and peed on the seat.

He climbed the ladder with the bottle in his right hand. Through the hatch he could see the glow of his computer screen and hear its quiet hum. The desk lamp was lit, casting a limited pool of light around the room. He could also hear an unidentifiable sound, a sort of thumping, like a pillow hitting the floor, soft and rhythmic. When he was high enough through the hole in the floor, he tucked his beer safely out of harm's way under the small table.

As he pulled himself up through the hatch, a shadow danced on the wall opposite. He turned to look behind him.

A man hung from a rope tied tight around his neck. The rope was suspended from somewhere above, Richie couldn't see where and did not follow the end of it much past the point of the darkness. The man's body swayed (serenely) lazily back and forth. Richie started and screamed, a child's scream in the night, ambushed, attacked, and like a child, he covered his eyes. *When I look up it will be gone.*

He kept his eyes closed and breathed heavily through his fingers, concentrating on slowing the too-fast beating of his heart. *I'm having a hallucination, like the other night. I'm drinking too much. Too drunk. When I open my eyes it will be gone.*

In the minute or so that passed, his heart stopped its relentless thudding against his chest and he calmed himself. Under the hum of his computer he could still hear the unfamiliar *thlump thlump* – of something soft on something hard?

He dared not open his eyes. If he could hear it he would see it. He did not want to look and see – *was it Dad? my dad?* – a dead man hanging in his attic.

It isn't really there. It's the drunk. I'm having a bad drunk.

'Richie.' He jumped again.

A voice, deep and silky, spoke from there. Richie sobbed. Without opening his eyes, he twisted his body round and jerked himself back down on to the ladder, finding a step with his right leg, fumbling with the other until he was on firm footing.

'Look,' the voice said. A man's voice, low and rich, loud without volume. Commanding. He turned his head, still poking through the attic hatch, and opened his eyes.

They met a pair of feet, held steady about a foot off

the floor. Black shoes, dark socks and trouser legs. He followed them up, not wanting to look, really, but unable – *it's not really there bad drunk* – to stop himself. The man wore a long coat or tunic of some sort that reminded him of the old West, some kind of ranching coat or maybe even a cleric's coat but it was of heavier material than that. He looked up, following the line of the man's body to his neck, cringing as if preparing himself for what he would see.

Not really there.

There was nothing to see, just a neck. He looked at the man's face. It was an old face, wrinkled and sad, with heavy pouches under two smallish eyes that were dark, too dark to be any colour at all, just pupils.

'I would like to talk to you,' the man said.

'Go away,' Richie slurred. His eyes followed the path back down. The man's feet were not touching the floor. He stood above it.

The man smiled, sadly. 'A moment of your time.'

Richie realized he was shaking. His hands felt weak as they clutched at the small ledge of the edge of the hatchway opening. His mouth was dry. He wanted to drink something. His eyes spotted the beer under the table.

'Please,' the man said, his voice an invitation. Richie shook his head, no.

'Come up and talk with me a while. I rarely get company. I'm off the beaten track, you might say.' The man smiled and seemed so sad even as he did that Richie felt himself relax slightly.

'Have your drink if you like.' The man opened his arms with such supplication that Richie was caught off guard. He began to pull himself up through the hatch again. His legs were weak and he thought, *None of this is happening*, but he was drunk. He pulled himself up far enough so that only his legs were on the ladder and he leaned over to grab his beer. Twisting his body to keep the old man in sight he grabbed the bottle and took a long, deep swallow. It did not go down easily, but he felt better.

'I'm drunk,' he admitted, to the room. He drank again. As he began to relax, he glanced around. As soon as he did, the image of the man began to waver, shimmer, as if through bevelled glass. The image went double, then seemed to fade. He squinted, focusing on where the old man had been. Where he had been was only dark now. Slowly, without conviction, he glanced around the rest of the room, but the old man was gone.

'Where'd ya go, old man?' he called. His voice echoed off the back wall. He shook his head. *Bad drunk*. And finished off half of the rest of the bottle in one swallow. The computer hummed. The light glowed from the screen. It was turned away from him, facing his chair. He pulled the rest of himself up through the hatch.

He stood up, unsteadily, and lumbered two steps over to his computer, kicking the leg of the little table and making computer and lamp shudder. An ashtray fell over the side, hitting the floor and sending up a cloud of ash, cigarette butts scattering. He hardly noticed.

He pushed the screen of the laptop open all the way and was not surprised to see something written there, but he swallowed and looked up to where the old man had been.

As he read, the oily, acrid smell from previous nights

clouded around his head, stinking up the air and making him nearly gag. The source of the smell came to him casually, as if it was something he'd known all along but hadn't realized.

Burning flesh.

He'd smelled it before. Once, completely baked (*pun intended, ha ha*) he'd fallen, hands first into a ring of campfire, badly burning an elbow as he tried to avoid plunging both hands into the flames. He'd singed his hair, and burnt his shirt, but mostly what he remembered from that booze-soaked evening was the smell of his flesh, blackened and blistered after the guys pulled him out, and ripped his shirt off him. He still had a scar.

A whole page, nearly, was on the screen this time. He squinted and read as best he was able, going back several times and rereading what he might have missed, his eyes widening, his stomach turning, the dulling effect of the alcohol losing its edge.

There was pain, much sweet lovely pain. And fear was also something I had learned to enjoy, such energy and life in pain and fear, the very excesses of human experience. So few understand the beauty of true real dear pain and fear. I would hide them. Tell them it would be all right. They would be so terribly afraid, so wonderful in their fear, that when it came time to hurt them, it was so much, and that much, sweeter. There is a certain fragrance to fear that cannot be described or reproduced.

I loved them even as I hurt them I loved them. I was always sorry to hurt them, but the pain was very important. It had to be branded upon the flesh. I had to consume it.

I cooked them up in a little stove, a wood stove, no gas to add odour to the scent, the scent of their fear and flesh. Afterwards I would take the knife, the same knife of course!, and sharpen the blade just so and run it across the fleshy parts of my body, my chest my face my arms and feel their pain becoming one with mine. Their sweet little cries ringing in my ears even then.

Pain is sweet like the flesh.

Even as I cried with horror at my actions I heard them crying inside me a part of me.

'Pain is a catalyst,' came the voice from the other side of the table. Richie looked up just as the man came close, gliding, his feet off the floor. He held something aloft in his hand and Richie did not want to look.

'Get away,' he said, backing up. The attic was pitch black behind him. Something small scurried past him and he glanced down automatically to see what seemed to be a small child scampering past, away, fast, like an animal. 'Get away,' he said, louder.

'Richie,' the man intoned, his voice resonating in the small space, 'pain is your good friend, is it not? Do you not invite him into your life, yourself? We are alike, you and I.' The old man smiled his sad smile and Richie saw not lines on his face, not lines of age, but scars. He was scarred, slashes on his cheeks so long they appeared to be flesh, wrinkled by age.

The man came closer. 'I had to die. They were coming for me. But I did it my way, a way that would extend my pain into pleasure and I would go out the way I chose.' He smiled widely. 'I hurt and hurt and hurt.' What seemed like a laugh came rolling out of the scarred face, the thing's eyes black without irises.

'Do you deny that you live your life, hurting all the people who love you? Your lady friend, your son, the people you hold dear and close? Do you deny that?' He tilted his head condescendingly to Richie.

Richie, unable to speak, stared.

'You hurt them, you hurt yourself, and then you blame others. All the while you are consuming your own flesh.' He clicked at him with his tongue, his mouth a dark cave, toothless, fathomless.

'You would never hurt anyone again, Richie,' he said, and he held high what he had been holding in his hand. A rope, held by the end, the other end, looped.

A noose.

Richie stared, unable to take his eyes from it. There was a full silence in the room, that waiting sound that he had heard before, breath held. It seemed to him that the attic was crowded with souls, listening to hear what he would say, watching to see what he would do. The rope dangled in front of him, close, just beside the table.

Your lady friend your son the people you hold –

A lifetime without smoothing the sharp edges.

He reached out, the rope a lifeline, his fingers stretched.

And the rope disappeared.

Like a switch being thrown, he was staring at a blank screen, the only sound in the room the hum of his computer, the screen white and pure.

In his hand was his beer. He felt his fingers around it. He raised it to his mouth, draining the bottle. *Salud*.

He cried self-pitying tears that did not last long. He was much, much drunker than he'd thought he was. Once convinced of that, and the conspiracy against him, he shut his computer off without bothering about details and went back down the hatchway, stumbling off the last two rungs of the ladder in haste to get out of the dark and into the light. The hall was dark too, the only light from the bathroom, through which he could hear the slow, steady drip of the tap. And he knew who would be in there.

Richie plunged into his bedroom and closed the door. He pulled the chair over to the door, the clock on it pulled off violently by the cord, and propped it in front of the door.

'Stay out,' he mumbled. And he crawled into the bed, fully dressed, and pulled the covers over his head, hiding away, like a little kid. He did not sleep. Not then. As the drink began to wear off, he thought less about the man and more about the rope.

The subconscious is a powerful thing, he thought, before drifting off, finally, in the wee hours of the morning, when the adrenaline began to subside and his body, too, began to succumb to exhaustion. *The subconscious can tell us things we really feel.*

Maybe it's trying to tell me something.

6

Richie did not bother with the pretext of writing. He had other things on his mind.

Carefully he went over each and every moment of pain that he had caused anyone, from his mother to his son. The things he had said to people, casually and deliberately. The million fights he'd had with Jennifer. The way he and Janis had broken up, when RJ was still Richie Junior and only a month old. He tortured himself.

Once (*drunk*, of course, everything bad could be traced back to some drunken incident or other, and he became relentless about admitting to himself the unadorned, naked truth) he had accused his mother of driving his father to his death. He had, up until this time, only an internal memory of the event, only his own thoughts, scattered and dull and one-sided as they were, but now he sat and looked at the terrible memory from the outside. How he had stood above her in the old house he shared with his brother Jimmy – the drunk tank they used to call it – he stood above her, the traces of a dinner she had cooked still on the table, his finger pointing, so close to her face that she backed away from it, spittle coming out of his mouth as he denounced her for her sins as unearthed by him. He remembered her own cries and the way she bent over nearly double as though there were a pain in her stomach, and the way she buried her face in her hands and was unable to speak for minutes, until she managed somehow to regain control and stood up without another word and left. She didn't talk to Richie for several months after that, something that he took as an admission of guilt; it was shame that kept her away. He and Jimmy had many drunken conversations about that, none sober. Jimmy lived in Los Angeles now, managing a successful restaurant; he was married, no kids, and was a Buddhist. Or as Richie described it to his buddies (when asked), 'a candy ass'.

He got himself a new girlfriend when Janis was nine months pregnant, and told himself it was because they were fighting all the time. But they were fighting because Richie was never around. He resented the fact that Janis, enormously pregnant, seemed to need something constantly. She, of course, never found out about the girlfriend, but when she finally kicked him out, when RJ had been just over a month on the planet, he told his buddies that it was a mutual decision. Then he dumped the girlfriend, to be free.

For two days, Richie wallowed in pain. His and everyone else's.

Upstairs in the attic, there were the sounds. Sometimes he heard them and wanted to go up. He did not drink. For the first day, he didn't even want to. By the second day he thought about it, but was terrified that, in drunken judgement, he would wander up into the attic again.

A terrible bleakness settled over him and the whole house. When dark came at night, he sat in it for hours, brooding, forgetting to turn on lights until he heard something from upstairs, or outside. Once he heard laughing. Like little kids playing. The tap dripped into the tub. Something thumped down and was dragged in the attic.

He had truly, truly loved Jennifer. She had not been a crutch, or a bauble to make him feel better when he was down. She had come into his life in a flush period, an extra in a time of abundance. He had never cheated on her; she'd never done it to him. On some level, even when things turned very, very bad, he had only been daring her to leave him, the feeling that she ultimately would so overwhelming that he couldn't bear the interim between her being his and then not his. By the time things started to go sour on him, when he couldn't write and drinking (his real love) became his crutch, his bauble, he had become tired, exhausted by the waiting, and expected her to book out on him with every drink. He wondered, in his gloom, if he had been pushing her to it, tired of waiting, deciding subconsciously to act.

Richie's first novel had an alcoholic in it. Those were the days before Jennifer, and after Jimmy; no roommates, no soulmates, just him and his computer. He'd worked then, full-time at a direct-marketing company, writing form letters, selling copiers, long-distance companies, upholstery cleaning, and spaying or neutering your pet. He'd get home at night, sometimes feeling like he was completely out of words. Come seven thirty, he would have wandered over to his typewriter and worked on something. He'd written a lot of short stories then.

The first novel had that alcoholic in it. He'd done a little bit of research on alcoholism. He'd talked to a guy at AA, who was aggressive and defensive. He'd gone down to the library and read dated periodicals on old research. He'd buried himself in the old man. It scared him some. That had been a pretty dry period.

There was a genetic element to alcoholism. They

were undecided as to how genetics played its role, it was complicated; at the time, that information was new. One of the complications was nurture. The child's environment might or might not have played as large, or larger, a role in developing an alcoholic as genetics. In other words, the times when (say) RJ visited and the house was full of empties and overflowing ashtrays, and the stink and reek of gone-over beer and spilled wine – that was nurture. And, genetically, the kid was covered. He had it coming or going.

When thoughts strayed too close to RJ, Richie mentally backed off. He couldn't face thinking about his son. Thinking about his son made him feel soiled and depraved; as though even if his thoughts touched the boy he, too, would be soiled and ruined.

Richie swathed himself in pain and dirt, tormenting himself with memories that were irreversibly bad; he was incapable of conjuring anything good from the past, and if, by chance, he happened on something in the course of the wretched accounting, it was only due to its proximity to something horrible, and it was then irrevocably tossed into the dirt with the worst of it, tainted for ever by one moment in time too close.

He did this until the space in which to breathe became smaller and smaller, and he felt unworthy even of the effort.

The phone went unanswered. Newspapers piled up in front of the door. The mail stuffed the box.

He brooded and wandered the house, unconsciously eyeing railings and ceiling fixtures, moving up and down the stairs with deliberation and reflection, going from room to room, never straying far from the truth.

*

Richie had not bothered to get out of bed when morning came on Wednesday. He lay there, as he had most of the night, thinking. By then his thoughts were undefined, jumping from topic to topic, anecdote to anecdote, in all of the stories where he came off poorly. In all the stories he was the villain. A scourge.

The light on the walls went from vague to diffuse to morning; he still did not get up. He got up instead an hour or so after light, when he could no longer hold his bladder. Even that seemed an afterthought. Unimportant. He went to the bathroom and relieved himself, feeling no different afterwards, no better, no worse, just less occupied with that one discomfort.

Between bathroom and bedroom, something caught his eye. Hanging on the knob of the banister, at the top of the stairs, something had been draped over the railing. He went closer and picked it up, expecting it to dissolve, disappear before he even touched it.

It was a rope.

It was very real. He held it in his hand, feeling its weight and the coarseness of the braid, smelled the chemically rich odour of the jute, so rough near his nose. Three strands twined together. A good strong rope. Richie sat with it on the top stair, moving it from one hand to the next, feeling its weight, its strength; its possibilities.

He looked up to the hatch on the ceiling in the hall. It was still closed, as he had left it the other night. 'What am I supposed to do with this?' he asked it. The attic was silent. Nothing moved, nothing fell from a height, as though cut down, and nothing was dragged across the floor. A half-dozen alternative questions ran through his mind with just a ghost of the famous Bramley wit: *what are you implying? what's the meaning of this?* There was no response to anything, and none was required.

He pressed it to his cheek, and curled himself into a ball, burying his head between his legs, the rest of the rope dangling there, a length of it running down the stairs, taking comfort in options and last resorts.

Richie played with the rope for more than an hour, trying knots and braids, his fingers and hands moving independently of thought. He fashioned a noose and undid it, several times, trying to remember where he'd learned to tie one. It was not simple. You had to have a very long piece of rope, at least six feet. You formed two loops in an S shape, running at opposite ends to each other, leaving the short side on the neck piece. The shorter piece was strung around the two larger loops, back towards the bottom, or second loop; successive loops are made, a deliberation that can only be confirmed as it begins to take its undeniable shape. The end piece, now short, is passed through the bottom loop; by pulling on the top noose, it pulls the shorter tie end through the successive loops and forms what is universally accepted as a symbol of death and punishment, pain.

What are you waiting for? Salud.

He held the noose, newly formed, his fingers sore and slivered from the coarse weave of the rope, lightly in his hands and thought how functional knots were. They each had a purpose. They were either easily undone, or nearly impossible. He'd had a book when he was boy, just about tying knots. *The Knotical Guide?* If that wasn't it, it should have been.

Nowhere in the book had they shown you how to tie a noose.

He tried to remember where he'd learned it. Couldn't. How was it he could remember every slight he'd perpetrated even on strangers but was unable to remember who had taught him a simple, and likely at the time, pleasurable pursuit, with its own dark attachments that young boys so adore, like tying a noose?

But he couldn't.

Intruding into trying to remember was the wondering. How would it feel around his neck? The jute would prick and jab his flesh, soft there (and getting softer), even with his near-beard. Maybe it wouldn't prick; maybe it would only itch, like wool. If he pulled it tight, it would pucker the thin skin on his neck and that would pinch. If he pulled it tight, the blood would be trapped in his head, the pressure intense. His eyes would –

The house seemed to take a breath and hold it. Richie could feel its eyes upon him.

And then the doorbell rang.

At first he wasn't even sure what he had heard. The sound might have been inside his head; it might have come from one of the rooms – there seemed so many of them, and they all had their sounds. He pulled the noose off his head, the jute catching in his hair and tugging, doing it quickly, like a child caught in the cookie jar. He listened.

The bell rang again. It chimed through the house loudly, so foreign in its temporal purpose that it sounded obscene.

'Mr Bramley?' someone called through the door.

Richie was terrified, scrambling down the stairs to the landing and peering out the side window, like a madman, the noose still in his hand. The scene was absurd. A woman stood on the stoop. An ordinary woman. Familiar, somehow.

She caught his face in the window and smiled, waved. 'Mr Bramley,' she said again.

He knew her. He blinked. Had no idea if he was to let her in. He couldn't seem to think. Was he to let her in?

The door opened of its own accord and she came in, bringing with her a burst of cold air and whirling flakes. She smiled and closed the door behind her, quickly, glancing only slightly behind the door, as though wondering how he had let her in. She brushed snow from her jacket, smiling broadly, sharing smiles between him and the house, which she glanced around, hungrily.

'Still snowing out there,' she said. She had an accent. 'Pretty, though. I see you've kept the floors nice.'

The realtor.

As if reading his mind, she said, 'Glenn Darnley. I sold you this house.' She glanced around it again, in a practised motion. 'I hope you don't mind my dropping in this way?' She looked at him squarely, as though really seeing him for the first time. Her face went slack, and he realized what she must have seen. Dark hollows under his eyes, pouches, three days of beard, patchy and dark. Eyes red-rimmed with drink and too-little sleep. She would have smelled him too.

Richie had not yet spoken. He stood on the landing holding the rope.

Her eyes dropped to it, and then back up again,

smiling, less sure this time. 'Have I come at a bad time?'

There was a pause and then it struck Richie as funny, and he half smiled, the motion unfamiliar, stiff.

He shook his head. He lifted the noose and looked at it. He let it fall to the floor. 'I can take a break,' he said.

She nodded. 'I've come to talk to you about something important, Mr Bramley.'

He stepped down the rest of the stairs. 'Would you like some coffee, Mrs Darnley?' he asked her, having some trouble forming words in his mouth.

She declined. 'Please, call me Glenn,' she said. 'It's Richard, is that right?'

'Yes.' The two of them stood awkwardly just before the archway into the living room. It was Glenn who first moved. She stepped into the living room with the curiosity of a first visit. She walked over to the fireplace and stood in front of it, as though the fire were alight and she was warming her hands. She was more familiar to him by then, but there was something remarkably different about her. Richie didn't follow the thought long; instead he looked up nervously at the ceiling. Nothing there. All was quiet above.

'Have you used this yet?' she asked politely, even though the fireplace was clean of ashes and there was no wood nearby.

'No.'

She turned to him and smiled a little smile. 'I'm sure you're wondering why I'm here.' She looked up at the ceiling herself, and ran a hand over the mantel of the fireplace. 'I don't want to ask you if you are enjoying the house.'

He stared.

'I'm dying, Richard. I don't have many months left.'
She spoke more quickly, to cut him off when he opened
his mouth to speak. 'I am going to present a most unusual
proposal, and I do hope that you'll consider it before
turning me down.' She looked pleadingly at him, and he
noticed what was different when her cheeks drooped so
hollowly and her flesh seemed to hang loosely around
her neck. She was thin. Very thin.

'I–' he started, but didn't have anything to add.

She raised her hand in any case for him to stop. 'I
don't know quite how to say this so I will be blunt,' she
said. 'I – I love this house. I always have, I think, from
the moment I first walked in, something in it has spoken
to me.' She blushed, looked away, embarrassed.

'I would like to die here.'

The words hung in the air between them, the space
filling up with unexpressed exclamations and *bons mots*
that occurred to Richie, but would not come through.
He didn't know what to say. But the frail woman in
front of him did not understand.

'You don't know what you're saying,' he said. 'This is
not a –' and words failed again.

But Mrs Darnley, this new Mrs Darnley, Glenn, so thin,
smiled knowingly and sadly at him. 'I know this house.
It's a special house.' She walked from the mantel into the
dining room and peeked into the kitchen. She gazed
upwards at the ceiling, seeming to see something there
that wasn't. She cocked her head, as though listening. She
turned back to Richie, who watched with disbelief. *She
can't know. She thinks it's all art deco and character, fires in
the living room, antique tubs and nicely done floors –*

'There's so much *life* here, Richard,' she said.

They locked eyes.

He nodded. Knowledge passed between them and Richie felt a slight change in the air. A warmth, and electricity. It seemed almost as though the house was leaning in to her. There was something about the air that seemed suddenly musical, without the sound. As though it were whirling and dancing, and it was, he could feel it move past his face, ruffle his hair. She smiled into the blank spaces of the house and saw. Her hand ran down the archway between dining room and living room, affectionately. She blushed again, furiously, searching his face for confusion, sympathy, fear.

'I would like to trade houses, if you will. I have a lovely house just outside of town, perfect, really, for a writer. It's quiet and rural, and very well set-up. If you would do me this small favour, I would leave you the house when I go. I have no family, you see. Some very, very good friends, but I have other things. No one wants someone's house.' She giggled. 'Except me, I suppose.'

'I couldn't –'

'Please, promise me you'll think about it before you answer – I know how outrageous it sounds. I know this is your house.' She looked down to the floor.

Richie exhaled. It was all he could do to stay in one place, not jump up and run out of the house; all he could do not to scream, *yes! take it! let me out!* But he couldn't do it. The woman didn't understand. She thought the house was full of life.

'The house likes me,' she said. 'It does. It wants me.'

He shook his head. 'You don't know.'

She nodded and the air danced around her, like little balls of light. 'Yes, I do.'

As if to prove itself, the house came to life. Music played in the little room under the stairs and footsteps clomped through the attic. Children giggled through the walls. A dog barked.

Glenn smiled happily and laughed. 'It wants me to stay, for ever.'

Glenn's Story

November was bleak.

Not much moved around the house at 362 Belisle Street, but not much moved on the street at all, except at prescribed times, when the children left for school, and parents left for work. The streets were silent and cold most of the day then. In the evening, cars pulled into driveways already dark with night. Children came in early.

Twice a day a young woman, who sometimes wore the anonymous pink uniform of the cafeteria worker, cleaning lady, nurse's aid, walked up the stone walk to the red front door at 362 and disappeared into the house. She came out an hour or so later, and sometimes people saw her. Leaving or arriving. No one was sure if she lived there, or if she just came and went. No one thought about it.

Grown-ups might buy and sell the properties, but children are the true denizens of any residential street.

The children know where the other kids live, and don't care about the places where there are none. They find the best bush for hiding under, the best trees for climbing. They know the shortcuts to everywhere: town, the store, the house with the sweet, soft crab apples. They know which yards have biting dogs, and where the good dogs are. Kids are the first to get wind of a fire, a break-in, a broken window, new car, pool, playground, the first on hand to watch the new neighbours move in. With a speed that would have been unthinkable in an adult, the children pass stern judgement, often well earned, on the status and progress of a neighbourhood.

Long before it was even empty, the children were aware of the house at 362.

The young woman who came and went there was of little consequence to the children who crossed the street to pass by the house, especially if they happened to be out after dark. They knew she didn't live there. And they knew who did.

Kids, if they saw the young woman coming or going, sometimes spat between their fingers. It was usually for luck, but was also a kind of charm, like warding something off.

Kathy Rossana, in her first year as a home-care worker, had already expressed extreme discomfort at the circumstances of the woman she cared for at 362 Belisle Street. She had told her supervisor not long after her first week that the woman was really too ill to be cared for at home.

'She should be in a hospital,' she told her supervisor, Madelaine Dufresne. Ms Dufresne, an RN of many years, listened to the girl sympathetically as she talked, nodding in all the right places, by rote, really, having heard the new girls tell the same story about very nearly every elderly person they cared for. The problem with these girls was that they were *so young*. It seemed to Madelaine that every one of them believed anyone over sixty belonged in either a hospital or a home, the connection between frailty and wrinkled skin and disability inseparable in their minds. They understood (yet) little of dignity and the right to manage your own health care. And the woman had a very good health plan.

'Unless we get a call from her physician, she is to stay where she is,' Madelaine said, obliquely. She did not look at the woman's chart. If she had, she would have seen the name of an unfamiliar doctor, and that might have set alarm bells ringing.

'Let's just see how it goes for a while longer,' she told Kathy.

Kathy heard the dismissal in her supervisor's voice, and her youth and inexperience prevented her saying very much more, but she did allow herself (and Nurse Dufresne) a small uncertain look before she left the office.

Kathy, only a home-care worker for six months, had twelve people to care for. There was not a lot of time to be spent thinking about Mrs Darnley.

But sometimes she did.

Mrs Darnley was tall but thin-thin, her flesh sapped of tone and shape so that it might only have been a sheet strewn aesthetically about her. She was yellowed and unhealthy-looking, but so were most of Kathy's cases, ill or elderly as they were. It was a terrible job in many ways, but terrible in that it yanked on Kathy's still tender heart for hours after she left her last home. She sometimes cried on her boyfriend's shoulder, but he was getting less understanding and lately she had been keeping it to herself, holding it close like the resentment she began to feel against her boyfriend. Lots of times she felt terribly alone, like the people she served. She was very tender with them.

She left her supervisor's office that day, deeply concerned, because in spite of her youth, she had an instinct, and her instinct told her that something was very, very wrong with Mrs Darnley. With the whole situation, really.

For instance, sometimes when she arrived, letting herself in with her own key (feeling each time she did it like an intruder or robber, as though she hadn't any right), she had the feeling that she was interrupting.

Murmurs of voices coming from upstairs.

'Mrs Darnley,' she would call out, but not too loudly in case the woman was sleeping. She slept a lot, clearly quite ill in spite of other opinions. Each time she heard the voices, she expected to meet members of the family, upstairs, standing around the bed, dark looks of sorrow and concern on their faces (and, well, expected the questions to fly at her, angry and confrontational, *why isn't our Glenn in hospital?*). Each time, she mounted stairs to walk into an empty hall, and an empty room, the silence as foreboding as the murmur of voices.

She arrived later than usual at Mrs Darnley's and as she approached up the walk, she saw a figure pass in front of the large, lighted front window, through the curtains. A large figure, a man, she had been sure, and her heart had pounded just a little faster as she thought, This is it, the family, the confrontation, *why isn't our Glenn in hospital?*, and because of her youth, she felt an instant guilt, even though it was not her responsibility and she *had* brought the matter up more than once. She braced herself, took deep breaths, and let herself in with her key.

But no one met her at the door.

'Hello?' she called out, thinking that a preoccupation

with *why isn't our Glenn in hospital?* had made the family member miss the sound of the key turning in the lock, the door swinging smoothly and quietly open. Footsteps, the careful placement of the bag on the floor.

'Up here,' had come back weakly, in answer to her call. From upstairs. The voice, however, had not been masculine at all, but had been her own lady, Mrs Darnley.

She could not resist a quick peek into the living room. But before looking, even, she knew she was mistaken (overtired), because there were no lights on downstairs. If she was spooked then, it was only at the thought that a man was wandering around in the darkened rooms.

Upstairs, she found Mrs Darnley in bed, as usual, in the yellow room that smelled like illness and Kathy's own grandmother's washing room. Disinfectant. It was as familiar to her as the smell of urine and vomit. A consistent part of the job.

'How are you today, Mrs Darnley?' Kathy had asked, as usual, but she could see exactly (in spite of what Madelaine Dufresne would later tell her) how she was: she was a dying woman.

Mrs Darnley smiled weakly at her. 'Right as rain.'

'Have you family here today?' Kathy asked softly, gently running a warm damp cloth over sunken flesh. Flesh moved with the cloth if Kathy wasn't very, very gentle and she was aware of this. She did not soap the poor woman, her skin seemed beyond that kind of cleaning, filtering as it did, her own cancer from inside. The room smelled unpleasantly of it.

Glenn's eyes danced at Kathy, the only part of her that still seemed to live.

Had she winked? In any case, she did not answer,

but soon after closed her eyes and either rested, or feigned sleep.

That same day, Kathy had noticed Mrs Darnley's dinner tray from the Disability Meals was untouched, more so than usual. Even the tea was still lidded and had grown cold.

'That's not what I hear from Disability Meals,' Madelaine had said to Kathy, when she claimed Mrs Darnley was alone at all times. *She doesn't have family there*, she'd said.

'The way I understand it, a man answers the door and takes the tray up,' Nurse Dufresne had said, reassuringly. 'If at any time that door is not answered by someone, they will call us. They're the first line of defence. Twice a day they are there; twice a day you are there. You're not to worry so, Kathy. There's plenty of years to worry yet.' And she had been dismissed.

It all became a moot point, anyway. Because the same day that Kathy expressed her last concern to Nurse Dufresne, a man called the office and told her that Mrs Darnley's family had arrived to take her home.

'Home where?' Kathy said, suspicious. Nurse Dufresne shrugged. 'I don't know. You said she had an accent. Maybe England.' The thought had long run out of her head. Since the call, as far as she was concerned, the case was over. It was someone else's affair now.

She did not mention to Kathy how strange and distant the call had been, or how in the background there were odd sounds that invoked smoky, beery memories of youth.

Of course, Disability Meals got the same call.

*

The pain was often unbearable. When it was like that, Glenn would fade away into her mind. There were things there that were pleasant. There were things there, also, that were mercifully blank.

Her arms and legs were numb much of the time. On occasion she would drift back from a pleasant place to find the bed shaking with a gentle motion and see the dark outline of someone at her feet, rubbing, stroking, coaxing life back into her flat limbs.

Sometimes she spoke. *Kathy?* she might say. Or *Is that you Mrs Parkins?* And a voice might come back, or not. *Staizer*, would sometimes come, a firm reply. Or a kindly *Ssssh, Mrs Darnley, go back to sleep.* Sometimes, Glenn would just smile and say nothing, but fade back into summer, or on a boat, floating serenely on a lake, with her laughing man telling her stories she'd already heard while waves lapped (kindly) against wood.

She was aware, blissfully, of humanity in the room. There was, it seemed, always a murmur of kindly voices, whispers not of concern but anticipation, quiet and low so that they never disturbed her. She was unaware, blissfully, much of the time, of her sundered appearance and the lingering presence of death.

They came in and out, heedless of time. Time followed them. It was sometimes 1922 and music played. It was 1972, 1985, 1944. The room would swirl around her, a bedroom, a sitting room, the walls changed, grew photos and pieces of art, curtains billowed with summer air, or did not, a flap of solid blind blocking out the gloom of November. A little dog sometimes sat beside the bed. If Glenn opened her eyes, he would be there, the little yellow dog, panting happily to see her, his wiry tail thumping up and down against the wooden floor.

Sometimes she would find herself in a field of tall, rolling grass, where the air was fresh and the sun warm. A woman would come to her and say, over the muffled laughter of children, *Oh my, Mrs Darnley, we have to get you back to bed. They'll be coming soon*, and she would gratefully take her hand and the two would go back to bed, Glenn smiling questioningly at her, and *Staizer not Parkins* would say *Soon, dear, very soon*. Her smile was bright and calm and like the sun of endless summer.

Glenn woke on Thursday with the light slanting nebulously against the far wall. There was no way to tell what time of day it was, but there was a feel of morning to it. She would have liked then to sit up. Her limbs and any will to use them had long departed, however, so she lay on her back thinking about sitting and enjoying even just that.

She was, she realized, pain free. Her body had little feeling at all, although she was cold. The room was empty. The yellow walls that she had once found so disturbing and falsely bright seemed pretty then, an imitation of sunlight, made more real by the slant of white light on the wall opposite her bed. The ceiling above her was an old pressed-tin roof – much sought after by period purists who would never truly be able to appreciate the charm and quality of something that had withstood time and occupation in quite the way of a resident of the era. The whole house was that way. It had stood, waiting, passing the time, moving forward

reluctantly, but defiantly pulling along its past as a gesture to endurance as well as dignity.

The muscles of her face were averse, but Glenn smiled
into the air. 'Hello, house,' she whispered. Or may not
have.

She felt surprisingly well. And that was how she
knew.

Sometimes she closed her eyes. And sometimes she
held them open for a while.

They gathered.

Around her, when she opened her eyes, were the
people of the house. They smiled down on her kindly,
sweetly, hopefully, and with a perfect intimacy. They
watched over her.

In time, the old woman, her smile only a tug of
flesh at the corners of a worn-out face, the permanent
inhabitant of the yellow room, reached out her hand.

Behind her, children watched, wide-eyed but not
frightened. The warm, kind woman from the field rested
her hand on the thick hair of a red-headed child. She
smiled, too.

'Come with us, Mrs Darnley,' the old woman said.

The tall man who had taken care of so many details
for her – although she sensed a naughty, unhealthy
streak in him – said affably, 'We officially extend your
invitation, my dear. We've waited for you.'

The old woman's hand, a claw nearly, but the age
tattooed there was one of love and children and care,
reached over and rested her hand very near Glenn's so
that she need do nothing but –

Glenn took her hand.

The light on the wall shifted and changed until it was